Story By: Author Everlazt

I0634164

Dedication page

The Rev. Ted Attles

Domonique Brown

De'Sean Theo-James Attles

Jayden Brown

Leron & Duron Pinkney

O.G.

Gail Tidball-Cowart

Dream the dream, Live the dream. If the dream looks unreachable, stretch your arms some more. If the dream loses it sound, change the beat. If the dream looks dark, give it some light. Do what you have to do to achieve the dream. Don't stop, Won't stop…#realalwayswins

WINNERS NEVER QUIT

QUITTERS NEVER WIN

R.A.W. 2

Written By: Author Everlazt

Special Edition with part-1

Today is the day.

On a nice sunny day Karmen felt strong enough now to face the world, and so was her new baby boy Tyrel. Karmen fed Tyrel, got him cleaned up and dressed him in a baby Guess farmer suit and a pair of soft bottom Adidas.

Every since the two crackheads found Karmen on the roof of the building that night Ne'Sean shot her, she had been keeping a low profile. She rarely went outside for anything, and she kept her visitors to a two-person limit with Adina and Mimi being the only ones on the list. Once the news spread about Ne'Sean being killed and De'Quan going to jail for shooting a cop, Karmen chose to stay out of sight, out of mind.

After lying up in the hospital for a week, Karmen had a lot of time to replay the events of the night Ne'Sean shot her, and she was convinced something psychologically went wrong with Ne'Sean. It showed in his eyes that night. The way he looked at Karmen was as if he didn't know who she was anymore. It wasn't that he wasn't in love with her anymore, Ne'Sean just freaked out over the thought of them having a baby and him not going to college because of it. They argued, got into a struggle and the gun accidently went off.

Over the months Karmen blamed herself a lot of nights for his death even though she wasn't there. She could not duck the feeling that she was the one who pushed Ne'Sean over the edge. Why else would he fight her so hard on the issue of having the baby? Karmen knew the shooting itself was an accident from them fighting, but she couldn't understand why he left her on the roof when she passed out.

This is where Karmen felt the need to defend Ne'Sean again for his extreme actions that night. He was scared.

Adina and Mimi said nothing but good things in front of their fragile friend, but Karmen knew. She could feel it. They were calling her a fool behind her back for defending her baby daddy who shot her and left her for dead on that cold roof.

Karmen shook her head and smiled down at Tyrel, "What do they know...Your daddy was a good man boo-boo", Karmen said with a bright smile. If she believed, then so would her baby, and she didn't want Tyrel growing up with ill feelings towards his father for one mistake.

Tyrel made a sound as if to cheer his mother on, "That's right baby, now let's go."

She packed a small baby bag and made the trek to the Myrtle side of Marcy projects. Some people were surprised to see Karmen, but she kept everything on a light tone with quick hi and bye's and proceeded on her mission.

Karmen took a deep breath as she stepped up into building 105 and took the slow elevator ride up to the fifth floor. She knocked on the door and was so nervous she almost walked away, but the lock clicked, and the door swung open.

Seeing Meika for the first time in months made Karmen take a step back. Meika was beginning to grow and it showed. "Hi Meika, I'm sorry to bother you, but is Mama K home?"

Meika was surprised to see Karmen. Word on the street was something bad happen to Karmen and her family sent her away. "Wow, Karmen?"

Karmen smiled, "Yes".

Meika beamed, "Where have you been? Come in…come in". She opened the door wider to allow them in. "And who is this?'

Meika closed the door, as Karmen removed the light blanket covering the baby face, "This is my little man, Tyrel".

"Yeah", Meika said looking into the blanket. "Come sit down, Mama K will be here in a minute. She went to the store to pick up something. So where have you been? We haven't seen or heard from you in months".

Karmen sat down and got herslef and Tyrel comfortable, "That's what I wanted to talk to you and Mama K about. I would rather tell the story once though, cause it's long and hard to tell without crying and getting all emotional".

"Oh okay, well do you want something to drink, and what about this little man?" Meika asked cooing at the baby.

"Nah, I'm alright. I fed Tyrel before we came over. You want to hold him?" Karmen asked.

"Oh yeah, come here mister", Meika said as she took him into her arms.

A key jiggled in the door. "There she goes right there", Meika said looking toward the front door.

"Ok Meika, I got the nutmeg, so we can…" Mama K stopped in her tracks and made eye contact with Karmen. "Karmen?"

"Hi Mama K."

Mama K almost broke down and cried as momeries of Ne'Sean bringing Karmen to the house began to flood her thoughts. "Oh, my goodness, come here and give me a hug".

Karmen stood up and they hugged, "Where have you been at…We haven't seen you in months."

"That's what I'm came to tell yah."

"Look Mama." Meika beamed.

Mama K looked from Karmen to the baby, "Aww, who's this?"

Karmen took a deep breath and said, "This is Tyrel, Ne'Sean's son."

Mama K and Meika looked from the baby to Karmen, then back to the sleeping baby. "Are you for real?" Meika asked with a shocked look on her face.

"Yes, I'm for real", Karmen said. "I wanted to wait until we were strong enough to come over here. I'm sorry for staying away for so long, but I was scared, and I didn't want to intrude."

Mama K looked back at the baby and began to see her sons face in Tyrel's face. "Let me hold him", Mama K said in a soft voice careful not to wake him.

There was an awkward silence as the room awaited Mama K approval. "He is so handsome Karmen. Please sit and tell me why you stayed away for so long. I didn't even know you were pregnant."

"Well when we found out Ne'Sean wasn't a big fan of it."

Mama K began to frown, "what you mean?"

Karmen told them her tale about the night on the roof, all the way up to her sitting on their couch at that moment. By the end of her story they all were crying and tried they're best not to wake up Tyrel in the big bubble of emotions they were wrapped up in. By the time she left karmen had assets her day as one full of happiness and sadiness all in one pot. But she felt better about finally introducing Tyrel to his other half of his family. Now maybe they all can begin to heal alittle better, together.

Chapter 2

The scene was set for De'Quan's trial and it was brewing up to be a long and hard one to fight, but he was determain to come out of this with some light time or no time at all. Which ever worked out better for him, he was with it at this point. Being on Rikers Island was really taking a toll on De'Quan and his family. Months of going back and forth to court was boring him. The DA office refuse to revival who is the witness they have in hiding, but De'Quan had a feeling he knew exactly who it is. He was just patiently waiting for that day to come when that person must actually take that witness stand and point him out.

After a year and half of hearings and delays the DA's office was ready to rumble and send De'Quan to hell for good. For back up to their claims that he is a menace to society the DA's office is going to use De'Quan's bad jail record and how he has joined a gang since his stay on Rikers Island.

Before they brought him out into the courtroom, De'Quan had a moment to himself in the holding cell. He paced back and forth trying to curb his rage for the system that was going to try him and put his lights out for good with a guilty verdict.

De'Quan paused for a moment, closed his eyes and did something he hadn't done since he was a kid and Grand-Ma Trina tried to teach him there was a higher power covering all of us.

"Dear God, I know you don't hear from me a lot...but I just wanted to say I'm sorry man. I never meant for all of this to happen. Tell Ne'Sean I love him." A tear slipped out the corner of his eye. De'Quan quickly opened his eyes and wiped them. The sound of keys made him straighten himself up.

Two court officers walked up to the cell, "You ready?"

De'Quan took a deep breath, "Only time will tell. Come on, let's do this." He said as he stuck his hands out and the officer put the cuffs on him.

They escorted De'Quan out into the courtroom and over to the defense table where Mr. White sat going over some papers. The officer removed the handcuffs from De'Quan's wrist and sat down behind him and his lawyer.

"Morning Mr. Short", Mr. White said as he looked up from the paperwork.

"What's going on Mr. White, how we looking today?" De'Quan quickly asked as he looked over his shoulder to see who was in the crowd.

Mama K, Grand-Ma Trina, Meika and Shakia were all in attendence. A few other familiar faces were spread out in the packed courtroom, but he didn't care about them. All he cared about was his home team of cheerleaders sitting behind him. De'Quan winked at Mama K and the rest of the family, and then turned his attention back to his lawyer.

"Well today we will begin with opening statements and I'm going to present this motion to the court to dismiss the charges against you. It's just a standard motion that I know the judge is going to deny, but I have to file it just in n case", Mr. White said as his eyes bounced around from De'Quan, to the papers in his hand, and then quickly scanning the courtroom.

They had a couple of attorney-client visits while De'Quan waited for his trial to start, but he was impressed by Mr. White's attention to detail and everything moving around him whenever they were in the courtroom. De'Quan didn't know how Dre found the lowkey, but effective lawyer, but he was greatful he did, because De'Quan didn't know the first thing about being in a courtroom. The entire scene was foreign to him. Sure, he attended court appearances for Pop and Dre, but to be on this side of the courtroom, facing life in prison never came across De'Quan's line of vision, and this was not the time to be looking like a deer caught in headlights.

This is where Mr. White came in.

Mr. White was a seasoned lawyer on the New York City criminal court circuit, standing at five feet eleven inches tall, with a scruffy beard, and golden-brown skin, he gave off the look of a person who is very humble, but don't test that humblity in a courtroom. His trial record of seventeen wins and three losses spoke volunms in the Manhattan D.A.'s office.

To go up against Mr. White the D.A.'s office sent in one of their top convictor's A.D.A. Dolen, a whiteman in his late forties who rose to the top of the office conviction rate by riding the backs of low level drug dealers who took cop-out deals to turn on their bosses and connections for a lesser sentence or no jail time at all.

A.D.A. Dolen knew De'Quan was apart of a crew of robbers who stumbled on a police force ran operation that went bad. What he didn't know was where is the missing member Andre Jones, who got away on the night of the shooting. Not having the forth member of their crew was hurting Dolen's case from the inside of the crew. He had a talking witness, but a dead passenger in the car, a silent De'Quan, and a missing member made him have to rely of police testimony. Not a bad thing in a police officer involved shooting, but you always want all the elements in place when a trial starts to avoid surprises.

"All rise, the honorable justice Demarcus is presiding", The bailiff spoke in a loud tone, causing the entire courtroom to stand as the judge walked in and headed for his seat on the bench.

"Please be seated", judge Demarcus said as he put down a stack papers and book he was carrying.

The entire auidence and jury took their seats as the court officers remained standing and took up positions around the room.

Justice Demarcus had thin white hair to match the lightly shaven beard under his pale skin. He looked like a ghost floating around in his black robe. He put on his reading glasses and quickly shuffled through his stack of papers.

"Good morning all", the judge said as he scanned the courtroom. He flashed a smile toward the jury and the prosecution table, then turned his attention to the defense table with his back to business attitude, "Mr. White are you ready today?"

"Yes, your honor".

Justice Demarcus adjusted his glasses and said, "Very well, today ladies and gentalmen we will begin the trial of the people of the state of new york vs De'Quan Short, and he is charged with murder in the second degree, attempted murder in the second degree, robbery in the first degree, weapons posession, and drug posession. Mr.

Dolen you can begin with your opening statement when your ready".

"Thank you, your honor,", Dolen blurted out as he hoped out of his seat and button the top button on his suit jacket in one smooth motion.

Dolen turned his attention to the jury and began, "Good morning ladies and gentalmen, my name is James Dolen and I am the leading prosecutor on this case, which means I work for you", he pointed at the jury for his dramatic effect. "The people of the greatest city on earth. I'm here to serve you. In return I'm going to ask you to listen to the evidence of this case and return with a convincing guilty verdict against the defendant".

Dolen gave his opening spill for twenty minutes, when he was done De'Quan sat there thinking about the events that lead up to that night, but he could remember bits and pieces of the night of the incident. A.D.A. Dolen's account of what happened that night from pure word of mouth had De'Quan thinking he really did everything they were charging him with, but all those negative thoughts quickly began to fade once Mr. White approached the jury box with his Crouching Tiger style and laid out his blueprint of the night in question.

"Good morning ladies and gentlemen, I am Tyrone White and I'm here to make sure my client Mr. Short receives a fair trial. I know the process will be long because Mr. Dolen has a long list of so called witnesses and experts. But I assure you by the end of this trial you will return with a not guilty verdict. Please people remember I don't have to prove Mr. Short didn't commit the murder and the rest of the charges on this indictment. Mr. Dolen must prove beyond a reasonable doubt Mr.

Short committed these crimes. I know he can't prove that. Because his account of the night in question can't possibly be right…" he let the thought longer in the air as he mumbled a 'Thank you' in the judge direction and made his way back to the defense table.

"Okay, aww Mr. Dolen you may call your first witness", Justice Demarcus said as he leaned back in his chair and tried to get comfortable for the big show.

"The state calls Lieutenant Hardy to the witness stand", Mr. Dolen said as he looked down at his note pad. He wanted to start out light with the first commanding officer on the scene, then build his case from there.

When Lieutenant Hardy took his seat on the stand, Mr. Dolen cracked a grin and said, "Thank you for being here today Lieutenant. Can you tell us how many years you have been with the N.Y.P.D.?"

Chapter 3

Alabama was different speed from New York and South Carolina, but Dre had to adapt to the new resting spot. He knew being on the run wasn't the ideal way of life with a girlfriend and two kids, but he was determined make life work for them and moving to a place where they could blend in until they came up with a more long-term plan would work for them in the mean time.

Getting Tammy on board with this sudden change in life wasn't an easy task for Dre either. Tammy was broken when they had to flee New York city, leaving her mother behind. Dre was able to calm Tammy when he hooked up with Mr. White and decided to run all communication through him, with Tammy's mother sworn to secrecy about having contact with her daughter. Dre figured who's going to question a lawyer about his client's and their dealings? Which covered Tammy's link to her mother.

That's when Tammy really became married to the idea of them living away from everything they knew back in New York and build a new life in a foreign city.

What Tammy didn't expect is to be doing at the same time is raising two kids in the mist of the madness of living on the run. Before they left her family in South Carolina Dre showed up in the middle of the night with a baby boy, saying it is De'Quan's son and he told her the whole story of De'Quan and Melissa and how De'Quan asked Dre to take the baby and raise him as his own. De'Quan lost his brother and knew he would lose contact with his child forever once Melissa had to take the witness stand against him in his trial.

Tammy cried for a long time at the thought of being a part of the kidnapping of someone's baby, but when she stopped, Tammy looked at how much time and their lives had changed since she hooked up with Dre that cool night in Marcy, and now no matter how bad things may look this is her family and she had to step up as such to keep it in tact.

They named the baby boy Ne'Sean and Dre was able the buy new birth certificates and I.D.'s for everyone to make their move smoother from state to state Tammy was able to put together a small case with section 8 with the fake I.D. and they helped her find housing. Dre laid low and stayed out of town until the caseworker backed up off Tammy, then he moved into the apartment full time and they kept to themselves.

Once they settled in Alabama Dre would make short runs to check in on Tammy cousin in South Carolina and keep their money flow going. Then turn around and meet with Mr. White in New Jersey to exchange messages from the New York family and give him any money he needed for De'Quan defense.

All the running was taxing on Dre and it showed, "Dre what's wrong Baby?" Tammy asked as they laid in the bed under the night light of the low playing t.v.

"I'm just thinking about De'Quan trial", Dre said as he turned over to look into Tammy's eyes.

"You worried he's not going to win?" Tammy asked as she ran her fingers through his low haircut.

"It's not that…it's the protected witness they have. I know it's Fat Per, and if it is, he let his words trail off as Tammy took a deep breath for both of them and said, "Dre don't let a rat take you out of character. We all know he can't be touched, and you going to give yourself high blood pressure thinking about him. I know he was a very special friend to you, but he crossed the line".

Dre chuckled., "I know baby…I didn't go soft on you in the last 24 hours".

Tammy kissed him, "you better not, cause we need you".

"You three are my everything, you know that," Dre said as he moved a piece of her hair from her face.

"Wwaann…"

"Who is that", Tammy asked in an annoyed tone.

"Sound like Andrea, I'll get her, "Dre giggled as he got out of the bed and shuffled into the next room.

"Okay, okay, okay," Dre hushed her as he picked his daughter up. "What's wrong, you want to wake your brother up?"

Andrea began to calm down as Dre hugged her and walked her around the room, "I got you mama…it's ok…what u had a bad dream".

He sat down on a rocking chair they had in the room and rocked back and forth just thinking about everything that has happen to him since he was released from jail.

When Dre stepped back on the scene he knew he had to elevate his game because Tammy was pregnant at the time. Dre's inner thoughts on how he was going to raise and protect Tammy and the baby were so strong at the time that he wasn't thinking straight the night they decided to rob the last drug house. Now his friend is facing life in prison, his friend brother is dead, and their trusted third member of the crew is a cooperating witness.

Dre came home with thoughts of going legit, he just didn't know how or where to start. Not having a male role model in his life was really beginning to show. Dre didn't have anyone older who could drop a jewel on him or give him some direction when things got a little sticky in the life department. Sitting there rocking Andrea back to sleep he looked at her beautiful face and a thought crossed his mind. 'How can I give them direction, if I don't have none myself?'

Dre closed his eyes and let the question hang in the wind as he drifted off to sleep with his daughter in his arms.

Chapter 4

With everything that was going on with her family Mama K knew she needed to get away and build with her other half. Mama K hadn't been upstate to see Pop in almost two years and her spirit woke her up and guided her in the direction to go to him.

They had always been a tight couple, but Pop going to prison hurt their bond. They still wrote to each other, and whenever Pop had the money to call, he would. But life just wasn't the same between the two anymore.

Losing Ne'Sean broke their hearts and his funeral was the last time she actually laid eyes on Pop. Mama K was mad at the world for months after the funeral, causing her to isolate herself. When Pop heard the news, his anger boiled over into the messhall where he used a food trey to shut someone up, because the guy was talking too much at the dinner table. Pop ended his night in the box where he stayed for seven months for his transgressions, but he was still allowed to attend his son funeral. A day Pop will never forget.

Mama K refused to visit Pop while he was in the box. Seeing him in prison hurt her to the core and she thugged it out because they had contact visits; but visiting him from behind a caged window was just too much for her swallow. So, she waited for him to finish his box time before she decided to go see him.

Mama K took the long bus ride to Attica correctional facility feeling positive vibes about being able to touch her husband again after such a long time. To keep a clear mind on her ride she tried to read 'Journey to the Kingdom of Soul', but thoughts of all the questions Pop will ask her now that they were face-to-face made her loss focus on the book and she closed her eyes to rest them.

*****

Pop went through his daily ritual of being woken up at 5:45 in the morning by the sound of a loud fire alarm ringing through the halls and tiers of the entire prison for the morning count.

Once he was counted, Pop cleaned himself up, said his morning prayers, and got ready for the breakfast run to the messhall. After being in prison for nine years Pop hardly ate anything they served in the messhall, but breakfast is mandatory, and Pop could not afford to have another disciplinary incident on his record when he is getting short to going to the parole board.

When he returned to his cell after breakfast Pop laid down on his bunk and started watching the Martin reruns on BET when his cell door cracked open.

Pop hopped up off the bed and quickly stuck his head out the cell to look down the tier. "A Short, you got a visit", an officer barked from behind a thick plexiglass window.

Pop waved his hand, "Aight, let me get in the shower", Pop said as he grabbed his shower gear and hustled down the tier to take a quick shower.

*****

The ride to the jail was long, but the trip always got longer once they reached the jail, and the guards would start with their degrading treatment of the visitors. Outfits were scrutinized, and some visitors were asked to change certain clothes, or they would be denied entry.

Mama K stood on the line and tried to block out her negative thoughts about the guards as one of the c.o.'s called her over to take her information. Then she was told to walk through a metal detector. Once she walked through a c.o. that looked like a female, but the hair on her face confused Mama K.

"Step over here Ma'am, so I can give up a quick pat down", the c.o. said.

Mama K hesitated, staring at the light hairs on the guard face and shook off the thought of it being a man doing these hand searches of women and stepped to the side.

Mama K raised her hands and the strong smell of stale coffee floated out of the c.o. mouth as she ran her hands down the side of Mama K 's body, then ran her fingers along Mama K bra line.

"I'm not suppose to let you in here with this metal bra on", the c.o. said as she continued to rub her hands along Mama K curves. "I'm going to let you slide today," the c.o. said as she stood face to face with Mama K.

Mama K put her hands down and cracked a slight smile, "Thank you", she said before walking away. The whole exchange was disgusting and unnecessary to her, but Mama K refuse to let the c.o.'s mess up her visit with here husband before it even starts.

*****
———

Saturday is a busy day in the visiting room with short lines at the vending machines, light conversations carrying across the room, and prisoner's entering the visiting room two at a time. Pop went through a pat down search before he stepped through the sliding metal gate and walked into the visiting room. He walked to the c.o.'s table at the front of the visiting room and handed the officer his visit card, then he quickly scanned the crowd looking for his wife. He saw her sitting at a table at the far right of the room and made his move.

Mama K watched Pop walk through the gate and a smile quickly crawled on her face. When Pop made it to the table Mama K stood up and gave him a deep kiss and hug before their close encounter is interrupted.

"Ok have a seat", the c.o. sitting at the front desk barked.

Pop sucked his teeth, "Come on baby, let's sit down".

"How are you?" Mama K asked looking into his eyes. Pop had aged a little bit around his eyes and collected a few grey hairs, but he still looked the same to her.

"I'm good baby…how are you, how was the ride?" Pop asked as his smile warmed her heart.

"It was okay. Tried to get some rest but all I could think about was seeing you", Mama K said as she reached across the table and took his hand. Pop missed that soft touch.

"Oh yeah, sounding like that teenage love I met twenty years ago", Pop joked.

Mama K chuckled and said, "I'm always going to be your teenage love. So, you better not be looking for a new one".

"Why would I do that, when I have all this sexiness coming to see me?" Pop said as he rubbed her hands.

"All of this sexiness is getting old, you might want to go young or something", Mama K said looking down at their hands.

Pop raised her chin up so see could look into her eyes and said, "Mama K you will forever be my number…now let's start thinking positive. I'm about to go to the board soon, so we need to be ready".

"Oh, I'm ready", she said with a sly smile. "And I have a surprise for you".

"Yeah, what's that?"

"A new baby", Mama K said and watched his reaction.

Pop felt confused, "What you talking about Mama?" He asked as he looked around the table at her stomach.

"Not me silly".

Pop felt relieved and said, "Oh you talking about De'Quan's baby with that cop chick".

"I'll get to that story in a minute, but no not her", Mama K said shaking her head.

"Mama K if you telling me Meika…"

She quickly cut him off, "Pop would you stop it, you know I will kill that girl if she walked up in our house pregnant".

Pop chuckled, "Okay, so who?"

"Remember Ne'Sean old girlfriend Karmen, from the Flushing side of the projects?" Mama K asked.

Pop frowned, "I think I remember Ne'Sean talking to me about her on the phone, but I never met her".

"I know you never met her, but he did talk to about her?"

"Yeah, I can't really remember the whole conversation, but I remember the name", Pop said.

"Well she showed up at the house with a baby, and said Ne'Sean is the father", Mama K said with a big smile on her face. "And he looks like him too".

"Hold up, Ne'Sean has been gone for almost a year, where she been at all this time with this baby?" Pop asked with a suspicious look on his face.

"I asked the same thing and her story broke my heart Pop", Mama K said biting her lip to hold back the tears.

Pop quickly recognized the change in her mood and reached over the table to give her a hug. He looked over her shoulder at the officers at the front desk to see if they would say something to him, but they were too engaged in their own conversation to care.

"Mama K it's okay, tell me what she said", Pop said in his soothing voice.

Mama K began to melt in his arms. She hadn't had a strong hug like this from him in a long time. Mama K exhaled feeling safe again; even if its was only for a moment. Pop had always been her protector, but when he was arrested and sent away to prison Mama K had to become her own protector of her feelings. A job she was tired of.

"She said Ne'Sean shot her and left her on the roof".

Pop was shocked, "What did you say?"

"She said he was scared she was pregnant. They were on the roof arguing and they got into a scuffle and the gun went off. She woke up in the hospital and saw on the news Ne'Sean died the same night".

Trying to find the words that would make sense of what his son did was impossible for Pop. He sat there with a blank stare on his face and said, "Damn Mama, what the hell happen to our kids? Girl tells him she's pregnant and he shoots her", he shook his head.

"It was an accident Pop, I know my baby didn't do that on purpose. He probably thought she was dead and that's why he left her up there", Mama K said trying to help Pop make sense of it all.

"What's the baby name?" Pop asked.

"Tyrel and he is so handsome Pop," She said beaming like a proud Grandmother. "I know nothing can take the place of Ne'Sean, but the minute I laid eyes on him Pop, I felt his spirit. It's like Ne'Sean was there".

"Yeah…well if you approve then I'm on board," Pop kissed her hand and said, "How's the trial looking?"

Chapter 5

Ever since her baby was taken from Harlem hospital Melissa lived a dark life and it showed in her appearance. Melissa was always known for her nice figure, beautiful flowing black hair, and her butter pecan colored skin always looked tasty with a heathy shine to it. Now her hair stayed in a ponytail with a few grey streaks in it, her skin color was looking dull, and her figure still hadn't recovered from the baby weight making Melissa 210 pounds in a five-foot four-inch frame. A far cry from her super model figure of 5'4, 160 pounds.

Her contact with the outside world had limit itself to sporadic conversations with her cousin Suge and the lead investigator in her son missing persons case. She took a leave from the force and after months of no word about her son disappearance Melissa was beginning to lose faith in the system she dedicated her life to.

Melissa tried to go out and search on her own, but always came up empty. She would start her search at the hospital and end up outside staring at all the many ways to get away from Harlem hospital. The 2 and 3 trains run underground, so someone could jump right on the train. A cab could easily be hailed right at the curb, and there were plenty of places to park a getaway car.

Melissa knew after months of no word being heard about her baby, the chances of her ever seeing her baby again were very slim, but Melissa refused to give up her search. Even though she didn't know what her own baby look like because she never had the chance to hold him.

The phone rang snapping Melissa out of her zone, "Hello?"

"Hey Mel, what you doing?" Suge asked, sounding like her usual cheerful self. Her energy always put a smile on Melissa's face.

"Nothing, I was just about to go for a walk, I need some air," Melissa said as she sat on the edge of the bed staring down at her sneakers.

"Yeah, did you open the curtains in there today?" Suge asked.

"Yes Suge…"

"Ok, I'm just asking. You need that sun light Melissa," Suge said sounding concerned.

"I know Suge, and I woke up today feeling like I have to start taking better care of myself," Melissa said as she stood up and walked to the mirror.

"Now that sounds like a plan. You know what, we should go to the hairdresser," Suge said.

"When?"

"This weekend. I'll make our appointments for Saturday," Suge said feeling good her friend was ready to function with the rest of the world.

Melissa began to smile at her reflection in the mirror, something she hadn't done in a long time. "Okay, let's do it."

"Great, I'll call you later, I have to go, my lunch is almost over," Suge said then hung up the phone before Melissa could change her mind.

Even though Melissa agreed to go, Suge tried numerous times to get Melissa to go to the beauty salon, and Melissa always backed out of their meetings. She worried about Melissa, but she couldn't force her to come out do something nice for herself. Melissa had to be ready and willing to make that move, not forced.

Melissa put on a pair of sweatpants, a light jacket, and a New York Yankee cap and went out to take a walk down Broadway.

Since the shooting, Melissa hadn't been uptown Broadway by the scene of the crime. As she walked from 142 street heading uptown thoughts of that night flashed in her mind.

When Melissa approached De'Quan and his friends she didn't know they would try to shoot her, and she certainly didn't think the situation would escalate to an all-out shootout and car crash.

De'Quan blamed the entire incident on her and Melissa couldn't blame him. She should have never brought De'Quan with her to the coke house. He was able to map out the apartment and its lay out when she did, but De'Quan didn't know they were undercover cops.

Before she knew it, Melissa had walked up Broadway and was coming up on 160th street. Flashes of the jeep fleeing the scene and getting side swiped in the intersection crossed her vision. The impact that night was deafening.

Melissa remember taking cover when the shots began to fly out of the crashed jeep. Then one of the passengers hopped out of the front seat and made his way across Broadway and down 161st street toward Riverside drive.

That's when the thought hit her.

What happened to the guy Andre who got away?

*****

A.D.A. Dolen called numerous police officers who responded to the scene of the shooting, but he didn't have a positive I.D. on De'Quan shooting a gun that night. Sitting at the prosecution table Dolen looked down at his notes and knew it was time unleash his secret weapon.

"Whenever your ready Mr. Dolen, you can call your next witness," Justice Demarcus said as he leaned his chair back.

"Yes, your honor, the people calls Perry Long, a.k.a. Fat Pee, to the stand," Dolen said and watched as the temperature of the courtroom heated up. A.D.A. Dolen made a living off of getting people to snitch on their friends and family, and this moment would be no different.

The bailiff wheeled Fat Pee into the courtroom in a wheelchair and the entire place went silent. Then a low mummer began to got loud real fast. Justice Demarcus quickly snapped his chair forward and grabbed his gavel.

"Order…Order in the court," the judge barked to get the ruffled crowd back under control.

De'Quan knew this was coming and he tried to prepare himself for this day, but who could prepare themselves for a childhood friend taking the stand on them. He figured Fat Pee flipped on him once De'Quan was indicted and Fat Pee wasn't listed as his co-defendant but seeing him being wheeled into the courtroom to carry out the deed was a hard sight to see.

The bailiff wheeled Fat Pee to the space next to the witness stand and the jury box then stepped out of the way so Fat Pee could be sworn in.

Fat Pee looked like he lost 100 pounds and was on the verge of reaching his 50th birthday, instead of looking forward to his 22nd birthday.

"Now, Mr. long, please tell the court where you are from and your current address," A.D.A. Dolen said as he stood at a small podium with a few papers scattered on top of it.

Fat Pee shifted in his wheelchair and kept his line of vision planted on his sneakers. "I'm from 626 Marcy avenue, and I'm currently in the hospital under watch because of my condition".

"That nigga ain't from Marcy no more!" A voice barked from the crowd causing the rest of the room to murmur in agreement.

Justice Demarcus quickly banged his gavel, "I will have order in this courtroom. One more outburst like that and I will have this entire courtroom cleared out. Now please Mr. Dolen continue".

"Thank you, your honor. Now what condition is that?" Dolen asked Fat Pee.

"I'm paralyzed from the waist down," Fat Pee said with a sadness in his voice.

"I'm sorry to hear that, did that happen to you before the night of March 3rd, 1996?"

Fat Pee began to sweat. When he agreed to testify against De'Quan he was angry because of what happen to him, and he didn't think the courtroom would be packed with all these people from the neighborhood watching him tell this story. He swallowed hard and said, "No it happened when I crashed the car that night".

Dolen turned his attention to the jury then back to his witness to engage the two parties. "Now, are you familiar with the neighborhood around 160th street and Broadway in New York county?"

"Yes sir", Fat Pee said as he raised his eyes to meet A.D.A. Dolen eyes.

"Okay, so on the night of March 3, 1996, around 4 a.m., were you on the block of 160th street, between Broadway and Amsterdam avenue?"

"Yes sir".

De'Quan stared at Fat Pee and waited for him to look his way, he couldn't believe his friend from childhood was crossing the line like this. He shared corner store sandwiches with Fat Pee. Let him sleep in his room when his mother kicked him out. Did robberies with, talked to girls with. De'Quan was hurt, but he maintained his blank stare in Fat Pee's direction as Dolen continued his line of questions.

"How did you get there?"

"A stolen jeep," Fat Pee said.

"And were you alone…or were there other people in this jeep?" Dolen asked as he walked around the space between the prosecution table and the jury box.

Fat Pee looked at De'Quan out the corner of his eye and said, "It was me and my three partners at the time".

A.D.A. Dolen walked to the table to give Fat Pee a clear line of vision to the defense table, then unloaded his next question, "Can you please tell the court, who were those three partners and if the defendant is one of them".

Fat Pee looked around the silent courtroom and cleared his throat o make sure he was still breathing, "It was me, Ne'Sean Short, Andre Jones and the defendant De'Quan Short was in the car that night".

A light rumble vibrated across the courtroom, but De'Quan acted unaffected as he scribbled something on his note pad and turned his attention back to the action.

"And what were you all doing parked on that block in a stolen car, at 4 a.m.?" Dolen asked trying to set the scene for his audience.

"We were loading up our guns and planning on how we were going to rob this drug spot upstairs in that building," Fat Pee said.

"Is that building number 57?"

"I didn't know the building number, he just told me to pull over by the building", Fat Pee said.

Dolen looked at his notes and said, "So did you go upstairs with the defendant and your other two partners, or did you wait in the car?"

Mr. White wanted to jump up and object, because they never established De'Quan going into the building. But he remained seated. This might help the case in the long run he thought to himself as he scribbled some notes on his pad.

"I was the getaway driver, so I never went upstairs," Fat Pee said as he glanced over in De'Quan's direction.

De'Quan was staring so hard at Fat Pee it felt like he was looking through Fat Pee's soul. De'Quan wanted to scream on him and ask him what is he doing? But it was too late. Fat Pee had crossed the line and he could never show his face in Marcy projects ever again.

"So, you never saw what happen upstairs in the apartment?" A.D.A. Dolen asked as he faced the jury to watch their reactions.

"No sir".

"Okay, so tell us what happen when you waited out side in the stole jeep", A.D.A. Dolen said to move the action along.

"When they came out of the building, De'Quan was carrying Ne'Sean because he was shot. Dre tried to get into the car, but some women came up the block with a gun in her hand. We all froze, then somebody started shooting".

The judge and the entire courtroom was on the edge of their seats and Dolen knew it, "How many people did you see shooting from the car?"

"From the car…Just Dre…and me", Fat Pee said putting his head down.

"So, the defendant and the other partner, aww Ne'Sean Short didn't fire any shots from the jeep?" A.D.A. Dolen asked as he paced the floor.

"Well when the shooting started I got scared and stepped on the gas pedal. I think De'Quan fell but Ne'Sean pulled him into the jeep while I was driving off. Then next thing I know it, a car comes out of nowhere and hits us and we crash", Fat Pee said as he shifted in his wheelchair.

Fat Pee wasn't the best witness Dolen ever had on the witness stand, but he had the courtroom attention, "At that point what did the defendant do?"

"He was knocked out in the back".

"Then what happened?" Dolen asked.

"Dre was the only one that could get away, so I shot out of the window to give him some cover. He grabbed the bag and jumped out of the car. I was shot after that and I woke up in the hospital,"

"You shot what out the window?" A.D.A. Dolen asked.

"A gun", Fat Pee answered with his voice trailing off like he was embarrassed by his actions.

"Oh, I see, and how many shots did you shoot?"

Fat Pee was feeling uncomfortable about this line of questioning. He thought they were there to talk about De'Quan, but it seems like A.D.A. Dolen only wanted to focus on the stuff he did that night.

"I don't remember", Fat Pee said with an attitude.

"Okay, your witness," A.D.A. Dolen said as he looked in Mr. White's direction. He scooped up his papers from the small podium and sat down at the prosecution table feeling incomplete about establishing De'Quan as a killer, but he still had better witnesses on his list to call.

Justice Demarcus spoke first, "Aww, I think we should take a short recess and continue at 2 o'clock". without waiting for a response, the judge stood up and headed to for the judge's chambers in the back.

"All rise!" The bailiff said causing the courtroom to stand and file out the back door.

*****
─────

After a short recess it was Mr. White's turn to cross examine Fat Pee and De'Quan was ready to watch him squirm. During the recess De'Quan held a short meeting with his lawyer in the holding cell area, and it was agreed that Mr. White will continue the path A.D.A. Dolen paved with Fat Pee not really seeing De'Quan do anything. He was just there and not the mastermind of this crime like they are saying he is.

Mr. White got his thoughts together, then walked over to the side of the jury box to begin his line of questioning, "Mr. Long, you say you stayed in the stolen jeep, but you don't know what building my client went into?"

"Nah I don't know the building. It was dark man", Fat Pee said feeling annoyed.

"Okay, so what floor and apartment did he go to?" Mr. White asked looking from the jury to Fat Pee to keep their focus on him.

"Aww, I think the top floor, I don't know the apartment", Fat Pee said.

"You think the top floor," Mr. White said more to himself, then he asked, "So in this apartment that you said my client went into, how many people were in there?"

"I don't know, I told you I didn't go up there," Fat Pee said feeling frustrated.

"So, you can testify to my client killing anybody in an apartment, in a building that you don't remember the building number to, am I correct so far?" Mr. White said.

"Objection!" A.D.A. Dolen blurted out from behind the prosecution table.

"Sustained, get to the point Mr. White," Justice Demarcus sternly said to the lawyer.

"Okay, sorry your honor…I'm just trying to establish some type of picture that has my client in it committing a crime, besides riding in a stolen car according to this witness".

Justice Demarcus hesitated; he knew Mr. White was right. Fat Pee didn't testify to De'Quan doing nothing more than riding in a stolen car and possessing a weapon. But in his courtroom, you are guilty until proven innocent, so Mr. White had to work harder than that. He cleared his throat and said, "Okay, continue".

"Thank you, now you say you pulled away from the curb before my client could get into the car?" Mr. White asked as he looked down at his notes.

"Yeah man, I got scared when all the shooting started," Fat Pee said in De'Quan's direction with pleading eyes.

De'Quan maintained his neutral stare in Fat Pee direction, but on the inside De'Quan was boiling. Nothing hurts more in the street life than a friend ratting out another friend, and he never thought one of his friends would do it to him.

Mr. White had coached De'Quan on how to suppress his anger when a witness like Fat Pee takes the stand and tries to send emotional signals through their testimony to him. Mr. White assured him if he maintained a neutral look he would be able keep the jury focused on the facts of the testimony and not the fluff that A.D.A. Dolen will feed the jury.

"So, you get scared, pull off with my client hanging out of the car, was my client shooting a gun?" Mr. White asked.

"No man, he was dragging outside the car and his brother pulled him in before we got hit by another car," Fat Pee paused, "and his brother died".

The entire courtroom seamed to stop breathing. Mama K put her hand over her mouth as Meika put her head on her mother shoulder. They didn't know how exactly Ne'Sean died and hearing it for the first time in a packed courtroom made De'Quan want to jump over the table and choke Fat Pee. His reckless driving got his brother kilt and him in jail

"Mr. Long what kind of plea agreement are you receiving for today's testimony?" Mr. White asked knowing he had enough to show Fat Pee didn't testify to anything really incriminating to get De'Quan life in prison.

Fat Pee fidgeted in his wheelchair and said, "Ten years flat".

De'Quan shook his head as Mr. White said, "Thank you for your time," and made his way back to the defense table.

Chapter 6

A.D.A. Dolen was feeling like he needed a better back-up witness, so he went looking for the key to the case; Detective Melissa Sanchez.

A.D.A. Dolen had lost contact with Melissa when the trail got cold on the disappearance of her baby. Being that her baby was snatched before he could even meet his own mother, the search for the baby went cold after ten hours of no word. Last time A.D.A. Dolen tried to reach out to Melissa he didn't get an answer, and he let it go. But now he needed her to come in and help him put De'Quan away for good. What he didn't know is what kind of shape he would find Melissa in.

A.D.A. Dolen brought his assistant Paula and an armed escort to wait in the car while they headed upstairs. Melissa lived in a rough part of Washington Heights and the last thing Dolen wanted is someone recognizing him from a courtroom and seeking retribution on his way out of the building.

Melissa was sitting in her living room watching a talk show when her bell rung. She hopped up off the couch and shuffled to the intercom.

"Who is it?"

"Aww, A.D.A. Dolen".

Melissa looked at the intercom as if not to let him in. She took a deep breath and buzzed the buzzer to let him in.

Melissa hadn't heard from anyone at the D.A.'s office in months, so for someone to come to her house it must be serious. She quickly moved some cups and newspapers off the coffee table, then looked in the mirror to check her look. A knock at the door snapped Melissa out of the mirror and she shuffled to the door.

Melissa open the door and looked at her visitors up and down, "Hi".

"Hi detective Sanchez, this is my assistant Paula, may we come in?" A.D.A. Dolen asked.

Melissa stepped to the side and pointed to the couch, "Sure have a seat."

She locked the door and said, "Can I get you something to drink?"

"Aww, no I'm fine and this will only take a minute, what about you Paula?"

"No. I'm okay, thank you", Paula said with a bright smile.

Melissa sat down on a chair and said, "So what can I do for you Mr. Dolen?"

"Well that murder case with De'Quan Short and his crew is in full swing, and I know your involved with it in a lot of different ways, and for that reason I tried to try this case without having to call you in to testify," he said.

"And what has changed?" Melissa asked as she crossed her arms across her chest. She thought he would have some news about her baby. Not her baby father who don't want anything to do with her.

"Well we need to establish De'Quan went to that apartment that night knowing what was in there and you are the one who showed it to him".

"Won't that open up the door to our personal relationship", Melissa asked causing A.D.A. Dolen to shift in his seat.

"Aww, yes it will. Why is that a problem?"

Melissa tried to control her anger, "Of course it's a problem. I made a stupid decision to be sexually involved with a person who is charged with killing officers I was doing a sting with. To the rest of the force that looks like I set my own partners up. Then my baby gets stolen before I could even kiss him hello, and those same colleagues put in zero effort to find him, and it look like that's my punishment for this damn case," A tear slide out the side of her eye causing Dolen to look over to Paula for help.

Paula quickly caught the hint, "Aww, don't cry. Here." She got up and gave Melissa a tissue.

"Thank you," Melissa said as she wiped the corners of her eyes. "I'm sorry, I just get so emotional when I think about my baby, and why nobody can find him".

"I'm sorry about that detective. I thought they would have better results by now," A.D.A. Dolen said shaking his head. "We're not giving up hope something will turn up".

He thought his words would be more comforting, but his words had the opposite effect as Melissa got up and rushed off to the bathroom, "I'm Sorry".

Paula stood there in silence not knowing what to do. A.D.A. Dolen knew Melissa was still shaky since they didn't find her baby yet, but to witness her break down first hand had him feeling like he would have to win this case another way. "Paula, why don't you go check on her…see if she's okay".

"Yeah, sure," Paula said and headed down the hallway toward the bathroom.

Chapter 7

If you told De'Quan two years before he would be sitting on Rikers Island, New York city county jail, facing a murder charge, in the mist of a racial war he would have laughed at you. Standing at the cell bars trying to look out onto the tier wasn't looking too funny after all.

De'Quan walked in the door with a street rep of being a shooter from his highly publicized case, that easily elevated once he came to jail and got into his first fight.

What De'Quan didn't know about was the wide spread gang network that had a strangle hold on the giant floating jail. Being from Marcy projects in Bed-Stuy Brooklyn De'Quan was already a part of a home town gang. But when people from different home towns gangs and city housing projects get placed into a large cage the rules change.

Things went from claiming a hood or repin your boro to it being a black against Spanish thing, with the blacks electing to adapt the lifestyle of the well-known west coast Bloods gang, and the Spanish guys falling under the strong Latin Kings or the Neita's. A lifestyle De'Quan only saw on TV. But very much real in the jail system. Coming in De'Quan tried to play neutral in the war going on around him because he had other matters on his mind. What he had to learn is everybody on Rikers Island has problems and some try to avoid their reality by making others around them uncomfortable.

Looking out onto the empty tier De'Quan found himself thinking about how he got caught up in the gang culture on the Island.

"You are going in seven cell," The female c.o. said to De'Quan as she looked at his floor card.

De'Quan nodded then dragged his two plastic bags full of his personal property down the gallery. Before he was moved to the new housing area De'Quan already got the 411 that he was being moved a Latin King house. The beef on Rikers Island between the Bloods and Latin Kings had escalated from small fights in dorm rooms in the jail's, to shoot outs on the streets. Things were getting serious around him and he tried to play each situation accordingly, but some situations don't warrant a calm response.

As De'Quan made his way down the gallery, he only saw four black faces in the dayroom when he passed it. That didn't alarm him. De'Quan wasn't a full-blown

Blood member at the time, and still had the mentality of being neutral in the war.

When he got to the cell the door was locked and he had to wait for the c.o. come and open it. Standing with his back to the closed cell door, De'Quan looked up and down the gallery watching the activity going on at the prime-time hour of eight o'clock at night.

Magazines were being traded, food shared, conversations about the streets and court cases flooded the air waves, and a light aroma of weed smoke lingered in the air. As De'Quan turned to look toward the back of the gallery he peeped someone coming his way. He didn't recognize him, so De'Quan didn't take it as an immediate threat.

"A man, you Dawg?"

Dawg was a slang word for being Blood, but De'Quan played the fool. "Nah man, do I look like a dog to you?"

The guy was five feet, six inches tall, but he looked up and down at De'Quan's six-foot frame as if he was the short one there and said, "I don't know homes, they all look different," He screwed up his face and said, "But I know you can't deny it if you are".

"So, what that mean, a Dawg can't live up here?" De'Quan asked already knowing the answer.

"No, they can't," and with that he spent off on his heels and walked down the gallery toward the dayroom.

De'Quan knew they would send somebody at him to see where he stood in the war. By now De'Quan was tired of the oppression and pressure the Latin gangs where putting on black people in the jails. Some of the Blood members where friends of his and living in a house where none of them could live was not a go look on his resume. Especially if one of them is suddenly moved to the housing unit.

The front gate opened, and a few guys came on to the gallery. The c.o. closed the gate behind them and one of the guy's spotted De'Quan standing down the gallery.

"Yo was up De'Quan?"

"Chilling…What's happening Ish," De'Quan said as they gave each other a pound.

Ishmael is Muslim, which put him on the outside of the racial war with the Spanish gangs, but some people didn't pay things like religion any mind when it is time to get bizzy. Ishmeal is one of those people. Standing at 6'2 tall and weighing close to 240 Ishmael was no small guy to tussle with when it had to go down.

"Ain't nothing God, I'm coming from the law library. You just came up here?" Ishmael asked as he looked down at his bags.

"Yeah man, I been waiting for like a half an hour for the c.o. to come over here and open this cell, so I can put my shit in here," De'Quan said.

Ishmael looked around and said, "Man you alright up here?"

De'Quan knew what he meant. "Nah, they already sent somebody my way to see if I'm Blood".

"Word, yeah they on it up here. A Blood kid from Queens got into it with them this morning up here, so they on point up here," Ishmael said.

"Yeah, well as soon as I can get my shit in this cell and lock it, it's going down Ish. I can't stay up here".

"Okay cool, it's like four other black guys up here who will step in if shit gets thick," Ishmael said looking around, trying to make sure no one was listening to their conversation.

"Yo Ish, I don't want you getting into no shit over me God. I got this," De'Quan said confidently.

"I hear you, I still got you, even if them other niggas don't do nothing…hold up, let me try to get the c.o. over here to open the cell," Ishmael said and headed down the gallery toward the c.o. booth.

Ishmael returned with on of the c.o.'s who quickly open up a few cells and disappeared back off the gallery.

"Ish hold me down real quick," De'Quan said when he pulled his bags into the cell.

"I got you God, do your thang," Ishmael said as he took up position in front of the open cell door.

De'Quan quickly dug into his bag and grabbed a pair of pants. He went to the lining of his pants and pulled out a razor wrapped in plastic and electrical tape. He put on his black hoodie and black Tim's, took a deep breath and said, "Aight Ish, I'm ready".

Ishmael stepped to the side and De'Quan stepped out onto the gallery, "You sure you got this?"

47

"Yeah God, good looking man, where you going; in the dayroom?" De'Quan asked as his eyes scanned his surroundings. A small group stood in the back smoking weed and cigarettes, while a few others hung out by open cells talking.

"Okay just holla if you need me," Ishmael said before he gave De'Quan a pound and walked away.

De'Quan stood in front of his cell with his hand in his hoodie packet, waiting for an opening, and one happened five minutes later when one of the guys smoking in the back walked off from the pack.

He looked really high and De'Quan saw opportunity knocking, "A man, I can ask you something?"

The guy stopped and looked up at De'Quan as if this was the first time he laid eyes on him, that didn't stop him from poking his chest out. It was a Latin King house and if you weren't apart of the rush then you were looked at as a peasant.

"What you want man?"

De'Quan kept his neutral look as he said, "I was looking for some weed man. If you got it, I go on a visit tomorrow...I can hit you back when I come back feel me".

The guy looked De'Quan up and down and said, "Yo Bee, you don't got money?"

"Nah man, but like I said," Before De'Quan could finish the guy waved his hand in the air and said, "Fuck out of here. Nigga with no money".

He tried to walk away giving De'Quan the opening he wanted. De'Quan pulled his hand out of hoodie and rubbed the razor across the guy cheek splitting his face open, spraying blood on the wall. Blood immediately ran down his neck soaking his shirt as his eyes open like he just got electrocuted.

"The fuck, Mineto! Mineto! He cut me!" The guy screamed as he ran toward the back of the gallery to the rest of the group, holding his face.

De'Quan went the other way toward the front. The female c.o. sitting in the control booth saw the commotion and watched De'Quan run to the front.

"Open the gate," De'Quan said as he watched the group get hyped up and start making their way down the gallery coming for him.

The female c.o. picked up the telephone as she waved to her partner on the other side of the housing unit, "Yeah this is 2upper, we have a red dot," she barked into the receiver then hung up. "Stand right there!"

De'Quan saw she wasn't going to open the gate to let him out, so he went to his plan b. De'Quan grabbed a plastic chair with his free hand and walked toward the crowd ready for anything.

Before he made it pass the third cell on the gallery De'Quan was blindsided with a hard punch to his temple.

"Shit," he blurted out as he bounced off the cell bars and wildly swung the chair. The chair connected with one of his attackers, but it wasn't enough to stop the onslaught coming his way. Somebody grabbed De'Quan by his hoodie and pulled him down to the ground. De'Quan quickly cut the guy on his forehead with his razor, sending blood squirting across the floor.

"Awww! He cut Me!" The guy cried as he grabbed his face and was pushed out of the way.

"Get the knife!" Someone barked as they jumped on De'Quan, hurting each other in the process.

"Get the fuck off of him!" Ishmael barked as he grabbed one of the Latin Kings by his long braids and threw him into the wall.

An all-out brawl started with the other black guys running out of the dayroom when Ishmael did and started hitting anybody on the gallery who was against them with a chair.

Before someone could get the razor out of De'Quan's hand he felt the pile on top of him get lighter, then Ishmael grabbed him and pulled him far enough from the group for De'Quan to get himself together.

"Come on God...Yah niggas back the fuck up!" Ishmael yelled over the confusion as he swung the chair at on of the Latin Kings head, connecting with a loud thud.

De'Quan hopped to his feet and swung his razor to cut another one of them. He missed and was suddenly knocked off of his feet again, but this time it was from the blow to his head by a riot squad stick.

The bad part about the incident is De'Quan woke up in the infirmary handcuffed to the bed, with a big knot on his head, and new assault charges pending. The good side of the incident is he received an offer on the table for him to join the N.Y. Bloods gang for his latest performance. De'Quan never saw himself being a part of a large gang, but he took their offer to join and hadn't looked back since.

"Yo De'Quan, you up?" A voice coming from the cell next door snapped him out of reminiscing trance.

"Yeah Mikey B, what's Poppin homie?" De'Quan asked as he stared out the little window on the cell door.

"Eastside Blood," Mikey B saluted De'Quan with a groggy voice.

"All da time blood," De'Quan said.

"You going to the yard today?" Mikey B asked as he rubbed his eyes.

"Yeah…They're running it now. They're at the front of the gallery", De'Quan said.

"Oh word, let me get ready," Mikey B said as he ran over to his sink and started brushing his teeth.

Being in 23hour lock down wasn't De'Quan's idea of chilling in jail, but it was the reality he was living because of his numerous assaults and gang affiliation tickets. Awaiting trial while on Rikers Island and not out on bail made De'Quan change his mind set about a lot of things in life. Being locked down for 23hours had him reading books and getting into himself more than he would if he was still running the streets.

De'Quan could feel his growth everyday as he read books on the Black Panthers and other black liberation groups who stood up for the people and their rights in this country. Being Blood meant De'Quan had to learn about his people, where they came from and their history in this country, more so now because he was involved in a racial war in the jail that was finding it's way out onto the streets of New York. He always saw himself as a general, no matter what army he's a part of, and good leaders educate themselves, so they can teach their troops.

The sound of keys jingling made De'Quan get on point. Even though he could see out the little window on the cell door, he could not see who was coming up the gallery, "Yo Mikey B, I think we next".

"I'm ready homie", Mikey B said as he put on his sneakers.

A tall dark skin c.o. appeared in front of De'Quan's window, looked him up and down, then asked, "You going out?"

"Yeah", De'Quan said as he stuck his hands out of the slot in the thick metal door.

The c.o. put the handcuffs on De'Quan, "put your back to the door...Open 23 cell!"

De'Quan turned around as the cell door slide open. The c.o. grabbed De'Quan by his waist band and backed him out of the cell, then he escorted De'Quan down the gallery, so he can get stripped searched. De'Quan never understood the logic to strip searching a man that is going to be put in a 9x6 steel cage by themselves for one hour, but those are the rules if you some fresh air.

Once he was searched, De'Quan was place in a pair of shackles and escort down the stairs. Walking out to the box yard was like walking on the red carpet if you were a celebrity gangsta. Shout outs and salutations would be shot in your direction to let those know, that didn't know who you are and what you look like exactly who you be. De'Quan put on his New York lean and walked down the aisle that had a row of 25 metal cages on each side of him.

"031 Blood", one of the homies in cage saluted De'Quan on his walk by.

"031", De'Quan responded as he walked to the cage and a c.o. closed it behind him. The c.o. took the shackles off De'Quan wrist and ankles, connected the handcuffs to the gate, then walked away.

Two minutes later Mikey B stepped into the cage next to De'Quan and had his shackles removed. "What's good homie?" Mikey B said with a smile, as he subconsciously rubbed his wrist.

After being in a cell by yourself for over 20 hours a day De'Quan witnessed firsthand how important human contact is. Even if your having an hour-long conversation with a friend, you had metal bars between you two.

"Ain't shit homie, I just been stressing about my case", De'Quan said as he paced around in the small cage.

Mikey B took off his jacket, laid it down on the ground and started doing push-ups on top of it, "When the next time you go back to court?"

"Tomorrow. I think they trying to get this chick I was fucking with to testify", De'Quan said as he grabbed onto the metal gate and did 10 pull-ups.

Mikey B stood up from his set of push-ups and said, "Damn homie, first your man tells on you, now your chick…They must really don't want you in the street". Mikey B shook his head then got down to do another set of push-ups.

"Yo De'Quan what's poppin homie?" The question came from across the aisle.

De'Quan walked to the gate, "031 eastside Jah", De'Quan flashed the signature gang sign.

Jah Red returned the salute and said, "All the time Blood. Yo you heard that fool Omar coming out today".

Mikey B came to the gate breathing hard from doing his set and said, "Eastside Jah".

"All the time Mikey B", Jah Red said as he saluted him.

"That's the dude that's locked up for killing the little homie on in Brownsville?" Mikey B asked.

"Yeah that's him. He trying to say he didn't do it, but niggas is saying he was there. So, he knows what's up", Jah Red said, then looking down the walkway he continued, "Here he goes right there, coming down".

They all stood in silence as they watch Omar walk pass their cages. He could feel the heat coming up off the bars as they stared him down. Omar had been on Rikers Island for 10months, and so far, his stay has been filled with people talking about him or trying to make a move against him. He was used to the tension, and at this point in the game he had beef with one of the most ruthless gangs in New York city; he couldn't fold now.

Omar went into his cage, had the shackles removed, and went about his business of working out without saying a word to anyone in the yard.

"Yeah so, Jah when the next time that boy Tye going to shake out on the V.I.?" De'Quan asked changing the subject. They couldn't get to Omar right now, but seeing his face was enough for future run inns in the jail system.

"He went on a visit yesterday, but he fucked around and went back down there this morning", Jah Red said.

"Word, yo tell that nigga I'm going to send my chick up there tonight", Mikey B said then walked off to do another set.

"I got you homie", Jah Red said as he looked down the walkway. "Police coming".

The c.o. walked up to the cage De'Quan was in and said, "Short, you got a visit", and unhooked the handcuffs off the gate.

"Okay playa…Give her a kiss for me", Mikey B joked.

De'Quan smiled, "Stay away from my chick Blood".

Mikey B laughed, "Come on homie, just tell her to find me a friend and I'll call it even".

De'Quan laughed as he let the c.o. put the shackles on him and took him out of the cage, "Call it even; I don't even remember owing you".

"Come on, let's go", the c.o. said as he grabbed De'Quan by his arm and lead him down the walkway.

*****
———

Shakia sat in a small cage that had two plastic chairs and a small table in it waiting for them to bring De'Quan downstairs. She knew De'Quan was stressed out about being locked up, but she couldn't understand why he had to get into so much trouble while he is in there and end up locked down for 23hours a day. Visiting him in a tiny cage felt ridiculous and unnecessary to Shakia, but the department of corrections disagreed.

Sitting there looking around the cage feeling like a bird Shakia knew she could never get used to going through the whole being searched and questioned, then placed in a tiny cage process that comes with visiting someone for too long.

Shakia loved De'Quan, but this whole jail thing was putting a strain on their relationship and ever since the trial started Shakia was learning things about De'Quan and Dre that upset her and made her feel uneasy. She knew they were in the streets doing things; but killing people and learning De'Quan had a baby with the cop chick who set them up was a hard pill to swallow.

De'Quan was escorted out onto the packed visit room wearing a red jumpsuit and black Nike slippers, smiling and talking to everybody like he was the damn mayor of the jail. Shakia shook her head and said under her breath, "He make me so sick, he can't just bring his ass to the cage".

The visit floor was a mixture of 5 small visit cages for one on one visits, 5 larger cages for family visits, and 10 small visit tables outside of the cages for less violent prisoners and their visitors.

De'Quan was a homie on the rise in the Blood ranks so him coming on the visit floor like he was running for office was a must. When the c.o. put him in the cage and took the shackles off him De'Quan turned to Shakia with a big smile.

"Really De'Quan, you had to say hello to the whole place before coming in here", Shakia said an attitude.

De'Quan kissed her and sat down, "Well hello to you too".

Shakia smiled, "I'm sorry baby, I just miss you and waiting for you in this cage, is crazy".

De'Quan hugged her over the small table and said, "I'm sorry Shakia, I know this whole jail thing is hurting us".

"Yes, it is", She countered.

"Well hopefully it'll be over soon", De'Quan said with a touch of confidence.

"You think you can still win after Fat Pee got up there and told on yah like that?" Shakia asked frustrated.

"Shakia we have to have some faith baby; Yeah he told, but he can't say he saw me do anything but get in and out of the car", De'Quan said as he held her hands and looked into her eyes.

Shakia was the same complexion as Dre, but that's where the comparison stopped. It took De'Quan along time to look at Shakia in a sexy way because she is older than him by 4 years and she never paid her younger brother friend any mind just for that reason; he was her brother friend.

"What about your…girlfriend", Shakia asked, "Won't her testimony hurt you?"

Talking to Shakia about Melissa was a hard subject to deal with while he was in jail because he cheated on Shakia with Melissa. Shakia would have never found out about the affair if it wasn't for Melissa getting pregnant and De'Quan getting Dre to take the baby. Shakia didn't know where her brother was at, but she had a feeling he had something to do with the baby disappearing.

"I think she's going to testify, but she wasn't there either, so she can't really say I killed anybody", De'Quan said trying to keep his voice down in the small cage.

"I'm scared for you De'Quan, I love you, but I can't do no life in prison bid. I'm going to lose my mind", Shakia said squeezing his hands.

"Don't worry, I'm not getting no life in prison, and that's real", De'Quan said and kissed her, then he changed the subject.

Chapter 8

Not knowing where her baby was really took a toll on Melissa mentally, and at some point, she felt herself feeling like she needed to use her police training and find her own baby. She just did not know where to start.

A.D.A. Dolen coming to see her made Melissa break down, but when they left her house she started brainstorming about De'Quan and the whole situation with the case. Two things bothered her about it all; investigators haven't been able to find Andre Jones, and her baby was missing and De'Quan hadn't made any noise her way about it. Melissa didn't care about putting De'Quan away for the rest of his life. All she cared about is getting her baby back, and the D.A.'s office wasn't talking about that, so she didn't want to talk anymore.

Melissa knew she was up against the eight-ball going to her colleagues for information, but she had to something. They blamed her for the De'Quan murder case because she brought him to the apartment and he returned with his friends to rob their undercover operation. A lot of days Melissa blamed herself for her partners deaths, but that was no excuse for the force to turn their backs on her. Her baby is an innocent bystander in all of this and the least they could've done is help her find her baby. Melissa had always been a good detective, she just didn't use her skills because she hadn't been thinking straight for months. Now it was time to change.

The first-person Melissa went to see is the lead investigator in her baby disappearance case to get copies of everything he had. The detective was reluctant to give her his files, but Melissa came in his office determine to get what she wanted, and he was cold on the case anyway, so why not let her give it a try.

Melissa took the files home, pulled out the files she had on the De'Quan case and looked over everything until her body forced her go get something to eat.

*****

After having a long conversation with Tammy about the direction they were going in and their future plans, it was decided Dre would stop selling drugs with her cousin Boogie in South Carolina. Their main concern is the babies and their safety, and Tammy cousin was the only connection to them and their old life who still physically sees one of them.

Problem with getting out the game with Boogie is he didn't have a solid connect, and Dre had him open off of selling the good stuff from New York. When Dre came to him about moving on with Tammy and the kids to live a more secluded life Boogie was in agreement with them parting ways, if it was the safest thing for him to do for them and the babies. But he needed Dre to plug him in with his New York connect. Dre wasn't a fan of doing that, but he owed Boogie that much after everything he did for them when they came to South Carolina. He helped Dre maintain a money flow and Dre needed to hook him up to his own flow, it was only right. But it was easier said then done because his connect didn't trust anyone.

"Who is you friend Dre?" Roman asked when they cleared the front door security and was lead to his desk. Roman usually met Dre with a smile and hug, but new faces didn't make him so friendly.

"This is my cousin Boogie, he good people Roman. I can't make too many trips uptown anymore. I need him to come for me", Dre said, giving it to Roman as if he still was going to be involved with the operation, just not visible anymore.

Roman looked Boogie up and down, then turned his attention back to Dre, "He come for you Dre…I don't like problem…He come alone".

Dre looked over to Boogie, who quickly responded, "Yes, of course, that's not a problem".

After a brief silence Roman motioned for them to sit down, and asked, "Now what can I do for you?" as he leaned back in his chair.

*****
___

Melissa's Washington Heights neighborhood was full of Spanish and Dominican culture, making her coca complexion and long wavy black hair an easy fit in when she moved in and became an undercover cop. Once the incident happened with De'Quan she was advised by the department to move, but Melissa was comfortable at that point and she was pregnant making her want to have the baby first then think about moving.

Walking through the neighborhood, snacking on a slice of pizza Melissa began to get the feeling it might be time to move and let everything go. She didn't want to feel like she was quitting, but there was nothing around here to look forward to anymore.

Walking down Amsterdam avenue she found herself looking at a red Lexus GS300 double parked in front of the store on the corner of 138th street. New York city is full of Lexus', but it was something familiar about the red Lexus that made Melissa stop and watch as the driver came out of the store shaking a juice. He looked at Melissa as he opened his juice, took a swig, then opened the car door. When he opened the door, the light came on in the car and Melissa could see the passenger face. Her heart almost stopped. That can't be.

The driver slammed the door, shifted the car in gear and pulled off; it seemed like all in one motion without giving her much time to think. Melissa watched as the car pulled off and quickly pulled out a pen and wrote the license plate number down on her hand. JIC8768 South Carolina.

Melissa speed walked back to her apartment to write down the license plate number on some paper and get on her job of tracking down the two people she saw in that Lexus. If her eyes didn't deceive her, Melissa just saw Andre Jones riding in the passenger seat of that Lexus. The South Carolina plate on the back was throwing her off, but if she had to bet on it, that car looked familiar to her because she used to ride in it when De'Quan owned that Lexus.

Chapter 9

Going court had to be the most tiring ordeal De'Quan ever had to go through in his life so far. First; he is woken up at 4:30 in the morning to eat breakfast (usually a small personal box of corn flakes and an apple), and by 5:30 he should be searched and escorted downstairs to the holding pens to wait for transportation to pick him up.

Transportation to the court from Rikers Island can be fast or slow, depending on the status of your case and in jail record. De'Quan was labeled high risk because of his case, and red I.D. for his bad jail record, awarding him transportation by a team of elite E.S.U. correction officers who get an adrenaline rush from beating on high level prisoners before they bring them to court to face the judge.

By 7:40 E.S.U. rushed up into the busy holding area, got De'Quan searched- again- shackled, pushed their way out of the building without answering to many questions about skipping the line and taking their prisoner before the other buses and vans waiting.

E.S.U. got De'Quan to Manhattan Supreme court within an hour and he was ready to fall asleep in the holding pen when Mr. White showed up to get the day started.

"Morning De'Quan, how are you today?" Mr. White asked as he grabbed a chair and pulled up to the cell bars. He sat down and started pulling out some paperwork.

"Tired as shit man, I can't understand why they have to wake me up at 4:30 if court don't start until 9", De'Quan said with an attitude.

"Well don't let it get to you. They want you off balance like that, so they can get a bad reaction out of you in the courtroom. If your too tired you might fall asleep at the defense table, or someone testimony might set you off because of fatigue. All tricks they use to get under the accused skin", Mr. White said.

"I feel you Mr. White. So, what's going on today?" De'Quan asked as he lit up a cigarette.

"Today the A.D.A. is going to come with a deal", Mr. White said.

De'Quan was surprised, "A deal? Why, I thought they wanted to give me life"?

"I'm pretty sure A.D.A. Dolen would love to give you three life sentences, but his evidence doesn't support that type of sentence. Now his next move is to offer you deal of something along the lines of 17years to maybe 22years."

"Damn, and they call that a deal", De'Quan said with disgust as he pulled on his cigarette.

"All of this is just back door news for now, we'll know when court starts today if their serious about any offers", Mr. White said.

"Why you think they want to stop the trial and give me a deal now?" De'Quan asked.

"From what I'm hearing their having problems with one of their witnesses", Mr. White said.

"Who, Melissa?" De'Quan said knowing the answer already.

"Yes…Apparently she's not mentally stable enough in their eyes to testify. She's still broken up about her baby being stolen. I personally seen people with bigger problems come in and give a good testimony anyway, so my guess is they don't want it to come out that you were in a relationship with Ms. Sanchez and the baby issue," Mr. White said, playing the story lines in his head.

"If she doesn't testify, then who else do they have that can point me out?" De'Quan asked feeling confident there was no one else.

"On the D.A.'s witness list it says a few more officer's names, but as far as any civilian names…no. There were a lot of officers who responded to the scene that night, so I'm pretty sure they all have something to say about what they saw that night. As long as no one saw you with a gun, we should be fine".

The sound of keys jiggling made them pause as a c.o. appeared and said, "Counselor we have to being him out, judge is ready for early motions".

"Okay, thank you", Mr. White gathered up his things and said, "I'll be outside," to De'Quan as he walked off.

Manhattan Court building is a maze in the back settings of the building. A part Mr. White hate navigating through to get to the right courtroom. As he turned a corner he bumped into A.D.A. Dolen looking like he also was lost and looking for the right door to walk threw.

"I'm sorry...oh morning Mr. White," A.D.A. Dolen said with a bright smile.

Mr. White never trusted a white man from the D.A. office with a smile, especially when they were sworn enemies on opposite sides of the courtroom. "Good morning Mr. Dolen, you look refreshed today. Does that mean I can look forward to some good-news"?

A.D.A. Dolen chuckled and said, "You know me so well by now Mr. White. I'll tell you what, you tell your client I'm in a good mood this Monday morning, so I'm going to offer him 20 years flat. If he turns me down and we have to keep wasting tax payer's money on the inevitable, the Justice Demarcus is going to show no mercy".

Mr. White looked A.D.A. Dolen in his eyes and he knew he didn't have a strong enough case like he was putting on he did. He wants De'Quan to cop out to 20years, then he must think they can't get De'Quan on the murder charge like they want.

"Okay, thank you. I'll talking to Mr. Short about this offer", Mr. White said as a court officer pushed threw one of the doors in the wall. Mr. White didn't bother to see if it was the right courtroom he was walking into, he didn't want to be in that small hallway with the enemy any longer than he was.

*****

"All rise, the Honorable justice Demarcus is residing", Justice Demarcus made is way into the packed courtroom, took his seat, "please be seated, then he addressed the jury, "Morning ladies and gentlemen, I hope you all had a splendid weekend".

Everyone in the jury box smiled as a few nodded in agreement. "Great. Now, is the prosecution ready to call its next witness?" the judge asked ready to get things moving.

"Yes, your honor, the people call detective Steven Torres to the stand," A.D.A. Dolen said as the side door next to the judge chambers swung open and the detective limped to the witness stand.

De'Quan thought he was watching a ghost limp across the floor. The last time he saw this guy he was laying in a pool of his own blood by the table where the drugs were. De'Quan whole insides was screaming at him to stop everything and reconsider that flat 20year deal the A.D.A. Dolen offered. He wasn't a fan of giving away

20years of his life without a fight, but that was before witnesses starting returning from the dead.

"Detective Torres, please tell the court how long you've been with the N.Y.P.D. and what is tour job description with the forced?" A.D.A. Dolen asked as he set up shop at the small podium. He knew he was in good shape already because when the detective walked out into the courtroom De'Quan turned pail.

Detective Torres cleared his throat and said, "I've been on the force now for 11years, and I'm apart of an undercover drug unit that was operating out of the 33rd precinct".

"And you were involved in an operation on the night of March 3rd, 1996", A.D.A. Dolen said trying to set the scene.

"Yes sir. It was me, detective Mike Kozak, who went by the alias Bear, and an informant named Thomas Fernandez, who went by the alias Bolo", the detective said as he kept his eye contact with A.D.A. Dolen.

"Please tell the court, what was the nature of this operation you guys were conducting".

The detective looked over to the jury as if they were the only people in the room and said, "Well our operation was to run a fake drug house out of apartment 4a. Whenever we have buyer's, usually a few buys go down then the task force steps in to make an arrest when we have enough evidence and information on the subject".

A.D.A. Dolen paced the small floor and said, "now did you meet the defendant running this operation, and if you did, Why?"

The detective looked over in De'Quan direction and back to the jury and said, "he was brought up there to use the bathroom and that's when we believe he scoped out our operation ".

"Objection! Making assumptions about what was scoped out during a bathroom run is pure speculation", Mr. White said as he half stood out of his seat.

"Sustained, move on Mr. Dolen", Justice Demarcus said.

"Sure, your honor. Now detective if you were running a drug house, you saying the defendant came to purchase drugs from you?" A.D.A. Dolen asked. He knew he was riding on a slippery slope, but he needed this conviction and the only way he was going to get it is if he established De'Quan had been in the house and knew who was up there.

Detective Torres knew he didn't see De'Quan's face that day, but it had already been established their investigation it was De'Quan and his friends who came up there later that night and shot him and his partners. At this point detective Torres didn't need to see his face, he just needed to put someone away for the crimes.

"No, he came in with one of our C.I.'s and he used the bathroom".

"And that's when you saw him", A.D.A. Dolen asked to make sure.

"Yes sir".

"So, when is the next time you saw him?"

Detective Torres took a sip of water and said, "When they came into the apartment shooting".

The judge, jury, and the courtroom audience were on the edge of their seats.

"And that's when they shot you, and what happened after That?"

"I blacked out. I woke up two weeks later in the hospital", he said.

A.D.A. Dolen felt like he had enough to get a conviction. The detective just placed De'Quan in the apartment, "I have no further questions at this time, tour witness".

Mr. White stood up and wanted to pounce right on his target, "detective Torres, you say my client was up there early in the day to use the bathroom right"?

"Yes sir".

"Who brought him up there"? Mr. White asked. He felt something wasn't right with this case and it had a lot to do with the meeting.

"A confidential informant", detective Torres said looking over to the prosecution table.

"Oh, I'm sorry, I thought a detective Melissa Sanchez brought him up there in the morning", Mr. White said as he looked around the courtroom. He wanted to know why they were trying to keep her a secret if she's the link to De'Quan and this apartment.

"Well aww…yeah the undercover brought him there", the detective said trying to keep his answers light.

"And did my client know she was an undercover?" Mr. White asked as he got closer to the witness box.

"I don't know…you'll have to ask him," he said with a smirk on his face.

"Did he know that was an apartment that conducted drug transactions in it"? Mr. White asked.

"Again, I don't know. I never heard of him until he walked through the door that day to use the bathroom", Torres said feeling frustrated from answering the same questions he answered already.

"Do you remember what he was wearing that day"?

Torres was stuck for a moment, "aww, no. Sorry".

"Why did the undercover, Ms. Sanchez come there early in the day"? Mr. White asked.

"To drop something off", Torres said.

"So, you didn't witness my client commit any crimes during the day right…but you say he returned later that night with other people and started shooting, so how many of them came in?"

"I think 3 or 4 of them".

"So, tell us detective when these three of four people rushed in were they white, tall, short, black, big or slim?" Mr. White had the entire courtroom confused from the question, but only detective Torres had to answer it and from the look of the sweat sliding down the side of his face he didn't know how he was going to answer it.

A.D.A. Dolen jumped up, "Objection!"

"Over ruled", Justice Demarcus barked, "answer the question".

"Aww I don't know…it happened so fast…I only remember the tall one that shot me, and I shot him as I was going down. When I fell I blacked out, I'm sorry", the detective said feeling cornered.

"So, you never saw my client that night", Mr. White said as he eased up on the jury box.

Detective Torres looked to A.D.A. Dolen for help, then to the judge, but the judge wasn't giving out sympathy breaks today, "Answer the question detective".

Detective Torres looked defeated as he lowered his head and said, "no I didn't see him that night".

"If you didn't see him and he didn't shoot you, can you tell us if he did shoot anybody that night…no sorry withdrawn…this witness didn't see my client commit any crimes…I have no further questions at this time", Mr. White said as he grabbed up his papers and went back to the defense table.

De'Quan wrote on the legal pad 'Good job' and slide it to his lawyer as A.D.A. Dolen stood up to use his rebuttal. He didn't like how that line of questions went with the detective and he needed to clean it up, but the damage was done. Detective Torres didn't finger De'Quan like A.D.A. Dolen wanted him too.

Chapter 10

After a long day in court De'Quan just wanted to take a nice hot shower, smoke a blunt and lay down on a soft bed. All wishes and a far cry from the same daily routine of waiting in the holding pen until 8:30p.m. Around this time the transportation team comes to get him and take him back to Rikers Island. Once he arrives back to the jail he is placed in a holding cell where he is strip searched, feed a semi warm feed up trey, then escorted up stairs to the housing unit. By the time De'Quan makes it to the cell and is able to lay down it is 12 something at night. A few hours of rest in between and the c.o.'s we're right back at the cell door at 4:30 in the morning to put him through the motions all over again.

Since De'Quan started trial all of the waking him up and keeping him up all day had him feeling like he was on team no sleep- hustling for his life. A draining task that needed to recharge on the daily. The fight for his freedom shouldn't be so hard, but it is and every night when they brought him back to that cell, he could feel the souls in the other cells wishing for the same thing he was. To win his freedom.

"031 Blood", Mikey B saluted De'Quan once the c.o. took the shackles off of him and walked away.

"031 homie, what's popping?" De'Quan said as he took his sneakers off.

"That five…how it look today at court"? Mikey B asked.

"Brazy homie…I'll have to tell you in the yard", De'Quan said as he came closer to the steel door.

"No doubt. Yo, I'm about to set this one thirty off. I know you mad tired from today, so I want to get to it", Mikey B said with a grin. One thirty is a code for their war anthem that they chant daily as a ritual before everyone takes it down for the night.

"Yeah Blood I'm tired, but I will never be too tired for that one thirty". De'Quan said with a smile on his face. Chanting their war cry with the rest of his comrades on lock was that adrenaline rush he needed everyday to continue in his legal battles.

"That's what I'm talking about…UP TOP!" Mikey B shouted loud enough for everyone on the housing unit to hear him and take notice.

"Down Low!" De'Quan responded, catching the attention of other Blood members on the unit.

"Down Low!" "Down Low Blood". "Down Low, I'm here", the acknowledgements began to rain down the unit as everyone let their presence be heard.

Mikey B smiled and said, "I love this shit…I'm going in…PEACE ALMIGHTY!"

"PEACE BLOOD!" The response from the other members to Mikey B call was thunderous.

"PEACE ALMIGHTY!" Mikey B shouted at the top of his lungs.

"PEACE BLOOD!"

"OPRESSION!"

"BLOOD!"

"RESISTANCE!"

"BLOOD!"

"WAR!"

"BLOOD!"

"HOW ABOUT SOME HARDCORE!"

"THE BLOODS LIKE IT RAW!"

The building shook as other Blood members on other floors of the box began their own role call, chanting sounds camaraderie, and death to their enemies out their cell windows into the cool night sky.

Chapter 11

Ever since she saw the red Lexus in front of the store Melissa was on a mission to find that car and who owns it. She knows that was Andre Jones She saw in that car, which means this a sign. Melissa had been so down for so long that seeing Dre gave her a sense of hope again

She hadn't had in months and She wasn't trying to let that feeling get away.

Melissa made some calls and found out the car is registered to a woman named Monique Brooks, in Orangeburg South Carolina. From everything Melissa had in front of her, she could not tell what the connection would be between the woman and Dre, but after sitting alone in her living room under a dim light Melissa made up her mind. She had to go find out.

Melissa knew she needed a plan and rider with her. She threw some clothes on the bed, grabbed her gym bag and stocked it with a few things she was going to need. When she was satisfied with her bag Melissa picked up the phone and called her cousin Suge.

"Hello".

"Ola Suge…what you doing?" Melissa asked trying to sound regular.

"Laying here, watching t.v., what's going on, you okay?" Suge asked as she sat up on her bed.

"Yeah, but I need your help", Melissa said.

"What's wrong…do you need me to come over?" Suge asked ready to get out of the bed.

"No actually I need to come and get you. I need you to take a trip with me", Melissa said not wanting to explain herself over the phone. "I'm about to get in a cab and come to your house".

Suge was fully up now, "This must be serious if you calling me this late talking about going on a trip".

"It is Suge, now pack a bag and can you please be ready", Melissa said.

"Okay, okay. Let me get myself together", Suge said as Melissa hung up on her.

Melissa went into her closet to get her lock box. She opened it and grabbed her badge and gun out of it and put them in her purse, then grabbed her gym bag and headed for the door.

Melissa paused at the door when she heard the phone ringing but brushed off the caller. She didn't want anyone calling her right now and slowing up her process. She had to make moves.

*****

After another subpar day in court A.D.A. Dolen knew he had to come with the big guns in order to win this case. When he started the case Dolen was confident about it being a slam dunk conviction. De'Quan had been arrested on the scene, in the backseat next to his dead brother. There were guns in the car, and his clothes he had on that night had gun powder residue on them. But now after a few weeks of testimony he wasn't so sure about getting that conviction.

A.D.A. Dolen felt he had enough evidence to convict De'Quan without having Melissa testify in the trial. She was intimate with De'Quan, and the snatching of her baby had sent Melissa into a bad mental state. Dolen didn't trust Melissa would get on the witness stand and hold up long enough under questioning without falling apart about their relationship, or the baby being taken out of the hospital without her being able to name him.

Two weeks into the trial and A.D.A. Dolen was ready to change his tone and take his shot. Before leaving his office for the night he picked up the phone and dialed Melissa's number. The phone rang out and the answering machine picked up, "Hi this is A.D.A. Dolen, can you give me a call back on my personal line, or I will be in my office at 8a.m. Looks like I'm going to need you for the Short case". The machine cut him off before he could say anything else.

He gathered up his things and cut off the lights in his office before walking down a row of cubicles thinking to himself she's not going to call.

Melissa thought Suge would put her through the motions when she told her about seeing Dre and how her gut is telling her to track him down. Suge knew he was an important piece to the case she is involved in, but she didn't want to get involved with a wild goose chase for a criminal when the baby is still missing.

"I know it sounds strange Suge, tracking down that Lexus and finding Dre might be the answer what happened to the baby", Melissa said as she stood in Suge bedroom. Suge had clothes spread out on her bed like she didn't know what to take with her on the trip.

"Yeah but how Melissa, why would he know about the baby if he's been on the run since that night of the shooting?" Suge asked not convinced by her cousin story.

"I don't Suge…but I do know I haven't heard a word, seen a sign, or got a message about my baby since he disappeared, and when I'm ready to give up and just leave it all I see Andre Jones sitting in a car on Amsterdam. You remember Grandma used to tell us to look for the signs in life whenever you feeling lost?" Melissa asked.

Suge stared at her cousin and knew there was no stopping Melissa. Once she started quoting Grandma it was impossible to change Melissa's mind on anything. "Ok, so say we go all the way down there and he is there, then what are we supposed to do?"

Melissa smiled, she knew Suge was down once she started asking questions like that, "Then we just get in contact with the locals and let them take him in. Once he's in custody then I can get some answers".

Suge shook her head and said, "Ok, you're the cop, so you more about this stuff then me. I'm only going because my little cousin is involved in this some how and we have to find him…but if it wasn't for him you would be on your own sister".

Melissa chuckled and asked, "Why?"

"Because I'm too pretty for that cops and robbers shit. That's your deal. Now help me pack this bag before I change my mind", Suge said causing Melissa to bust out laughing. Suge hadn't seen her cousin smile and laugh in months and it felt good seeing her finally break out of that down state.

"That's why I love you Suge", Melissa said giving her cousin a hug.

"You Better, now come on and help me", Suge whined as she grabbed a hand full of halter tops.

Chapter 12

Growing up in the projects no one thinks about the only way of getting out is to be on the run from the police and Dre was no different. As he sat in the passenger seat of the Lexus thinking about the current state of his life Dre started getting thoughts of not being able to do this much longer. He didn't feel like giving up, but he didn't expect to be living this kind of life with Tammy and children in the mix with him.

When Dre and De'Quan came up with the idea to do robberies for money Dre didn't have clear picture on what his life would look like 10years later. They were young and only living for the day; now looking out the window as he watched the country side roll by at 65 miles an hour, he knew that way of thinking was a mistake.

Pop was the only male figure in their lives and once he went to prison they had no one to give them a real sense of direction. Dre knew that was no excuse for their actions, but when the streets raise you all logic flies down the highway like the Lexus was doing.

Snapping out of his trance Dre looked over to Boogie and said, "yo slow down bro".

Boogie gave Dre a quick glance as he maintained his speed and said, "Dre you really need to get off of that paranoid shit. We are 5 hours away from New York and you still worried about somebody following us".

"Nah bro, I just got a lot on my mind that all", Dre said.

"Hey man I can dig it. That's why I'm not going to disappoint you on this move man. That's all I needed Dre is a reliable connect. Whenever I had to wait for you to make the move it took too long, and I would have to pick up something light from them Atlanta boys, and that shit be so-so. Now with the connect I'm going to hurt this town".

Dre sat back listening to Boogie and he knew it is a good decision to get out of the game with him. Dre learned from Pop, when you mess with too many different people in the drug game your business suddenly starts leaking out to the streets. Next thing you know the wrong people is knocking at your door at the wrong time and Dre couldn't afford those problems. They had a good thing going for a while, but all good things come to an end.

"Pull over at the next rest stop so I can drive", Dre said as he looked out the window at a passing sign. They were almost in Virginia.

Boogie chuckled and said, "Okay scary".

✻✻✻✻✻

When Melissa and Suge landed in South Carolina they rented a car and made their way to the address Melissa had. She didn't want to waist anytime going to a hotel when the address was a three-hour drive from the airport. Melissa wanted to get right to it, because if she is wrong about the whole locating Dre thing, and him being there in the south, then she will just cut her loses and get back on the plane.

They took turns driving to Orangeburg and when they got there Melissa was far from tired even though she'd been up for almost 20hours.

"So how you want to do this?" Suge asked as they drove through the neighborhood looking for the house.

"If we don't see the car, I think we should sit for a while and just watch the house", Melissa said as she navigated the rental and looked at the house numbers as they passed them at the same time.

"You think their back from New York already?" Suge asked.

"Yeah they should be. That was like two days ago when I saw them, and I don't see them hanging around New York city for too long," Melissa said as she slowed the car down on a long stretch of road that had a few houses scattered about on both sides of the street. None of the houses were higher then two stories, with short driveways in front of each one.

"This one says 29", Suge said as she looked out her side of the car. The houses on the block each had a fence around its property, and enough space between them to park three cars. Some yard had toys and jungle Jim's in them, while others had garbage cans and chairs as their front yard decoration.

"Yeah the numbers are going up. What is it again?" Melissa asked like she forgot, but truth was she remembered the address the moment it was told to her over the phone.

"41, it should be around here...slow down Lissa", Suge said as she looked at the yellow house with a brown roof. "It's that one right there".

Melissa slowed the car down as they looked at the property that was partially blocked from being fully scene by two large trees, and an old fence. Melissa stopped the car to look down the side of the house. There were two cars parked on the side of the house. An old four door Cadillac that looked like it hasn't moved in years, and next to it was the red Lexus with a South Carolina plate on it.

"Oh shit, that's the car Suge", Melissa said as she pulled the car away from the curb.

Suge got excited, "what you want to do?" She asked as she started tying up her long flowing hair.

Melissa glanced over to her cousin as she turned the first corner they came too and said, "Suge what are doing, this isn't no street fight".

"Shit girl you never know. You got me out here in the middle of nowhere chasing down bad guys that may know where my little cousin is; it might go down today", Suge said no play no games.

Melissa ginned as drove around the entire block, then rolled through the block of the house again to see where they could park at. Parking on the street in Orangeburg was rare because most people parked on their property, but not unheard of as Melissa pulled over one house down and across the street from house number 41.

Melissa turned the car off as they both stared at the house on their radar, "You want to wait, or go knock on the door?" Suge asked looking over at Melissa.

"I don't want to tip them off if Andre is in there, so we should wait and see what happens," Melissa said as she leaned her seat back to get a little comfortable.

Dre woke up feeling like he needed to get back to Tammy and the kids. His business with Boogie was all squared away, and once he got his rest after their drive from New York, Dre was ready to get it moving again.

Dre went into the bathroom to wash up and change his clothes, then he went to the front of the house where Boogie's girl-friend Avena was laying on the couch in a pair of stretchy shorts and one of Boogies t-shirts watching t.v.

"Hey Dre", Avena said in her southern twang.

"What's up Avena, where Boogie at?"

"He went over by the block, or something. I don't know. He just said he'll be back, "Avena said as her attention stayed locked into the talk show she was watching.

Dre sucked his teeth, "Damn, I'm about to get up out of here. I can't be waiting for Boogie all day", Dre said as he walked off to go get his bags and put them in the car.

*****

After sitting in the car for two hours Suge began to get hungry, "Melissa when we gonna take a lunch break? I'm starving".

"Yeah, me too. What you have a taste for?" Melissa asked.

"Depends", Suge said with sly smile.

"On what Suge?" Melissa chuckled.

"On if you treating, duh", Suge said and they shared a quick laugh until Suge looked toward the house. "Ooh shoot, somebody is coming out".

They stared at the house in the distance and Melissa broke the silence, "That's him Suge", she said as she pulled her gun out of the bag.

"Hold on Lissa, what you about to do?" Suge asked with fear in her eyes. She was cool with finding Dre and letting the locals arrest him, but Melissa looked like she was about to do it herself.

Dre popped the truck of the Lexus and put two bags in it.

"He's going to leave", Melissa said as she stared at him, ready to jump out of the car.

Dre slammed the truck, looked around, then walked back to the house. He looked up and down the block, but Dre didn't see anything out of place as he climb the steps and went inside.

"You think he saw us?" Suge asked sounding scared.

Melissa looked at her cousin and said, "No, but we have to do something before he leaves".

"Yeah let's get to a phone and call the local police like you said", Suge said.

Melissa looked at Suge and knew her cousin was scared, but she wasn't going to pass this chance up. She couldn't understand why her colleagues at the department, had so much trouble trying to track Dre down, but there he was in the flesh. "Suge by the time we get to a phone he will be gone, I can't let that happen. I have to do something".

Before Suge could respond, the house door swung open and Dre walked out. He didn't bother to check up and down the block as he headed to the car and got in.

When Suge turned to Melissa to see what they were going to do, Melissa had slid out of the car and raced across the street in a crouching stance. "Oh shit", Suge blurted out as she quickly got into the driver's seat and turned the car on.

Melissa's heart was pounding out of her chest as she made her way across the street in three steps, then ran down the dirt sidewalk to house number 41.

Dre started the car and popped open the arm rest to look for a C.D. when the passenger door suddenly snatched open and a gun was pointed in his face. "Don't Move!"

Dre froze as he looked up from the arm rest and focused on the face behind the gun. This has to be a joke Dre said in his mind. The last time they encountered each other on the street uptown, Dre tried to kill Melissa. Now she was standing there with the drop on him thirteen hundred miles away from 160th street, he had to be dreaming.

It took Dre all of five seconds to realize Melissa was standing there by herself, which made him want to try her, but she could shoot him by mistake.

"Don't shoot", Dre said as he slowly raised his hands. He didn't know what to do.

"I said don't fucking move!" Melissa said as she contemplated her next move.

Suge saw Melissa make her way into the yard, with her gun drawn, and snatched open the passenger door to the Lexus. "Oh shoot", Suge almost peed on herself as she put the car drive and drove down to the front of the house blocking the driveway.

Dre hands froze in mid-air, "Okay, you got it. So, what you want to do?"

"For starters take you to jail, now get out the fucking car!" Melissa spat as she gripped the handle ready to shoot Dre.

"Okay, relax", Dre said as he slowly climbed out the car. He quickly took notice to there only being one car in the driveway. No swat team. No back-up, and the driver in the car didn't even get out of it.

Melissa kept her gun aimed on Dre as she made her way over to the driver's side of the car, "Put your hands on the roof of the car…don't get no ideas. You have any guns on you?" She put the gun to his head and ran her hand across his waist line to check him for a gun. Then up and down his arms and legs.

"Nah man".

Suge got out of the car and slowly walked up on the scene as Melissa searched Dre. "Come on Melissa, hurry up", Suge said like a paranoid look out.

Dre could sense this wasn't your average arrest on a fugitive. Knowing Melissa was from New York she probably didn't have jurisdiction to be arresting him. "What you gonna do now, take me to the county?" Dre asked as Melissa stepped back, but kept the gun aimed at his head.

"Yeah Melissa, let's go before somebody comes out", Suge said as she watched the front of the house.

Melissa grabbed Dre by his collar and said, "Come on you going with us".

*****

Avena heard Dre start his car, but when he didn't move after running for five minutes she got up from the couch to glance out the window. Avena almost chocked on her own spit when she saw Dre standing there with his hands on the roof of the car, "Oh shit".

She watched as Melissa searched Dre, then Suge pull up. But that was it. No sirens. No banging on the door. No commotion. The next thing that came to her mind is the girls outside were trying to jack Dre. Avena went under the couch and grabbed the 380 pistol she was sitting on and ran to the front door. When she snatched open the door, Melissa was trying to put Dre in the backseat of their car at gun point.

Suge saw the door swing open first, "Oh shit", Suge didn't even think after that. She jumped right in the driver's seat and put the car in gear, "Come on!"

Melissa saw Avena run out onto the porch with the gun in her hand and knew she meant business. Melissa didn't talk, she just pointed her gun at Avena and let off two shots.

"Shit!" Avena blurted out as she fell to the ground trying to duck the bullets.

That gave Melissa time to jump in the backseat with Dre and Suge slammed her foot on the gas pedal.

Avena climbed to her feet and started shooting at the back of the car as Suge spun out of the dirt sideways and skidded onto the street screaming, "Oh my God, Oh my God!" the whole time.

Two of Avena's bullets shattered the back window causing everyone in the car to scream. Suge swerved and almost fell in a ditch on the other side of the street.

Avena squeezed off five more shots before she stopped, "Damnit!", She cursed as she watched the car gain control then speed off down the long road.

"Are you okay?" Suge asked as she looked in the rearview mirror at Melissa.

Glass had shattered on their heads and clothes, but other than that they were fine, "Yeah I'm okay".

"Where are we going?" Suge asked as she just followed the way of the road without a destination.

"So, what do yah call this…Yah kidnapping me or something?" Dre asked not sure what was going on at this point.

"No, we taking you in. It's just your girl-friend seemed to have a problem with that", Melissa said as she kept her gun aimed at him.

"Which way?" Suge asked as they came to a big intersection.

"Just go straight Suge", Melissa said feeling annoyed with her. Why can't she just drive the car Melissa asked herself as she turned her attention back to Dre.

Dre knew they either did not know where they were going, because the county jail was in the opposite direction. Or they really were kidnapping him.

"So, what's this all about?" Dre asked trying to see where their heads were at, so he can plan his next move.

"I already told you, we taking you in to face your charges", Melissa said.

"You can't tell me you wanted me so bad, that you followed me down here, just to take me back to New York. Since when you became the warrant squad?" Dre asked.

"When you decided to take a shot at me on 160th street, you opened the door to me finding you and bringing you back", Melissa said like she was doing something.

Dre stayed quite for a while as Suge continued to drive in the wrong direction. He had to do something, because going to jail was not on his agenda for today.

"I'm sorry about that", Dre said looking sincere.

Melissa wasn't trying to hear him apologize. Criminals will say sorry for everything when they get caught, "Whatever", She turned to Suge and said, "Suge where are you going?"

"I don't know! You told me to go straight…I don't even know where the hell we are," Suge barked clearly frustrated.

"Listen you don't really want to take me to jail," Dre said sizing up the situation. It was clear these two didn't have a real plan or some type of direction, but he was sure if they found the county jail or a local precinct they were going to drag him in there.

"And why not?" Melissa asked.

"Because then you'll never see your baby again," Dre said and watched her reaction.

Suge spoke first as she pulled over to the side of the road, "What did you just say?"

"Listen ladies, I'm not going to jail today," Dre said confidently.

Melissa had other thoughts about the situation as she put the gun in Dre's face and said, "If you know where my baby is, and you don't tell me, I'm going to blow your head out that window".

Dre knew she was serious, but he still had the upper hand, "Then you'll never know what happened to the baby. Now like I said, I'm not going to jail today. So, let's talk about an alternative".

The car was silent as Melissa weighed her options. She wanted to shoot Dre just because, but he was right. If she did shoot him then she won't know what happened to her baby. Melissa knew tracking him down would benefit her somehow, but she would have never guessed he would know where her baby is.

"You gonna rot in hell for this", Suge snapped as she looked in the backseat with disgust.

"Suge!" Melissa yelled at her cousin, then turned to Dre, "What Alternative?"

Dre kept his cold stare on Melissa, but inside he was smiling in her face, "One baby, for my continued freedom".

"You must be crazy…you definitely going to jail now", Suge said.

"Suge would you stop please and let me think", Melissa snapped.

"You not taking him serious, are you?" Suge asked with a voice full of anger. "We take his ass to jail and he's going to tell us about the baby…what's there to think about?"

"Don't be so sure about that sweetheart. Yah take me to jail, I'm not telling you shit and that baby disappears forever", Dre said looking at Suge, then turning back to Melissa. "Now if you let me go, you can be reunited with him and everyone is happy".

Melissa looked from Dre to Suge. Suge was angry, but Melissa knew she will ride with any decision she would make. She looked back to Dre and cursed herself, but her baby comes before that oath she took with the N.Y.P.D. "Take me to him".

Chapter 13

When A.D.A. Dolen didn't hear from Melissa by noon the next day he sent out a uniform car to go look for her. To drag it out in court, A.D.A. Dolen called a few crime scene expert witnesses to keep everyone busy until he found his main witness.

At the end of the day A.D.A. Dolen was on the phone in his office when the uniform officer showed up at his door. He motioned for the officer to come as he spoke into the phone, "Ok, hey let me call you back", he slammed down the receiver without listening for response.

"Come in, what happen, did you find her?"

"No sir. There was no answer and we waited outside all day. Before we returned here we took another crack at it by knocking on the door, but still no answer," the officer said.

A.D.A. Dolen face turned red, "and her family hasn't heard from her?"

"Her emergency contact couldn't be reached either", the officer reported. "Sorry sir".

A.D.A. Dolen stood up and escorted him to the door and said, "thank you officer", as he shook his hand and closed his office door behind him.

It was after 8:00pm leaving majority of the district attorney's office empty for the night. A.D.A. Dolen walked over to his office bar and poured himself a drink. Before court adjourned for the day Justice Demarcus could sense he was dragging it out and warned him to keep things moving or rest his case and turn it over to the defense. Thinking about how the judge spoke to him, made A.D.A. Dolen so mad, he threw his glass at the wall.

"Fuck!"

*****
_____

Another day went by with A.D.A. Dolen not hearing from Melissa, causing him to rest his case and turn the podium over to the defense. A.D.A. Dolen didn't know what to make of Melissa disappearing at a time like this, but he also had to weigh the option of her being depressed and needing to get away for a little while. He couldn't understand why nobody knew where she went or when she was coming back, but he ran out of time to call her as a witness and that might hurt his case in the long run.

Mr. White did not have line up of witnesses ready to come in and proclaim De'Quan's innocence and he wasn't going to put De'Quan on the witness stand. It was up to the prosecution to prove De'Quan was there and did the crime. The only thing the prosecution did establish is De'Quan was there. That didn't mean he killed anybody or is responsible for anyone's death. Mr.

White knew a victory is this case was an uphill battle, but he was confident he could pull one out with a great closing argument.

Mr. White showed up to court, ready to display his A-game in a sharp charcoal grey colored suit, with is signature scruffy beard cut down some. His closing argument had been playing in his head for a few days and he was ready to let it go. He walked over to the jury box and began.

"Good morning ladies and gentlemen, like you I sat through this whole trial and tried to convict De'Quan Short of murder, and like you I couldn't. The prosecution did not prove to me beyond a reasonable doubt Mr. Short committed murder in the first degree.

"Let's go through the evidence presented to us. Yes; the evidence puts Mr. Short at the scene, because his unconscious body was pulled from the back seat of the car, but that's about it.

"No one places Mr. Short in the apartment at the time of any crimes. No one testified seeing my client go any further than the front steps of the building. There is no evidence of him possessing," He stopped to look down at his notes, then continued, "It just says over two kilos of cocaine", He said to the jury like he was sharing a secret.

"Looking at this report I can't understand how things was going in this so-called drug set up apartment, but I can tell you if I was selling something, I would have to keep an exact count of everything. Which makes us question what…if anything…was in the apartment", Mr. White said as he walked around the to keep his entire audience engaged.

"No one places a gun in Mr. Short hands, beside a guy who admitted to shooting a gun himself, then pulled the stolen car away from the curb, all while dragging my client with the car. So, if Mr. Short was getting into a moving car, lost his footing and was dragged down the block before the car was rammed into, when did he have time to hold a gun? I've seen a lot of movies ladies and gentlemen, but never have I seen one like that.

"Now I did not come here today to play with your intelligence", Mr. White got closer to the jury box like they were a group of friends talking. "We know Mr. Short was there, but how many people are standing in the wrong place at the wrong time in their lives and it turns out to be a bad call of judgement. That does not mean he went upstairs in that building and participated in any actions against anyone in apartment 4a. Use your better judgement, if he was just looking out, is he guilty of murder? No, he's not".

De'Quan didn't know Mr. White was going to label him a lookout, but he understood. Mr. White would have looked crazy trying to convince the jury De'Quan was an angle that did nothing, so he labeled De'Quan for a crime he wasn't charged with in this case.

A.D.A. Dolen wanted to object to this whole closing argument as he thought about what Mr. White was saying, and he knew when it was time for him to preach to the jury, he was going to put De'Quan in that apartment at the time of the incident. He wasn't going to let Mr. White pull that stunt on him today. Fat Pee told the D.A.'s office De'Quan was the mastermind of this whole plan and that what he wanted the jury to see.

"How could Mr. Short know what was going on up stairs if he was downstairs? He's not responsible for anything he didn't witness, and wasn't apart of", Mr. White said feeling confident he got his point across as he spoke for 10 more minutes to hammer out some points. Mr. White wrapped his closing argument up and turned the floor over to A.D.A. Dolen who jumped out of his seat and fixed his blue suit as he got ready to send De'Quan away forever.

Chapter 14

Before they went off on a wild goose chase Melissa and Suge took Dre to a phone and made him call to confirm about the baby. Dre and Tammy had prepared for a few scenario's in case things got out of their control, and this was one of them as he called her and told her in code they had him.

Melissa snacked the phone out of his hand and said, "Hello? Hello?"

Tammy stood silent for a second then said, "Yes, who is this?"

"Do you have my baby?" Melissa asked wanting to get right to it.

Tammy froze up, "You have my husband?"

Melissa looked at Dre with pure hate in her eyes and said, "Yes I have your husband, and he's going to prison for a very long time".

"That's not going to get you the baby back", Dre said loud enough for Tammy to hear him.

"I'm telling you Melissa, we should just take him in and let them track her down", Suge said, mad Melissa was considering this without any official help.

Melissa ignored Suge, "We coming to get my baby", Melissa said firmly into the receiver.

"Let me talk to Dre", Tammy ordered.

Melissa looked at Dre and said, "Tell her, we coming to get my baby".

Dre took the receiver and said, "Baby we going to make the switch".

"You ok?" Tammy asked scared their run was coming to an end.

"Yeah I'm cool, listen we'll be around the north pick up in about 7 hours", Dre said giving her the code for one of their drop off points only Tammy would know.

Tears started to run down her face as Tammy said, "You sure Dre? I know that's his mother right, but what about us?"

"We'll be fine…Bring Ne'Sean to that spot and we'll make the switch, okay?" Dre said feeling Tammy crying on the other end.

Melissa and Suge were practically breathing down Dre's neck as they tried to follow the exchange between the two kidnappers.

Tammy bit her bottom lip as she said, "Okay", and hung up.

"What happen?" Melissa asked when he hung up the phone.

"Fare exchange, no robbery sweetheart, now let's go", Dre said as he walked back to the car.

Dre was never a fan of taking the baby from Melissa, but the plan went further than that. De'Quan knew she was the only one who could finger De'Quan as the person who put the whole robbery scheme together. Melissa brought De'Quan to the apartment, making it look bad for his case. But if Melissa doesn't testify because she is preoccupied, De'Quan had a strong chance of beating his case. What Dre didn't count on was Melissa finding him in South Carolina, and them having to use the baby a bargaining chip to stay out of jail.

In-order to drive any further than the South Carolina state line they needed to switch rental cars. Suge rented the second car, and they left the other car in a mall parking lot. Suge set off the trip by driving for s few hours, then Dre took over until they made it to Alabama.

*****

Deep down in her heart, Tammy knew it would be hard for them to live a life on the run with two babies, but for Dre, Tammy was willing to go to the extremes. The love they had for each other was unique and it showed in the ways they cared for each other and had each other's back.

Tammy cried for an hour, before she got herself together, then got Ne'Sean ready to see his mother. At 8 months old Ne'Sean was beginning to form a face of his own with a mixture of De'Quan's features. Tammy never saw Melissa before, but she was pretty sure the baby shared some of his mothers features in his face too.

Tammy put the baby in the playpen with their daughter, then she went to pack a few bags. The way how their life has been set up for almost two years Tammy was always ready to move at the drop of a dime. She got the important stuff together and put it in a coach backpack to keep with her at all times. A baby bag for Andrea and a few things for her and Dre went in two gym bags, then Tammy was ready to roll. By eleven o'clock Tammy put all the bags in the trunk of her car, strapped the sleeping babies in their car seats and went off to the meeting.

When they moved to Alabama, Dre made sure he quickly learned the area, while Tammy worked with the housing and shelter services agency to get the apartment. Dre knew it would be hard living on the run with De'Quan's son with them, but he was willing to try anything to save his friend. Dre picked out four locations they could use in case they have a family emergency, and this constituted a real family emergency.

When they got to the town it in was one o'clock in the morning, making it a ghost town except for the occasional passing car. Street lighting was limited and that's why Dre this location. The north side of the town was lightly populated with an area that housed a couple of old factory's and a lot of woods in the background.

Tammy knew the area well because they planned this place as one of their spots just in case things out of control. Dre and Tammy agreed if they got trapped they would be able to get away through this abandon area. Using the woods in the distance as an extra escape route. The woods had driving paths that would lead you to one of the interstates, and walking trails that stretched for miles.

Tammy sat in the car and watched the road as the babies remained sleeping in their car seats in the back. She found herself dozing off until a car appeared in the distance and started making its way down into the area. Tammy snapped out of it and got on point as the car slowed down and stopped forty feet from where she saw parked. Tammy picked up her 380 pistol that was sitting on the passenger seat and she readied herself for anything.

Dre stopped the car and looked over to Melissa, "I know once we give you the baby, you going to call the police on us because you are a cop".

"Me being a cop don't have nothing to do with this. I just want my baby back. I don't care about you Andre and what happens to you after this", Melissa said with real sincerity in her eyes. When she originally found Dre, she was ready to take him in, but words of her getting her baby changed all of that.

Dre nodded and said, "Okay, let's go".

They got out of the car and stood in the front of it as Dre waved to Tammy. Tammy watched them get out of the car and Dre wave to her. Tammy put her gun in her jacket pocket and got out of the car. She unhooked Ne'Sean's car seat and carried it half way. She put the car seat on the ground and said, "Let him go", as she put her hand in her pocket.

Melissa kept her gun in her hand as she said, "Go head and walk to her. I'm right behind you. Wait here Suge".

Suge nodded, "Okay", as she walked over to the driver side of the car and open the door. If they had to get out of there fast, Suge wanted to be ready.

Dre walked to Tammy, with Melissa hot on his heels. As she got closer to the waiting baby Melissa felt like her body was floating to him. She never thought this day would come when she'd get to see her baby again, and now that the moment had come, Melissa was a bag of mixed emotions with a strong taste of loose insides all in one. She didn't know if she was going to cry or laugh once she gets to hear his little voice. All she knew was she had to get him back safety.

Dre looked down at little Ne'Sean sleeping face for one last time as Tammy began to slowly back up. Melissa put her gun in her pocket then quickly grabbed the handle to the car seat and hustled back to the car.

"Come on", Dre told Tammy as they jumped in the car and Dre quickly put it in reverse. The spent around in a half circle, he snapped the gear in drive then drove around the abandon factory to head toward the interstate.

"You okay baby?" Tammy asked when she felt they were far enough away from Melissa.

"Not really. You know how much I love that boy", Dre said as he tried to focus on the dark road.

Tammy rubbed his head and said, "Me too baby, but remember us three always comes first".

"I know…I didn't forget", Dre said.

"Where are we going?" Tammy asked as Dre drove pass the exit to their house.

"First, we got to get to a payphone and call Boogie. We need to get back to S.C., all my stuff and the money is in the car. Boogie is probably going crazy right now cause these bitches started shooting at each other in front of the house", Dre said shaking his head, thinking about his last 24 hours.

When Melissa got the baby to the car Suge got out and watched Dre back up and speed away. Then she turned her attention to Melissa as she put the seat on the hood of the car.

"Oh my God! Look at you!" Suge beamed as they looked at the sleeping baby.

"Suge I never thought we'd find him again", Melissa said as tears ran down the side of her cheeks.

"I know Lissa, but you never quit. Even when the department gave up on their search, you still believed, and I love you for that", She said as she hugged Melissa.

"Now can we get out of here, this place gives me the creeps", Suge said as they strapped the car seat in and Melissa hopped in the back seat with the baby. Suge drove to the highway and headed straight for the nearest airport.

Chapter 15

De'Quan paced in the court holding cell taking a pull off his cigarette every two seconds, trying to keep his cool. They were working on day three of jury deliberations, making the stress surrounding the trial too much to handle for most people. De'Quan's mind had been swirling with old memories, costly decisions and bad nightmares for the pass few weeks, and he was at the point where he just wanted a verdict in this case. It was taking a toll on his mental and his body was tried from the lack of sleep and consent travel.

Justice Demarcus made a ruling if the jury didn't come back with a verdict soon, he would have to declare a mistrial. De'Quan couldn't afford to get a mistrial because he knew the D.A.'s office would make sure Melissa testifies the next time. They're not going care about not finding the baby, they're going to want that conviction on him, and she will be the key to it next time.

De'Quan smiled to himself as he thought about how he played that whole Melissa situation. Once Dre took the baby, De'Quan was feeling real confident about Melissa not showing up to testify. He wanted Dre and Tammy raise his son better then Melissa would. She probably would have taught their son how to be a cop, De'Quan thought to himself, then chuckled. "Yeah right, imagine that".

The sound of keys jingling brought De'Quan out of his private thoughts and he walked over to the cell bars to see who was coming.

"Hey Short, get your stuff together. They have a verdict", A big brown skin complexion c.o. said, as a white court officer, sporting a crew cut, came around the corner hot on his heels. The white court officer didn't like bringing De'Quan out in front of the judge without any shackles on, but the rule was nobody can be shackled in front of a jury.

He put a pair of handcuffs on him, then escorted De'Quan from the holding cell and up a short flight of steps, trying to make small talk, but De'Quan paid his nervous ass no mind. All he could think about is what would be his fate when that jury read the verdict.

When he brought De'Quan out into the courtroom, which began to fill up as word spread about the jury reaching a verdict. Mr. White came in with Mama K, Shakia, Meika, and Karmen who brought Tyrel with her. They had been camped out in Mr. White's office across the street from the court house waiting for this moment. All of them showing a touch of nervousness on their faces as they made their way to the front pews of the courtroom.

Mr. White sat down at the defense table and leaned in toward De'Quan and said, "Listen, no matter what the verdict is, just remain calm".

He tapped De'Quan's arm and he nodded his head as the whole courtroom rose to the bailiff's command, "All Rise!"

Justice Demarcus came out and took his seat, "Bring the jury out please".

The jury came out and took their seats as the media and sketch artist went to work on describing the scene for their respective articles.

"Ladies and gentlemen of the jury, have you reached a verdict?" Justice Demarcus asked.

The entire courtroom was still as the foreman stood up and said, "Yes your honor, we have".

Justice Demarcus motioned for the bailiff to take the folded-up piece of paper from the foreman and pass it to him. The judge glanced over it, then passed it back to the bailiff, who in turn gave it back to the foreman.

"No matter what the outcome of this verdict is, I will have order in this courtroom. Will the defendant please raise", Justice Demarcus said, letting it be known who was in control now.

De'Quan and Mr. White stood up and faced the jury. The judge spoke to the foreman, "To count one, murder in the second degree, how do you find the defendant?"

"We find the defendant...not guilty".

It felt like the entire courtroom shifted in their seats, causing the judge to give the audience a stern look before he continued. "To count two, murder in the second degree, how do you find the defendant?"

"Not guilty".

"To counts three, four, and five attempted murder in the first degree?"

"We find him guilty on all three counts".

The judge looked down at his sheet and said, "As to count six, robbery in the first degree?"

"We find him not guilty".

"And count seven and eight, possession of a deadly weapon?" the judge asked.

"We find the defendant guilty", the foreman said as he looked from the paper to De'Quan.

"Well I would like to thank the jury for their time and service...please escort the jury out", Justice Demarcus said causing the men and women in the jury box to get up and leave.

De'Quan didn't know how to feel in that moment. He beat the top counts, but still ended up convicted of something. He turned around and looked at his family. Mama K held her brave face, as Shakia and Meika broke down crying into each other arms. Karmen hugged Tyrel as a tear rolled down her cheek and she got up and left the courtroom.

The court officers moved in on De'Quan and quickly put a pair of handcuffs on him. Mr. White tapped De'Quan to get his attention, "Look, I'm going to talk to your mother and them first, then I'll be back there to talk to you".

De'Quan felt like he was dreaming as he nodded his head and the court officers took him back into the belly of the beast for a long stay.

Chapter 16

The van ride back to Rikers Island felt longer than usual to De'Quan as he stared out the caged window at the passing city. When he heard not guilty to murder in the first degree, you couldn't tell De'Quan he wasn't going to walk out that courtroom and into his family's waiting arms.

Ever since he heard guilty to the attempt murder charges, De'Quan felt like he's been running on auto pilot. Mr. White spoke to De'Quan briefly before he left the court for the night, but De'Quan just sat there nodding his head like he understood what the lawyer was saying to him. Truth was De'Quan didn't remember nothing Mr. White said to him after the trial was over.

When transportation brought De'Quan back to the jail the receiving c.o.'s was put on point about De'Quan losing at trial, and how he might want to lash out with some form of aggression towards them. But truth was he was drained mentally and physically from the three-week trial that he just wanted to lie down and sleep for two days. De'Quan didn't have it in him to start nothing with the c.o.'s, or anybody else for that matter.

De'Quan was searched as soon as transportation turned him over to the receiving c.o.'s and he refused the cold dinner feed-up tray they were trying to give him.

"Nah, I don't want to eat, I just want to go upstairs", De'Quan said looking defeated.

"Ok, sit tight, I'm going to make sure they take you up next", the c.o. told him, then went to call for an escort.

When De'Quan was brought to the housing unit, Micky B was standing on the gate in his cell having a long-distance conversation with someone who was ten cells away from him.

Micky B heard De'Quan's cell door open next to his, so he put a hold on the conversation, "Yo, hold on homie, they're bringing De'Quan back".

"I got you, hit me back when the police leave", A voice said back to him.

"Okay", Mikey B said, then he stood in silence as the escort walked De'Quan to the cell, the cell door closes, and the c.o. unshackled De'Quan. The c.o. closed the slot in the door and walked back down the gallery.

"De'Quan, eastside Blood", Mikey B saluted him.

"All the time Blood", De'Quan said as he stared out the little window on the cell door.

"What it look like homie?" Mikey B asked, wanting to know how De'Quan's day at court went.

"It's over homie. I blew to the attempt murder and gun charges", De'Quan said.

"Word…Damn homie. What about the body charges?" Mikey B asked knowing those charges held the most time if he's convicted.

"I beat both body charges. But this other shit got me sick right now", De'Quan said shaking his head. He really didn't see himself looking out that small cell window anymore. He would have beat the house on him winning his trail out right and walking out the court room doors, never to return.

"Here get this", Mikey B said. De'Quan heard something sliding on the side of the cell door.

De'Quan looked down and saw it was the white envelope they use to pass each other small things that can fit the tight space under the door. He grabbed the envelope and opened it. Inside was two rolled joints, and three match sticks.

De'Quan smiled, "How did you know I needed this right now?"

Mikey B chuckled, "You my brother Blood, and I feel your pain. I can't buy you a drink right now, but I can send you to the sky for a little minute, feel me".

"Good looking homie", De'Quan said as he grabbed a striker and lit-up one of the joint's.

"Look man, I know this shit is looking crazy right now, but just make sure your lawyer put in that appeal, feel me", Mikey B said.

De'Quan coughed off the weed and said, "Yeah man, he's on it. I think he spoke to me about that tonight. I don't really remember. This whole shit got me all fucked up".

"Well fall back then. Don't worry about roll-call tonight homie, I got you", Mikey B said giving De'Quan a pass to sit out their war chant for the night.

De'Quan took a pull from the joint and nodded his head as if somebody could see him and said, "Good looking…Eastside Blood".

"All the time…holla at you in the a.m.", Mikey said.

De'Quan walked away from the door and sat down on his bunk to smoke the rest of the joint. Awaiting the unknown was probably going to be the hardest part of this whole life changing experience he reasoned with himself. Not knowing how much time Justice Demarcus is going to give him. The unknown on how his family is going to handle him going away for along time. And the biggest unknown is, where are they going to send him when he leaves Rikers Island. The horror stories De'Quan heard about the prisons up-north was about to become his reality and he didn't know what to think about it.

His thoughts were suddenly broken up from the loud voices of his neighbors as they woke up the night sky with their gang anthem.

"Peace Almighty!"

"Peace Blood!"

De'Quan laid down and stared up at the ceiling, as he let the roll call put him to sleep like a lullaby.

Chapter 17

Making sure Melissa and the baby got back to New York safely was Suge's only concern when they made the trip back, but once Melissa and the baby was settled in, Suge wanted to make sure they would be safe from any future attempts against them.

The phone rang three times before he picked up, "Hello, A.D.A. Dolen".

"Hi, I have some information for you", Suge said.

"Okay, and what is your name?" A.D.A. Dolen asked as he grabbed a pen and scrap paper.

"That's not important. What's important is the guy your looking for Andre Jones, I saw him in Orangeburg South Carolina", Suge said.

A.D.A. Dolen snapped to attention when he heard Dre's name, "Did you say South Carolina?" He asked as he jotted down what she said.

"Yes", Suge knew Dre would head back to his car and belongings in South Carolina.

"Do you have an address for me?"

* * * * *

When they made it to South Carolina Boogie and Avena were so happy to see Dre was alive they put together a cookout to celebrate. Dre was surprised because Boogie wasn't a big fan of letting too many people know where he lived.

"Aww man cuz, when Avena told me two chicks kidnapped you, I was bugging", Boogie joked as they sat at a card table playing domino's. "I'm like you sure it wasn't the police? Bitch was like, nigga I let off on them bitches and they didn't come back with back-up...so no they wasn't no damn police".

Laughter bounced around the table as the music blared in the background.

Dre smiled as he took a pull off a blunt he was smoking and said, "Yeah man, shit was crazy. But I got up out of that".

"So, what you going to do now?" Boogie asked as he slammed down a domino on the table.

Dre didn't like sharing his plans with an audience, and Boogie knew this, but the weed, BBQ, and alcohol had them feeling it and talking a little too much. "We might head down to Miami. I got a cousin down there who got a good connect bringing somethings across the water".

Boogie chuckled, "Nigga, I thought your ass wasn't fucking with this drug shit anymore".

"Man, I need to make some cash. We can't go back to Alabama, and we can't stay here, so we need a change", Dre said slamming a domino down, "That's game!"

"Damn man, I didn't think you saw that", Boogie joked.

"I'm out man, we need to get up early", Dre said as he stood up and gave everybody a pound, then went into the house.

Dre woke up at five in the morning feeling refreshed and ready to get out of South Carolina. When they got there, he was so tired he just wanted to sleep for a day before they moved on, but Boogie threw the cookout causing Dre to lose sleep and his focus.

He woke up Tammy and told her to get ready, while he packed the car. Dre wanted Boogie to sell the Lexus for him, because he wasn't coming back to South Carolina, and they flew better under the radar in Tammy's Honda Accord.

Dre went outside to get the rest of his stuff out of the Lexus. He walked out onto the porch and caught the flash of someone moving fast out the corner of his eye.

"Shit", Dre blurted out as he felt the presence of other people around him. The early morning fog covered what he knew was watching him and he had to make a move.

"Freeze!"

Dre made a dash for it and snatched open the car door.

"Don't Fucking Move!"

"He Got A Gun!"

Pop. Pop. Pop. Pop. Pop. Pop.

The sounds of gun fire outside sent Tammy into a panic as she grabbed Andrea and hit the floor, knocking over the kitchen table. Baby bottles and glass plates shattered on the ground sending the rest of the house into a frenzy.

"The fuck is going on?" Boogie asked as he ran out of his room wearing a do-rag and boxer shorts, carrying a 9miller meter pistol in this hand. Avena was hot on his heels clutching her silk robe as they both had sleep all in their eyes.

"Tammy!" Avena screamed when the gun fire stopped, and they saw her laying on top of Andrea. She grabbed Tammy and pulled her up. Andrea was crying, and Tammy looked shaken.

"Tammy you alright?" Avena asked as she checked her to see if she was hit.

"I'm okay, where's Dre?" Tammy asked as tears suddenly rolled down her cheeks. "It's okay baby", Tammy said to Andrea to calm her down.

Boogie ran to the door and snatched it open, "A man!"

"Drop the weapon!"

"Fuck you man!" Boogie spat when he looked to the side and saw Dre laid half way in, half way out of the Lexus. Motionless.

Boogie got off two shots before getting hit with a barrage of bullets from guns he couldn't clearly see; but knew were there.

"Boogie!" Avena screamed, as she watched Boogies lifeless body fall into the doorway. Tammy was crying hysterically as she hoovered in the corner hugging Andrea like this was going to be the last time she would be able too. The world was ending around them and she didn't know what to do.

Avena ran to Boogie's body and began crying on top of him as the local police and New York warrant squad rushed up in the house to make sure no one else was ready to die today. The heavy smell of gun powder and sounds of walkie-talkies flooded the air, as Avena was quickly taken from Boogie's body and escorted out of the house.

"Ma'am are you okay?" An officer asked Tammy as two of them approached her in the messy kitchen.

Tammy's emotions were all over the place at the moment, but she remembered what she and Dre promised to each other. Andera is their main priority no matter how bad the situation may get. Looking around the kitchen, hugging Andrea, Tammy knew Dre was dead. She could feel it and so could his daughter because she wouldn't stop crying. There was nothing she could do right now, so Tammy stood up and nodded.

"Please step outside Ma'am, so we can search the house and remove the bodies", one of the officers said to a dazed looking Tammy.

Tammy wanted to break down when he said bodies, but she had to keep it together for the sake of Andrea. Tammy tried to hold it together until she stepped outside and saw them covering Dre's lifeless body with a sheet.

"Oh my God...No!"

A female officer quickly grabbed Tammy and guided her and Andrea over to a waiting cop car. She helped Tammy and her daughter into the backseat of the car and drove them away from the bloody scene.

Chapter 18

Due to him being confined to a wheelchair, Fat Pee was shipped off to Greenhaven correctional facility, a maximum-security prison equipped to house people with medical issues, to serve out his ten-year sentence for his involvement in the botched robbery with his old partners.

Fat Pee tried to keep a low profile by going to school everyday and avoiding going out to the yard, any entertainment he needed he had in his cell, or he would do without. Greenhaven is a big prison, that housed over two thousand prisoners, and Fat Pee wasn't trying to get to familiar with them. He had the tag of being a rat and De'Quan's name was floating around as having a bright future in the gang lifestyle in prison. Fat Pee had to be careful.

Being in a wheelchair gave him room service for breakfast, lunch and dinner, because wheelchairs weren't allowed in the mess hall, but Fat Pee could leave the cell for everything else. He sat in his cell listening to his radio when one of the few friend's he had rolled up on his cell in his own wheelchair.

"A Pee, what's up man", Dee-Jay said snapping Fat Pee out of his mode.

Dee-Jay was Spanish, and in his late twenties. He was also confined to a wheelchair from taking a bad fall on the train tracks one night running from the police in the Bronx.

Fat Pee looked up and said, "Ain't nothing Dee-Jay, what you about to get into?"

"Man, I'm about to roll out to the yard and cop me a bag or something. Why don't you roll with me? All you have to do is buy a philly from Black-Ty for a stamp. I got the dough for the trees". Dee-Jay said.

Fat Pee turned his radio off and said, "Dee-Jay man, you know I don't be playing that yard like that".

Dee-Jay pressed on, "Aww man, you got to get out and get some fucking air man. It's hot as hell in these cell blocks and your skin needs some sun Pee...now let's ride out, I'm trying to get high today".

Fat Pee was reluctant to leave his cell for the yard, but he started to reason with himself that Dee-Jay might be right. "Man, I don't want to go, but your right. It's hot as hell in this cell and it feels like the walls are closing in on me".

Dee-Jay smiled, "That's what I'm talking about. I'm going to tell the c.o. to crack your cell".

"Yeah, but I'm not smoking in the yard. I want to wait until we come back", Fat Pee said full committed to go.

Dee-Jay shook his head and said, "Damn man, you didn't smoke shit yet and you already paranoid. Aight whatever", he chuckled, before rolling down the tier towards the front. Fat Pee got his stuff together to get ready to roll out.

"On The Rec!" A c.o. barked over a loud speaker.

The ringing of opening cell doors was heard through the entire cell block, and voices started to rise as people made their way out onto the tiers. Fat Pee was in 34 cell, on a fifty-cell gallery. He had to be on the bottom tier which was a mixture of wheelchair prisoners and walking prisoners.

Fat Pee wheeled himself out onto the tier and started to make his way down the tier. He tried to look for Dee-Jay but too many people began to come out of their cells, making it hard for Fat Pee to see over the small crowds forming on the tier.

Suddenly a dark-skin guy with a ski hat pulled down to hide the top of his eyes stepped in front of Fat Pee.

Fat Pee looked up to see who cut him off, but he came face to face with an ice pick. The man stabbed Fat Pee in his chest three times and said, "Rat bastard, that's for the homie".

Then he spent off into the crowd that was flowing toward the yard door. Fat Pee grabbed his chest as he felt the air leaving his body. He couldn't scream for help over the loud talking and ruckus of the entire cell block trying to come out for the yard, and he didn't want to let his chest go as he gasped for air.

People walked pass Fat Pee, as his body went lifeless in his wheelchair, as if he didn't exist. Until somebody kicked the chair to the side and it rolled into an empty cell.

"Watch the closing doors!" The c.o. in the control bubble barked over the loud speaker as the cell doors started closing one by one, and the crowd disappeared off the tier and out into the sunny yard.

Chapter 19

Life felt like it was going in slow motion for De'Quan ever since he lost at trial. The news of the police catching up with Dre in South Carolina crushed De'Quan. He wasn't ready for that one and it showed in his attitude leading up to the day of his sentencing.

The courtroom was buzzing with activity when they brought De'Quan in. The trial was over, so all bets were off, and it was back to him being escorted around with a full set of shackles on.

De'Quan immediately notice his support team of Mama K, Meika, and Shakia sitting behind the defense table. He gave everybody a weak smile, and they returned a weaker one as they wondered about his fate.

Justice Demarcus was already sitting on the bench conducting court business when De'Quan's number was called. The judge watched as they brought

119

De'Quan to the defense table and began, "I'll hear any motions before I sentence the defendant".

Mr. White stood up and said, "yes, your honor, I would like to begin by submitting a motion to vacate this judgement against Mr. Short. On the grounds of the jury inability to come back with a unanimous verdict".

Mr. White brought on his argument about how unfair the trial was, and numerous violations committed by the prosecution. His argument went on for ten minutes before Mr. White turned the floor over to A.D.A. Dolen.

The prosecutor objected to Mr. White's objections and asked for the harshest sentence the Judge could give to De'Quan, then he sat back down. He didn't like the verdict neither, but there was no way to bring back charges De'Quan was found not guilty of. Why argue.

Justice Demarcus acted like he was in deep thought about what both lawyers said to him, then he said, "I believe the jury did a superb job, and I don't see any real reason why this verdict should be over turned. Motion to vacate this conviction is denied", the judge concluded by slamming down his gavel.

"Now, as for sentencing in this case, will the defendant please rise", Justice Demarcus said as he shuffled through some papers in front of him.

De'Quan and Mr. White stood as the judge continues, "As to the charges of attempted murder in the first degree, I hear by sentence you 12 ½ to 25years. To the possession of a deadly weapons charge, I sentence you to 8 to 16 years in prison. Because this is your first offense these sentences will run concurrently".

When the judge was finished Mr. White spoke first, "I am submitting our verbal appeal to this conviction and sentence".

"As you wish, please remove the defendant", Justice Demarcus said without a real care for what the lawyer was talking about.

De'Quan quickly turned to look at his family. He mouthed 'I love you' to Mama K, who wiped away her tears and said, "We love you too", before a court officer grabbed him by his arm and pulled him to the exit.

Chapter 20

De'Quan was moved from Rikers Island to Auburn correctional facility not knowing what to expect. Auburn is one of the oldest maximum-security prisons in New York state, with a reputation of being a gladiator school. Being surrounded by a thirty-foot high wall, the 90year old prison had the look of a haunted castle in the middle of a small town.

De'Quan was lead off a none descript bus with 30 other prisoners and hustled into a receiving area where their shackles were removed. De'Quan felt like a fish out of water as he was pushed into a holding cell, and he listen to hick c.o.'s talk to guys any kind of way.

"Hey Nigger! I said go in there!"

"We got some hard head ass nigger's huh Billy".

"Do worry, you new guys will get it right, or we will get it right for you", a c.o. said from his seat, sparking chuckles from his co-workers.

De'Quan knew he just entered another world. White country c.o.'s calling guys nigger like it's nothing. He shook his head and remained silent as they searched him, then moved De'Quan to C-block.

"A Short, your going in 23cell. Grab a set-up of two sheets, one pillow case, two towels, and two rolls of toilet paper. Anything else you need, ask the porter for it. Now take it down and lock in", the c.o. at the control bubble said, as he watched De'Quan take his set-up and walk down the tier.

De'Quan looked down the tier of fifty-cells and figured it had to be as long as a city block. He took his walk down to 23cell with a sick feeling in his stomach as he passed the 8x10's. Smells of cooked food, cigarette smoke hit his nose, as different sounds from loud radio's playing different songs and loud conversations danced on his ears when he walked pass the other cells.

Before he walked into the open cell, De'Quan looked up at the number, then walked inside. The cell door closed behind him with a loud clank! Putting an end to a long travel day that started at five o'clock in the morning. Looking around the empty cell he figured it had to be nine o'clock at nine. De'Quan was beat.

De'Quan cut on the light and the roaches scurried to their designed corners and holes as the bright light shined light on his new dirty dwelling. He lifted up the thin plastic mattress and shook it out as best he could then laid it back down. He sat on the bed and pulled out a pack of cigarettes he was allowed to take on the trip with him and cracked them open. Then he remembered he didn't have a light.

De'Quan tapped on the wall and said, "A 24cell".

"Yeah, what's going on brother?"

"I don't mean to brother you, but do you have some matches?" De'Quan asked.

The man in 24cell thought he heard that voice before, "yeah give me second", but didn't think nothing of it as he grabbed a pack of matches and passed them over. "Here you go".

"Thanks man".

"A what's your name brother?"

"De'Quan, what's your?" De'Quan said as he sparked one of the matches.

The man in 24cell froze, then quickly grabbed his hand-held mirror and stuck it over to look at De'Quan's face.

De'Quan was surprised when he saw the mirror come out, "A man what's up. I asked for a light not an audience".

The man in 24cell shifted the mirror so De'Quan could see who was holding it and he almost chocked on the cigarette smoke.

"Pop?"

"Yeah son, it's me", was all he could say as he pulled his arm back into the cell and sat down on his bed. Pop couldn't believe what he just saw. His son is in the cell next door to him. Pop's worst nightmare had finally come true, all from making R.A.W. moves.

The End...

DEDICATIONS

To my mom Jeanette Brown Josey and the rest of the Brown family, thank you for always holding me down. To my St.Thomas family, thank you for your support. To my sister…and brothers, Wastelandz we did it.

To my projects people's worldwide, I am your voice.

Be real and you shall win.

R.A.W.

REAL ALWAYS WINS

Part 1

The Beginning

<u>Prologue</u>

As a light drizzle soaked the rotten apple, the stolen Jeep Cherokee rolled to a stop in front of building 57 on 160th street, between Broadway and Amsterdam Avenue. Everyone in the jeep had butterflies in their stomachs. That wasn't enough to stop tonight show.

"Check your watch Pee. We will be out of there in 5 minutes tops. When we go in, Sean you grab the money and drugs; me and Dre will hold the spot down." De'Quan said looking down at his watch. It was 4:47a.m.

"Pee give us to 4:52."

Pee nodded, and then set his digital guess watch, as his three passengers hopped out of the jeep and headed for the front door of the five story walk-up. They took the steps two at a time all the way up to the fourth floor.

De'Quan held up his hand to motion to Dre and Ne'Sean, as they caught their breathes. Then De'Quan eased up to the door and put his ear to it to listen for any sounds of movement on the other side. He heard a few voices that were rolling over the voices coming from the TV. De'Quan looked at Dre and Ne'Sean and nodded his head then pulled out his 40 caliber automatic. Dre and Ne'Sean followed suit by pulling out their own weapons and readied themselves for what was to come next.

De'Quan performed the secret knock he watched Melissa do earlier and took up his kick in the door stands, as Dre and Ne'Sean stood off to the side in anticipation. Suddenly an eye appeared in the peephole then quickly disappeared with the sound of the locks clicking from the other side.

Bolo snatched open the door surprised to see De'Quan there so late, "what do you..."

Bolo was cut off by the 40 caliber pistol which was shoved in his mouth with enough force to crack some of his front teeth. Dre wasted no time as he pushed past them and ran into the apartment with the fire raging bull and his eyes, "Get the fuck on the floor Poppy!"

'It Started When We Were Young'

'From A Seed, Grew A Forest'

'How Strong Are Your Root's'

Chapter 1

1989

"Quan and Sean get your asses up and ready!" Mama K. yelled as she passed their open door on her way to the kitchen. De'Quan sat up and wiped the cold out of his eyes. He hated getting up in the morning more than anything in the world. At 12 years old, De'Quan already had a bad taste in his mouth for school. Once he learned how to read and count De'Quan began to get the feeling that everything else in school was useless.

"Sean, Mama K. said get up."

Ne'Sean rolled off the top bunk with an attitude and headed for the bathroom. Ne'Sean loved his brother but he covers De'Quan in his head as he walked by him. Just because De'Quan was two years older than him, that did not give him the title of ruler of the bedroom.

The bathroom door was closed, forcing Ne'Sean to knock on the door, "what is it?"

"Meika it's me. Come on I have to use the bathroom," Ne'Sean whined as he hopped from foot to foot.

The door opened and Meika walked out the bathroom ignoring her brother as she headed for her room. Ne'Sean shot darts at the back of her head as he held his tongue and rushed into the bathroom to do his business.

De'Quan put on a pair of blue Levi's, a matching sweatshirt, and a pair of fila sneakers. Looking into the mirror, he began to comb his hair when Ne'Sean came back into the room smelling like toothpaste. Something the younger brother thought his older brother better go use, before going all up into Mama K. face this morning.

"Quan are you going to school today? Or are you going to that hooky party?"

Quan continue to comb his hair wondering the same thing. "What you know about that hooky party?"

Ne'Sean poked his chest out and said, "People got loose lips in these projects that are how I know about it."

De'Quan smiled himself and said, "Your right. That's gonna be a lot of these people down fall around here. Anyway, you're not going. You my man is going to school."

"Why I can't go? I'll be in I.S. 205 next year. That just about makes me grown now."

De'Quan frowned, "look, if you miss school there gonna call here and top wheelchair bowlful of asses up. He'll know if you didn't go, then I damn sure didn't go to school. Now get dress so we can bounce."

Ne'Sean sucked his teeth and said, "Whatever, if I was you I would go sleigh that Dragon before you burn Mama K. eyebrows." They both laughed as De'Quan headed for the bathroom.

It was a slow morning and Marcy projects, the heart of Bed-Stuy Brooklyn, but Andre Jones was wide awake. He always felt best was the only way you were going to survive in New York City. Especially Brooklyn.

Andre was the same age as De'Quan and they have been friends since they were five years old. Andre waited in front of De'Quan's building thirsty to roll back over to the Flushing side of the projects for the highly anticipated hooky party. Andre lived on the Flushing side of Marcy projects and he could not figure out why De'Quan couldn't meet him in front of his building for change. Breaking up his thoughts was a burst of chatter from De'Quan, Meika, and Ne'Sean talking a whole bunch of nothing as they marched out the front door of the building.

"What's up Dre?"

Andre hopped in step with them and said," We have a little time to burn before we slide over there, so let's hit arcade."

"I didn't know junior high had an arcade in it", Meika said butting into the conversation.

De'Quan looked over to her and said, "mind your business and you'll live to see junior high".

"Oh yeah…

"You'll keep quiet regardless", De'Quan countered as he dug into his pocket for the $.50 anyway.

Dre snickered and said, "Meika you going to be one hell of a gold digger when you get older. You just got to switch your style up from ratting on everybody."

"Word" Ne' Sean added, as De'Quan just shook his head.

"Here, now poof- be gone!"

Ne'Sean and Meika crossed a street to go about their way, while Dre and De'Quan did a quick dip to the arcade. As 845 approached, they started to make their way over to the hooky party.

It was a Friday and everybody who was somebody from IS 205 was up in there. Tyshawn and his crew was deep in there, as well as Sabrina and her girls rolling hard. It was 40's of Old English being passed around, with bottles of Cisco, and some heads who where ahead of their time were smoking weed. Everybody wasn't ready for the Weed yet.

Around 11:30 am, the party was jumping. De'Quan had a Carmel complexion shorty in the corner of an already crowded couch. He was rubbing up on her half-trained breasts and kissing on her neck when he heard a ruckus jumping off towards the front of the apartment.

De'Quan came up for air long enough to see Dre going at it with a kid from Tompkins projects. Dre was getting the best of the kid as he grabbed him by his shirt and swung the kid into the stereo. The impact scratched the record so hard the music shut off and a dark-skin girl barked, "What the fuck is wrong with yah!"

The few who were high off of the weed started to laugh, as De'Quan finally began to focus on what he was watching. He jumped up off of the couch and ran over to help out his friend.

B. Range came out of the back bedroom with a girl tight on his heels, "Yo man! What the fuck yah doing? Yah fucking up my mom's crib!"

At the end of his sermon, De'Quan picked up a lamp and smashed a kid across his face, because he looked like he was going to jump into the fight. At that site of this B. Range lost it, "Oh hell no! Everybody get the fuck out!"

Half of the party was already making their way out the door before he could finish his temper tantrum. De'Quan grabbed Dre by his shirt, as Dre continued to stomp on the kid.

"Yo man, let's get the hell out of here!"

Dre and De'Quan ran out the door and headed down the staircase, "let's go to my side of the projects where is safer. Them niggas won't come over there knowing my pops run that shit", De'Quan said in between breaths.

"Yeah, but what if your pops sees us?" Dre asked.

De'Quan thought about this for a second then said, "It's like 12 something now. So it's lunch time, he won't say nothing."

They walked over to the big park on the myrtle side of the projects, where damn sure enough pop was walking back from the weed spot taking a shortcut through the park.

Pop was a force on the murder which side that nobody really wanted to deal with. He stood at 6'1" tall with a golden brown complexion. His 175 pounds didn't make him as menacing as his temper did and that's what scared people. He met his chocolate sundae Mama K when they were young, and they had De'Quan shortly after a few episodes while his mother was at work.

Pop was America's nightmare. 30 years old, black, smart, and will kill to feed his family. Pop's soft spot had always been for his first born. De'Quan was Pop's mini-me when it came to him looking like his daddy. On the other side of the coin Ne'Sean and Meika came out as splitting images of Mama K.

Pop saw his son and Dre sitting on a bench across the park, oblivious to his approach from they're blindside. Pop smiled himself about the loyalty the boys had for each other. He knew that loyalty will run deep for some years to come.

"Aren't you two far from your school?"

Startled and mad at himself for not seeing Pop coming De'Quan said, "its lunch hour and we didn't want to be in the schoolyard, so we came to hang out in the park."

Pop just stared at them. He knew they were lying. He sidestepped their words and asked, "Dre why is your face all red with that scratch on it?"

Being a high yellow complexion, the slightest abnormality to his body will always show without warning. Dre looked over to De'Quan for help.

Pop said, "Yah were fighting, weren't you? You can tell me."

The two boys looked at each other again, causing Dre to speak up. "Pop, some cat from Tompkins's tried to front on me over a girl".

"Yeah so we gave them Marcy day", De' Quan added.

Pop laughed and said, "Yeah, well make sure you don't have that school calling me to come up there. You know I like to think in peace during the day." This meant enjoying his weed high without any disturbances.

Pop looked at his gold watch given them his silent signal it's time to go back. "Yah have any money?"

De' Quan reached into his pocket, "I've about $.70 left. What about you Dre?"

"I have a dollar left."

Dre was Pops son by another mother, as he liked to think of him. Dre father stepped off long before he could walk, making

Pop the closest thing to a father he ever knew. Pop pulled out a knot of money and he peeled off two ten's. He gave one to each of them and said, "This better last yah until at least Sunday. Yah hear me."

The two boys nodded their heads.

"Now get back to school."

Boys quickly hopped off the bench and headed in the direction of their school, knowing full well they will not be going inside.

Chapter 2

That summer emerged as a hot one, with Ne'Sean graduating to the six grade. This Open the door for him to start hanging around De'Quan and his friends now. This did not sit too well with De'Quan, who just turned 13 and was feeling like nobody can tell him anything anymore.

At this point in his life, De'Quan was beginning to pay more attention to Pop whole style. To Quan, Pop was the most Gee up person in the world. When Pop spoke, everyone who were supposed to listen- listened, even those who pretended to be minding their business.

Pop was grinding at a fast and heavy rate in the hot projects, as well as having control over a welfare hotel out in Queens. He made a new connection with some brothers down in South Carolina, and he was preparing to set up shop down there as well.

While Pop was out making the money, Mama K was holding down the home front and keeping the troops in line. Meika stayed close to Mama K. Ne'Sean on the other hand started going out more and sticking with De'Quan and Dre, when they would let him.

On the morning of the first day of school, Ne'Sean was the first one up in the house. It was his day to start at IS 205 and his nerves would not let him sleep. By the time, he made it into the kitchen Mama K was getting ready for her morning rush hour. "Hey baby, what you doing up so early?"

"I couldn't sleep." Ne'Sean mumbled.

She smiled to herself. Another one of our babies was growing up. "Well I want you to learn all you can when you start 205 today, and be conscious of what's going on while you're learning. Because they teach us a lot of things in schools that isn't always true. Something like a bent up truth. I'm going to let you in on something that you won't learn in school. The Indians discovered America." She winked her eye at him and he laughed.

"You don't believe me?" Mama K asked.

"I believe you Mama K. I knew something was funny because they kept saying Columbus ran into the Indians when we got here", Ne'Sean said cheesing.

"Good. Always remember things we learn can be researched. Now go get cleaned up and get dress."

"Yes Mama."

De'Quan was still in the bed dreaming when Ne'Sean walked into the room. Watching his brother's sleep, Ne'Sean thought to himself, 'I should do something to him now, because he's going do something to me later being that his freshman day'. He went into the bathroom and grabbed the toothpaste. Easing up on his brother Ne'Sean sprayed some toothpaste on his pillow, then began to snicker as De'Quan rolled his face over into the glob of toothpaste.

Watching his brother smear toothpaste all over his face Ne'Sean could no longer hold it and burst out laughing. Mama K began to come down the hallway barking orders into the rooms to wake up her little troops. When she walked into the boy's room, she saw what Ne'Sean was laughing at and smacked him in the back of his head

"Quan get up!" Mama K yelled, walking over to the window to raise the shade. She let the sunlight and could not hold in her own laughter, as De'Quan rubbed the toothpaste across his face.

"No... No, don't touch the bed", Mama K said.

"What the hell." De'Quan blurted out once he began to realize what was happening.

"Don't you cuss in this house? Now go wash your face," she said with a chuckle.

Ne'Sean stepped to the side with a smirk on his face, as his brother mumbled, "you'll pay for that."

"I know Colgate."

Ne'Sean made it school without incident, then coolly eased his way into his first period class. He took a seat in the back of the class and looked over to the kid that was sitting next to him. He recognized the kid from the playground in Marcy. "What's up, my name is Ne'Sean."

"What's up, my name is Jamel. You from the Myrtle side of Marcy, right?"

"Yeah, building 105. What building you from?" Ne'Sean asked.

"Building 101. My brothers are the Moore twins." Jamel answered.

"Okay, I've seen them around."

Jamel was a light brown complexion and he weighed 70 pounds with rocks in his pockets. He was looking fresh for the first day of school, with a new Levis suit on and a low haircut. Ne'Sean always thought Jamel was younger than him, because he was so small. They stopped talking once the teacher came into the room and their day began.

Ne'Sean and Jamel stuck together for the whole day like they've been hanging out together for years. Listening to the words spreading on how the freshmen were going to get it today. No matter who they were related to.

Jamel said, "Man, I hope they don't rip my shirt. My mom will flip if I come in the house with my clothes ripped."

Ne'Sean looked over to him as they made their way toward the front door of the school. "Can you run fast?'

Jamel put on a weak smile, "Man my life is on the line once we out there. I'll do anything to get away from them vultures."

They looked out the windows to the front door before heading outside. Ne'Sean pointed to the right and Jamel nodded his head in agreement. They popped open the doors and ran straight to their right as soon as their feet hit the top step. It was straight pandemonium outside, as girls screamed at boys not to mess up their hair, and kids running every which way. Either throwing eggs or trying to get away from the egg throwers.

Making their way away from the action, Ne'Sean spotted De'Quan, Dre and Fat Pee waiting on the side of a parked van. Before he could change direction, they jumped out and began to bomb Ne'Sean and Jamel with eggs all over the faces and clothes.

"I told you, you would pay for that!" De'Quan screamed as Jamel slipped and fell, paying for that with eggs on his hair. As they hammered Ne'Sean, he stopped to grab hold of Jamel's book-bag and pulled his fallen comrade back to his feet.

"Come on man...Let's go!"

De'Quan, Dre, and Fat Pee caught cramps from laughing so hard at the fleeing freshmen.

Chapter 3

Things were running smoothly around Pop. Too smoothly. The money coming in from Marcy had always been up and down throughout the years, and now it was at the $4,000 a day mark. The hotel in Queens Pop had to leave alone, because the place got too hot for the headaches, and the money wasn't worth it. South Carolina seemed like good money for now, but Pop was beginning to feel the eyes of the hood burning holes in the back of his head. When that started to happen people usually paid a heavy price for their debt. The issues were beginning to outweigh the money some days to Pop.

On the home front, Pop liked what he was seeing. Mama K was representing the name of e true thug's wife. The troops stayed in line, and every female that was about something wanted to know Mama K's formula. Pop never disrespected her by messing with, or even talking to another woman in Brooklyn. Unless it was business orientated, and even then, he would go to Mama K first. He knew how the chickens liked to sit on the benches and create delusions.

When De'Quan was born, the couple made a deal with each other to be true to one another, no matter the cost. Pop would take care of their financial well being, and Mama K would keep the home front going, in or out of Pops presence. As far as life for the moment, things seemed to be in order, but something was troubling, Pop and Mama K could sense it. She could tell when something was bothering her husband.

Their room was beyond the look of a project bedroom in 1991, with a king size, super soft bed, laced with red and black sheets, and a red comforter to match. Off to the side a wall unit housed a 35' T.V., VCR, stereo system, and a new five track CD player. All made by Sony. On the side of the wall unit was a big dresser-mirror set, with a chair in front of it. Mama K sat in the chair brushing her hair, feeling sexy in her black silk lingerie set, with the silk jacket draped over her back.

Mama K didn't miss a beat on brushing her hair when she asked Pop, "What's on your mind Ryan?" Mama K was the only person on the planet- beside Grand-Ma Trina- who could call Pop by his government name and get away with it.

"I feel like something is lurking in my mist. I just can't put my finger on it", Pop said, as he blew out a cloud of smoke.

Mama K stayed out of the business part of their lives, but when it came to Pop's well being Mama K was his best listener, and sometimes his best problem solver.

"Maybe you should slow down and watch people from the back for a while. If you just flip your routine, people will have to scramble to catch up with you. Then maybe you'll see a difference."

Pop thought about this and said, "My next move is to open up the close down store on Lewis ave and Green Street. That way we will finally be legal. The only problem is something is poking at me, telling me dudes won't let me go legal."

She put down her brush, got up from her seat and started toward him. He had to smile- God she was sexy. She sat on his lap and kissed his forehead, as she slowly ran her hand with the waves in his hair. "We've been in this for a while now and I'm slowly getting tired of worrying about you. So please, think of something that will ease my mind as well as your mind. Shit, we getting older by the day, what you think?"

They both laughed, and he said, "You right. If I was to change my hold shit around tomorrow, niggas won't know how to cover me. Then I might get some answers. And yes, we are getting younger, making you the sexiest shorty in the world.

"You so silly."

He put his blunt in the nearby ashtray and laid her down as gentle as a feather. He kissed her passionate, but hard. She pulled his T-shirt off over his head, and then pulled him back down to her for more of his Kisses. He only had on his boxers, which were useless with his manhood peeking out of the slick. She flipped him down to the bottom and began to perform her famous strip show for his eyes only. By the time she was down to her all-black thong, his manhood was watching the show from the slit in his boxes. She slipped off her thong and swooshed it pass his nose for quick sniff. She pulled his boxer shorts off as smooth as her masterful hands could, and then she turned the scene into channel 69.

*****

After a night filled with good loving, Mama K always woke up with a pep in her step. This meant getting the kids up and ready for school with no arguments. Then push them out into the cold world. Once that was done, she got dressed and went on her nursing job as a home attendant to Ms. Betsy's house in Brooklyn Heights.

Pop woke up at 10:40 AM and felt a breath of fresh air knowing everyone was off to their daily whereabouts. This was his time to sit back and think in peace. Pop was given what Mama K said last night a lot of thought. The more he analyzed it, the more it made sense to him.

He got up, shit, showered and shaved. Then rolled his morning blunt and went to his closet. He moved the boxes of shoes and sneakers out of his way then click the fake panel on the back wall. Then he pulled some money out of a sneaker box in the hole in the wall. Pop made sure, when he had this stash spot put in you would never know was there. Unless he showed it to you or you started kicking the whole wall out. He counted out 30,000 cash, put it in the Nike plastic bag and put the rest of the money back in the wall. Then he picked up the phone and dialed out a number he had gotten out of the newspaper a week earlier.

"Hello, Miller rentals".

"Yes, my name is Ryan Short and I'm interested in the store front on Lewis Avenue and Green Street that is up for rent.

I was wondering can I take a look at it with someone that's in charge of its sale".

"Yes…Yes Mr. Short. I can make an appointment for you to meet with the building owner...aww…hold on a sec".

When he returned to the phone Pop said, "I'm sorry, who am I speaking with, so I'll know who's putting this together?"

"No, I'm sorry. My name is Bill Conners, and I've found the owner information for you. I will give him a call and take care of all the arrangements for you two to meet. Let me have your day and night time numbers so we can reach you please".

"Ok. 718-555-3572, if I'm not in, then you can leave a message with my wife".

"Okay, we'll do".

When he hung up the phone, Pop put on his bullet proof vest, polo knit sweater, and his black leather jacket. He grabbed his 16 shot 9mm, checked it, and then slid it in his inside jacket pocket. He put on a black ski hat, grabbed the Nike bag of money and headed out the door.

When Pop stepped out into the cold winter air he found himself thanking God the snow stopped coming down. He trekked over to the pay phone on the corner of Nostrand ave and Park ave. He dropped a quarter into the phone and dialed a number he knew by heart. A deep accented voice came over the line after two rings.

"Ola?"

Recognizing the voice, Pop responded, "This is Pee. I need to see you".

The man said, "Ah Pee. My friend. Come see me at 4:00".

"Ok. I need to see two mommies today", Pop said.

"Si. I have the perfect sweeties for you", the man said, then hung up.

Pop walked down to his parked 300E Mercedes Benz shoveled the snow out of his way and off his car. Then he peeled out and headed for the weed spot and Bushwick.

He checked to see if anybody was following him several times, but he did not see anything unusual. He decided since the store was in Queens and he had about two and half hours to burn, he should go to his down low chicks crib on the Corona side of Lefrak City, and hang out there until 4 PM.

As he waved through traffic on the Interboro Expressway smiling to himself on how more and more his plan was beginning to look better as the day went along. He was going to buy two keys of Coke. Stash one and give the other one to his lieutenant Uni. Pop can tell Uni he had other things that needed his attention and to just bring him back $40,000 off that key. Uni was a good worker and very reliable. He'd jump at the chance to prove himself without Pop breathing all down his neck.

His next step would be to get the building owner to rent him the store front. Then he came get Mama K to help him build up the store's clientele. He didn't like her working as a nurse attendant, but she always said it kept her busy.

He stopped at Deidra house on 57th Ave, at 2:40 PM. As usual, she was ready to smoke some weed and fuck. He caught the time at 3:55, and he couldn't afford to be late. He jumped out of Deidra and told her to keep the pussy warm; he'll be back when it got dark outside. She knew he was bull shitting her, so she hit him up for $200 to go shopping and he slid out for his meaning with Cabesia.

Cabesia was a small round man, with big bodyguards and some big guns. He was always happy to do business with Pop, because Pop never came short and he was always about his business.

Pop parked three cars from the front of the small grocery store on 102nd St. and Roosevelt Avenue. When he's stepped up into the store an old Hispanic man, with a bad receding hairline was behind the counter. He gave Pop the nod and the finger toward the back. The old man pushed a button under the counter as Pop walked through a curtain and up to a door.

An eye appeared in the peephole and the door suddenly open. A big Hispanic man with a shoulder holster carrying of 45 automatic in plain view stepped to the side and let Pop in.

In the back of the small room, Cabesia sat at his table with at least 4 kilos' on one side of him. There was an open key on the other side of him, with a triple beam scale resting next to it, and a 38 snub nosed rested close to his hand, which was count in a stack of money in front of him.

He stopped counting his money and jumped up to greet his guests, "My Friend. Nice to see you".

With a half grin Pop gave him a quick business pound and a hug and said, "Cabesia how's life treating you in this hole of yours? You need a bigger office Mr. cheap man."

Cabesia laughed and his bodyguard grunted. Cabesia grabbed two keys off his mini stack and said, "For you-straight from the boat".

Pop pulled the money out of the night bag and put the stacks on the table. Cabesia took his seat and Pop said, "You have anything to drink around here? It's going to take you a good minute to count that 30. That's another thing to invest in- a money machine."

"Yes…Yes." Cabesia waved Pop off as he picked up a phone that rested by his foot and started to bark out orders in Spanish.

"I know you like turkey and cheese hero, yes? So I have one coming for you, okay?" He said then jumped right into counting the money.

"Good, because I have been eating all day", Pop said.

When Cabesia finish counting the money and Pop dusted off his sandwich and juice, Cabesia picked up the phone again to check and see if the front was clear for Pop to leave.

"Okay my friend it is all clear out there", Cabesia said standing up to give Pop of pound and a hug.

"Good looking Cabesia, that sandwich hit the spot", Pop said on his way out. He jumped in his 300E and weaved through the rush-hour traffic headed back to Brooklyn. Pop felt like someone was we even through the traffic with him. He pulled his gun out and put it on his passenger seat. Then he turned down his music. Check in his rearview mirror, he saw nothing unusual.

Pop drove to his stash house on Halsey Street and Malcolm X and took his time parking out front of the brownstone. When Pop turned the car off his peripheral vision caught a glimpse of something that didn't feel right. He snatched his gun off of the seat and pushed his door open with a quickness he didn't know he still had.

The first person Pop locked eyes with was a white man dressed in jeans and an army jacket. He charged at Pop with a 357.magnum, screaming something that didn't register to Pop until it was too late.

Pop squeezed off two quick rounds knocking the charging man off his feet. As he crumbed to the ground, he squeezed off three rounds of his own shattering the car window and denting Pop's car.

Pop ducked down behind his door when a barrage of bullets started going off all around him. He couldn't grasp what was happening; feeling like everyone within eye shot is an enemy, Pop spun around to his blind side to squeeze off four more rounds.

Suddenly, a bullet hit Pop in his arm and one slammed him in his chest, causing him to fall backwards into his car. Another bullet hit Pop in his leg, causing him to scream out in pain as he lost the grip on his gun, and fell down to the pavement. They rushed him like hyenas on its prey, yelling words that began to sound clearer to Pop now that the shooting had stopped. He knew he was assed out.

"Police! Freeze Motherfucker!"

"Man down! We need two buses right away!"

Those were the last words Pop heard before a walkie-talkie connected with the back of his head and he blacked out.

Chapter 4

At 2:00 in the morning, Mama K found herself lying in bed watching TV with the sound on mute. She was thinking about all the good times she had with her husband through the years, but a bad feeling was brewing in the pit of her stomach. It was late and Pop always called her to let her know if he was going to be out later than usual. Mama K had not heard from Pop all day, and she was on the border line of worrying. Then the phone rang.

"Hello?"

"Yes, is this Karolyn Short?" A male voice asked.

"Yes, who is this?"

"This is Detective Robert Kelly, from the 87th precinct. Ma'am there is a matter we have to speak with you about concerning Ryan Short."

Her body snapped into attention, "Matter. What kind of matter?"

He said, "Your husband was involved in an incident earlier and he is currently in the hospital in stable condition, but no one can go see him right now without me or another detective as an escort. So I'm asking you to come down to the precinct so we can sort some of this out."

She was already getting dress when she asked, "Why can't I go to the hospital without a police escort?"

"Security reasons ma'am."

"Alright… Alright. I'll be down there in a minute", she said and hung up the phone.

Mama K called next door to her friend Linda's house and asked her to watch to kids while she ran down to the precinct to find out what happened to Pop. She promised she would be back before the kids woke up. Linda was all right with it because our own kids were sound asleep, and her boy friend was over for the night, with the two of them they could handle two houses full of kids. Linda through on her robe and went over to Mama K's house to stretch out on her couch.

Mama K arrived at the 87th precinct by cab, and as soon as she crossed the precinct threshold, a chill ran up her spine. She went to the sergeants Desk and asked to speak with Detective Kelly. She was ushered into the detective's domain of the precinct, which looked to be in full swing at 3 o'clock in the morning.

"Mrs. Short?" He motioned to her, "please right this way".

Detective Kelly was a big balding white man that looked as if football was his calling, but he insisted on law enforcement. He didn't look tired for person that had been up since five in the morning the day before. When he got close enough to her the distasteful smell of coffee, rolled off his breath and smacked Mama K in her face hard enough to let her know he had been having a long night. So she got right down to business.

"I don't have a lot of time, so can you please explain to me what's going on with my husband", Mama K said, looking around at her surroundings.

Detective Kelly thoughts himself 'get a load of this one'. "Well, your husband is in Kings County hospital right now under arrest. We have been following him for some time now and when we tried to arrest him today, he opened fire on us. Shot one of my offices and I'm not too happy about that. When the confusion was over Mr. short was still conscience, but he was shot three times. I believe he's alive because he was wearing a bulletproof today.

"Now, while he is in the hospital he won't be allowed any visitors until he's moved to a more secure place, even though he's up and in stable condition. He gave me your number and asked me to call you."

Mama K sat there soaking it all in, then asked, "Well what is he being charged with?"

Detective Kelly took a sip of his coffee and said, "At the moment attempt murder on a few officers, weapons possession, and drug possession".

"You can't tell me this over the phone? I mean – being that you're saying I can't see him without you being a part of our conversation. So, what's the real reason for the getting me out of my bed at three in the morning Mr. Kelly?" Mama K I asked with a slight attitude. Pop had taught Mama K not to panic if a situation like this ever occurred. Just take charge, and don't trust the police.

"We were hoping you might want to help your husband out here. If you look at the bigger picture your husband is in a lot of trouble right now, and any information you might have for us..."

She cut him off, "Listen Detective, you're barking up the wrong tree. I don't have any information about nothing but children's school clothes, and attending to old people who's, sex life been over years ago".

He said, "Come on Mrs. Short. You expect me to believe you don't know anything about the drugs your husband has been pushing to kids and..."

She stopped him again, "Look, what did I just tell you? Now you are insinuating things in my direction, and I'm not comfortable with this line of questions. Which is giving me the impression I'm going to need a lawyer".

Talk of a lawyer threw the Detective off. Usually he would have cracked a dealer wife by now. The thought of him being in the station for the last 14 hours crossed his mind and he made up the decision to shut this interview down. He was too tired to tussle with this one right now, but he had to take one last shot at her.

"I'm just trying to give you the opportunity to come clean about your husband's dealings, because the bottom line is, in the long run, we can charge you with accessory to his dealings".

She chimed in, "Well, I'm not being charged tonight for shit. If I were, I would be over there in that cell. So if you're done, I would like to go now".

He gave up and pulled out one of his cards. Handing it to her, he said, "Only if you change her mind".

She took the card and got up without saying another word. Stepping back out into the cold night the wind blew harder enough to carry the Detectives card up in the air as she flung it into the night sky.

Chapter 5

Mama K did not want to say anything to the kids until she spoke with pop first. She woke them up as if nothing happened and got them ready for school. Then she waited for the phone to ring.

By 11 o'clock, she could not wait any longer and started calling around to see if pop was still in Kings County Hospital, or if they had moved him yet. When she finally got straight answers from a lady, who sounded Haitian, she learned he had been released from the hospital and taken down to central booking.

Mama K kept their lawyers number in her pocket for days like this and it was time to use it. She called Ruben Schollof's office and he was ready for her, because he had seen the 6 o'clock news when he woke up that morning. He told his secretary to put her through, "Hello Mrs. Short".

"Hello Mr. Schollof. I'm calling because my husband has a problem right now and we need your assistance", she said.

"Yes, I saw it on the news this morning and it will be better if we met at the courthouse tonight. I already checked into when he would be brought into the court and arraigned. I'm going to fight for a bail, but it's going to be an uphill battle from what I'm hearing." He said.

"What time should I be there?" She asked.

"Night Court starts roughly at 6 o'clock."

"Okay I'll be there". Then she hung up.

Mama K got her thoughts together and went into damage control mode. Things were looking real bad right now, so she went into their bedroom and open the closet. She moved all of the sneaker and shoeboxes out of her way and opened up the stash spot. Inside were a Timberland box with money in it and a Reebok box with 2 guns in it. She took out both boxes and counted the money first.

Her total came up to $42,077, and ten hurt fingers. She felt relieved Pop never kept any drugs in the house. That was one headache she wasn't in the mood to deal with. Mama K thought about moving the money and said why not. She packed the $40,000 into her purse and dug out the keys to her mother's house. Going into the other box with the guns in it, she took out her trustee 380 Beretta, checked it, and put it in her purse. Anything can happen on her short trip to Bushwick, so she had to be ready.

Mama K went downstairs to her old Maxima, she only like driving when she had to, and dug it out the snow. Her thing was to ride shotgun in Pops Benz, riding around in New York City with the rest of the crazies is not something she liked to do.

Her mother was still at work when she got Hancock & Evergreen. As soon as she opened the door, Mama K was greeted by her mother's big ass Rockwaler Ginger, who was in the hallway.

"Hey Ginger!"

The dog barked and rubbed up on her leg, as she scratched behind Gingers ears and proceeded to go upstairs. She went into the back bedroom where Pop had a secret stash in our mother's floor. Only Pop, Mama K, and Ginger knew about this stash spot.

She moved the bed and the night table to the side, went to the corner, and started pulling at the rug until he gave way. Under the rug was a wooden floor that had two movable floorboards. She moved them and saw it was money down there already. She didn't have to count that money to, so she left it alone. She figured if it's down there then Pop knows how much it is already. She put the $40,000 down there, closed it up and turned around to all watching Ginger. "Shhh... don't tell mommy. She might go to Atlantic City on us."

Ginger balked as she put everything back and played with Ginger a little bit on her way over to the telephone.

"Hello?"

"Kim? What's up girl?"

"Mama K? Girl where are you? The streets are talking crazy right now." Kim said.

Kim was one of Mama K's closest cousins wool was of brown skin 5 foot, with a bigger chest then back. Kim always was first in the hood to know all the doubt, and it was usually accurate. It helped a lot that she was reliable when it came to watching the kids.

"I'm trying to get a hold on it now. That's why I'm calling you. I need you to watch to kids tonight while I go down to the courthouse." Mama K said.

"I got you. What time you need me there?" Kim asked.

"Around 4-4:30."

"Aight. I'll be there."

*****
———

Mama K arrived at Brooklyn criminal courthouse and a line was already forming outside in the brisk winter cold. Looking around at the other faces on the line, she noticed other wives, girlfriends and some even brought their children with them. Some hood dudes with big gold chains with medallions the size of hands were also on line. She thought to herself 'they might as well be holding up an sign saying yeah we getting money and we here to bail our homie out'.

Mr. Schollof was waiting inside the courtroom stationed off to the side conversating with another man in a suit. Mama K walked in and took a seat in the middle of the courtroom audience. Mr. Schollof caught her eye and gave her a nod to step outside.

"How are you doing?" He asked once they were in the hallway.

"I'm worried Mr. Schollof. Can you tell me something good right now?" She asked with her face full of stress.

"I was just talking to the ADA, to see if we can at least agree on a reasonable bail, being that Mr. Short is injured."

She cut in, "how injured?"

"He was shot in his leg, that wasn't too bad. The bullet went in and came out missing the bone and his arteries. He has a broken arm from a bullet, and he was also shot in his chest. The bullet proof vests stopped that one."

She gave a sigh of relief to the sound of that as he continued, "I went back there to see him and he's definitely going to need something to wear".

"Where are his clothes?" She asked confused.

"He told me EMS cut them off of him and the police took them, which is typical in a case like this."

"Okay, so what about his bail?" She asked.

"The ADA won't budge. He wants a remand, and he might get it tonight." He said clearly aggravated with the prosecutor. "I'm going to fight for at least hundred thousand dollar bail."

"$100,000! Where am I supposed to get that kind of money from?" She blurted out.

He said, "Listen Mrs. Short, I don't have a lot to work with right now. These are some serious charges and with the news coverage, it's not making my job any easier. The judge is going to side with the DAs office tonight just to get us out of his face, but like I said, I will definitely do my best and we'll see what happens. Just stay calm okay?"

"Okay", she agreed then they went back inside the courtroom. Mama K went back to her seat and watched Mr. Schollof coal back over to the ADA and make his pitch again on Pops bail.

It seemed like forever had come and gone to Mama K, as she watched the faces and crimes come and go until that time came. "Docket number 3577/91, people v. Short. He is charged with attempt murder (four counts), possession of 2000 g cocaine and possession of a weapon and the first and second degree."

Without looking up the judge asked, "How does the defense plea?"

Mr. Schollof spoke, "The defense pleads not guilty Your Honor".

The judge looked up real quick from the paperwork he was reading to look at Pop. Pop looked like he was in a lot of pain carrying his cast and bad leg at the same time across the room.

Mama K put her hand across her mouth to stop herself from screaming. To her Pop looked like a wounded bird. He had a deep limp all the way to the table, and he was wearing a pair of dirty sweatpants she had never seen before. A hospital gown and hospital slippers rounded out his outfit for his late-night appearance.

"Bail?" The judge asked looking in the ADA's direction, who jumped right into his sermon about how Pop, was a threat to society, who was facing some serious charges, and therefore should get nothing but three hots and a cot.

"Your Honor, my client is seriously injured, and we are axing for bail to be set at $50,000. This way my client can receive medical care from his personal doctor upon making bail."

The judge looked at Mr. Schollof and said, "Counselor, you're not serious right? Your client tried to kill four police officers. There won't be a bail ahead at night. Remand! Next case."

With that said Pop turned around and caught eye contact with Mama K, before he was led back into the belly of the beast.

Chapter 6

Mama K left the court feeling defeated. She thought she would at least hear a bail that wasn't outrageous enough to break them... She was still debating on what to tell the children as she drove back home. The boys were old enough to understand, but Meika will be a problem. By the time she got home, it was 9:37 PM, and Kim was trying to put the kids to bed. He heard Mama K come in and it was like that energy took on a new level. Meika ran up to her and of their saying, "Mama K, I want a piece of cake."

Mama K looked over to Kim, and Kim said, "She won't go to bed tonight if she eats another piece of sweets."

Mama K looked down at Meika and smiled, "Oh yeah, so we had our sweets for the night already."

De'Quan wandered over and asked, "Where's Pop at Mama K?"

Mama K had made up her mind the car. She was going to keep it real with our kids and tell them what happened. She needed their strength right now, just like they needed her strength every day.

She said, "Everybody come here in the living room and sit down. I have to tell you something."

All of her little troops and Kim filed into the living room. De'Quan, Ne'Sean, and Kim sat down on the big leather couch, Meika sat on Mama K's lap on the loveseat. She began with, "I don't know how to tell y'all this, so I'm just going to come right out and tell y'all. Pop is in jail-"

De'Quan jumped up stunned, cutting her off, "What!"

"Please sit down." She said, but he didn't so she continued. "He also was shot really bad. He's okay though. I saw him tonight at the courthouse," she said with as much's composer as she can muster without crying.

"Mama K can we go see him to?" Meika asked before anyone else could.

"Yes of course baby," she said. "I have to go see him tomorrow and find out what's really going on, because honestly I don't know why he's in jail or what happened."

After sitting there in silence, Ne'Sean looked like he was at the point of crying. Kim noticed this then put her arm around for comfort. "When is he coming home?" De'Quan asked.

"I don't know when he's coming home baby, and when I go see him tomorrow, I'll find out when we can go all go see him, and if we can bring him stuff", Mama K said as she looked from face-to-face to give them some assurance.

"Can I sleep which shoots and night Mama K? I'm scared", Meika asked with tears forming in the corner of her eyes.

Mama K wiped because face with her hand and said, "Sure baby. Now come on y'all is time to go to bed.

Kim took Ne'Sean hand and used the other one to guild De'Quan as they gave Mama K a hug and made their way down the hallway to their bedroom. Once the children were in the bedrooms, Mama K and Kim met up in the kitchen and sat down at the table.

"Damn its times like this when I needed a drink." Mama K said. They did not keep any alcohol or drugs in the house, because they knew how kids love to experiment.

"What you need me to do?" Kim asked. She reached out to hold her cousins hand across the table.

"I'm going to bring him some clothes tomorrow and see what's up. He looked so sad and hurt tonight. I don't want the kids to see him like that", Mama K said.

Kim said, "Damn, what about his bail? What did they say? You know I'll run up on *Uni and them, and tell them to get that money up. Speaking of which Uni and Rock called here a few times tonight wanting to know was going on? I told them whenever they know is what I know. They said they'll call back to see what's up."

"Those motherfuckers won't even give him a bail." Mama K said rubbing her eyes as she continued. "I'll deal with Uni and them when I speak to Ryan. I'm going to need you to hold me down tomorrow while I am at Brooklyn house."

"What time are the visits?" Kim asked.

"I'm going to call tonight before I go to sleep, so I'll know what my day is looking like while the kids are at school. If anything, I will call you in the morning. You going out tonight?"

"No. Trevor is coming over later. I ain't got my freak on in like a week." They chuckled, which somewhat relived Mama K. Kim continued, "Anyway, I might hang around here for the next few days."

"Would you", Mama K said feeling touched.

"You know I got your back girl. Tomorrow I'll bring some clothes over." They stood up and hugged. "Don't worry; it's going to work itself out."

Mama K put on her strongest smile of the night and said, "I pray that your right."

Chapter 7

Pop was lead back through the doors after losing the battle of trying to get a bail. Handcuffed and disgusted, he was taken through few underground tunnels over to Brooklyn House of Detention. There he was processed and given an I.D. number. Pop didn't make it to a cell with a sleep-able bed until three in the morning. By that time, the doctors had fed him with enough pain killers to make Pop pass out as soon as his head hit the hard mattress.

8:00 in the morning the cell doors popped open, waking Pop up to pain all over his body. He brushed his teeth, swallowed a few pain killers and stepped out of the cell. Pop looked down the fifteen cell gallery from seven cell, and then slowly made his way down the gallery to the dayroom area to use the phone.

"Damn! You alright homie?" A dark skin brother asked, as he looked up from the morning paper.

"I've seen better days. Anybody using that mic?" Pop asked.

"Naw, go ahead."

Pop picked up the receiver and dialed his house number. Mama K picked up on the second ring, "Hello?"

"What's up Mama?"

She jumped up from her seat at the table, "Oh baby, are you alright?"

"Half and half. Listen I need some clothes. Them…"

She cut him off, "I know. I just sent the kids to school and I was just about to call up there again to see when I could come up there and take care of all that."

He tried to get comfortable as he leaned up against the wall and saw there was a visit schedule taped next to the phone. "Oh shit, here go a schedule right here. It says I can get a visit today from 1 to 9."

"Okay. Let me get my stuff together and I'll be up there by 3."

He said, "Alright, we'll talk more then."

"I love you Pop."

"I love you too K", and they hung up.

"Yo Black, let me talk to you for a minute", the dark skin brother said from his seat at a round plastic table large enough to seat four. Pop limped over to the table and grabbed a seat looking from the guy who called him to a Latino kid with long brides.

"What's your name?'

"Pop."

"Ok. Ok. My name is Shabazz. You want a cigarette?"

"Yeah." Pop took the out stretched cigarette, lit it, took a long pull, and slowly sat back in his seat as he released the blue smoke into the air.

"Yo where you from?" Shabazz asked.

"I'm from the Myrtle side of Marcy projects. Where you from?" Pop asked.

"I'm from Brownsville. Yo, as a matter of fact, you was on the news for the last two nights, right?" Shabazz said.

Pop let out a slight laugh and said, "Shit you know more than me. I went from K.C.H., to central booking, then to here in like 48hours."

The Spanish kid final spoke, "Yeah that's him. Yo, my name is B.R., and I'm from Williamsburg." He gave Pop a pound.

"Damn, I heard about you holding down Marcy. I got some wears for you if you need some things", Shabazz said, looking Pop up and down.

B.R. chimed in, "Word. I saw a new nigga come in last night rocking a Polo outfit that will fit you."

Shabazz and Pop burst out laughing.

"Naw, I'm good. I'm going on a visit in a few hours. I just need to lie down and get my head together. My body is mad sore."

"I bet you are. I got some soap and eats for you. You don't have to pay me back or nothing", B.R. said.

Shabazz said, "Here hold down this pack of cigarettes".

Pop gave both of them a pound. "Good looking", he said, then slowly got up and made his way back down the gallery to seven cell.

*****

Mama K called up Kim and told her what time the visits started. Kim felt relieved it wasn't in the morning, because she was still in the bed recovering from her late-night rodeo show with Trevor. Kim told Mama K she would be over by noon to prepare to receive the kids when they came home.

When Mama K got to Brooklyn house, it seemed like déjà vu from the night before at the court house. The line was full of wives and family members, all with the same tired and stressed out look on their faces like her.

Pop walked out onto the visit floor and it seemed like all conversation stopped for a moment. He put on his hardest gangsta bop he could muster to mask the limp he was walking on. Mama K stood up with a bright smile, hugged him and kissed him. As they sat down, she bit on her bottom lip to stop herself from crying. With his good hand, Pop moved the hair away from her eyes and smoothed her cheek.

He broke their silence, "How did you like my gangsta lean just now".

She smiled and shook her head, "Damn Pop. What the hell happen out there?"

He sucked his teeth and said, "Mama K, I thought them niggas were stick-up kids, or some dudes trying to hit me up. I didn't know they were cops. When I shot the first one, they just rained down on me from everywhere. God was definitely watching over me."

"I spoke with Schollof and he told me you might not get a bail or anything. How do you want me to pay him? And what about Uni and them, they called last night asking me what's up?"

He said, "I'm going to get the price from Schollof when I speak to him in a few days. The money Uni has for me, tell him to give you half. That's 25thou. You use that to pay Schollof. In the house I have…"

She cut him off, "I know. I counted it and took it to Moms house, and I found some more over there. "

"Good. That money is our future. All together it's close to 90gees, maybe a little more. That's got to hold us down until we see what's going to happen with this case. Tell Uni with the other half of the money he can do what he feels, that's on him. Between me and you, this is our out. Out of the Game. I've had enough. These crackers might try to hang me behind this shit. I just hope Schollof can pull a rabbit out of his hat." Pop said feeling weigh of a heavy career on his shoulders.

She said, "I brought you enough clothes to last you a few days and I put a $1,000 in your account. The kids want to come see you too".

"Bring the kids next time you come. Remember Mama K, it's just us now. Once you get that dough from Uni, all of our street ties are severed as far as money is concerned. That's why that dough was in Moms house. With that, you're going to have to flip it on a legal tip. Just until I can come home and help you out, okay?"

A tear rolled down her cheek and he caught it with his finger, then he kissed her on the forehead. "I know it's going to be hard, but remember it's been just me and you since before De'Quan was born. We can do this. Just be strong, okay?"

"Yes", she answered.

"Table 12, your visit is over. Say you're good buys", A chocolate c.o. barked from her chair across the small visit room.

Pop said real low, "I got to go babe."

More tears rolled down Mama K's face as they stood up and embraced. "I got you, and I love you". They kissed, and he said, "I love you too", Before walking off with a heavy sadness in his eyes.

Chapter 8

De'Quan

Pop was locked down now and being the oldest sibling in the house De'Quan felt a little weight on his shoulders to step up. If not now, then definitely in the near future. De'Quan knew he was next in line to become the man of the house at 16, and there were moves to be made. How to start is where he was lost at.

De'Quan was going to Grover Cleveland high school, on the border line of Brooklyn and Queens. The school was like no other to him. Nobody went to class that wasn't important to them. The strong aroma of chocolate ty hung heavy in the bathrooms. The staircase is where the robberies went down at if you weren't on point, and the coolest females hung out in the lunchroom for at least 2 periods in a day if they weren't outside in the school park.

De'Quan had a small crew now consisting of Dre, Fat Pee, and a dark skin brother named Rahkem, who was bigger than his age of 16 suggested. Rahkem wasn't one of the fliest guys in the school, but Dre liked his style, so they put him down with them.

Q was the other new edition to the crew, who was a pretty boy from Jamaica Queens. De'Quan liked him because Q gave him some competition when it came to bagging girls in and outside school. They like going at each other on who could get the prettiest girl for the week, and the bonded from there.

All five friends were standing on the back staircase, smoking cigarettes, and talking a whole bunch of nothing when the question came up, "Yo Quan, what's sup what your pops?" Fat Pee asked.

De'Quan blew out some smoke and said, "He's alright. They're still trying to sort through the bullshit. They saying he might be on the island for a while".

Pop had been on right is Alan for seven months and things were changing. De'Quan's crew and other kids in the hood looked up to De'Quan because of his father. Pop was a legend in Brooklyn and all the older Gees made it their business to look out for De'Quan and his friends whenever they saw them.

Rahkem asked, "So you think he's coming home soon?"

"I hope so. Mama K be looking mad stressed-out when she comes home from the Island. Sooner or later we going to have to get this money thing popping", De'Quan said.

Dre added, "Word! My pockets are hurting right now".

"We'll talk about that later", De'Quan said, ending the conversation as the back door open and five girls came strutting through it. Being the closest one to the door made Q speak first as he moved to the side.

"Oh shit. The Glamour of girl's have arrived. Let's make it happen ladies". Being from Queens made Q a hot commodity Grover Cleveland H.S. Being in his presence Eisha made hers felt immediately. "Hey Q. What's it gonna be this afternoon. Us or class?" The light coming through the dirty window still did justice to Eisha's honey complexion.

Q looked her up and down. 'Sexy' he thought to himself as the rest of the girl's took up position in front of their respectable pick for the afternoon get together. Tee-Tee stepped in front of De'Quan causing a smile to creep into the corners of his mouth. Tee-Tee stood at 5feet, with a Toni Braxton haircut, and a thick body for her sixteen years of age. De'Quan liked what he was seeing.

India was a dark skin slimly who had had her eye on Dre for a minute. She stepped in front of Dre and whispered something in his ear that put a bright smile on his face. Dre was on board.

The last two girls Torry and Scarlett silently debated on who would take Fat Pee or Rahkem. Tee-Tee broke the silence, "Yeah, Eisha's mom won't be home until eight tonight. That's more than enough time to chill."

India eyed Dre as if they were the only ones on the staircase and said, "So it's like our own little party".

De'Quan took charge and said, "That's what I'm talking about. Let's head up to the bus stop. Eisha what your moms got to drink in there?"

"Nigga, B.Y.O.B." she said.

"What the fuck is that?' Fat Pee asked.

Eisha and the girls looked around at each other and slowly realized none of the boys knew what she was talking about. "Bring your own bag!" causing a barrage of chuckles as they headed down the stairs and out the side door of the school.

$$*****$$

Eisha lived in building 106, on the corner of Park Street and Marcy Avenue. It was like pulling teeth getting everybody to chip in for the liquor and when the money was right, the kids got one of the old drunks from the neighborhood to go in the liquor store for them and pick up two bottles of gin. They grabbed a bottle of orange juice and a pack of cigarettes from the corner store and made their way upstairs.

Eisha lived in the standard ghetto crib, with plastic on the couches, entertainment center resting in a big ivory color wall unit. In the kitchen hung the big wooden fork and spoon on the wall, causing everyone to ask did their mothers buy them at the same clearance sale. "Yah motherfuckers better not break nothing, and don't drop any cigarettes on the plastic", Eisha said with chuckle in her voice, but a dead serious look on her face.

"Tee-Tee and Quan come in the kitchen", Eisha commanded and lead the way.

"Let's get this party started", Dre said walking over to the stereo system. He popped in a mix tape he was carrying, releasing the sounds of Large Professor 'Live at the Barbecue' through the speakers.

De'Quan, Tee-Tee, and Eisha mixed the drinks and handed out the cups, as everyone got comfortable. Two hours, bottle, and half later things started turning into a full blown good time. Eisha had Q in her mother's bed as if she was the Queen of Sheba, crying out his name as he bent her up like a bike frame.

Tee-Tee encouraged De'Quan to join her in Eisha's bedroom, while Dre and India set up shop in the bathroom. Rahkem, Fat Pee, Torry, and Scarlett sat at the dining room table engaged in a heated game of strip spades. All four of them were drunk and the girls were winning the game. Fat Pee and Rahkem were down to their boxers and socks, with Scarlett and Torry sitting comfortably in t-shirts, panties, and socks.

In the bathroom, Dre was getting his very first blow job, "Damn girl!" Slurp…Slurrrpp. She stopped, licked all around the head, and then looked up at him. Dre looked like he was going to pass out. India smiled and went back to work. Slurp…Slurrrpp.

Tee-Tee and De'Quan explored each other with kisses for an hour before things got real heated. De'Quan pulled his pants down to his ankles, as he smoothly undressed Tee-Tee down to her bra. She laid down on her back, missionary style and De'Quan slid inside her. They rocked back and forth until they got a nice rhythm going like they knew what they were doing. After some good stroke's De'Quan began to tense up and his body shook a little bit. Tee-Tee grabbed onto him tighter then a girl ever grabbed on De'Quan before making him melt into her embrace. When the earth stopped shaking, they laid there lost in each other sex, as De'Quan tried to figure out what just happen to him. He never felt a sensation like that before and Tee-Tee seemed to love every minute of it.

By 7:00p.m. Eisha was done turning Q out, and it was time to air the house out. Scarlett and Torry won the game of strip spades. Fat Pee and Rahkem thought once they got naked the girls would want to do something with them. The boys didn't expect to be sitting there when it was time to get out being laughed at by their two drunken opponents.

"Sorry guys. Party over".

*****

After the clean up, De'Quan, Dre, and Fat Pee made their way over to De'Quan's house. Mama K moved about in the kitchen, as Ne'Sean and Meika sat at the table eating their dinner.

"There he is and his tag a-long's", she said with a smile on her face. "You boys hungry?"

De'Quan said, "You know Fat Pee is hungry. What about you Dre?"

"Man, I'm starving", Dre said rubbing his stomach.

Mama K moved around the kitchen flexing her nose, then asked, "What the hell is that smell?"

The boys spilt a pack of tic tac's in the building lobby to cover the heavy smell of alcohol. Before any of them could answer her, Mama K made her move over to them. She sniffed each one of them causing a panic in their teenage chest. She stopped and 'hummed' to herself as she made her way over to the stove. The three boys looked at each other, and then slowly sat down at the table.

"Where you been at Quan?" Meika asked. Lately his young sister had been acting like Mama K's watch dog and it was beginning to annoy him.

"Mind your business", De'Quan shot at her with the evil eye.

Mama K cut the fight short. "Boys go wash your hands. Meika set more places at the table for me please."

"Yes Mama."

The boys jumped up and made their way down the hallway with Ne'Sean in tow. When they made is safely into De'Quan's room Fat Pee was the first one to speak.

"Yo man, what gives with Mama K sniffing us like that?"

"Sean come here", De'Quan said. Ne'Sean walked over to his brother as everyone else watched in silence. De'Quan blew his breath into Ne'Sean's face without warning.

"What the hell you do that for?" Ne'Sean asked with a frown on his face.

"What my breath smell like?"

"It smelled like peppermint dummy", Ne'Sean asked irritated with the exercise he was just put through.

"What you think she smelled?" Dre asked.

De'Quan thought for a second, and then said, "I don't know. Mothers are strange people man. Forget that, let's wash our hands and go eat. I'm starving".

Once they finished eating De'Quan said, "Mama K we going downstairs for a little while."

"Yah be careful. Quan, I want you back up here no later than 11:30."

"Ok Mama", he said as they walked the door.

Mama K and Meika were cleaning up the kitchen when Ne'Sean put down his video game and came out his room looking to follow his brother and his friends. Without turning around from the sink Mama K said, "Where do you think you're going?"

He stopped in his tracks. 'I almost made it', he thought to himself.

"I'm going downstairs with De'Quan and Dre".

"No, you're not. You're going back into that room. It's already 9:00 o'clock, and you have no business down there. Go find something on TV and we are finished in here we'll come in there and watch it with you".

"But Mama K", Ne'Sean whined.

"Boy what I said", she snapped.

Ne'Sean knew it was time to get out of dodge. He sucked his teeth, turned on his heels and moped back down to his bedroom.

De'Quan stood in front of Dre and Fat Pee who were sitting on the bench in front of De'Quan's building. A light breeze moved through the project court yard as De'Quan looked around a few times before pulling out his pack of cigarettes. He gave one to Dre and lit up his own. Fat Pee didn't smoke.

"De'Quan what's up, you said you had a plan. So, what is it?" Dre said.

De'Quan lowered his voice where only the three of them could hear him, "I got a place we can rob". He stepped back and watched their reaction.

Fat Pee said, "Rob? Shit man, I thought we was going to sell drugs out here".

"Word, what gives Quan...I mean the whole Marcy respects Pop, and I know we can get some crack heads on the strength of Pops name. People out here know you not going to sell them no bullshit, so we can get sales". Dre said as Fat Pee nodded in agreement.

De'Quan took a pull on his cigarette, blew out the smoke, and said, "Listen that's the problem right there, the whole projects know us. I don't trust people out here anymore. Somebody told on Pop, and we still don't know who did that. Shit, we set up shop and motherfuckers tell on us cause we getting Pops clientele. Then we be right on the Island with him. I'm not trying to see that".

"Shit, neither are we", Dre said. "We don't even have a gun, and what's the place anyway".

De'Quan knew if he could sell Dre on the idea then Fat Pee will roll without argument. "I got a gun. You know Pop had mad guns and before he got locked up, I took one and stashed it. I've been scoping out the store on Nostrand and Walt, and I know the perfect time to hit it".

"How much you think we can get?" Fat Pee asked.

"About five hundred or more", De'Quan answered with a gilt in his eyes.

"Shit, for ten minutes of work. That sounds pretty good", Dre said lighting up to De'Quan's plan.

De'Quan smiled and said, "See, that's what I'm trying to show yah. We can hit something, and we won't have to stand in no park all day or be ducking Mama K and her friends all day. She find out we out here selling drugs she will try to break my neck and yours, but if we hit stores and shit like that how will she know about that. Like you said it's only like ten minutes of work and we can be back in the crib chilling before she even realizes we were gone".

Fat Pee said, "Shit Mikey B and them be in the park all day and damn near all night and Tech only pays them $400 a week".

"You see what I'm saying? So yah in?" De'Quan asked rubbing his hands together.

"Fuck it Pee, let's do it", Dre said sounding convinced.

"You know I'm riding. My mom's ain't giving me shit." Fat Pee said and they all laughed. Reality was Fat Pee's life was no joke. Living in a single parent home with three other siblings and no fathers in sight had put a tight grip on any dollars and cents that came through their front door. Being the oldest of his siblings put Fat Pee in a position where he knew he had to do something before they starved in their crowded apartment.

Dre was a second child of a mother who was married to Jack Daniels. Most of the time she forgot Dre and his sister was alive. That is why Dre spent so much time over at De'Quan's house.

De'Quan said, "Tomorrow is a Saturday, a big day in the store business. We get some ski mask, dark clothes and ride up there at 10:00p.m. Pee you be the doorman when we in there. You watch the street and make sure it's safe for us to run out of there. I'll hold down the spot with the gun. Dre, you hop over the counter and get the money out of the register, and that niggas pockets. He might have a Philly blunt box behind there with money in it too. Get all that shit. Oh, and rip the phone out the wall while you back there, that will give us some time to get away".

"What kind of gun is it?" Dre asked thirsty to see the new hardware.

De'Quan said, "It's a 38 caliber, with six shots. I only have six bullets too. I guess Pop didn't care about that gun, cause I went looking for more bullets and there wasn't any".

"We can buy some bullets Ju on the other side", Fat Pee said.

De'Quan asked, "You sure he will sell them to us?"

"Man, as long as we got the dough we can get whatever we want from that nigga. Even another gun".

"Word? That's what I'm talking about", Dre chimed in with a taste of excitement in his voice.

As a guy and a girl walked past them De'Quan asked them for the time and found out it was 11:05. "I'm going up stairs. I'm crazy tired. When yah get up, come to my crib".

"Aight. Come on Pee let's bounce", Dre said hopping off the bench.

They gave each other a pound, and then Dre and Fat Pee went to the other side of the projects.

When De'Quan walked into his house and went straight for the refrigerator and made himself a glass of juice. Mama K walked into the kitchen and said, "Hey baby, you alright?"

"Yeah", he answered in between sips of his juice.

"Come here and let me talk to you for a minute", she said taking a seat at the kitchen table.

"Where's Meika and Sean at?'

"They fell asleep while we was watching a movie", Mama K said, smiling to the thought of how her two babies looked sleeping, while the big one in front of her was growing up right before her eyes.

"What's up Mama K?"

"I don't know how to ask you this, so I'm just going to come right out and ask. Quan are you having sexy?" Her voice was so smooth and low De'Quan felt at ease at anything Mama K wanted to talk to him about without being sacred to respond. It still was weird for a boy to be talking to his mother about sex. He just blushed and stayed silent.

She pressed on, reaching across the table to take his hand. "Quan, I know it's hard to talk to me about something like this, but I worry about you. And I smelled it on at least two of you when yah came in here tonight".

He put his head down feeling a little embarrassed. "You got me Mama K".

"I know…So here", she said reaching in her robe pocket and pulling out some condoms. "I want you to wear these. You know it's a lot of diseases out here and you better not come in here with some baby mama pregnant.

They shared a laugh and De'Quan said, "Don't worry about that, I'm not trying to be no baby daddy".

She giggled, "Okay, okay…just be careful please. Another thing is Pop might be starting trial soon, and he wants us to be prepared for the long haul".

"What do you mean; I thought Pop was coming home soon?" De'Quan said with a puzzled look on his face.

To get her thought's together Mama K got up and got some water out of the refrigerator. De'Quan just sat back and watched her in silence. When she sat back down she said, "I know I can talk to you about this. Your brother and sister are too young to understand how this whole thing is happening to us. Baby, your father is going to have to do some time out of this. He shot a police officer and they shot him. It's not much he can say to that. Therefore, his next order of business is to try and get the smallest amount of time he can get.

"All this means is we have to be ready. We have a little money put away and I'm going to use it to open up a store front. It's Pops idea, so I have to talk with him a little more about it. In the mean time money is going to be a little tight around here", Mama K said.

De'Quan wouldn't dare tell his mother what he and his friends were planning, so he kept quiet and nodded in agreement as she continued, "I know you and Dre are growing up now, and the people in these projects is going to be looking for yah to step up in Pop absence. I don't want yah selling drugs out here, you hear me".

He shook his head and said, "Mama K we know somebody told on Pop, and they will tell on us too, if we give them the chance".

She smiled, "Ohhh, smarter than Mama thought, huh. That's good. Well I still want yah to be careful out here. That's why I have to get this store thing going, so yah can come and work with me and stay off these streets".

She yawed and stood up, "Now go wash up and go to bed. I'll see you in the morning".

"Ok Mama".

Chapter 9

Saturday

Click...Click.

Ne'Sean heard the sound, but he thought it was his subconscious mind playing tricks on him. He rolled over and felt movement in the room. Lying on his stomach, Dre slowly open his eyes, and began to focus on the figure sitting on the bottom bunk.

"What's that?" Ne'Sean asked in a groggy voice.

De'Quan was startled by his voice. He quickly tossed the gun under his pillow and blurted out an angry, "Go back to sleep man".

"Let me see", Ne'Sean pressed, hopping down from the top bunk.

"Look, I told you to go back to sleep", De'Quan snapped.

"Man, it's time to get up any way, and I'm not a baby or stupid Quan. I saw the gun. Let me hold it".

Thinking about what to do next, De'Quan looked at the door as if he didn't already lock it and push the dresser on it. He picked the gun up and said, "You better not tell anybody I let you hold this. Not even Jamel".

Ne'Sean's eyes lit up, "I swear I won't tell anybody".

De'Quan made sure there weren't any bullets in the cylinder, then handed it to his brother. Ne'Sean held the gun lost in his own world for a moment. He cocked the hammer, pointed the gun at the window and pulled the trigger. When it clicked, De'Quan spoke and moved on his brother at the same time, "Man give me that".

"Why you snatch it like that?" Ne'Sean asked clearly upset about what just happened.

De'Quan said, "Stop asking so many questions. All you need to know is if something happens to me, and Pop doesn't come home, then you are the man of the house you dig. Then you will be able to carry one of these".

"Let me go with you", Ne'Sean asked out of nowhere.

De'Quan chuckled, "Go with me. You don't even know where the fuck I'm going".

"Where you going then?"

De'Quan ignored his brother, put the gun and bullets in one of his sneaker and slid it under the bed. "Don't touch that gun again unless I say so, you hear me?"

Ne'Sean sucked his teeth, "yeah I hear you". Feeling disappointed, Ne'Sean moved the dresser from in front of the door and headed off to the bathroom.

De'Quan went out into the kitchen and found Mama K in there making pancakes and turkey bacon, "Good morning baby".

"Morning Mama K...did Dre call yet?" He asked, sitting down at the table.

"No. Where yah going so early on a Saturday?" she asked.

"We might go down to Fulton Street to hang out then go over to Fort Greene to play some ball" he answered.

"Yah be careful out there", she said moving toward the ringing telephone on the kitchen wall. "Hello...Morning Dre, hold on".

De'Quan hopped up and grabbed the receiver, "What's up...ok...yeah I'll be ready in 10 minutes. Yea she's cooking," De'Quan said loud enough for his mother to hear.

"Tell Dre I'll make a plate for him", Mama K said as Meika wondered into the kitchen rubbing her eyes.

"Come through, she said she got you", he said then hung up.

"Meika, you all up in that refrigerator like you brushed your jibs already". De'Quan said, taking an early morning shot at his sister.

"Shut up! Mama tell him to leave me alone". Meika whined.

"You do look like you missed the washcloth on your trip to the bathroom this morning, with all that cold in your eyes. But, you still my baby- come here and give me a kiss". Mama K said with a big smile on her face.

De'Quan just shook his head and walked out of the kitchen, "Unbelievable Mama K".

*****
———

De'Quan, Fat Pee, and Dre hit Fulton Street by 11 o'clock to pick up their ski mask from the army and navy store. Then they stepped in Dr. Jays to buy three sets of black Nike gloves. Once they finished picking up their supply's the boys walked over to Fort Greene projects to play a few games of basketball.

"A Yo...we got next", Dre barked as they crossed the court and headed for the bleachers to change into their b-ball gear.

"Check it out, the police make their rounds at 9:40p.m. We go in there at 9:50p.m. on the dot, and we're out of there in 3 minutes", De'Quan said. He looked up from tying his shoe to see if they had any feedback.

"So which way we gonna run too when we come out?" Dre asked.

De'Quan said, "We run to Marcus Garvey, then make the left and try to jump in a cab, since Pee won't be able to make it back to the project on foot".

Dre laughed, and Fat Pee took offense, "Fuck you Quan, I ain't that slow".

"Ok, my bag", De'Quan chuckled, then he got back down to business. "The meet spot is Dre's crib, cause he's the only one with his own room and his moms is hardly there".

"That sounds cool", Dre said nodding his head in agreement.

"NEXT!" Someone yelled from the basketball court.

"Ok…now let's go bust these niggas asses", Fat Pee said as he hopped off of the bleacher and they took to the court.

*****

Mama K took Ne'Sean and Meika up to Rikers Island to see Pop, while her oldest son hung out with his friends on this clear and sunny Saturday. Prison officials made Pop status C.M.C. (captain escort) because of his case and all of the publicity it was drawing. Pop was being held in N.I.C. (north infirmary clinic), on the high security third floor until his trial.

Mama K did not mind coming to visit Pop while he was in N.I.C. because she only had to wait 15 minutes after she was processed to see him. Compared to the horror stories she heard from other visitors having to wait for an hour or more to see people in other buildings on Rikers Island.

Mama K loved to style on the female c.o.'s whenever she came to see her husband, like she was doing on this busy Saturday with her Gucci skirt suit and matching loafers. The hateful stares she received walking through the steel gates spoke volumes to Mama K as she ignored them and helped her two kids through the process.

Meika wore a pink Gap skirt, a white Gap sweater and pair of pink Reebok sneakers, while Ne'Sean rocked a stonewash Levis suit and pair of Reebok pumps. They were waiting in the C.M.C. visiting booth when the captain escorted Pop into it.

Pop locked eyes with his family and his face lit up as usual. No matter what was going on behind the steel doors, Pop never brought those problems down to the visit room. His mind set was to always enjoy his one-hour visit with his family.

Meika jumped up first with a 'Daddy!' already coming out of her mouth as she bear hugged him. Pop kissed his daughter on her forehead, "Hey baby girl".

Mama K stood up and collected her hug and kiss, then he turned to Ne'Sean, smiled and said, "Give me five".

The c.o. locked them in the booth together and they all sat down. The officers took up their positions on the other side of the glass window and their time began.

Where's De'Quan?' Pop asked.

"He's out running around with Dre and them on Fulton today. I'll bring him on Wednesday night when I come back", Mama K said.

"Okay. So how is everybody doing?" Pop said with a bright smile.

Meika spoke up first, "I got a B in math." She sat there with her top lip poked out. Pop chuckled. Only his daughter would have an attitude about not getting an A in one of her classes.

After an hour of idle conversation about family matters and what's new in Brooklyn the captain knocked on the window and signaled to Pop that his visit was over. Meika began to tear up and Pop wiped them from her eyes. "Don't worry baby girl. It will be over soon, ok."

Meika nodded then Pop turned to Ne'Sean, "take care of your sister for me, Ok".

Ne'Sean stood up and took his sister hand, "Yes Pop." Pop gave him a hug and a pound, then he turned to Mama K.

They hugged and kissed, "I'll call you in about two hours".

"I'll be there", Mama K said with a reassuring smile. "Don't forget I brought you a package".

Suddenly the door unlocked, and the c.o. asked Pop was he ready. Saying yes to his dumb ass question wouldn't have felt right to Pop, so he stepped to the side so his family could leave first, then he let the captain handcuff him as they led Pop back behind the big steel door that was only for prisoners to walk through.

Chapter 10

De'Quan, Fat Pee, and Dre hid in the yard of a house directly across the street from the store. There were no light's on in the house, which made their concealment even better. Fat Pee looked at his watch and it read 9:49p.m.

"One minute", Fat Pee reported in a low voice.

De'Quan was sweating from the anticipation. "Fuck it", he said and pulled down his ski-mask. His two partners followed suit and they made their move. They dipped across the street as quick as possible, looking in every direction. De'Quan rushed into the empty store first and pulled his gun out on the owner immediately.

"Put your fucking hands up!"

The store owner thought about going for the gun he had under the counter, but Dre jumped over the counter to fast freezing the owner in his tracks. Dre pushed the owner into the rack on the back wall spilling candy all over the floor. The owner caught his balance and put his hands in the air.

Dre hit a few buttons on the register and it chimed as the money tray slid out. Dre open a black book bag he was carrying then emptied the entire money tray in it. Dre looked under the counter and saw three Philly blunt boxes stacked in between a few cartons of cigarettes. He grabbed them and found one filled with money, the second had Philly blunts in it and the last one had a 38 special in it. He dumped all three boxes into his bag as fast as could just as Fat Pee said, "One minute!"

Dre turned to the owner and shook him down. He took the owners wallet and searched his socks, "Nothing else?"

The store owner looked at Dre like he was crazy, "Come on guys—you got everything. Now please leave."

"Shut the fuck up!" Dre snapped, and then he turned to the telephone and kicked the whole connection box off of the wall. Dre jumped back over the counter and De'Quan stepped up close to the counter, "lie down on the floor and count to 50".

The owner sucked his teeth and laid down on the floor. The three robbers were out the door by the count of two. They cut corners and ran until Fat Pee almost passed out. By the time they realize it they were two blocks away from the projects. The running turned to walking until they reached Dre's building and onto the elevator.

When they got off the elevator, they heard music coming from Dre's apartment. Before Dre put the key in the door he said, "Just go straight to my room".

Dre open the door and they tried to avoid the living room action of Dre mother doing a drunken two step with a guy the boys knew from Marcy Avenue. De'Quan took the book bag from Dre and made a bee line to Dre's bedroom. Fat Pee followed De'Quan half way down the hallway until Dre's mother voice made him stop in his tracks.

"What you got for me Dre?" His mother asked with a slur.

Dre was used to walking in on scenes like this, but now they were getting tiring and it didn't put any food in Dre's stomach. His mother always used questions like these as a forum of checking up on her son in front of her company, but once they left things would go back to her ignoring him and his sister while nursing a bottle of Gin.

Dre said, "Ma, I don't have nothing and I'm starving. Did you make something to eat?"

"Shiittt…boy you old enough, go make your own food", she replied. Then she turned her back on him and went back to entertaining her date.

Dre shook his head, and then walked down the hallway to his room. De'Quan stood on the side of Dre's bed, still holding the book bag as if he was ready to run back out of the room, "What did she say?" De'Quan whispered like anyone could hear them over the loud music.

'Never mind her. Let's count this paper", Dre said trying to forget what was going on in his living room.

Fat Pee moved the dresser onto the door and De'Quan quickly dumped the bag content's out on the bed. De'Quan sat down on one side of the bed, while sat down on the other. Fat Pee pulled up a chair and they formed a triangle around their booty on the bed.

Dre grabbed the gun and De'Quan snapped at him, "Man, empty that shit".

"I know…be cool".

"Fuck that. Let's count this", Fat Pee said with a big Kool-Aid smile on his face.

De'Quan and Fat Pee separated the bills from the change and Phillies, while Dre continued to play with the store owner gun.

"Dre you got a good hiding spot in here?" De'Quan asked.

Dre looked up and around his room then it hit him, "Yeah check this out".

Dre went over to the radiator that was underneath the window and he began to remove the door off the radiator. Inside the radiator was a small space at the bottom of it. Then Dre went over to his closet and pulled out an old Nike box and brought it over to the bed.

When they finished counting the money Fat Pee said, "$653.22".

"Yeah! That's what I'm talking about. Not bad for 10minutes worth of work", De'Quan boasted proudly.

"Hell yeah, and we got a new gat for the stash", Dre added.

De'Quan split the money three ways and said, "I'm only taking $50 of mines. I want you to put the rest in your window spot Dre".

"I'll stash my dough in my own crib", Fat Pee said.

"We know, just don't go crazy at Burger King", Dre said sparking a chuckle around the room.

"So, what yah want to do now?" De'Quan asked.

"Let's go to that party over on Flushing", Fat Pee answered feeling hype about how the rest of his night was supposed to go.

Dre's eyes lit up, "Word, I'm with that. Let me change real quick".

Fat Pee stood up said, "I'm going to run down stairs and change too".

Once Dre finish getting dress they went down stairs and collected Fat Pee, who lived in the same building as Dre. Then they went over to De'Quan's house so he could do the same. It was almost 11:00p.m. When they walked into the house. Mama K was sitting on the couch on the telephone and said into the receiver, "Oh here he is. Here, say something to Pop before they lock hi in for the night".

De'Quan ran over to the phone, "What's up Pop?"

"I've been looking for you all day. I'm going to call you back in the morning, alright", Pop said more as a statement than a question.

"Okay Pop".

Pop said, "I love you, and tell Mama and them I will call back in the a.m.".".

"Okay. We love you too Pop", De'Quan said, and then hung up.

Mama K stood back and analyzed the three amigos, "And where do yah think you're going?"

"We were going to this party over on Flushing ave for a little while Mama K", De'Quan answered.

"Yeah Mama K, just for a little while", Dre said quickly backing up his friend.

She looked from De'Quan to Dre. Then she looked over to Fat Pee and he added his piece to their argument, "We'll be back by one. That's not too late for a Saturday Mama K".

"Boy you don't have to tell me what today is", she snapped and looked from face to face again then said, "Yeah well, you boys be back in these projects by one. I'm only saying okay because it's a Saturday".

"Thank you, Mama K,", De'Quan said with a big smile. He kissed her on the cheek then ran down to his room to change. Dre and Fat Pee followed suit by kissing Mama K on her cheek and heading down to De'Quan's room before she changed her mind.

Chapter 11

Stepping onto the visit floor on a Wednesday night always felt electric to Pop. Wednesday and Thursday night visits on Rikers Island were usually reserved for the wives or the baddest girl-friend a prisoner had, and they always came dressed to impress.

Mama K lit up as usual when Pop was escorted into the visit booth. She stood up, embraced and kissed her husband. All of the tension Pop had in his body from being constantly on point flowed right out of his body and he was ready to sit with his family.

Pop turned to his left and locked eyes with his oldest son and smiled, "What's up champ".

De'Quan beamed as he gave his father a hug. Mama K usually went up to visit Pop by herself on Wednesday and Thursday nights, but De'Quan missed the last visit and asked to take the ride with her tonight.

"What's up Mama?" pop asked with a look of concern in his eyes.

"Ain't nothing. I'm just tired", she said as she reached out across the table to take his hand.

He took her hand and said, "I know…we all are tired." Pop looked over to his son and said, "De'Quan why you so hard to catch now a days?"

For a moment, De'Quan got nervous. Sometimes you didn't know what Pop had on his mind, or if he already knew you were doing wrong behind his back. Pop always had eyes on his children in the projects and De'Quan knew the eyes had be out extra hard now that Pop wasn't out on the streets to watch for himself.

"I be around the building or on the other side with Dre and them. When you getting out Pop?" He said to change the subject from him.

Pop looked from De'Quan to Mama K and said, "They offered me a better deal. I called my lawyer today and he said they are offering my 7 ½ to 21 years. I told him I will have an answer for him by my next court date. What do you two think?"

Mama K gently closed her eyes, then open them. "That's a long time Pop. But, it's better than the time they're saying you going to get if you lose at trial".

Pop looked at De'Quan and said, "Can you hold your mother down for me for 7years?"

De'Quan stuck his 17 year old chest out and said, "Yeah Pop".

Pop smiled and said, "Mama I know it's a long time, but I'm starting to look at this situation realistically. I got caught at the scene with a smoking gun in my hand. I'm not going to beat that. Even in Brooklyn Supreme court they'll find me guilty of something, and I already have a year and a half in on the island".

"All of that time counts right", Mama K said to make sure.

"Yes…it counts. So, this is what I want yah to do. Open up that store front. The one I was looking at when I was home is still on the market. Put it in your mother name as the person leasing and financing it. That way welfare won't be sniffing around asking where you got the money from. Me and your mom already spoke to the owner of the property and it's going to cost $1,300 a month to lease it. Have you been reading those books I told you to read on how to get the candy and food from the vendors?"

"Yes, and I spoke to a delivery company that will give me a good deal on the newspapers. The boys and Meika will help me clean it up and stock the place, right De'Quan".

"Yes Mama".

"That's good. That's how I want yah to handle it, strictly a family thing. Quan always close the store with your mother", Pop said.

"Yes, of course Pop. I have Dre and Fat Pee on point too".

"Before I take this plea I'm going to see if I could get it lowered, but I doubt it. It's worth a try though".

The captain tapped on the window and signaled to Pop he had 5 minutes left. Pop shook his head then turned back to his family. "She's so fucking miserable".

They all laughed, and Mama K said, "Okay, be nice yah. We're getting short on money too Pop".

"I know…I know that's why the store is so important. It will generate money while I'm up north".

De'Quan sat there thinking quietly to himself on how he could make things easier by giving Mama K his robbery money, without her asking him all types of questions. At the end of the day that's what the money was for anyway, so Mama K wouldn't have to stress for dough while Pop was locked away.

Suddenly keys jingled in the door and it swung open. They all stood up and Pop gave De'Quan a pound and a hug before he turned to Mama K. "I love you", they kissed in a warm embrace.

"Remember, yah always close the store with Mama K", Pop said staring into his son eyes before he was handcuffed and lead back through the big steel doors.

<u>Chapter 12</u>

Pop stalled the D.A.'s office for two months, but the offer stood. Either Pop was going to take the 7 ½ to 21years they were offering him, or they were prepared to go trial. Pop said, 'fuck it', took the time and the trip up north before things got out of hand with the court system.

De'Quan, Dre and Fat Pee did two more robberies within that two-month time frame and things were beginning to look up for the young trio. De'Quan held strong on his thoughts of Mama K going to need him to step up for the family while Pop was away, so he used Dre radiator to hold onto his stash of $1,300. Taking notes from Pop over the years De'Quan knew the key to a secure future was to keep stacking his dough.

Ne'Sean began to develop a love for playing basketball and it showed in the dedication he started putting into it with Jamel. They would go to the park every day, and play with the other kids in the projects to sharpen their skills. Word began to spread around Brooklyn Tech High School about Ne'Sean and Jamel being a good duo on the basketball court, prompting the junior varsity coach to put them on the team.

With one of her boys growing up faster than she can see and focus on, and her other son showing a new love for a gift they did not know he had when his father was home, Mama K was beginning to feel the pressure of having two boys in the house and no father around to keep them grounded. Everyday Mama K got the feeling of opening the store as an important piece to the entire family growth. No matter what state they were in Mama K knew she had to trust in Pop's plan and stand by his side until he is able to come home and take them to the next level.

Mama K put $5,000 in Pop account when he was shipped upstate, so his commissary would be fat. Mama K had to laugh to herself, thinking Pop will try to figure out a way to flip that $5,000 while he's in there, instead of spending it on its intended purpose.

Things were pretty stable in Mama K's eyes, with a stash of $38,600 tucked in her mother house in Bushwick. She lined up a few vendors who were willing to supply her with the candy, food and drinks at a start-up discount. The only delay was coming from the real estate company, who were shaky about leasing the store front to Grand-Ma Trina at such a late age. Making the acceptance of the check by the real estate company, the only thing left standing in Mama K's way.

Until one of life's curve balls was thrown her way.

Ring...Ring.

Grand-Ma Trina hustled from her stove over to the ringing telephone hanging on the wall. Grease popped out of the frying pan, as the rag she was using as pot holder brushed across one of the open flames, but she thought nothing of it as she dropped it on the counter and answered the phone, "Hello?"

"Hi Trina." It was her long-time friend Emma.

"Oh…hey Emma. I was just thinking about you".

Grand-Ma Trina talked with her back turned to the counter, as the rag caught fire and the flames quickly jumped onto the kitchen window curtain. She smelled smoke, quickly turned around and panicked.

"Oh Lord!"

"What's going on?" Emma asked as the phone receiver left Grand-Ma Trina hand. The long slinky cord let the receiver hit the floor without bouncing back up into the air.

Grand-Ma Trina grabbed another rag, as the flames began to spread faster than she could move. She hit the flames with the rag, and her plan quickly began fail as that rag caught fire.

She blurted out another 'Oh Lord', and then she took off for the bathroom to get a bucket of water. Her dog Ginger began to bark historically from the back yard, repeatly scratching and ramming into the screen door. Smoke seeped out of the cracked kitchen window as the wall and ceiling started to catch fire.

Grand-Ma Trina ran back with a bucket of water and tripped on an old rip in the rug in the hallway. As she was falling, Trina cursed herself for promising to get that rip fixed and never doing it. She paid for it today by spilling the bucket all over the hallway rug instead of the fire on the other side of the wall.

'Oh, please not my kitchen', was all that was going through Grand-Ma Trina mind as she scrabbled to her feet and ran back into the bathroom to refill the bucket. A loud crash almost made her heart stop as she hustled out of the bathroom to see what just happen.

Emma got scared when she heard Trina fall with the bucket of water. Emma quickly hung up the phone and dialed 911. When Emma finish explaining her story to the 911 operator, she hung up and quickly called Mama K before she put on her slippers and hurried herself over to Trina's house which was only two blocks away.

A police squad car cursing the area responded to the call. As the police pulled up in front of the house smoke began to float out of the living room window. Officer Benson hopped out of the curser and ran for the burning house, while his partner Officer Jimkoski radioed in for more help.

Officer Benson ran up against the locked door and began to pound on to see if he would get a response. When he didn't Officer Benson began to kick on the door until the locks gave way. He rushed pass a whiff of thick smoke, "it's the police, is anyone here?'

Grand-Ma Trina threw the second bucket of water into the kitchen from the doorway to avoid the thick smoke. "Yeah, I'm back here. Help me please".

Officer Benson saw her through the smoke trying to feel her way back to the bathroom with a bucket in her hand. He quickly ran up on her and started pulling her down the hall.

"No…No. We have to save my kitchen!" Grand-Ma Trina protested as she tried to fight her way back into the thick smoke.

"Ma'am the fire department is on the way. Please let's go!"

Grand-Ma Trina began to cry as the smoke began to take a toll on her. Office Benson led her out of the burning house and into an EMS worker hands. As they put an oxygen mask on her face, Trina was able to blurt out Ginger's name.

"Who is that ma'am?" Officer Benson asked.

"My dog, she's in the backyard".

Officer Benson turned around and told the fire fighters about the dog as they ran into the burning house.

Mama K had to park the car almost a block away from her mother house. Police officers were pushing people away from the scene, as fire trucks and police cars clogged up the street. Mama K rushed over to the yellow tape barricade with Ne'Sean and Meika hot on her heels. Her mind was racing double time as she pushed her way through the light crowd.

"This is my mother's house!" Mama K barked when she was stopped at the barricade.

"Okay, let them through".

Mama K and the kids ran over to the EMS truck parked half way on the sidewalk, with its doors open. Grand-Ma Trina was crying with the oxygen mask on her face, as Emma held her hand and tried her best to console her friend.

"Ma what happen, you alright?" Mama K asked with confusion in her eyes. The kids ran over to their grandmother side as she sat on the back step of an ambulance. Tears streaming down her eyes as she breathed into an oxygen mask.

Grand- Ma Trina tried to speak but the oxygen mask made her words come out to distorted for Mama K patience. She turned to a fireman wearing a white helmet with a clip board in his hand and said, "Excuse me, can you please tell me what happen to my mother's house".

He stopped looking over his reports and said, "As far as we know the fire started in the kitchen".

"Where's Ginger? Her dog", Mama K asked.

"She's in the backyard, she's fine, just won't stop barking. The only way out of the backyard is through the house, and I'm not letting my men open that door. That dog is not a puppy and she's very upset. Once we get the house secured, you can go in and bring her out." The fire chief turned to Grand-Ma Trina and asked, "Ma'am can you tell me what happen?"

"I don't know! I turned around to answer the phone, and when I turned back around the curtains were on fire".

"You can go in and get the dog now. But you need a leash." One of the firemen said to Mama K. She reached in her purse and handed Ne'Sean ten dollars to go see if he could buy a leash in the corner store.

Grand-Ma Trina recapped her story and the fire chief said, "Well Ma'am, you're very lucky. I suggest you lock up the house and rest at your daughter house tonight. Give your house some time to air out. The backroom upstairs is intact, but the kitchen ceiling fell. So, the bedroom still has a floor, but it's very unsafe to go in. You might want to call someone to check it out before you go in there.

"We believe the insulation that's placed in-between the ceiling and the upstairs floor caught fire, and it accelerated when some money caught fire in the same area. The money is burned up and unusable." His walkie-talkie started going off and he turned his back to answer it.

Grand-Ma Trina sat on the step of the EMS truck with a confused look on her face, "Money? What money?" She asked herself in a low tone.

In that moment, Mama K felt like she was just punched in her gut. Ne'Sean ran back to the truck with a leash he got the store owner to let him borrow and he pocketed the ten dollars his mother gave him. Two firemen escorted Mama K through house, so she could get Ginger out of the back yard. She tried her best not to look through the ruins of her mother's house as thoughts of her real lost danced around in her mind.

Chapter 13

Once the area was cleared out, and the streets of Bushwick went back to normal, Mama K and Grand-Ma Trina went back into the house to grab some things, before they all piled into a cab and headed back to Marcy for the night.

De'Quan and Dre had been out all day planning their next hit and had no idea what was going on in his apartment. When they walked in it immediately felt like walking into a mad house. Meika and Ne'Sean were playing with Ginger in the living room with bags of clothes all over the place. Mama K,

Grand-Ma Trina and Kim were in the kitchen making a big ruckus about getting Grand-Ma Trina house fixed, and De'Quan could swear he smelled smoke in the house.

"Where have you been?" Mama K snapped at him.

De'Quan just smoked a blunt of chocolate Ty from Marcy and Gates with Dre, making him slow on his feet. "We was…ah…we was on the other side. Why does it smell like fire in here?" De'Quan asked to shift the attention from him to something else.

"There was a fire in my house tonight," Grand-Ma Trina said with some sadness in her voice. She stood up and he gave her a hug.

"Wow Grand-Ma, what you going to do?" De'Quan asked.

Mama K spoke up, "they going to be staying with us for a while, you boys hungry?"

"Yes, but where yah going to sleep?"

Mama K snickered, "Don't worry your bunk bed is safe from Ginger. They sleeping in Meika room, and she will sleep with me. Tomorrow I want you to go with me and mommy over to her house so we can see what has to be done over there".

"Come on Dre, let's go in my room".

Mama K excused herself and went into the room behind them. She closed the door behind her and said, "I know you know everything Quan knows Dre, so both of you have a seat. I have to talk to yah".

"What's up Ma?"

She paced back and forth for a second, as De'Quan and Dre stared at her from the bottom bunk. Mama K took a deep breath and said, "The money is gone". Her voice almost broke down.

De'Quan and Dre snapped right out their high, as they both thought the same thing at the same time. 'How did they find the money in Dre's radiator?'

She continued before either of them could speak, "The fire started in Grand-Ma's kitchen, and it just so happens her bedroom is right on top of the kitchen. The whole damn ceiling fell on top of the fire and burned up the money Pop had in Grand-Ma floor".

Shaking her head, Mama K sat on the edge of the dresser craving a cigarette. Then she remembered she didn't smoke.

The boys breathed a sigh of relief that their little stash was still safe. "I didn't know Pop had money over there. I thought we were broke". De'Quan said feeling confused.

"Yeah well...It's gone now." She said clearly upset. "I needed that money to hold us down just in case the store plan didn't do too well".

"What you want to do now Mama K?" Dre asked.

She couldn't answer him.

De'Quan asked, "How much did you need for the store?"

"The down payment was 3,500.00, and that's already in the bank. The money in the floor was the just in case the store doesn't make enough money to cover or bills and inventory. Only until we did start to make a profit".

De'Quan looked over to Dre and they gave each other a slight nod. "By tomorrow we'll think of something Ma".

She nodded and said, "Yeah. By tomorrow, I'll have a plan together. I just wanted to let you know what's going on. Dre, you part of this family too. So it affects you too".

Her statement made Dre feel good inside to be recognized as a part of a more stable family.

She stood up and said, "Well you two go wash up and get ready to eat". Before she walked out of the room, Mama K took a look around like it this was the first time she walked into the boys room and said, "And clean up this damn room...place is a mess".

*****

Once Mama K was gone, De'Quan's mind went into over drive. "How much we got in the stash?"

"About 4,300, why, you want to give it to her?" Dre asked.

De'Quan jumped up and started pacing the room. "Shit! I got too. If I don't, this house will fall apart. We can hit that spot we scoped out, and we'll still be on top. That spot got at least five gees of better in it. We piece off Pee and we'll still have a little stash. What you think?"

Dre said, "I'm with you however you want to do it. But where we going to tell her we got the dough from?"

"Easy. We just say we spoke to G-Eyes that used to work for Pop, and we told him she was fucked up and we needed some work to get on, but instead of giving us drugs, he gave us the cash and we brought it straight to her. What you think?"

Frick and Frack is at work.

Dre said, "Yeah...that shit might work. It's hard as hell to find G-Eyes. She might not run into him for months".

"By then the store will already be jumping", De'Quan added with a smirk.

"Word". Dre said as they gave each other a pound.

"Let's go eat something. I got the munchies like a motherfucker".

Chapter 14

10:00a.m. the next morning Grand-Ma Trina, Mama K, De'Quan, and a neighborhood mister fix it name Mr. Jackson did a look over of the damaged house. Mama K felt a sharp pain in her stomach when they made their way into the kitchen. She had to remind herself to move on or fall apart. The money was gone.

De'Quan took one look at the inside of the kitchen and knew he was going to be out of $4,300 by the end of the night. Grand-Ma Trina had to hold onto Mama K's arm for strength as they made their way around the house.

Mr. Jackson went upstairs to assess the damage in the bedroom and came back down with the same warning the fire chief told them the night before. Upstairs would not be safe for Grand-Ma Trina to be in until they get the ceiling downstairs fixed first. After a long conversation it was established Mama K and Grand-Ma Trina would take care of the clean up. Once the ceiling was fixed, De'Quan and his friends will take care of the painting of the house to save them some money. It will take some time, but it was doable.

After a long day of skipping school and running with his mother De'Quan was ready for some action. He picked up Dre and they went downstairs to pull Fat Pee away from his cheeseburger and TV so they could handle their business. Their robbery G.A.M.E. was getting serious, making them put some money together, and purchased some new guns from Ju the gun seller from Dre side of the projects. They added a 16shot 9mm Taurus, a 15shot 9mm, and a 12 gage shotgun.

To make their getaways go by a little smoother Fat Pee learned how to steal cars, and in a short time, he became a good getaway driver, since his running skills were so suspect. Fat Pee kept the 12 gage in the car with him to give his partners great cover on the outside.

De'Quan and Dre had been watching a coke spot in Williamsburg for a couple of weeks and now the time was right to try their luck. To stack the $4,300 they had stashed, they had to rob too many stores. With each time feeling like it was getting harder and harder to get away. Robbing a drug spot would be more dangerous, but they all agreed the payout will be worth it. That's when De'Quan got wind of the under-man spot in Williamsburg.

Fat Pee stole an Acura legend from Saratoga and Halsey, and they drove to Williamsburg in a nervous silence. No music, no smoking, and only thoughts of surviving this next hit silently flowed through the car.

Fat Pee parked a block away from the private house and all three of them got out. They walked with a purpose through the shadows, unnoticed by anyone out on the cold winter night. After taking one last nervous look around De'Quan knocked on the door.

A sliding peephole slid open and a pair of eyes appeared, "What you want little nigga?"

"I work for Jah. He sent me to pick up for him", De'Quan said.

The peephole man thought for a second, and then said, "What Jah?'

"Tompkins Park Jah", De'Quan said with a slight attitude in his voice. If you act like you know what you're talking about, you might catch him slipping. The slot was slammed, and locks started clicking.

De'Quan stepped to the side making way for Fat Pee to lead the way with the shotgun. Fat Pee jammed it in the doorman face, "Don't even fart", he whispered, as Dre and De'Quan rushed pass them headed for the back room.

A brown skin man wearing a bent up New York Yankees hat sat behind an old card table counting money. He looked up in mid count and it took him too long to register what was about to happen him.

"Put your fucking hands up!" Dre screamed.

The man flinched in the direction of his gun that rested on his table filled with money, drugs and paraphernalia, but

De'Quan was a step ahead of him. De'Quan knocked the gun on the floor with his left hand, and with gun wielding right hand he hit the man on the side of his head with the butt of his 9mm. The man fell out of his chair and crashed to the floor with a, "OWW…What the fuck man!"

"Shut the fuck up!" De'Quan said, as he stomped on the man's face, breaking his nose. Blood splattered all over the floor.

"Bring that other nigga in here", De'Quan yelled over his shoulder.

Fat Pee still had the shotgun in the doorman face as he led him to the back room, "Walk fucker".

De'Quan made the two dealers lay down on their stomachs, as Dre filled up his book bag with everything that was on top of the card table. De'Quan patted the two men down taking their money, keys and any loose change they had in their pockets, "take that jewelry off…and those shoes too".

"What the fuck you want their nasty ass shoes for?" Fat Pee asked shocked De'Quan was into taking dudes shoes now.

"So, they can't follow us", Dre answered.

That's when a light went off in De'Quan's head, "Yo F.P. go start the car".

"Why the fuck did you just say my name?" Fat Pee said, fuming.

De'Quan snapped back at him, "Man, just do what I said. We right behind you".

Dre knew something was up. Fat Pee looked around the quiet room, sucked his teeth, and then ran out the door to go start the car. Dre put the heavy book bag on his back and asked, "What's up?"

De'Quan picked up the dealer's gun, "We do them with their own guns, and throw these shits off the Brooklyn Bridge. What up, you down?"

Dre searched De'Quan's face for a trace of a smile. He couldn't find one. De'Quan was dead serious.

"I'm…I'm saying…It's on you", Dre said. He tried to swallow after saying it, but his throat was drier than Arizona.

To make sure Dre was down, De'Quan said, "I hit one. You hit one."

Before Dre could answer him, De'Quan stepped up and shot the doorman point blank in the back of his head. Everybody in the room jumped at the loud sound of the dealer gun. The table man began to plead his case from the floor.

"Hey listen young blood, I didn't see".

"Shut the fuck up!" De'Quan barked, as he handed the gun to Dre.

"Hey listen, just let me go and I'll forget your faces and this whole shit. I'll even get rid of Ol Tuffy over here."

"Man if I to tell you again. Dre shoot this fagget!"

The man began to piss on himself. "Aww come on little man, you do have to do this," He cried.

"Dre, the nigga saw our faces. They will come to the projects and kill us. So shoot this nigga and let's go."

Dre began to sweat like he just took a shower with his clothes on. His hands were so clammy, Dre just wanted to let the gun slip out of his hand and he run up out of there.

"Let's Go! Shoot him Dre!"

Dre pulled the trigger three times silencing the whining table man. The action brought a smile to De'Quan's face. No matter what Dre will always be his brother. "Come on!"

They ran out of the house and hopped into the waiting car. Dre laid down on the backseat floor as Fat Pee pilled off into traffic. Fat Pee dropped them off at Dre's building, and then drove to Queens to drop off the stolen car.

It was 11:10p.m and all was quiet in Dre apartment. His sister was in her room asleep, and Dre mother wasn't home. De'Quan sat on Dre bed and began to roll a blunt, as Dre paced the room. They were waiting for Fat Pee to return before they counted their booty.

Dre tried to keep his voice as low as possible, "Damn Quan, I didn't' know we were going to kill them dudes."

De'Quan tried to look cool as fan when he looked up from the blunt he was rolling and said, "Just chill Dre, them dudes were some serious dudes who saw our faces. When I thought about it, I said 'shit what would I do if I was them?

"Then it hit me, find out where they from and go kill their asses. They saw our faces and we couldn't get in there wearing masks. Give me a light, shit got my nerves all fucked up."

Dre grabbed the lighter off the dresser and handed it to him, "I guess you right. Shit just caught me off guard."

"You think that caught you off guard, wait till you smoke some of this chocolate ty."

By the time Fat Pee got back from dumping the car Dre and De'Quan were sitting in a chocolate ty stupor. Fat Pee grabbed the crate to sit on and said, "Yo what happen in there? I thought I heard shots when I was starting the car."

Dre and De'Quan just stared at him. Then they looked at each other and burst out laughing.

"What the fuck is so funny?" Fat Pee snapped.

"Man, you sounded like you was about to cry just now," Dre said still chuckling.

Fat Pee looked around the room with a stupid look on his face making them laugh at him harder. "Matter of fact, where the weed at, niggas ain't going to be laughing at me all night."

De'Quan gave Fat Pee what was left of the blunt and said, "Nah, but on some real shit, we had to smoke them dudes."

Fat Pee took a long pull of the blunt and almost chocked, "What…what the fuck for?"

Dre said, "Because they saw our faces Pee, and they would have come looking for us. That's how big time dudes get down son."

De'Quan jumped in, "Yeah Pee…and when you left the boss nigga asked who we said we came for again. That alone tells you they would have come looking for us."

Dre continued the double team, "The last thing we need is for some big time dudes to come through the projects looking for us. And what's up with you acting like there's some love lost for them niggas?" Dre said flipping it on Fat Pee.

"Naw man", Fat Pee took a strong pull from the blunt clip and said, "It was on my mind that I thought I heard shots, and maybe they tried to move on yah when I left. That's all. I really don't care what happen to them, as long as we got away and we get to count this dough."

"Yeah, that's what I'm talking about", De'Quan said with a big smile. "Counting that dough." He grabbed the bag and dumped it's contains out on the floor. Dre pushed the dresser onto the door and they all just stared at all the money and drugs on the floor.

Dre broke the silence, "Damn! I ain't never seen so much dough before in my life."

"Word! We are fucking rich now dawg", Fat Pee said with a big Kool-Aid smile on his face. Dre and De'Quan started laughing and they all dug into stacks of cash and started separating it.

When they were finished, they were staring at $35,753 in cash, and $11,240 worth of cocaine. Everyone was lost in his own thoughts for a minute until De'Quan finally broke the silence, "Ok, this is how we freak this. We do our usual split of the dough, but the drugs, I say we flush it."

Dre snapped out of his high real quick, "What? Why the fuck would we do that?"

"For one we ain't no drug dealers, and for two how we going to look coming out of nowhere with 11 thousand dollars' worth of drugs to sell all of a sudden. Shit and where would we sell it at if we could?" De'Quan said in Dre's direction. De'Quan knew Fat Pee will go with any plan that sounds good to him and Dre.

Dre said, "Naw man, I say we sit on it for a rainy day. What if we go out, and get crazy and spend all of our dough, we going to be fucked up if we can't find another spot to rob, but if we have this coke to fall back on we good for a minute."

Fat Pee added his two cents, "Now that sounds like a plan instead of flushing it down the toilet."

De'Quan scratched his head, "Alright, it makes sense. We sit on it then. Pop taught me a long time ago coke won't go bad as long as we keep it cool."

They did their split of the money and when they were finish, Fat Pee looked like he was ready to run out the door. Dre eyed him hard, "Pee why don't you leave some of that in the window stash".

Fat Pee blinked, and got on the defensive, "For what".

De'Quan approached him from another angle, "Pee we know about you and Sugar. The streets are talking".

Fat Pee looked like he just got caught stealing out of the candy jar. "Yeah, so what. I don't care about what the streets is saying".

"Yo keep your voice down before you wake up Shakia", Dre snapped. "Anyway, it's your money and you can spend it on anything you want, but 12gees is a lot of dough Pee. The last thing we need is for Sugar – or anybody else for that matter – to be questioning where we get dough from, you feel me".

Fat Pee remained on the defensive, "Fuck I look like telling some chick our business?" He stood up and started stuffing money in his pockets. "Yah acting like a nigga pussy whipped or something".

De'Quan stood up to face him, "Nah Pee it ain't like that. We just saying now we playing with some real money, and we don't need anybody asking us shit about shit".

Fat Pee sat back down on the crate and lit up a cigarette, "Yeah yah said that already".

De'Quan put his hand on his shoulder and said, "Pee, we brothers man, and we're only watching each other's back".

Dre jumped in, "Yeah, that's all I'm saying Pee. So, if you want to leave some here, you'll be alright is all I'm saying".

Fat Pee sat there thinking about it as De'Quan put a new agenda on the table, "Before I forget, we have to buy some new guns too. Dre make it happen with Ju and see if we can get some new nines for a good price. We all can put a gee to the side for that".

They each counted out a thousand dollars and Dre rubber band it together. De'Quan took the $4,300 out of the stash, then he and Dre put ten thousand each of their money back in the stash spot. Fat Pee watched all of this and thought to himself 'fuck it'.

Fat Pee counted out five thousand and said, "Here, put this in there".

"When we going to dump these dirty guns?" Dre asked.

"Tomorrow, so get on Ju", De'Quan said.

"We should get some big joint's from him", Fat Pee suggested.

"We will", De'Quan stuffed the $4,300 in his pocket, and his $1,000 of spending money in his other pocket. "What you going to do with all that dough Quan?" Fat Pee asked.

"Mama K is fucked up right now. My Grand-Mom's crib caught fire the other day and Pops money burned up in there. So I'm blessing her with this so she can still open up the store".

"Word, damn", Fat Pee said.

De'Quan put on his jacket and said, "I'm tired. Come on Pee, let's bounce".

"Word. I'm mad hungry too".

Dre walked them to the door and said, "Don't eat five gees worth of White Castles in one night".

They all laughed, "Whatever man. Later". They gave Dre a pound, and then headed down the stairs.

*****

De'Quan crept into the house and was surprised to run into Mama K sitting at the kitchen table nursing a cigarette, something he never saw her do. He locked the door and went into the kitchen to sit with her.

"I thought you would spend the night at Dre's house tonight when I didn't see you at 11". Mama K said, surprised he was coming in so late.

"Sorry Ma. We was chilling and I lost track of time", De'Quan said.

Mama K put the cigarette out as De'Quan dug into his pocket and pulled out the money. He slowly put it on the table and Mama K's eyes grew wide under the dim kitchen light.

"Where did you get that?"

De'Quan shifted in his seat and said, "Me and Dre went to see G-Eyes".

"I know yah ain't been out here selling drugs, after I told you not too", Mama K said trying her best not to raise her voice.

De'Quan put on his performance face and said, "No Mama. I'm not going to lie, we went to him to get something from him, but he gave us the cash instead. I know what you told us, but we can't just sit back and watch you struggle on your own all the time. The store is important to you and Pop and we was just trying to help, if we could".

She slowly took the money and began to count it. As Mama K counted her anger began to subside and was replaced with amazement, "4,300, wow Quan, I needed this. Tell him thank you", she said reaching across the table to take his hand.

"You know I love you, and I don't want you boys out there doing no crazy things. I can't lose yah to these streets. I already lost Pop, and losing yah will break my heart even more".

"Don't worry Mama, we'll be here", De'Quan said with a tired smile.

She stood up and gave him a hug, "Thank you baby. Now go get some rest. I'll see you in the morning".

Chapter 15

"Welcome To The Rucker New York City! The junior tournament is in full effect today!" The crowd roared with approval over the background music in New York City's infamous Rucker Park. The screaming crowd stretched from the bleachers out onto the street. Heads hung out the windows of the school, and surrounding buildings shouting out their hood, but were out done by the spectators who let their presence from the roof tops be heard in the famous park.

"In the red jerseys we got the visitors representing Brook-nom! Let me hear it for the Bed-Stuy Heat!" The M.C. said, igniting a loud chant of 'Brooook-lyn!' from the hot summer time crowd.

"And in the black with white trim we got The Squad-representing The B.X. baby! Uptown give it up!" The crowd screamed even louder for its uptown favorite.

"Okay, yah know the rules…let your game do the talking and the losers do the walking!" the M.C. had the crowd in a frenzy, as LL cool J told all the girl's out of the park speakers how they were 'Jiggling Baby'. The bleachers were packed with a mixture of New York City's elite, basketball fanatics, high class honey's, baller's, and kids just out to have a good time.

8th Avenue was like a ghetto car show. Whips were freshly waxed as heads from up and down the east coast flocked to New York City traditional basketball tournament, where stars where made and bums was sent home with a broken heart. The atmosphere at the Rucker is always live and full of energy.

De'Quan, Dre, Fat Pee, and Rahkem sat in the bleachers absorbing the whole Rucker high as they watched Ne'Sean and his team the Bed-Stuy Heat represent on the New York stage. De'Quan also had in mind to scope out some of the big time dealers who felt the need to pull out their most expensive car, and shiniest jewelry for this festive event. They needed a new vic and what better place to find one on a hot Saturday afternoon.

"Now this is it yah. Let's bring it back to Brooklyn!" The coach barked from the middle of the huddle.

"Yeah, that's what I'm talking about!" Their center Lay Lay yelled in the huddle. He stood at 6'4 and was lanky, but what he lacked in size he made up with speed and skill on the court. "B.K. on three…1-2-3!"

"B.K." and the starting five took the court. Ne'Sean was big enough to be the team starting forward. Jamel was the point guard, Lay Lay at center, Taz at power forward, and Bliz at shooting guard. They jumped right into their business by winning the opening tip and scoring the first two points of the game.

De'Quan was into the game, while Dre sat back and analyzed the action that was popping on 8th Avenue. Dre focused on a dark skin brother with a fade, sporting a pair of Gucci shades. He was dipped out in a grey Nike suit with the uptowns to match. He was all smiles as he sat on the hood of a blue 325i BMW, with two summer bunnies standing in front of him, ke-keing at his every joke.

Dre nudged De'Quan in his side, "You see son sitting over there on that blue three and a quarter?"

De'Quan took his eyes off the game for a moment and scanned the action on 8th Avenue, "Yeah I see him. What about him?"

"You don't recognize duke?"

De'Quan was on the verge of being aggravated. Dre was disturbing his game watching. "No Dre, I don't know that dude, now what."

"That's that dude Shaborn from that hood in Queens...Lefrak", Dre said.

De'Quan stared at Dre with a lost look in his eyes, so Dre pressed on, "The dude from that club we were at, when those bitches were running their mouths about how son paper is long and how he got a section in Lefrak on lock. You don't remember that?"

De'Quan looked back over in Shaborn's direction with a different focus in his eyes. "Ohh yeah...I remember who son is now, but we don't know shit about him".

"Nah we don't; but peep the chick on his left-hand side", Dre said with a smirk on his face.

De'Quan looked over at the girl and he wasn't sure about who he thought he was looking at, "Damn, she looks like Tasha from here".

"That's who that is my man", Dre said grinning. "I see it like this, we keep an eye on her ass, cause Tasha always gets her man. We follow her to duke, and Bam we got an easy, but official vic. What you think?"

De'Quan's mind started clicking with his partner until a smile finally crept on his face. The crowd around them erupted forcing them to turn to the basketball court. Fat Pee and Rahkem were losing all of their cool point's as they jumped up and high fived each other, Oh Shit! You saw what Sean just did to son ankles?"

"Word", Rahkem said giving Fat Pee another pound.

"My brother is going to the NBA one day", De'Quan said only loud enough for Dre to hear him.

Dre shook his head in agreement, "Yeah I can see it. He got mad ups now, so imagine in...Oh Shit!"

Ne'Sean shook the kid guarding him and threw an ally-op to Taz, who finished off the play with a monster slam sending the park over the top as it exploded into another round of cheers and chants of 'Brooook-lyn'.

*****

"Mama! Mama where you at?" Ne'Sean loudly called down the apartment hallway. His loud entourage rolled in behind him and flooded the living room with replays of the game still fresh on their minds.

"What happen?" Mama K asked as she shuffled down the hallway with Grand-Ma Trina hot on her heels.

Ne'Sean wore a big smile as he held up his trophy he won with the Bed-Stuy Heat at the Rucker.

"Oh, my goodness, yah won", Mama K said giving him a big hug. "I'm proud of you baby".

"He put on a show out there today Mama K, but now we have to change and go to the victory party", De'Quan said.

"Well not before I get my hugs and kisses", Grand-Ma Trina said coming down the hallway. "I'm proud of you too baby", she said as she pushed Mama K and De'Quan to the side to get to Ne'Sean sparking a round of laughs throughout the house.

The victory party was held in building 520 in Marcy. No one cared whose apartment it was, all they cared about was

Brooklyn beat the Bronx at the Rucker and brought the trophy home. E.P.M.D. was giving everybody the business out of a set of large speakers that could be heard throughout the building. The atmosphere was soaked with weed smoke, laughter, and game being shot by both sexes in all directions.

De'Quan sported his brother to all of the girls in the party until he set his eyes on a coco brown cutie. She was dipped out in a sandy brown D.K.N.Y. velour suit, as she held up a back wall. She whispered something to her friend at her side and when she turned back around, she locked eyes with De'Quan.

De'Quan stepped to them with Ne'Sean at his side, "Excuse me ladies. I don't mean to disturb your conversation or anything. I just wanted to introduce yah to my brother Ne'Sean. The star of the Rucker show today".

Coco brown had been eyeing De'Quan all night and she was wondering when he was going to notice her. She had butterflies in her stomach when she said, "Yeah we heard. Sorry we missed your game".

De'Quan lightly pushed Ne'Sean in the small of his back toward her friend, "What's your name pretty?" Ne'Sean asked the friend.

A big smile crawled into the corners of her mouth, "Janet and this is my friend Mecca".

Ne'Sean looked over to Mecca and said, "Hi, can I borrow your friend for the dance floor?"

Mecca giggled, "As long as you not trying to steal her away from me. I know your brother can keep me company until yah come back".

They all chuckled and Janet said, "Girl, I hope we both get stolen".

The two girls snicker as De'Quan whispered into Ne'Sean's ear, "We definitely fucking tonight". The brothers laughed then partied the night away with their two new friends.

Chapter 16

Two days after the party, Dre sat on the back of the park bench waiting for De'Quan to come downstairs. It was almost noon and it was already a scorching summer day out front of De'Quan's building with the usual activity of crack heads coming and going at a steady pace. Dre paid all this activity little mind because it had nothing to do with him, until the chaos unfolded before his very eyes.

"T-N-T…T-N-T! Don't move motherfucker!"

"Freeze!"

40 ounces dropped, crack heads were quickly tackled as they cried their innocence, and two T-N-T officers got into a fist fight with one of the dealers in De'Quan's lobby. Dre quickly snapped out of his trance and tried to make his way off of the bench to head in the opposite direction.

"Don't fucking move asshole! Get on the ground! Get on the ground!"

Dre turned to the screaming voice and he was surprised to come face to face with the nozzle of a 38 special. Dre was knocked off of his feet by the 250 pound officer and slammed down to the ground. The officer speed searched Dre with his free hand as he kept his gun aimed at Dre's head.

When he reached Dre's waist band he pulled out a 9mm browning pistol, "I got one! I got one!" The officer called out over his shoulder. He threw Dre's gun to the side, holstered his gun and hand cuffed Dre.

De'Quan was coming down the stairs when he heard scuffling going on in the lobby. He thought it was the usual scene of a dealer beating up a crack head for being short on the money, until he heard the squawk of a walkie-talkie goes off. De'Quan did a 180 and ran back upstairs to his house.

When he ran inside De'Quan ran straight for the window. When he looked to the right of the benches, he saw a big white cop lift Dre off of the ground as if he only weighed only 20 pounds.

"Mama K! Mama K! Come quick", De'Quan called out over his shoulder as he kept his eyes on the scene playing out in front of his building.

Mama K shuffled down the hallway and over to the window, "What's wrong?" She asked, then took a look out the window before he could answer her. Mama K came just in time to see the officer hit Dre in his head with the walkie-talkie, as he was stuffing Dre in the back of a caravan.

Mama K turned from the window without saying a word and ran out the door. She ran down the steps two at a time and came out the front of the building like a young sister ready for an after school fight.

"What hell are yah doing to my son?" Mama K said as she stepped to the small crowd by the caravan. "What's going on here?"

"Who's your son ma'am?" A Latino officer asked as his directed the scene.

Mama K looked through the tinted windows of the caravan and pointed to Dre, "Him".

She made a move to open the door and the Latino officer stepped in between her and the door, "Hold on ma'am, if you talking about little Billy the kid back there, we just found a 9mm on him, so he's going to see the judge about that".

Mama K blinked and said, "A gun". She quickly thought about what she walked into and knew there was no way she was going to get Dre out the back of that caravan.

"Yes, ma'am a gun. Now what is his name?" The officer asked her thinking she was ready to talk to him.

Mama K looked him up and down and said, "Ask him", and with that she turned on her heels and headed back to the building. When she got back into the house De'Quan was all over the place, "Mama K we have to get him out. Damn!"

"Quan calm down. We're going to get him out. We have to wait for him to see the judge first, which will probably be in two days".

"Two Days!"

"Boy, stop yelling up in this house. Now go sit down somewhere, while I go call his mother and see if she can get some bail money together". As soon as she said it, she wanted to take it back. Everyone knew Dre's mother drinks her money away and she didn't have any friends who were worth more than wine money.

De'Quan sucked his teeth and said, "I'll get the money".

"Now don't you go out there and do something stupid. It's bad enough yah running around here with guns and shit". She cursed some more under her breath and walked into the kitchen to use the phone.

De'Quan did not want to tell her they had money stashed in Dre's room. He just stood there quiet thinking about how he was going to get into Dre's room. He got an idea and slipped out of the house while Mama K was still on the phone.

*****

Fat Pee was on the Flushing side of the projects trying to get in a good sweat on the basketball court when De'Quan found him. De'Quan stepped right onto the court, "Yo Pee, come here for a minute".

Fat Pee looked over and saw De'Quan walking on to the court with a purpose, "What's up. This game is almost-"

De'Quan cut him off, "Nah, we got to talk right now".

Fat Pee saw the seriousness in his friend eyes and he knew his game was over, "Yo Jah, take my place son". Fat Pee walked off of the court with De'Quan and as soon as they were out of ear shot Fat Pee asked him, "What's up Quan?"

"Dre got knocked like 20 minutes ago in front of my building by T-N-T".

"What do you mean T-N-T? Dre don't sell no drugs", Fat Pee said with a lost look in his eyes.

De'Quan filled him in on what happened to Dre in front of his building. "Look we have to bail him out. The problem is our money is in his house. We can't let his moms know about the stash, she will dead us on the rest and drink it away. His sister I'm not too sure about. Damn, I never thought this shit would happen".

Fat Pee grabbed his pants off of the bench and started getting dressed. De'Quan hopped on the bench and fished out a cigarette. Just when he put a flame to his cigarette, an argument broke out over the basketball game.

A little skin pretty boy type started arguing with a tall brown skin brother over a foul. The pretty boy walked over to another section of benches and said something to a girl that sitting by herself.

"Check the ball then nigga!" The pretty boy said as he walked back onto the court.

The brown skin brother through the ball at him faster than the pretty boy could react, and the ball slipped through his fingers and popped him in his chest.

Pretty boy lost his cool, "Toi, give me that!"

The girl quickly hopped off the bench and ran toward him like a cornered cat. He snatched the coach bag out of her hands and pulled out a 9mm berretta. Chaos engulfed the parkas the automatic barked across the afternoon sky.

Pop, Pop, Pop.

"Yeah you bitch ass nigga. What's up now?" The pretty boy yelled as everybody scattered, ducking for cover.

Fat Pee had on his pants, but his sneakers were still untied. When the shooting started Fat Pee followed De'Quan to the nearest park exit, but 10 feet from the gate, he tripped on his laces and fell face first on the black top.

De'Quan felt something wasn't right behind him and turned just in time to see Fat Pee getting up in a cross fire. De'Quan pulled out his 45 and let off two rounds in pretty boy direction. "Come on Pee, I got you".

"Oh you want some of this too?" Pretty boy barked as he aimed his gun at De'Quan.

Fat Pee got behind his friend as De'Quan stood his ground, "Nah son, we just going to go about our business. That's it". De'Quan and Fat Pee began to back their way out of the park.

Toi snapped her man out of his trance, "Pooh the police is coming!"

Pooh turned from his stare down with De'Quan, "Oh shit, let's go", Pooh said and ran for another hole in the park fence with Toi hot on his heels.

Fat Pee and De'Quan made it to Fat Pee's house and walked into another chaotic scene. Fat Pee mother stomped through the house beefing about something, while his two younger siblings tore up the living room like they were playing in the sand park. Fat Pee ignored the drama and walked straight to his room with De'Quan following him in a daze. The whole projects had gone mad.

De'Quan sat on Fat Pee bed and said, "This day is getting crazier by the minute. Yo what the fuck is going on in your living room dawg?"

Fat Pee peeled out of his shirt and said, "Who cares. Yo that nigga was talking shit all game".

De'Quan said, "Fuck that nigga. Anyway, like I was telling you we have to get Dre up out of there. You got any 45 bullets in here?"

Fat Pee open his closet reviling close to 30 boxes of sneakers and did a quick scan. When he saw the box he wanted, Fat Pee pulled it out and took it over to the bed. Inside the Nike box, he had a stack of money, two guns, and over fifty loose bullets. He took the money out and let De'Quan fish through the sea of bullets for what he needed.

When Fat Pee finished counting the money he said, "I got a little over thirty five hundred. If we need more than that, then I guess one of us is going to have to promise Dre's sister a good time, in exchange to let us in his room for a minute".

De'Quan busted out laughing, took the clip out of his gun and replaced the two shells he let off in the park. "That should be enough. Man, we got to start spreading this money out. We can't have this shit happen again. You got some weed?"

"Yeah. Yo where we go to pay his bail?" Fat Pee asked as he searched his secret stashes for his weed and Phillies.

I don't know. Mama K knows all that stuff. When I left her, she was on the phone calling about that stuff. We go see what she talking about after this blunt. I got to relax for a minute".

Fat pee chuckled and said, "We all do bro. These streets are crazy".

De'Quan laughed, "Nigga your crib is crazy".

Fat Pee laughed harder, "I know".

Chapter 17

Central Bookings in downtown Brooklyn is where Dre found himself roasting in a hot holding cell. Disgusted that he got caught slipping like that. He was currently sharing a cell with a dope fiend who must have the nodding record. Dre watched the dope fiend sit on the bench across from him and nod forward, with a long glob of spit hanging out the corner of his mouth, for four hours straight. Dre couldn't believe it.

Dre had been sitting in the same nasty cell for thirty hours and this stomach was doing back flips, because he hadn't eaten since he left his house. The police tried to feed Dre a baloney and cheese sandwich that looked half brown. Dre gave his away.

War stories were being told by other prisoners every hour on the hour like 10-10 wins, and Dre was tired of listening to it. He tried getting sleep, but every time he heard keys rattling, he would snap to attention in hopes of moving on to see the judge. Thoughts of having to use the bathroom kept invading Dre's mind, but one look at the toilet stopped him from taking a piss half the time.

"Alright, listen up!" The chatter floating down the small cell block quickly faded. "When I call your name, step up and step out. You will be cuffed, put on a bus and taken to court this morning. First man, Willie Johnson, Andre Jones, Michael Black".

Dre didn't care what the c.o. said after he called his name, as long as he called it. At Brooklyn criminal court house Dre was put in another holding cell for five more hours before he was put on a six-man chain gang and brought upstairs on an elevator to the second floor.

Dre and the rest of the chain gang were put into a much cleaner cell, and more action was taking place with lawyers pay guys visits.

"Andre Jones!"

"Yeah! Right here!" Dre made his way to the front of the cell. He was relieved to come face to face with a black man with a salt and pepper mini-afro. He was dressed in a brown suit and he looked like he hadn't shaved in three weeks.

"I'm Mr. Gordon Winston, here take my card", he said in a Caribbean accent. "Now Andre this is your first offense, so we might be able to get you an R.O.R. with no problem. Your mother and brother are out there", he said looking down at some papers. "Mama K and huh, De'Quan. They said they have bail money. I told them I might be able to get the R.O.R. So I'll see you out there", Mr. Winston said and quickly ran off as quick as he came. Dre didn't get two words in, just a bunch of head nods.

Ten minutes later Dre's name was called again and this time he was pushed out into the courtroom like he was being fed to the wolves. He walked over to the table he saw Mr. Winston standing at and stared down at the bright yellow arrow that was taped to the table that said 'You stand here' in bright red letters.

Dre did a quick turn around and scanned the faces in the crowd courtroom. He saw Mama K, De'Quan and Fat Pee sitting in the mist of the tired faces in the back. He felt a good feeling inside when they locked eyes.

Mr. Winston and the assistant district attorney went back and forth in a language of legalized bullshit Dre didn't understand until the judge said, "R.O.R. Clerk issue the defendant a return date and a slip please, next".

Dre quickly took his pink slip and made his exit through the plastic chain link barrier. He gave Mama K a hug, and gave De'Quan and Fat Pee a pound, as Mama K thanked Mr. Winston.

They headed out of the court building and walked to Mama K's car, but not without the sermon they all knew was coming. "I hope this is the last trip I'm gonna have to make to this court for one of you boys. Because I'm telling you now, yah better start being more careful out in these streets. Start thinking about what yah want to do with your lives".

The boys remained silent as the piled into the car and Mama K continued, "You boys are a month and some change out of high school and don't know what yah want to do. Well I'm going to tell you like this, yah better straighten up, and think about getting some jobs or come work with me in the store. I'm not going to lose one of you to these streets. Dre and Paul, you too are like one of my own and yah know this. Boys I love all three of yah and I don't want nothing happening to yah. You understand".

They all replied with low murmured 'yes's' and fell back into quiet mode. Mama pulled over the car in front of Dre's building and all three of the boys jumped out. Dre hesitated before he said, "Mama K why my mother didn't come?"

Mama K anticipated Dre asking this question, "I spoke with her and she was out trying to get some bail money, just in case we needed it. But we didn't, so everything is okay, right", she said, putting on a smile to relax Dre mind. Truth was Dre's mother was too drunk to go with them to the court house. Mama K knew it was best to keep that to herself.

Dre smiled, "Thanks Mama K". He leaned into the driver's side window and gave her a kiss on her cheek.

"Don't worry about it baby. You boys be careful and think about what I said about doing something with your lives". They all nodded as she pulled off from the curb.

*****

Dre tried to get his thoughts together in the shower, while Fat Pee and De'Quan played street fighter on his super Nintendo in the mist of large clouds of smoke. Spending thirty plus hours in the slammer gave Dre a lot to think about and it was time they stepped their game up. Mama K was right in her own little way. They definitely could not go on like this forever. They needed a real plan. They were some real niggas, and the way Dre saw it Real Always Wins in the end. A major plan was a definite must.

Dre dried off, wrapped the towel around himself, and shaved the little bit of facial hair he had. After brushing his teeth, putting on lotion, a white T, and a crisp pair of boxers Dre felt like a new man. Staring at himself in the mirror Dre felt a light surge of energy. "Yeah, I'm ready", He said to himself with a big smile.

Dre walked into his room into a loud cloud of smoke, and an atmosphere of cursing and kung-fu noise from the TV.

"Just what I needed," Dre said.

Fat Pee smirked and said, "What nigga, a shower?"

De'Quan started laughing. Dre said, "No nigga, this blunt", and with that, Dre snatched the blunt out of Fat Pee hand.

De'Quan laughed harder. His two friends always went at it for the entertainment in it, but if an outsider ever made the mistake of taking their cracks on each other as a weakness for their love for each other, they would pay for their mistake. De'Quan said, "What up Dre, did anybody try you for your kicks up in there?"

Dre blew out a deep cloud of smoke and said, "Hell no. Marcy is running shit up in there".

"Yeah, that's what I'm talking about. Pop didn't have any problems on the Island, and he was shot the fuck up. And niggas recognize Pop up north", De'Quan said with some pride.

Fat Pee jumped in, "That's word. Pop up in Clinton with my uncle Tech, from building 621. Tech said, 'they're living it up B.K. style".

De'Quan put down his joy stick and said, "So, what's next yah? We got to make a hit, and we have to change this situation with the stash spot. Dre, we was fucked up if your bail was more than five gees. I didn't know how we were going to get up in this house".

"I think we should put our bread in four different places", Dre said, sharing one of his thought's he brain stormed in the cell. "I did wonder how yah were going to get in here to get the money".

Fat Pee said, "four places, where we going to find four places' at?'

De'Quan said, "Well we can use our three houses, and we need one good stash spot we all have access to".

"What about a chick crib?" fat Pee said.

Dre said, "Hell no! I'm not trusting no female with my money, unless it's Mama K or my sister".

De'Quan said, "I can go for that. Mama K is the only female I would trust with my money too, but we can't go that route, so what's next?"

"I got it. We can make Rah the holder. Like our treasurer or some shit", Dre said.

"Now I can go for that. We put it to him like this; he holds the sneaker box for us. It will only have money in it, and if anything comes up missing, it's on him. We can't lose. Rah is scared of us, he'll jump out the window, before he spends some of our dough", Fat Pee said.

De'Quan agreed, "Word, that's a good idea. If any one of us gets in a situation like Dre did, then the rest of us still has access to the money to take care of bail and other things".

Dre started getting dress, "So we knock out the four places and just focus on one".

De'Quan said, "Yeah, I mean Rah's crib can be our major stash spot, and of course we all will have some dough in our own cribs like Pee did. Pee had a stash, and I had a gee to put with it for your bail".

Fat Pee said, "Yeah nigga, don't you forget who was coming to get your ass".

"Shut the fuck up. You know you my son. You better had came to get par-par out, or I would have put my foot in your ass", Dre said sparking a round of laughs around the room.

De'Quan calmed down and said, "what was you going to tell me before you got knocked?"

Dre looked at him with a lost look in his eyes, then it hit him, "Oh yeah. Remember the dude Shaborn from Lefrek we were watching at the Rucker?"

"The dude Tasha was all over, yeah I remember. What about him?" De'Quan asked.

Dre said, "Dig it, I ran up on her the other day on some trying to get some pussy shit right. She starts acting all high sadiddy and shit, so I took a stab in the dark and said, 'why, cause you fucking wit that nigga Sha?' and her whole face changed. She asked me how I know, but I side stepped the question with a, who doesn't know your business answer. Then I stepped off.

"Later on, I followed her to Queens and she took me right to his spot. He's in a three family house, in the back streets of Lefrek city. Shaborn lives on the third floor, and there's a family living on the ground floor. The middle floor is empty", Dre said.

De'Quan's mind started turning. He was the one who always figured out how they got in and out of a place. "Do you think they will hear us kick in the door?"

"Hell yeah, the wall's are super thin in a house like that", Dre said.

Fat Pee interjected, "Why don't we just stake it out, and see how we get in that way".

Dre said, "word, we can do that".

De'Quan said, "Aight, fuck it. We take shifts on him. This could be the big one, so we have to plan this one out to the tee. No fuck ups".

Chapter 18

Mama K was digging her new home away from home. With Pop making some calls from behind the wall, the paperwork finally cleared, and Mama K was able to open up the first legal family business. Mama K had a nice little grand opening at her new store on Lewis Avenue and Green Street. Even though a few people wandered into the store thinking she was opening a new weed spot in the hood, Mama K was still enjoying herself and the new people she was meeting every day.

Most of Meika's day consisted of her and her friends hanging around the store for the air conditioning, and to give Mama K a helping hand around the store. De'Quan helped on the close up like he said he would, while Ne'Sean tried his best to stay away from the store, unless he wanted something.

It was another hot summer day in Brooklyn and the action walking pass the store is what had De'Quan and Dre attention, as they sat on milk creates, sipping on juices. The two friends had been enjoying their pick of the many flavors of ladies that strolled by all day.

Dre eyed a brown skin cutie coming down the block in a yellow sundress, "I got this one", he said quickly staking his claim.

De'Quan shrugged her off, "Play on player".

"Quan, the phone!" Meika yelled from the back of the store.

"Aight", he answered and got off his create. "Dre don't hurt yourself out here".

"I hear you", Dre shot back as he watched sundress make her way closer to the store. When she got close enough Dre said, "Excuse me".

She stopped in her tracks and looked down at him. When it was obvious he wasn't getting up from his seat, she almost walked off. Dre reached out as he stood and said, "Hey, hold on a second. My name is Dre and I won't keep you long. Unless you in a rush".

With a straight face she said, "I might be, it all depends".

Dre thought to himself 'I got her'.

De'Quan picked up the hanging receiver, "Hello".

"Yo what's up?" Fat Pee said.

"Everything alright out there?" De'Quan asked.

"Yeah. A few trips in and out, but other than that, everything looks cool", Fat Pee reported.

"Where you at?" De'Quan asked.

"The payphone a few blocks from the spot. I'm about to bounce", Fat Pee said.

"Okay. We'll meet you at the crib", De'Quan said as the other line beeped on the phone. De'Quan clicked over and he was greeted by a pre-recorded message. "You have a call from an upstate correctional facility, caller your name...Pop. If you wish to accept these charges, please press 555".

De'Quan pressed the numbers and the line clicked over. "What's up Pop?"

"Quan, how's my b-boy doing?"

"I'm okay, just holding Mama K and them down today", De'Quan said feeling good inside to hear his father's voice.

Pop smiled, "That's good. That's good, have you been keeping your nose clean out there?"

De'Quan said, "Yeah, but I got so much going on that I don't know where to turn sometimes. They talking about sending Dre up-north too. That's going to kill me to have you and Dre in there".

Pop choose his words carefully, "Listen son, no matter what the outcome is in his situation, you have your brother and Pee at your side. I'm sure they have your back, and if Dre has to do some time, yah keep it true with him".

221

"Of course Pop", De'Quan said.

"Boy you still on my phone?" Mama K barked from one of her small aisles.

"Yeah Ma. I'm on the phone with your husband", De'Quan said with a chuckle.

Pop said, "Next time she comes to see me, I want you to come too. This phone thing ain't cool, and Mama K be beefing about the bill sometimes like I'm not the one who is paying for it".

They shared a laugh and De'Quan said, "Okay Pop. Hold on, let me give Ma the phone". When De'Quan put down the receiver and turned his back Meika came around the counter and picked it up.

"Hi Daddy!"

De'Quan and Dre stayed until Mama K closed the store and they made sure she and Meika were safely home. Then they went off to Dre's house to have their late night meeting.

Sitting in Dre's room De'Quan thought he should drop a bomb on Fat Pee and Dre before they get into the business at hand.

"I was talking to Ne'Sean the other night and he wants to get down with us".

Fat Pee looked over to Dre who looked shocked by this news. "I thought about it and I think we should pull him in", De'Quan said.

"Quan you sure? I mean, we talking about robbery with a mixture of other things in there. That can be some heavy shit on a nigga mind man", Fat Pee said with a lot of skepticism in his voice.

"I know, but he stepped to me and reminded me of the fact that we may be losing Dre for a minute, and it would be good to have extra hands on deck that we trust", De'Quan said as he got up and began to pace the room.

"What if Pop finds out?" Dre asked.

"How he gonna do that?" De'Quan shot back and lit up a cigarette.

Fat Pee said, "Shit man, the nigga got eyes all over the place. He might not be watching you that hard cause you the oldest, but he might be watching Sean".

De'Quan said, "He hasn't found out about us, if he did, oldest or not, he would have step to me. So adding Ne'Sean to the team shouldn't be a problem. This won't stop his basketball move and we won't let it. But the nigga is old enough to make his own decisions and we fuck around and do need him".

Dre spoke first, "Man it's on you. If you want to do it, then I guess it's cool".

They looked over to Fat Pee. He took a deep breath than shook his head, "Okay".

De'Quan put his cigarette out and said, "Fuck it, it's on then. Now what's up with this next bird?"

"Dude be in and out a lot, but what drug dealer isn't. Tasha comes and goes, and from the looks of it she has her own key now", Fat Pee said of his latest update.

Dre said, "Damn she works fast. She must have that superhead or something".

Fat Pee chuckled and said, "Word. Anyway, the family downstairs is deep and the traffic with them is all day. By about 7 or 8 o'clock that shit slows down though".

"Sounds kind of tricky", De'Quan said. "So what yah think is a good way of sliding in and out of there?"

"I think we can lay for the nigga on the stairs, and when he opens the door we'll be up close and personal with that heat in his face", Fat Pee said.

Dre smiled and said, "I like that shit. The nigga be in and out, so when he comes out we'll be waiting for his ass. And peep it, if the bitch Tasha shows up on the stairs before he opens the door, then we just put the heat to her neck and take the keys from her and walk right in".

"That will be proper", De'Quan added. "If we got the keys, he is going to think we Tasha, catching his ass off guard. You sure she's the only one with the keys Pee?"

"As far as I've seen, yeah, I mean don't get it twisted I saw dude bring other chicks there, but the only one I've seen come alone and dig for keys is Tasha", Fat Pee said.

De'Quan said, "Fuck it then, we go in tomorrow night. I'll talk to Ne'Sean and bring him with me".

Dre smiled for the first time in their meeting and said, "Good. Now let's go get some of that sticky and find some chicks".

"Word", Fat Pee said as their meeting concluded and they headed out into the dark streets.

Chapter 19

Fat Pee stole a Ford Explorer from the Corona section of Queens, and then drove to 102street and Otis Avenue to pick up De'Quan, Dre and a nervous Ne'Sean. When Fat Pee pulled up pumping Funk Master Flex on Hot 97, they came out of the shadows and piled into the jeep.

"Yo man, turn that shit off!" Dre snarled from the back seat.

"Calm down, I had to make it look good while I was stuck in traffic on 108street", Fat Pee said as he turned the radio off.

Fat Pee drove down four blocks and parked on the corner of Otis Avenue and Xenia Street. He cut the engine off and they all sat there in silence watching the late night calm of the dark street.

"Check your shit", De'Quan said, breaking the silence. Everyone in the car quickly checked their guns one last time before they slid out of the car. De'Quan and Dre headed for the house, while Ne'Sean took up his position a few houses away in the shadows. Ne'Sean was instructed to wait 20 minutes, then come in the house and wait with them on the stairs. Fat Pee remained in the car and watched the streets.

The front door of the house was unlocked giving De'Quan and Dre the easy access they needed to get in. De'Quan went into the house first, with Dre close on his heels. They crept to the staircase and were happy to hear the family on the first make enough noise to cover any creeks the staircase might have made. They made their way up to the third-floor landing without incident, and were greeted by music coming from Shaborn's apartment. De'Quan shook his head thinking they could have come in there pissy drunk, knocking over everything and nobody would have heard them anyway.

Dre put his ear to the door and took a quick listen. He could hear someone talking over the steady rhythm of the music, but he only heard one voice. Dre looked at De'Quan and gave him he's on the phone signal. De'Quan nodded and they relaxed a little, staying on the ready in case the door suddenly open.

While watching the street Fat Pee saw a cab pull up to the front of the house and Tasha climbed out of the back with her hands full with shopping bags. She stood by the cab driver window and paid him. Ne'Sean stood in the shadows watching the whole transaction. His heart was racing a hundred miles a minute. He knew they were going to tie Tasha up with Shaborn if she was in the house, but they did not tell Ne'Sean what to do if Tasha showed up while he was still outside.

Tasha said good night to the cab driver and made her way to the house. Ne'Sean found himself stuck, as he watched the cab pull away from the curb and drive off. Tasha pushed open the front door and pushed it close with her foot as she turned on her heels and tugged her heavy bags up the stairs.

Ne'Sean snapped out of his trance and sprinted to the front door. He took a deep breath and turned the knob. When he stepped inside Ne'Sean could hear Tasha making her way up the stairs. With the quickness of a cheetah, he quietly began to climb the stairs after her.

Dre and De'Quan locked eyes when they heard someone coming up the stairs with shopping bags in their hands. De'Quan pointed to a corner and Dre slid into the dark space. De'Quan stepped back onto the part of the staircase that ascended to the roof of the house.

Tasha walked up the steps, digging in her Gucci bag looking for her keys when she felt someone coming up the stairs behind her. Tasha tried to turn around, but it was too late, they pounced on her before she could realize what was happening.

Ne'Sean hit her in the back of her neck with the butt of his gun causing Tasha to let out an 'Ohhh', before she semi-blacked out. As she fell forward, Dre quickly jammed his gun in her mouth with enough force to break 5 of her teeth. The music was playing so loud in Shaborn's apartment, he never Tasha cry out in pain from the two hits she took.

She tried to focus as her eyes locked eyes with Dre's. "Shhh", Dre motioned with his free hand middle finger to his lips.

De'Quan snatched her Gucci bag and fished out Tasha's baby 380. All hope Tasha had left shivered right out her body. Dre grabbed Tasha by her collar and lifted her off of the floor with the gun still in her mouth. De'Quan fished the house keys out of her bag and dropped the useless bag on the floor.

Ne'Sean climbed the rest of the stairs giving Tasha a full view of her captures. Recognition of all three of their faces made Tasha break down and she began to cry. De'Quan stepped up to her left ear and in a calm, but sinister voice he said, "Tasha, shut the fuck up with all that crying and tell me what keys open this door".

Tasha gave him a stubborn look. Dre cocked the hammer back on his 9mm to show how real they were.

"Again, what key is it?"

She pointed to two keys on the ring. Before De'Quan put the key in the door, he looked over to Ne'Sean, who gave him his nod of assurance to go ahead. Very slowly and quietly, De'Quan slid the first key into the lock and unlocked it. He put the second key in and unlocked it. He listened for any movement and didn't feel any. He readied his 9mm then pushed open the door.

De'Quan and Ne'Sean rushed into the house and found themselves in the kitchen. They ran blindly through the loud music, quickly checking any empty room then turning to a second bedroom. When they ran up in the room Shaborn was lying on his back on the bed, with his eyes closed. A big titty Spanish mommy was riding him reverse cowgirl style. She looked to be in pure ecstasy, until De'Quan punched her in her face knocking her right off Shaborn's dick and into the corner of the room. She let out a little scream which caused De'Quan to rush her and hit her over the head with the butt of his gun.

Shaborn laid there in shock for a second, then snapped out of it when he saw De'Quan pistol whip his girl into submission. Shaborn reached for something on the side of his bed and Ne'Sean jumped right on the bed to stop him. Ne'Sean kicked Shaborn in his neck causing him to drop what he was reaching for and cry out in pain.

Ne'Sean didn't stop with his foot assault on Shaborn as he continued to kick him until he lost his footing on the bed and tumbled to the floor.

Ne'Sean quickly scrambled to his feet, as Shaborn tried to gather himself, but Shaborn was too out of it. Ne'Sean hit him over his head with his gun, then shoved it in Shaborn's mouth to stop his screaming. Once they got things under control, De'Quan silently thanked Shaborn for having the music on too loud and living on top on an empty apartment.

Dre brought Tasha into the house, locked the door and sat her on the couch. When he took the gun out of her mouth, Tasha spit blood and teeth on the floor, then she started sobbing, "Dre, what the fuck is going on? Why is yah doing this?"

"Tasha just be easy and shut up. Once we get what we came for, we outta here", he said. Dre grabbed a t-shirt from off a chair and wiped the blood off his gun.

De'Quan came out into the living room dragging the naked unconscious Spanish girl by her arms. He dragged her over to the love seat and gave up on trying to put her in it. Tasha's facial expression went from scared to angry in a New York minute, "What the fuck! What the fuck is going on here?"

Ne'Sean brought Shaborn out into the living room butt naked with the gun still in his mouth. When Shaborn locked eyes with Tasha, he wanted to turn back around and run back into the bedroom.

Ne'Sean pushed Shaborn onto the couch next to Tasha, who stared him down and wasted no time with the questions, "Who the fuck is this?"

Shaborn just stared at her bleeding face with a blank expression. Tasha caught the whole living room off guard by smacking Shaborn and screaming in his face, "Answer me dickhead!" she barked, with tears streaming down her cheeks.

De'Quan grabbed her by her arm and pulled her off the couch, "Chill the fuck out Tasha".

He moved her to an empty chair before she really went off on Shaborn, and Dre quickly pulled out the duck-tape. The first thing that had to be taped up was Tasha's mouth because she wouldn't stop crying.

As Tasha was getting taped up, De'Quan got busy with tying up the unconscious Spanish. Shaborn's mind started to click and spoke for the first time, "Wait a minute, how the fuck do you know her name?"

Dre turned from what he was doing and smacked Shaborn so hard Ne'Sean thought his hand had to be broke. "Shut the fuck up. No talking unless spoken too".

Dre finished taping Tasha up and all she did was cry and sob the whole time. He brushed it off and duck taped Shaborn's hands and feet together. When he finished Dre told Ne'Sean to watch them while he and De'Quan searched the house.

After five minutes of this, Dre got frustrated went over to Shaborn. He ripped the tape off his mouth and said, "I'm tired of this, where's the stash at Sha?"

"I don't have a stash dawg".

That answer awarded Shaborn another hard smack to the face. Tasha gave a mumbled cheer of triumph under her taped mouth. Dre said, "You know what Sha", and put the tape back on his mouth.

Dre turned to Tasha and said, "Listen Tasha, we didn't expect for you to be in the middle of this, and I know you didn't expect to catch this lame getting his dick suck tonight either. So how about we call it even and you tell me where the shit is at, and we might even piece you off".

Tasha's eyes lit up and she nodded her head. Shaborn mumbled a strong 'bitch' from behind his taped mouth. Dre smirked at Shaborn and took the tape off Tasha's mouth. She spit out a glob of blood in Shaborn's direction and said, "It's under refrigerator!"

"Thank You", Dre said with a smile, and then walked off toward the kitchen. He called out to De'Quan, but the music was still blaring through the house.

De'Quan finally came out of the back room with a bag full of jewelry, a few guns, and a couple of gees he found in the closet.

"Yo I didn't find any work in there", De'Quan said with a frustrated look on his face.

"That's because it's under the frig", Dre said.

They went into the kitchen and De'Quan open the refrigerator door. They took everything out until De'Quan noticed something about the bottom of the refrigerator. He pulled on it until it clicked, and he pulled the make shift door open. He pulled out three kilos of cocaine and a bundle of money plastic wrapped together.

"Yeah, now that's what I'm talking about", De'Quan was beaming as he looked up to his friend.

"Now let's set their asses on fire and bounce".

Dre said, "What about Tasha? I told her we would piece her off if she told me where the stash was at".

"Yeah right", De'Quan said, and then he turned to a knife set that was on the counter and snatched one out of its holder. "Piece her off with this. We can't leave that bitch alive son, you know that".

Dre scratched his head and said, "You right. She doesn't have any teeth anymore anyway. Let's stab them and set this place on fire".

"Word that sounds like a plan", De'Quan agreed and they went to work.

Dre found some oil in the cabinet and De'Quan turned on the gas burners. They went back into the living room and walked into Tasha giving the now woke Spanish girl an ear full.

"Bitch who the fuck is you? And why is you up in my bed sucking on my mans dick?"

The girl couldn't respond because of the tape on her mouth, but that didn't stop her from trying as she mumbled her responses. The whole scene had been making Ne'Sean nervous. He told Tasha the chill more than five times already and he didn't know what to do next. When his brother and Dre came back into the living room, Ne'Sean felt a sigh of relief rush over his body.

The sight of them made Tasha calm down for a minute and the only thing moving was the CD changer that had R-Kelly's 12play on heavy rotation. De'Quan stepped to Tasha and said, "Okay boys and girls, it's time to go. I heard you were promised a piece of this".

Before Tasha could answer him, De'Quan pulled the knife from behind his back and slashed her throat wide open. Ne'Sean and Shaborn watched the scene in shock as the Spanish girl started screaming under the duck-tape. Dre quickly went to work on her with his knife to shut her up for good.

"Here Sean, finish dude off", De'Quan said handing his brother the knife. Ne'Sean stood there wide eyed with his nerves shaking like a pair of dice. He only wanted to take the knife because his brother was telling him to take it, but his body felt froze to the floor.

De'Quan walked closer to his brother and said, "Listen Sean, they saw our faces, and Tasha knew where we from. Now stab him and let's go".

Ne'Sean slowly took the knife out if his brother hand and stared down into Shaborn's pleading eyes. De'Quan took the gun out of Ne'Sean hand so he could focus on the task at hand.

"Yo come on Ne'Sean, do this nigga and let's go. This place is going up in flames in a minute", Dre said as he doused the couch with the kitchen oil.

Ne'Sean nervously looked from Dre back to Shaborn. Without wasting another moment on his thoughts, Ne'Sean lashed out and stabbed Shaborn in his chest. Shaborn's eyes grew wide in fright as he felt his life slowly slipping away from him. Ne'Sean left the knife in his chest as he stepped back.

"Let's go!" Dre barked as his pulled out his lighter and set the couch on fire.

Fat Pee patiently held his position on the corner of the block. He had a clear view of the house and everything looked cool to him until he saw a spark of flames in the third-floor window. Fat Pee quickly started up the car and drove straight to the front of the house.

Ne'Sean was the first one to appear out the front door. He ran straight for the back door of the jeep, hoped in and slid over to give Dre the room he needed to hop in behind him and slam the door. De'Quan jumped into the front seat with their bag of goods, slammed his door and Fat Pee peeled off from the curb in a hurry. He blew the stop sign on the corner, made a quick right and headed straight for the Long Island expressway. Two blocks away Fat Pee could hear the faint sounds of sirens coming his way, but thoughts of those sirens coming for them was the furthest thing on Fat Pee's mind, as he hit the ramp at 45mph and cruised into ongoing traffic heading for the Brooklyn-Queens expressway.

Chapter 20

Fat Pee weaved the Explorer through the light late night traffic, as Ne'Sean stared out his window trying to get a grip on what he just witnessed. His brother, Dre and Fat Pee were laughing about what they just did, as De'Quan gave his version of the scene to fill Fat Pee in.

"Yo Tasha sees me dragging the bitch out of the back room and she looks at duke and says, 'who the fuck is that?' Yo Pee, you had to see the look on son face".

"Word?" Fat Pee says as they share a round of laughs from the amusing scene.

Dre caught his wind and said, "Word son! Homeboy looked like he literally shitted on himself when he saw Tasha sitting there".

"Word, and when he didn't answer her, she smacked the shit out of him!" De'Quan said as the three friends howled in pleasure.

Ne'Sean sat motionless staring out the window at the passing scenery trying to figure out what the hell was so funny. He was scared out of his mind and it could clearly be seen if someone was looking at him, but no one paid Ne'Sean any attention. Or so he thought.

"Yo Pee get off at Washington Ave", De'Quan said as he fished out a cigarette and lit it up. Getting off the highway wasn't a part of the plan knew anything about, but they stop questions De'Quan when he made sudden movements without informing the rest of them.

Fat Pee drove down the bumpy Brooklyn-Queens expressway and took his exit on their left. "Make a left at the light", De'Quan instructed as everyone sat in silence.

Fat Pee made the left, drove down two blocks then was ordered to make a right. They drove down the side of a school that was connected to a park that had some dark patches in it from bad lighting. "Pull over Pee".

When he pulled over, De'Quan hopped out of the jeep and pulled open the back-passenger door, "Come on Sean".

Ne'Sean looked at Dre and Fat Pee with a hundred questions in his eyes, but he couldn't fix the words to come out. Ne'Sean just shook his head and slowly got out of the jeep.

"Wait for me on the benches", De'Quan said to Ne'Sean, who walked off without saying a word.

When his brother walked away, De'Quan stuck his head in the window and said, "Pee drop Dre off with the bag and dump this jeep. We'll meet up at Dre's house in the morning. I need to talk to Sean for a while, feel me", De'Quan said informing his partners of his change their after-work plan.

"It looks like this shit is eating him up", Dre said with a worried look on his face.

"It's okay, I got this. Pee, don't forget to wipe this jeep down", De'Quan said as he gave each one a pound.

"I won't, come on Dre, get in the front. Fuck you think I am, your chauffeur or something", Fat Pee said.

When De'Quan reached his brother in the park, Ne'Sean was staring down at some ants making their way around his feet in the dark. De'Quan pulled out a Philly blunt and began to split it open.

"You can let it out anytime you ready. This blunt should be ready in a minute", De'Quan said with a taste of humor in his voice. At that moment it began to sink in how much De'Quan was beginning to grow into a young Pop.

"Quan, we didn't have to do that to Tasha".

De'Quan concentrated on putting the bag of weed on the waiting Philly in the dimly lit park. A properly rolled blunt would make his conversation with Ne'Sean go over a little smoother, than if they were sober. He could tell his little brother was caught up in his feelings at the moment and he needed to work those bad vibes out of him before they went home for the night.

"Quan seriously, what the fuck happen up there, you didn't tell me we were doing any of that", Ne'Sean said with some anger in his voice.

De'Quan lit up the blunt and sat down on the bench next to his brother. He took a strong pull off of the blunt, exhaled, and said, "Sean I told you we were into some serious things. Not any video game shit. This is what life out on the streets is about, and bottom line – Real Always Wins. Real smart, real gangster and real survival. It's hell out here some days and I don't want you riding with us if it's going to fuck you up in the end.

"We do this now to survive, but you the family's future. Just like the store is Pop's vision. Well that vision would've burned up in that fire at Grand-Ma house. I gave Mama K our stash to hold her down so she could get the store popping. That's real. We not out here doing this shit for fun. Niggas is trying to keep their heads above water, before these projects or streets drown us".

De'Quan passed his brother the blunt, then stood up and started pacing. Ne'Sean took his pulls of the blunt and tried to see the game through his brother eyes.

De'Quan continued, "Tasha knew who we were, and where we lived. Either that nigga she was fucking would have grew some balls or made her talk or she would have told the police about us. She was a good bitch, but a bitch with too much power over us and our situation. We can't risk letting people know who we are and what we do. That puts us in danger and Mama K and Meika, you feel me".

Ne'Sean felt his brother passion as he looked up from the ground and into his eyes. "Quan, I love you and I will do anything to help us survive out here while Pop is away. I'm not going to lie, that thing had me messed up, but like you said, 'it was either them or us'".

"That's what I'm talking about Sean. People out here ain't trying to give us or Mama K shit, but they claim to have love for Pop. Those motherfuckers don't give a fuck if we starve to death in that house. That's real".

De'Quan's words and the blunt began to take its effects on Ne'Sean as he said, "You right. I just didn't know killing someone was a part of it".

De'Quan sat back down next to his brother and said, "Sean I will do anything out here to make sure yah safe, even if that means killing the only witness to our crime".

"I guess you right. You know I will always have your back out here. I know things have been hard on Mama K since Pop been gone. So any help she can get from us is good, right", Ne'Sean said.

De'Quan smiled and said, "Right. So you with me".

Ne'Sean sucked his teeth and said, "Yeah man".

"Good, now let's walk. We have to find a cab on the boulevard or something", De'Quan said, leading the way out of the park.

"Quan, how long niggas plan on doing this for?" Ne'Sean asked.

"Shit, after tonight's hit we might be good until you get that first NBA check, you know what I'm saying", De'Quan said giving his brother a pound. He got a new rush of energy just thinking about counting the money they took.

$$*****$$

It was dark in his room as Ne'Sean stared up at the ceiling with images of the scene in Queens riding his thoughts. He tried to block it out and think about the future. This thing with De'Quan wasn't forever. Once he got his basketball scholarship, he will go to college and hopefully the pros. Those are the thought's he wanted to close his eyes with, not Tasha and Shaborn's face. Faces he knew he would never forget.

Chapter 21

The line in front of Brooklyn criminal court was extremely long and not moving fast enough. Dre found himself ready to walk off the line and say 'catch me when you can' on his way back to Marcy. He knew he would have to come up with a good story to tell his mother and Mama K when they question about what happen at court today, and he didn't have one. Without a good creditable story, he stuck on the slow moving line with De'Quan and Rahkem feeling as nervous as he was.

The three friends made it through the metal detector without incident and checked the docket list to find the courtroom. When they reached the courtroom, Dre spotted his lawyer talking to another white man in a suit.

"There he go right there", Dre said and they made their in his direction.

When Mr. Massinger saw Dre and his small entourage coming his way he cut his conversation short and guided the group over to the side. Dre picked up Mr. Massinger after firing Mr. Gordon for trying to get him to take 1-3years upstate.

"Mr. Jones how are you today?" The lawyer asked as he shook Dre's hand.

"Listen Mr. Massinger, what's the judge going to say today?" Dre said skipping the formalities.

Mr. Massinger thought to himself 'okay' and got right to it. "Well the district attorney is being generous today, so I got him down to six months with five years probation, when you get out. I think it's a good deal, being that you were arrested red handed with the gun, and you have no pyres".

Rahkem jumped in and said, "Then why can't he get a straight five years probation without the six months, since he ain't never been arrested".

Mr. Massinger looked over to Rahkem and thought he should choose his words wisely. "Because the D.A.'s office wants him to do some type of jail time. I was just talking to Mr. Crossmen and he won't go down any further, and since trial is out of the question, I say take the deal and run".

De'Quan said, "Can we get a minute here", and pulled Dre over to the side with Rahkem on their heels.

"So, what you want to do bro?" De'Quan asked Dre.

Dre mind was spinning, as he looked around at all the confusion going on in the courthouse hallway. People were barking orders at their lawyers or on the pay phones, court officer's dragging handcuffed people in and out of courtrooms, and someone's baby would not stop crying.

He sucked his teeth and said, "I can do six months, as long as I know yah going to hold me down".

"Of course we got you", De'Quan said. Rahkem nodded in agreement.

Dre thought for a moment then said, "Fuck it. As long as I don't have to go in today, and we should try to get that probation off too".

Rahkem said, "Shit, that cracker can get you at least 30 days out on the streets for some party and bullshit. If not we wildin on him in this hallway".

Rahkem was big for 17, standing at 6'3 and weighing 210 pounds. He would use his size when he needed too, especially on white people. However, to get him to run up in a spot to do a robbery was a whole another thing. Rahkem was too soft for a real drama scene.

They walked back over to Mr. Massinger with Rahkem stepping a little closer to the lawyer than he was before. Dre said, "I'll take some time, but I don't want any probation, and I'm not going in today".

Mr. Massinger looked at all three faces and quickly realized Dre wasn't asking him to make it happen. He was telling him to make it happen. "Oh okay, I'm going to see about getting you the straight jail time. The judge won't sentence you today anyway, that won't happen until probably next month. I'll go inside and talk to Mr. Crossmen and I should have this straighten out in ten minutes so you won't have to wait around all day", the lawyer said then ran off.

Dre left the court house feeling relived the judge gave him some more time to smell the fresh city air before they took him in for his bid. They hailed a cab and piled into the back.

"Dre, you think your moms will let us throw a party?' Rahkem asked as the cab weaved through traffic.

"Yeah that sounds like a good idea", De'Quan added.

"I don't know, but I'll talk to my sister. She'll take care of my moms'".

"Yeah, so it's on, I'm going to get my cousin Dog Time from Queens to DJ for us", Rahkem said excited.

"Your cousin who? Never heard of him", De'Quan said and Dre started laughing in Rahkem's face.

Rahkem smiled and said, "Okay, laugh now, but I'm telling you my cousin is going to be big time. You watch".

Chapter 22

"A Tammy, wait up a minute".

Tammy stopped to see who was trying to hold up her progress and was surprised when she saw it was Dre.

Tammy's insides lit up, but she tried to keep a straight face when she said, "Oh hi Dre, I have to go to the store for my mom, so she'll get off of my back".

Dre smiled and said, "Can I walk with you then?"

"If you want", Tammy said nonchalantly.

They headed up to Marcy Avenue with Dre watching Tammy out the corner of his eye. He found himself trying to put together a set of words that wouldn't make him look uncool. Dre never had any problems bagging a female. It was Tammy.

Tammy Brown was labeled in the hood as hard2get. Her chocolate complexion, chinky eyes, and long Indian hair made her a prize to bag on the streets, but whenever someone tried to rap to Tammy, she always claimed to have no time to stop. Dre figured walking with her would give him some time to get in her ear.

"You know, you shouldn't be walking around here by yourself anyway. Where's your man at?" Dre asked. It was too much talk on the streets; he needed to get his info straight from the source.

Tammy snickered and rolled her eyes, "what man?"

Dre felt his stock rise as he said, "the one I thought I peeped lurking around your building. I guess I was hallucinating".

Tammy smiled but remained silent. Tammy thought she was the only one watching him. To hear Dre say he be watching her made Tammy feel good inside. Watching Dre from the corner of her eyes Tammy could feel the butterflies in her stomach working over-time. She tried to relax so she wouldn't look to anxious as they walked up the long block.

"So, what you been up too Tammy, I haven't seen you in a while", Dre said after their awkward silence.

"I be in the house a lot. When I'm not here, I'm at my cousin house in Williamsburg. Ain't much in Marcy for me", she dryly stated.

"How do you know if you don't stick around to see?" Dre asked.

Tammy cracked a smile and said, "you might be right about that. What about you, where you be at?"

"Trying to lay low, shit is getting a little crazy out here. So I've been just trying to stay busy in my own little world", Dre said with a smile.

When they reached the store on Marcy Avenue, a small dice game was in full swing out front of the store. "What you got to get?" Dre asked her.

"Some milk and female things", Tammy said.

"Female things? I'll wait for you out here than", Dre said giving Tammy her privacy.

"Dre what's happening?" A light skin brother said he was watching the dice game from the background.

Dre stepped over and gave him a pound, "What up Tone, why you not playing?" Tone was a notorious dice player in the hood.

"Shiittt, not today. I got to finish this pack and head uptown, you feel me. Yo what's up with you and Tammy?" Tone asked as his eyes scanned the traffic rolling down Marcy Avenue.

"Yeah! 4, 5, 6 pay up motherfucker's!"

Dre thought about his answer and figured it would be good to put it out there for the wolves to back off. "Yeah that's about to be me", Dre said confidently. "So yah niggas back up off of that". Dre and Tone shared a laugh and gave each other a pound.

"It's all good homie. She's definitely a banger", as soon as Tone finished his sentence a crack head walked up on them.

"Tone I need four".

Tone did a quick look around and said, "Good, go around the corner".

"Tone I'll get wit you later", Dre said.

Tone wasn't listening his mind was on his business as he trailed the crack head around the corner.

"Okay bitches, make daddy proud", someone barked from the dice game as he shook the dice and rolled them out of his hand in a smooth motion.

Dre snapped out of watching the game when Tammy came out of the store stuffing her change in her purse. Dre took her bag from her to carry the load back to the building. On the walk back, Dre told himself it was now or never and said, "Tammy can I take you out tonight, to eat or something. I'm type hungry and that will give us some sit down time, if you don't mind that of course".

Tammy was a little taken aback by this. She thought he would just ask her for her number and run off. "Well I… When I drop this stuff to my mom I'll see".

"We can go to Junior's, so tell your moms I'll pick her up a cheesecake. How about that?" Dre said with a smile. Nobody's mother is going to turn down free cheesecake from Junior's.

She smiled and said, "That might do it. Moms loves her some cheesecake".

They chuckled, and Dre said, "While you up there call a cab, so she won't think I'm trying to kidnap her daughter".

She laughed and said, "Kidnap huh, I'm not worried about you. I can handle myself".

241

Dre had to laugh at her toughness. "Okay gangstress. I don't want any problems. I just want to eat and get to know who the real Tammy is".

She stayed quiet as his words rolled around in her head. She took the bag from him and said, "I'll be right back".

Dre sat on the back upright of the bench in front of Tammy's building and began to think about how he was going to incorporate Tammy into his near future plans. Dre knew he couldn't do a bid with the average bird from the projects holding him down. The thought has been on his mind ever since he agreed to take the short bid, to find a girl that would hold him down.

Dre had his eye on Tammy for some time, but he could never catch her at a good time. A shot rang out in the early night sky, invading Dre's thoughts of Tammy. From the sound of the shot, it came from the direction of the dice game. Dre shook his head and checked his hip to reassure himself of having his own peacemaker, then turned his thoughts back to the chocolate beauty he was going to make his official wifey.

When Tammy finally came out the front door of the building, she was wearing a blue Nike jacket to go with the blue Nike track suit she was rocking. Dre liked what he was seeing.

"My mom said, make sure that cheesecake got a lot of cherries on it", Tammy said, smiling as they hopped into the cab.

"Yes ma'am", Dre said with a chuckle.

On the way there, they talked about music and the latest videos out. When the cab pulled up to Junior's it was a regular car show outside. Three different sound systems were banging three different songs at the same damn time. Rims were gleaming, and the chicks were out in full force trying to bag them a balla for the night.

Dre and Tammy sat in a corner booth and scanned their menus. "What you want to eat?"

Tammy looked up from her menu and said, "I'm not really hungry. I just want a cheeseburger and fries".

The waitress popped up and Dre gave her Tammy's order, with a soda, and he ordered a chicken cutlet parmesan, and fruit juice. "Oh and let me get a cheesecake with lots of cherries to go please", Dre said with a wide grin.

"Thank you", Tammy said soft enough for only Dre to hear her.

While they waited for their food to come Dre asked, "What you going to do after high school, this your last year right?"

"Yeah, I was thinking about going to an all-black college down south. But I be worrying about leaving my mom in Marcy by herself".

"You don't have any brothers or sisters in another Boro or something?" Dre asked.

Tammy chuckled, "What you mean like the Ricki Lake show?"

They shared a laugh and she said, "Nah it's just me and my mom. I got cousins I hang out with, but I guess that's not the same. What about you, what you going to do?"

Dre said, "I'm done with school. I copped my G.E.D. so that's the end of that. I don't know what I'm going to do though. I'll have some time to think about it".

She skipped pass his last statement and said, "Sooo, what's up with you and Kimmie?"

The question caught Dre off guard for a second. He didn't let it show as he kept a straight face and said, "Me and Kimmie been old news. How do you say – we had a conflict of interest".

Tammy already knew all of this; she just wanted to hear it from him. Tammy had been keeping light tabs on Dre, so she knew more about him than he thought.

Dre stared across the table and told himself to put all his cards on the table and see how it goes. "Tammy, I know we only know each other from passing in the projects, but I'm feeling your vibe, and I would like to get to know you better than the average everyday p.j. life".

She smiled and said, "You mean we be exclusive".

Dre said, "No pressure. But I am feeling you like that".

Tammy blushed hard, but kept her eyes focused on her soda as she rubbed her finger over the top of the glass. She could feel his eyes burning a hole in her forehead.

"I'm feeling you too Dre, but I don't want to be apart no sideline drama. If it's going to be me and you, then we can swing that and see how it goes. But please Dre", she paused and looked up into his eyes. "Don't play me like I'm one of these lames out here with no future plans or anything like that".

Dre felt her sincerity and knew his gut feeling was right about her. "Come on Tammy, if you got my back, then I got your front".

She giggled, "Got my front huh. What's that some new slang or something".

"I can show you better than I can tell you".

Their food came, and Dre sat back to see how Tammy would eat in front of him. If she picked at her food like a bird, then she was fronting. Dre wasn't surprised to see Tammy throw ketchup on her burger and fries and dug right into it like he wasn't there.

By the end of their meal, both of them were feeling good about each other. They talked about everything except the fact that Dre only had 25days left out on the streets, and what he and his friends did for money. By the time they got out of the cab in front of Tammy's building the vibe between them was strong. Dre choose to ride with her up on the elevator. That's where he made his move and kissed Tammy until they missed her floor twice.

"Call me around 2 when I get home from school", Tammy said as she stepped off the elevator.

"Aight", Dre said as he kissed her one last time. His mind was already made up; he would go up to her school and pick her up instead of calling. Now that's official.

Chapter 23

With his head spinning out of control with crazy thought's, Dre found himself waking up every day and staring at the calendar on the wall. Ten more days before his final court date and it felt like those last hours were closing in fast on Dre. Some days he woke up and felt like running from New York City and its twisted system, but then the realization of not having anywhere to go would seep in.

Dre got up and went down the hallway to the bathroom. He cut the shower on and heard the phone in his room ringing.

"Hello".

"Hey you. I just wanted to see if you was up yet", Tammy said beaming through the phone.

"I'm getting in the shower now. I'll be over there when I'm done", Dre said.

"Oh, so you're in your birthday suit and wet right now", Tammy said with a snicker in her voice.

Dre laughed, "Yes sexy. Now make sure you ready when I get there please".

"Okay…okay. I'll be ready".

They hung up and Dre jumped into the shower. Thoughts of Tammy seemed to be the only Dre could think about lately. All of the bad questions would flood his mind and he would have to shake it off. Will she do the bid with me? Of course, she will, she's feeling me like that. Will Tammy mess around on me with another guy? Naw, I'll just have my boys keep an eye on her. Dre smiled to himself in the shower; yeah Tammy is going to hold me down while I'm gone.

He finished in the bathroom, went into his room and lit up a half of blunt while he threw on something to wear. Dark green Polo jeans, Nike shirt, some dark green Nike A.C.G.'s and a Nike hat to match rounded out his Saturday outfit. Dre grabbed $2,300.00 and his 9mm out of the stash spot, and he was gone.

When Tammy open the door, Dre found himself breathing again. It seemed like all of the drama he went through in his house and in the streets just disappeared. Tammy was the type of girl who could make a Gap suit look like a Prada suit.

Tammy loved looking her best everyday she spent with Dre and this day wasn't any different. She put on a big smile then step to the side so Dre could come in. She made a motion and said, "You like it?"

"You looking tasty in that skirt", Dre said.

"Oh ok, I thought I was going to have to put on something else", Tammy said.

Dre chuckled as he plopped down on the couch, "Oh no you not. You look good Tam. Seriously baby".

Tammy looked in the mirror and said, "I guess. So, I saw the shoes I want to get today in a store on Fulton".

"It don't look like you need any more shoes to me", Dre said as Tammy open the hallway closet revealing a stack of shoe boxes and coats.

Tammy fumbled in the closet for a moment than said, "Shut up silly. I need a pair of shoe to go with the outfit I'm wearing to your party. And for your information I got money to buy my shoes".

"If you got money, then can I get a pair of shoes too?" Dre said with a big smile on his face.

Tammy grabbed her purse and said, "Do unto others, what you want done for you. Let's go".

They walked up and down Fulton Street all day buying more stuff than they expected to get. Dre made Tammy hold onto her money and he paid for everything they picked out for the day. Tammy nothing about how or where Dre got his money, and she never asked. As long as Dre kept his focus on her and he was safe in the streets, Tammy didn't worry about anything else. She promised Dre she would come to see him when turned himself in to do his bid and the way Dre made her feel, Tammy had no thoughts of checking for another man while he was away.

The sky began to darken, so Dre took that as a sign to call it a day, grab some food and head back to Marcy. They grabbed some Chinese food and Dre stepped out onto the street to hail a cab. A brown Lincoln town car pulled over.

"Come on Tammy".

Dre open the door and the sound of someone winning some tickets on the radio flouted out of the car. Tammy jumped in and slide over in the backseat. Dre was putting the bags on the floor in the middle of the backseat when he thought he saw a glimpse of something out the corner of his eye. As Dre turned to get into the cab, he saw two guys coming at him fast. One had a big Rambo knife in his hand.

"Oh Shit!" Dre lost his balance as he tried to grab the gun off of his waist and jump into the cab at the same time.

"Yo Drive…Drive!"

The knife welding man tried to stab Dre but missed and stabbed the door panel as his partner quickly ran around to the outside and snatched open the door. "Give me the money bitch!" he barked as he grabbed Tammy's purse.

"Hey…hey!" The cab driver nervously yelled from the front seat.

Blam!

The sound was deafening in the body of the cab as the passenger side window blew out. "Oh shit, he got a gun".

"Get off of me!" Tammy cried out as she struggled with the robber for her purse.

The cab driver slammed down on the gas pedal, and Tammy's purse ripped right from her grip as the thirsty purse snatcher tumbled to the ground. Dre looked out the back window as the cab driver swerved through the narrow block with a purpose. The two robbers scrambled and dipped off into an alley way.

"Damn it! He got my bag Dre!"

"Damn!" Dre banged the butt of his gun on the car door as he watched the cab driver run a red light.

"Yo my man, take us to 506 Park Street". Dre said through the open partition.

"Hell no. Yah are getting out of my car at the next light. I can't deal with all this shooting and shit. Look at my got damn window", the cab driver angrily barked over his shoulder as he tried to keep his eyes on the road.

"Look motherfucker, take us to Park Street. Fuck you mean you throwing us out. We got money", Dre snapped as he threw a twenty-dollar bill through the partition. "Here man, keep the change. Just take us to Park man".

The cab driver pulled over at the next curb and turned to face his two passengers. "Please mister, don't leave us out here like this", Tammy pleaded.

"Who's going to pay for my damn window?"

"Man, my girl just lost her bag because you was bullshitting when I told you to pull off. So who you think is going to take the biggest lost today?" Dre said.

The cab driver looked over to Tammy who had tears streaming down the side of her brown cheeks. "Okay...but yah got to get out at Park". The car skidded from the curb without the driver saying another word.

Dre turned to Tammy and hugged her, "You alright baby".

"Them niggas got my bag Dre".

"I know this shit is fucked up. I should have been more on point", Dre said feeling his anger boil in the inside.

"My keys and everything was in there. We have to tell the police", Tammy said looking up at Dre.

"We can't do that Tammy", Dre said.

"Why not Dre. They robbed us!" Tammy barked. Dre never saw Tammy this angry before and he felt lost on how to calm her down in a short period time before the cab driver officially throw's them out.

"Tammy think for a second. I just let off a shot in the back of this cab, and I'm already going to jail in a few days for another gun charge. They going to pay more attention to me, than them two crack heads that snatched your bag". Dre said in a stern but calming voice.

"I'm sorry baby, but we just going to have to take this lost", Dre said gently taking her hand into his. With his free hand, Dre whipped the tears from her cheek.

The cab driver quickly broke up their hallmark moment by abruptly pulling the cab over and saying, "Hey, this is as far as I go with you two".

Dre quickly looked out the window to see where they were, "Come on Tammy".

Dre took Tammy home and after they went through the motions with Tammy's mother about how she lost her keys, Dre said his good byes and headed home knowing one day he will see them two crack heads again. Brooklyn was big, but not that big.

Chapter 24

"Bucktown!"

"Home of the original gun clappers!"

"Bucktown!"

"Home of the original gun clappers!"

The party goers chanted in unison with Smith & Wesson over the body popping beat. The apartment was packed, and Dre party was in full swing by the 11:00p.m. hour with hustlers, back-packers, fly girl's, hot chicks from outside the project's, and the gangsters all in attendance to pay homage to a person only a quarter of the apartment knew by face.

Dre's sister Shakia put the party together and no one argued with her on how she wanted to do it big for her brother. Dre's mothers moved to and from her bedroom to the kitchen to refill her glass every once in awhile, until the liquor put her to sleep.

The only piece of furniture they left in the living room was the couch and the loveseat. All the rest of the furniture was divided between Dre and Shakia bedrooms. Giving the living room all the space it needed to house the party goers. Rahkem's cousin Dog-Time came through for the small fee of $500.00, and from the way he had the place rocking he was worth every penny.

Dre sat back on the couch with Tammy up under his arm staring out at the people partying in his name and he couldn't believe the atmosphere. "If this is how they partying when I'm going in, imaging when I come out", Dre said to Tammy.

Tammy kissed him and whispered in his ear, "Dre I want you".

Dre pulled her closer to him and kissed her hard. Tammy's temperature had been rising all day, but they never had a moment to themselves. Tammy pulled back and stood up.

Taking Dre's hand, she maneuvered through the crowd and headed straight to Dre bedroom.

Dre bedroom was packed with stuff Shakia did not want broken and his bed looked like the coat rack with over twenty coats spread out across it. The only light in the room came from a lamp on an end table next to his buried bed.

Dre locked the door and put his back to it as pure lust took over them. They kissed with passion and fondled each other aimlessly until Dre stopped. Tammy thought something was wrong until he stepped over to the bed and with one sweeping motion; Dre knocked all the coats off his bed. Dre turned to Tammy and took off his shirt. He removed her shirt and brassiere and began to suck on her awaiting nipples. Tammy laid back on the bed and let his put his tongue to work as Dre sucked on her nipples, then eased his tongue down to her panty line. He smoothly pulled down her skirt and panties at the same time then opened her legs. Tammy's pussy was throbbing before he could even breathe on it. Dre smiled to himself then dived in.

"Ooooh Dre!"

Dre went to work until he felt her legs shaking and Tammy started calling out his name like she was in a trance. Dre quickly hopped out of his pants and boxers then entered her, as Tammy let out a soft moan. They rocked back and forth to the rhythm of the beat that was seeping through the walls, causing Tammy to get wetter and wetter with each stroke.

When Dre felt it coming, it felt too good to pull out this time. Dre climaxed, and Tammy welcomed it by grabbing him by his waist and pulling him tighter. For the first time in their lives, they were one.

They laid in each other arms panting and planting soft wet kisses on each other face until Dre pulled back to look into her eyes. A tear slid out the corner of Tammy's eye and Dre caught it with a kiss, "You know I love you right".

"I love you too", she said hugging him extra tight. "I wish you didn't have to go".

Dre smiled and said, "Me too".

The shared a laugh and Dre said, "Come on, we have to get back to the party before people start asking for us".

"I know right. You wanting to be all bad and stuff".

Dre busted out laughing, "Okay I'll take the heat for it, even though I remember the story was a little bit different from that".

"Whatever".

*****
———

De'Quan figured Shakia had to be five years older than him, and that might be the reason he never paid her any attention before. Older women never appealed to him that much like a woman his own age range. So why had he been watching Shakia all night then?

Shakia was a shade lighter than Dre and that was the closest the comparison came between the brother and sister pair. She had an ass and hips that made her co-worker droll at her all day, and a set of 36c cups that men stared at while they talked her. This always pissed Shakia off. She kept her weave intact and her nails stayed done. All of this made De'Quan question himself again – Why I didn't notice her before?

De'Quan played the corners as he watched Shakia move around the apartment. Getting her groove on out on the dance floor, mingling with the people that came in and out the door, and she kept the kitchen in order with every drunk and high person in the place asking her for something to eat every five minutes. Her people skills were surprising to De'Quan who never said more than hi and bye to Shakia in all the time he and Dre had been friends.

Having eye opening thoughts about his best friend sister was beginning to freak him out. De'Quan knew he needed to talk to somebody. He made his move through the party searching for somebody he could talk too in confidence about this.

De'Quan spotted Fat Pee and Ron-Ron over by the d.j. table talking to two brown sugar females and stepped over to them. Not wanting to bust their groove De'Quan stepped in and said, Hey, excuse me ladies for a second. I need to borrow Pee here for a moment and I'll send him right back".

The girls just gave De'Quan a whatever look as he put his arm around fat Pee's neck and guided him over to the side out of ear shot.

"Yo if you wit it we can get rid of that nigga Ron Ron and take turns on them chicks", Fat Pee said as he took a sip from his drink.

"Naw man, I got a problem".

Fat Pee thought it was beef and tried to quickly sober up, "Word, where they at. We can hit them".

De'Quan cut him off, "Naw man. It ain't that".

Fat Pee began to get restless, "Well spit it out nigga. This ain't no guessing game, what's happening".

De'Quan took one last look over his shoulder before he said, "Its Shakia man. I'm thinking about pressing her tonight".

"Fuck you mean press her?" Fat Pee asked with a confused look on his face.

"Look, I know that's Dre sister. That's why I had to talk to you about it. I've been eyeing her all night. I don't know if it's the fucking liquor, or that got damn perfume she's wearing, but every time she passes me shit feels crazy man".

To Fat Pee pussy was pussy, as long as it was above age, but this was close to home looking at each other sister. "Man, just ask her to dance. Can't much go down, cause she sees us as broke hoodlums who don't have a dime to our names. What's the worst that can happen from a dance to get her off your mind"?

*****
___

Two hours later the party was at its 2:45a.m. hour and De'Quan found himself in the bathroom doing the unthinkable.

"Oh shit! Oh shit!"

"Oh Quan fuck me. Fuck me!"

'Oh Shiittt!"

The world shook as they climaxed in harmony hard enough to almost break the sink off of the wall. The air stood still for what seemed like an eternity, until De'Quan's penis got soft and it slid out of Shakia. He stepped back and she slowly hopped off of the sink. They stood there for a moment just staring at each other until she broke the silence, "We can't let Dre know this happen".

"Aww, yeah…You're right", De'Quan said as he began to pull up his pants feeling embarrassed. She was his best friend sister and here she was making him promise to keep something from him.

"I have to use the bathroom", Shakia said.

"Oh yeah. Sure. I'm sorry, female thang right. I'll go", De'Quan fumbled with his words, then quickly got scarce.

Chapter 25

Since Dre had to turn himself in De'Quan tried to keep a low profile in the projects. He didn't want anyone getting any ideas because his partner in crime was on ice for a few months. Fat Pee always did his own thing outside of him hanging out with De'Quan and Dre, so it would not surprise De'Quan when he wouldn't hear from Fat Pee for a few days that usually meant some chick had his ear and they were laying up somewhere, but the thing that was troubling De'Quan was how Ne'Sean had been acting.

Since the robbery at Shaborn's house, Ne'Sean had seemed to be more closed in. Most days he would leave before De'Quan woke up, and afterschool Ne'Sean would become MIA for hours before finally showing up at the house and going straight to bed. Mama K was to focus on getting the store off the ground and making sure Meika stayed in eye sight to pay a lot attention to Ne'Sean and his constant mood swings, but not De'Quan. He had been watching his brother and he just wasn't himself anymore.

De'Quan needed to talk to Rahkem so he told him to meet him in the park. They sat on the bench and watched Ne'Sean and Jamel play a two on two game against duo who looked like they weren't any match for the much younger teammates.

"What the fuck you mean you had to spend a thousand dollars the other day Rah?' De'Quan asked heated. "You say the shit like it's okay to spend my dough on your escapades".

Rahkem was shaken by De'Quan's outburst. He figured he could take the money out like he did before and De'Quan wouldn't think nothing of it. Ever since Dre went to jail, De'Quan had been acting real up tight.

"Quan, I told you my brother was in a little trouble. You know he got a mad gambling problem, and them niggas was talking about killing him this time. That shit would break my mom's heart man if she found out I had a chance to save him and I didn't".

De'Quan lit up a cigarette and thought about what Rahkem was telling him as he kept his eyes on the basketball game.

"Rah you my man and all that, but don't try to play me son. We trusted you to hold that dough for us, and every time I turn around you got another situation going on in your crib that's costing us bread", De'Quan said clearly upset.

Sweat slid down the side of his face as he continued to explain himself, "Quan you know how my brother do. One week he's up and the next week he's fucked up. When he goes up next time, I'll make sure he puts the gee back".

De'Quan blew smoke in his face and said, "Yeah, you do that, and tell that nigga to go to AA or gamblers anonymous".

De'Quan looked back to the game just in time to see his brother score on a layup, "Yeah that's what I'm talking about".

Rahkem saw this as an opportunity to change the subject, "Yo Ne'Sean looks like he's getting better since last season".

De'Quan half listen to him, but still answered him, "Yeah, my bro is going to the pros one day".

"What's our count now Rah", De'Quan asked after a light silence.

"Like 27gees".

"You see Rah; this is where you be fucking up at. What the fuck you mean 'like'", De'Quan snapped.

"Come on Quan, it's just a roundabout number. The count is $27,670.00. Damn son, you need a blunt or something. You so uptight man".

De'Quan laughed to himself and said, "Yeah, I hear you. You better not be fucking with me Rah", and with that De'Quan hopped up off the bench and walked across the park to the court.

"Yo time out for a second. Sean I'm about to slide for a little while".

Ne'Sean passed the ball to Jamel and said, "Time out", and walked over to brother.

"I'm going to lay up somewhere for a little while. What's up you good, you need anything".

"Naw I'm good. I'm going to play for a little while then I'm going to take a shower".

"Alight. You know if you need to talk to me I'm here for you", De'Quan said wanting to break the mood, his brother has been carrying with himself for a few months now.

"Yeah I know bro".

"Yo I need you to find out what's good with Rahkem and his brother. And see if he been spending money on any of these chicks", De'Quan. Ne'Sean was always good info on people and not being on front street while he did it.

"Okay, I got you bro", Ne'Sean said and gave him a pound. Before he ran back over to the game he said, "Oh and tell Shakia I said hi".

"How the hell you know that's where I'm going?" De'Quan asked surprise his brother knew about his secret meetings with Shakia.

"Later Bro", Ne'Sean said with a chuckle and ran back to join his game.

De'Quan woke up one Sunday feeling like he needed to do something different. They had been getting away with the way they got big money in a short period of time without drawing any attention to themselves, but in order for them to really move around, they needed a vehicle to do that. If De'Quan started moving around now, by the time Dre came home, he can have something set up already.

After thinking about what he wanted to do for the day, De'Quan went into the kitchen and snuck up behind his mother.

"Muah", De'Quan planted a kiss on the side of his mother neck.

"Good morning baby".

"Ma can I borrow your car today?" De'Quan asked as he poured himself a cup of juice.

"To do what", She asked over her shoulder as she kept her eyes on the eggs she was frying.

"I want to go check something out at this store in Queens", De'Quan said as he sat down at the table.

"Check something out huh. Your check something's out be taking all night, and I want to close up the store at 8 tonight", Mama K said moving from the stove over to the counter to make their plates.

"Mama K I'll be back way before that".

"Ok, go wake your brother up", She said just as Meika shuffled into the kitchen rubbing her eyes. "Morning baby".

"Morning Mama", Meika said giving her a kiss and shuffling over to the table.

"He's not here".

"That boy left already on a Sunday", Mama K said giving them their plates.

"Nobody is in the park this early. He's probably down there shooting around", De'Quan said.

"Mama K I need some money", Meika said.

"Oh, so now I'm the ATM today", Mama K said as she poured Meika a cup of juice.

"No, but it's this shirt I want to buy for school. Ma, it's only 35 dollars ", Meika said ignoring her food.

"Oh yeah Erica Cane, if it's only 35 dollars, then why don't your rich self have the money", Mama K Joked as she sat down at the table.

Meika could not start eating until she had conformation on the shirt. "Oh, come on Ma, the shirt will go perfect with my D.K.N.Y. suit I want to wear. You know how it is Ma not to be matching and everybody is talking about you".

Mama K laughed and said, "So now I don't be matching and everybody be talking about me huh".

"No not you Mama. You know you the flyest mom in Brooklyn. I'm just saying, you know what I'm going through right now", Meika said.

Mama K thought for a moment then said, "Okay, I'll give you the money. But you have to go with your brother".

"What brother?" De'Quan asked with his mouth full of food.

"You...You said you're going shopping, or I should say checking things out at the store, so you can take your sister and she can grab her shirt. Everybody happy. Now Meika eat your food".

"Ma you can't be serious. Meika is going to cramp my style today", De'Quan said with a frown on his face".

"Boy you driving your Mama's car, you ain't got no style".

*****

"Where are we going Quan? I thought Mama K told you I had to buy a shirt off Fulton street", Meika said from the backseat of the car. She was steaming and wasn't afraid to let it be known.

To put Meika in the backseat, De'Quan picked up Q to take the ride with them to Queens. De'Quan figured he could put Meika in the back, turn up the music and tune her out. Today Meika wasn't having it so he had to set her straight before she really starting acting crazy.

"Look Mama K didn't say anything to me about Fulton street, cause she knew I was going to Queens today. Jamaica ave got all the same stuff as Fulton street anyway, so be easy", De'Quan said as he weaved Mama K's Honda through the light Interboro traffic.

Meika huffed and puffed but kept quiet. She knew when to push her brother buttons and when to leave him alone. De'Quan turned the music back up and they cruised to Queens.

They walked for an hour through the Coliseum and a couple of stores on 174 street until Meika found the perfect shirt.

Once he made sure his sister was straight, they got back into the car and drove down to 187 street and Jamaica avenue to 'Select your Car' dealership. When they pulled into the parking lot Meika went back into her investigative roll again.

"Why are we here? You going to buy a car?"

De'Quan laughed, "Damn little K, can I answer one question at a time".

"You are right. That's why we here, right", Meika eagerly pressed.

"Maybe, now you can stay in the car if you want, while I look around", De'Quan said as he opened his door to get out the car.

"No way Jose, I'm not staying in this car if you getting one of these", Meika said hopping out of the backseat.

De'Quan heard about 'Select your Car' dealership in the hood for having a nice selection of foreign cars at low prices if you had the cash on hand. Your paperwork would be fixed, and you will drive away without any problems. He wasn't too sure he would buy a car today, but just in case something caught his eye, De'Quan had $11,000 cash on him and Q who could drive his mother car back to Brooklyn.

They browsed through the car lot getting caught up in smell of every drug dealer dream sitting on chrome. B.M.W.'s, Benz's, Acura Legend's, Land Cruisers, and a few Jeep Cherokee's were just a few things they had shining on the lot.

"What type of joint you looking for?" Q asked.

"I don't know yet son, but when I see it, it'll hit me", De'Quan said as they kept walking through the aisle.

"Yeah I feel that, what about that three and a quarter over there?" Q asked.

"Yeah Quan, get a B.M.W.", Meika beamed as she stayed hot on his heels.

"Just because you want me to get one, don't mean I'm going to look good in it", De'Quan joked.

"Shit, ugly Sherry would look good in that three and a quarter", Q said.

"So what kind of car do you want?" Meika asked, and then said, "What about that red one over there?"

They walked over to the car and De'Quan felt it.

"Damn son, that shit is fly", Q said sizing the car up.

"Lexus GS300", De'Quan said as he stared at the front grill. Red with light tints on it and shiny factory rims on it. He walked over to the driver's side and scanned the price and mileage on the window.

Ron sipped on his cup of coffee and watched the lot from the confines of his office. From his window he can watch the reactions of people from afar, whether they showed interest in a particular car, or they are just browsing.

Ron watched two guys and a young girl hover around the Lexus, and thought it was time he made his move to see if their serious about it. He put down his cup, grabbed the master keys and stepped out into the lot expecting nothing, but always hoping for a sale.

"Good afternoon, my name is Ron. Can I help you?"

"My brother like this car", Meika said speaking for the small entourage.

Ron put on his winning smile and said, "Oh really".

"Yeah, looks real nice. How much are yah looking for?" De'Quan asked.

"Well this Lexus is in good condition, so we're looking for eleven-five. Would you be looking to put down a payment today?" Ron asked sizing De'Quan up. To many days, people come into the dealership just to ask a hundred questions and don't buy the car.

"I can do a lot can you open up the door?" De'Quan said ignoring his question.

"Oh yeah, sure", Ron said pulling out the keys. He gave De'Quan the key and let him open the door. He sat down and gripped the steering wheel to feel himself for a moment. Meika popped open the passenger side door and got in. De'Quan ignored her and scanned the dash board.

"Go ahead, start it up", Ron said as he stood in the doorway.

He started the car and it came right on. "Sounds good", Q said as he walked to the front. "Pop the hood Quan".

De'Quan popped the hood and looked at the lit-up dash, "53,000 miles on it".

"Yeah, and she handles these city bumps like a champ, trust me, my brother-in-law had one of these. Real nice car", Ron said.

Meika popped open the glove compartment and De'Quan snapped, "Close that, don't touch nothing, I didn't even buy it yet and you already touching shit that don't have nothing to do with you".

"Okay, damn. You don't have to yell", she said as she closed it and sat back in her seat with an attitude.

"Give it some gas", Q said from the front of the car.

De'Quan revved up the engine and couple of times until Q was satisfied. "Looks good, you said it got 50,000 on it".

"Yeah, and it smells like new money up in here son", De'Quan said feeling the excitement slowly creeping up on him. He got out the car and stepped over to Ron as Q sat behind the wheel.

"You said you want eleven-five for this."

"Yes, what does your credit look like?" Ron asked.

"How about I give you ten-five right now for the car? No credit check. Just me giving you the cash, and me driving away".

Ron had to laugh, "You got some balls Mr.?"

"De'Quan Short", he said as they shook hands for the first time.

"You got ten-five right now for this car, then we can do business", Ron said with a bright smile on his face.

De'Quan dug into one of his pocket's and pulled out a nice size brick rubber banded up. "Mr. Ron let's do business my man".

Chapter 26

De'Quan was beginning to feel the power of having your own car after riding around the city for three weeks. Now he felt it was time to flex that power at New York City elite night club The Tunnel. Q sat in the passenger seat with his Yankee hat pulled down low, while Ne'Sean rode in the back.

"Got damn son, look at all the chicks on the line", Ne'Sean beamed over the music playing in the car.

De'Quan rolled the Lexus down 27th street at 5 miles an hour so they could scope out the long line running up the side of the building, and the chicks on the line could see what they were sitting in. You couldn't tell De'Quan he wasn't a part of the New York elite now, and he didn't have to sell any drugs or put out a rap album to do it neither.

"Shit what Flex said, 'first five hundred bitches free'. Let me find a spot, I know that shit is already packed", De'Quan said.

The Tunnel was famous for Funk Master Flex spinning the latest hits every Sunday night. The hostess Mecca promoted the first 500 women free and the club was able to hold 3000 plus party goers, making The Tunnel New York City's grand finale to long party weekends.

Ne'Sean had never been in The Tunnel before, making his first glimpse of the large dance floor when they walked up in the club breath taking. Ne'Sean had been to plenty of house parties in his young years, but never to a club as large as this one. The three of them set up shop on the wall across from the bar and smoked blunt after blunt, soaking in the vibes and action that passed by them like a party train.

"I'm going to the dance floor to get up on some ass", Ne'Sean said as he broke away from his brother and Q.

"Aight. If you don't see us down here, then check upstairs", Q said over the load sounds of Mic Geronimo's 'I'm so High'.

Ne'Sean nodded his head then disappeared into the flow of the moving line that was headed toward the dance floor.

De'Quan bobbed his head to the music taking slow pulls off of his blunt when his vision was suddenly invaded by one of the baddest sisters he saw pass by him all night. Out of reflex, De'Quan stuck his hand out and gently grabbed her on her wrist. The girl froze, looked at his face real quick, and then stepped out of the moving line. The girl that was directly behind her also stepped off the moving line and by chance she had to occupy the small space that was in front of Q.

De'Quan leaned in close to her ear and said, "I didn't mean to grab you like that, but I could not let you pass me by without saying something".

She looked him up and down and liked red Polo teddy bear sweater and red Yankee hat set up he had going on. The club was to dark in the area for her to see what kind of sneakers he had on.

On the flip side of things, De'Quan was quickly analyzing the cutie he just pulled over. Versace shades, silk jacket, and he got a glimpse of a backside. Nice.

"Ok, so say something", she said snapping him out of his trance.

De'Quan smiled, "You a frisky one huh, my name is De'Quan".

"My name is India".

"Where you from India?" De'Quan asked pulling her closer to him.

"We're from Connecticut".

"Oh yeah, and what made yah come all the way down here on a Sunday night?" De'Quan asked.

"It's my birthday. So, I wanted to go where it was live at tonight", India said as she began to move her body to the beat.

"Oh word, you hear that Q, shorty here is a birthday girl", De'Quan said.

Q looked over from India's friend and said, "So I've heard."

De'Quan laughed and said, "You want to make a move to the bathroom".

"That will work", Q said then turned back to India's friend to give her an update.

"We never been here before, what's in the bathroom?" India asked.

De'Quan felt his stock rise to the ceiling. Bad chick - check, from out of town - check. It's her birthday, double check. She's got to be down for anything. De'Quan smiled and said, "Everything, couches, the bar, and more room to breathe".

India looked back at her friend who was all ears in their conversation and nodded her head.

"Lead the way then player", India said as De'Quan took her hand and did just that. He led the way through the live crowd that danced from the bar all the way up the lit-up steps, and down the hallway to The Tunnel's famous unisex bathroom, which had two full bars, couches lining the walls, and big speakers posted up in every corner. The bathroom itself began with a few sinks and mirrors, which lead off like a separate wing with close to thirty stalls in it.

The two couples found an empty couch off to the side next to the bathroom sinks and De'Quan asked her, "What you drinking?"

India smiled, "Whatever you have in mind".

De'Quan laughed and said, "Okay, we'll be back. Come on Q".

When De'Quan and Q walked away, India turned to her friend and said, "Kim what you think girl?"

"They cute, you think they getting money?"

"I think they're doing something, but it doesn't matter, it's my birthday and I just want to have a good time with some cool guy's".

At the bar, De'Quan and Q each ordered a bottle of Dom P, "what you think?"

Q popped in some tic-tac's and said, "Yo shorty was talking some things. We should try and fuck these chicks in the bathroom".

De'Quan thought about it and smiled, "word son, that way we don't have to pay for a hotel".

They both grabbed a bottle and two glasses and Q said, "Fuck it. Let's bet a buck to see who can fuck first up in here tonight".

They laughed and De'Quan said, "Hell yeah. That's a bet".

*****

The Dom P. and conversation flowed until India changed the subject, "I was thinking De'Quan, we should stop playing games and head into the stall and see what's good for tonight".

De'Quan tried his best to keep a straight face. Her directness caught him off guard, but he kept it smooth and said, "You know, we must have mental telepathy or something, because I was thinking the same thing".

"Or it might be something in this Dom P." India leaned in close to his ear, and purred in a sexy voice and continued, "Whatever it is, it has me extremely hot. Meet me in the last stall in five minutes".

India got up gently took Kim's hand and they disappeared into the stall wing of the bathroom. De'Quan and Q watched them walk away, then they looked at each other and smiled.

"This one might be a tie", De'Quan said.

Q laughed and said, "Fuck it, since you driving, I'll buy the breakfast. Now let's go handle this business".

De'Quan took a last swig of his Dom P. then stepped into the stall area. He walked down the short aisle that ended in a T shape and looked to his right. India was patiently waiting outside the last stall. De'Quan wandered over nonchalantly acting like he also was waiting for a stall to empty out.

Q wandered down to the top of the T and looked to his right. When he saw De'Quan and India waiting down that end, Q turned left figuring that had to be his route to go. Q was drunk but he was on point on what was supposed to go down. He staggered down the aisle not knowing where Kim was waiting at, but the fun and games were all good with him.

De'Quan stood two feet away from India laughing to himself as he watched Q's drunk ass wander down the aisle. He didn't hear the stall behind him open up, but he did catch a glimpse of somebody walk pass him. Before De'Quan could react, he felt a hand grab on his collar and pull him into the stall.

"Oh shit", De'Quan mumbled as India closed the stall door, dug under her skirt and pulled off her panties without any hesitation.

"Oh shit", De'Quan blurted out again as he stood frozen in the stall.

India moved in close and said, "You can't believe this is happening...can you".

Without waiting for his answer, India took charge and began to undo his belt and zipper. De'Quan quickly snapped out of it and pulled out his condom. India turned around put one foot on the toilet bowl, and one hand on the stall door. She put her other hand on the connecting stalls wall and arched her back. De'Quan stood back and watched her ass cheeks spread open like they had a mind of their own.

In the background, De'Quan heard the d.j. put on Mobb Deep's Shook Ones part2 as he was entering India from the back. The club erupted in a load roar like they were cheering him on. In his mind, De'Quan was doing this for all of mankind and he had to represent as he rocked to India's rhythm, while she bounced to Shook Ones part2.

India was in a zone as she stroked De'Quan's over excited ego with her moaning and dirty talk, "Ooooh, get this pussy nigga. Ooooh, get this pussy nigga".

Then he felt it. The point when he knew he should have pulled out of her, but he was at the point of no return, and it felt so good, De'Quan couldn't stop himself. Just a few more seconds and it will be over. They both began to climax at the same time, with India almost pulling down the stall connecting wall. De'Quan's knees buckled and he almost lost his balance.

De'Quan put his back against the wall to catch his breath, as India's shoe slipped on the toilet and she stepped inside of it with a big splash. "Shit".

As much as De'Quan wanted to laugh, his mind was somewhere else. They gave each other as much space as they could in the small stall and De'Quan gave her his back. He looked down at his dick and he was right about the feeling he felt. The condom broke.

He dropped the rest of the condom in the toilet and flushed it, and then he fixed his pants. When De'Quan turned around India was gone. At first, he thought he just had a good ass dream, but then her scent rose up off of his sweater. It was real, but where did she go so fast he asked himself as he stepped out in the T shape corridor and bumped into a girl who looked like she was on the verge of throwing up. She pushed pass De'Quan and quickly shut the door behind herself.

De'Quan walked down to the other side of the T, "Yo Q".

When De'Quan didn't get an answer, he walked down to the last stall and saw that the door was half open. He pushed it open and was shocked to see Q sitting on the toilet with his pants down to his ankles, passed out.

"Shit, Yo Q, get the fuck up son. Aww man this shit is crazy", De'Quan said smacking Q hard enough to wake him up.

"What the fuck man!"

"Man, pull your damn pants up so we can get out of here. Look at you man, I wish I had a camera", De'Quan said as he backed out of the stall and started laughing.

Q closed the stall and got himself together. The toilet flushed and Q emerged feeling disorientated, "Fuck is so funny".

De'Quan lit up a cigarette and said, "You might owe me a hundred dollars, that's what".

"How you figure that?"

"Because I bet you don't even remember if you fucked shorty or not", De'Quan said.

Q looked around to make sure nobody was listening to their exchange and said, "I fucked her. Why else would my pants be down like that".

"Because she fucked you!" De'Quan said and they burst out laughing. "Yo let's go find Ne'Sean and get up out of here".

Chapter 27

"Hello?"

"What's up Meika, its Dre. Is your brother there?"

"No, but Ne'Sean is here. You want to talk to him?"

"Yeah", Dre said and waited for him to come on the other line.

"Hello".

"What's the deal Dunn", Dre said.

"Yo what up Dre, how you doing in there?" Ne'Sean said.

Dre shifted in his seat and said, "Ain't nothing, just holding shit down. What's up with Quan?"

"Oh, he went away for a few days to go see Pop up in Clinton. You know he copped a Lexus, so that nigga been all over the place. I didn't even see him before he left".

"Damn, he didn't leave anything for me?" Dre asked.

Ne'Sean thought about it for a second, then said, "Nah, not that I know of. Like I said, I didn't see him before he left. Why you need some money or something?"

"Nah, I need you to make a run for me to this chick crib in Brownsville. She's waiting for Quan to bring it to her, but since he's gone I need you to give it to her".

"What you want me to bring her?" Ne'Sean asked as he grabbed a pen and paper.

"I need like ten body bags from Lewis, you feel me?" Dre said hoping he wouldn't have to break it all down to Ne'Sean over the phone.

Ne'Sean went into his room and went into his brother money stash. "Okay. I got some dough out of Quan's stash. Give me her number and address and I'll take it to her tonight".

Dre breathed a sigh of relief and gave him the info. When he hung up the phone, Dre walked to the back of the dorm and sat down on his bunk. Since he's been on the end side things had been going smooth for Dre. He had one fight his first day in the dorm for phone time. Once some of the other Brooklyn boys saw Dre could hold his own they welcome him with open arms and he hasn't had any problems since.

Dre stayed in contact with De'Quan whenever he could catch him in the house and he kept Dre up on what was going on in the hood. The gossip was cool with Dre but lately he had been feeling like they needed to do more with their lives. They had a nice stash of dough in Rahkem's house and Dre kept his separate stash with Tammy. Nobody wanted to leave any money in Dre's house without him being there, so Dre wasn't surprised to hear De'Quan brought a car. The last hit they did gave them a lot of breathing room to buy things they wouldn't normally buy. Dre knew if he was home he would done the same thing. Sitting in jail had him thinking they had to change that way of thinking or else they're going to be robbing drug dealers until they're old and grey.

Tammy stuck to her word and came through to see him no less than two days a week. Those hour visits were tough on the both of them at first, but once Dre got himself situated in the dorm he was able to focus more on their relationship and how far they could go if he came home with good plan.

"Yo what's good kid, what you thinking about?" Black Cee asked Dre snapping him out of his trance.

"What I'm going to do when I get out of here. Can't think about nothing else", Dre said.

"Soon as we smoke that next batch your mind is going to be somewhere else", Black Cee said and handed Dre a cigarette. "Here, bust me down".

"Yeah, I just called my man and he wasn't there, but I got his brother to drop it off to her. So, make sure Macho calls her, cause they're going over there tonight".

"Okay, how much they giving her?" Black Cee asked.

"Ten 20bags from Lewis", Dre said in-between pulls of the cigarette.

"Okay, I'm on him", Black Cee said as he stood up, took the half of cigarette from Dre and walked off to go handle his business.

That's why Dre liked Black Cee; he was all about his business. Dre could tell all Black Cee did in the streets was hustle. The first night Dre was in the dorm he beat a kid up in the bathroom for some phone time and Black Cee was the first one to pull Dre to the side and told him how the Brooklyn boys stuck together in there. Dre didn't want any free rides so he told Black Cee he came in with some dope and weed on him and he wanted to sell some to get some food and other necessities before they went to commissary. Black Cee hustled off all the dope and they smoked the weed, and they've been partners ever since.

Black Cee found Macho; whose girl was willing to bring in more drugs for him, and Dre had De'Quan drop the drugs off at Macho's girl house. Everything was going smooth until De'Quan brought the car and stopped coming home as much to catch his calls. Catching Ne'Sean in the house and getting him to make the run for him was the shot in the arm they needed, because they ran out of weed two weeks ago and Macho was short to go home. So getting a big package will be just what the doctor ordered to hold them down for a little while.

$$*****$$

When Ne'Sean hung up the phone with Dre, he called Jamel and asked him to make a run with him. Jamel was sitting in the house bored out of his mind, so he didn't have to ask him twice. Ne'Sean got dress and put on one of his brother leather jackets. He went into one of the Nike boxes and took one of De'Quan 9mm's and tucked it in his inside jacket pocket. Ne'Sean usually didn't like carrying guns, but he was no fool. Brownsville is a very harsh place at night.

Ne'Sean met Jamel downstairs and the hailed a cab. On their way to Lewis and Halsey to pick up the weed, Jamel pestered Ne'Sean the whole time about the trip being more than a business run for his brother while he was gone.

"Is she going to have any friends over there?"

"Jamel, I don't even know what the chick looks like", Ne'Sean said sounding uninterested.

"That don't mean she's not going to have any friends over there", Jamel said. He knew only good things could happen to them for stepping in for De'Quan.

"From what Dre told me shorty got a man or some shit like that", Ne'Sean said as he stared out the window.

"Jamel's face lit up, "Where, in jail with Dre? Aww man, that's even better. Her man is locked up and she's horny, don't you see".

Wondering what the hell made him bring Jamel on this mission, Ne'Sean said, "No, I don't see. Look we're in and out of there. I don't like being around them Brownsville niggas. Them niggas steal sneakers off dead people feet".

Jamel laughed and said, "You ain't lying about that, but don't be surprised if we walk in there and there's three Goddesses in there ready to get busy".

"Yeah I hear you", Ne'Sean said before he hopped out the cab to go grab the weed.

When they pulled up in front of 312 Saratoga Ne'Sean tried to get the cab driver to wait for them.

"Sorry boss, I'm not waiting for my mother out here longer than a New York minute. That will be 15dollars please", the cab driver said ready to get out of dodge.

Once Ne'Sean knew it was a lost cause he paid the man and they made their way to the building. As they walked past the late-night stares and glares from the people hanging out in the front, Jamel thought he saw saliva dripping from the corners of a few of the guys mouths. Jamel tried to keep his vision straight as he followed Ne'Sean into the building.

When they got on the elevator, Jamel said, "Damn Sean, them niggas looked thirsty as hell out there".

"Don't worry; I got one of Quan's biscuits on me. So, you don't have to tuck in your spaghetti chain", Ne 'Sean joked.

"Real funny", Jamel said as the elevator door popped open and they walked to the apartment door. Ne'Sean knocked on the door and the music that was playing inside turned down a little.

"Who is it?"

"Ne'Sean, is Ebony home?"

The door was opened, and Ebony looked surprised to see two people standing at her door, "Who is this?"

Ne'Sean stared at her for a second was taken aback by her beauty. Ebony's hair was pinned up in a dubee style, which brought out her smooth facial features. Ebony stood behind the door only revealing her face looking from Ne'Sean to Jamel.

"Oh, this is my friend Jamel".

Jamel put on his winning smile and waved to her. She looked him up and down then opens the door wider to let them in, "Sit on the couch".

When they sat on the couch, they were able to see what Ebony was wearing and it made both of their hearts skip a beat. Ebony was wearing a red silk Victoria Secret robe that was only thigh high and revealed more than she was supposed to be showing at the moment. The boys sat there stuck.

Ebony was thick for her 5'2 frame and whenever she walked, it looked like the robe was threatening to show more of her ass with every step she took. "So you got that?"

Ne'Sean snapped out of the trance she had them in and said, "Aww yeah".

"Come put it on the table", Ebony ordered as she sat at the dining table.

Ne'Sean dumped the ten bags on the table and he was caught by her powerful scent. It smelled intoxicating.

"You smoke?" She asked Ne'Sean.

"Nah".

"What about your friend?" She asked and they both looked over to Jamel. He quickly nodded his head.

Ebony walked over to the stereo and grabbed a bag of weed and philly blunt off the top of it. Her walk from the stereo over to Jamel was so seductive he caught himself catching a minor hard on.

"Here, roll this up", Ebony ordered handing it to Jamel.

Ne'Sean wasn't feel the direction this simple drop off was going, so he tried to stop it, "Ebony we need to call a cab, if that's okay with you".

Jamel snapped at Ne'Sean, "Damn Sean what's the rush. After this blunt we can call a cab".

Ebony walked over to Ne'Sean and touched his chest, "Yeah Ne'Sean, what's the rush? It's only 9:30, I know you don't have to run home this early".

Ne'Sean's heart felt like it was about to explode out of his chest. She was making him high off of her scent and the closer she moved in the more nervous he got. He looked over to Jamel, who looked like he didn't know whether to roll the blunt or watch them. Ebony slowly licked the side of Ne'Sean's ear. At that moment, Jamel knew it was going down; he ripped the wrapper off of the philly and went to work on the blunt.

Ne'Sean blushed and said, "Aww, can I have some juice?"

"Sure baby", Ebony said in the sexiest voice Ne'Sean ever heard and strutted into the kitchen.

Ne'Sean got up and went over to the couch. The nervous look on his face told on him before he could say it, "Yo man, did you see what she did to me?"

Jamel was all smiles, "I told you it was going down tonight, just chill man".

Ebony came out of the kitchen with two glasses of red kool-aid and gave it to them. She turned the music up a notch and sat on the couch in-between them. She gave Jamel the lighter and they sat there smoking until Ne'Sean was nice off the contact. Feeling good Ebony got up and started dancing in front of them. She could tell from the look on Jamel's face he wasn't leaving no matter what. Ne'Sean still looked confused about what was happening.

Ebony reached out and took Ne'Sean's hand, pulling him off of the couch, "Dance with me".

276

The dancing turned to grinding in the middle of the living room floor, while Jamel drooled on himself watching the show. Ebony stuck her down Ne'Sean's pants and grabbed on his penis like she owned it. He opened up her robe and started playing with her coco brown 36c's knowing there was no turning back now.

She undid his pants and started sucking on his penis as Jamel watched in shock. Ne'Sean was totally lost in the moment as he fucked her face like they were the only people in the room. When he came Ebony swallowed every drop causing Ne'Sean's knees to buckle.

"Oh shit", He fell to the floor tangled up in his own pants from not taking them off and stared at Ebony as she moved on to Jamel like a professional porn star.

Jamel was so excited he almost came in his pants before she even touched him. Ebony went in a small drawer and pulled out a condom. "Pull your pants down", she told Jamel, who wasted no time undoing his belt and pants. She put the condom on him, pulled her panties off and took Jamel on the ride of his life until they both climaxed.

"You can call that cab now", Ebony said before walking off to the bathroom, leaving Ne'Sean and Jamel stunned and spent in her living room.

Ne'Sean and Jamel waited for the elevator in silence, lost in his own thoughts about what just happen. When they stepped onto the elevator, Jamel broke the silence, "Now that session was official!"

They started laughing and Ne'Sean said, "Yo don't tell De'Quan what happen up there. He's going to flip if he finds out we did the drop instead of him, and Ebony turned out to be cold freak".

"What, are you serious? You think Quan ain't fuck that chick too? She's a freak son, I know De'Quan hit that", Jamel said feeling confident about what he was saying. The elevator stopped on the first floor and Jamel pushed the outer door open to walk out first. When he stepped out into the lobby, a hand suddenly reached out and snatched his chain.

"Oh shit!" Jamel blurted out as he fell back into Ne'Sean, and they fell back into the elevator. Ne'Sean stepped back and pulled out the 9mm as they both rushed back off of the elevator and watched the tail end of the chain snatcher running up the stairs.

"That motherfucker snatched my shit!"

Jamel flinched like he was going to run after him, but Ne'Sean quickly grabbed his arm, "Nah son, fuck that shit. Let's get the fuck out of here".

"What…That nigga got my shit!" Jamel said fuming from the incident.

"Man, that shit ain't worth it and this might be a set up. Let's get the fuck out of this neighborhood", Ne'Sean said. He looked out the front window of the building and saw the cab sitting by the curb with the engine running.

Ne'Sean put the gun back inside his coat and they walked out of the building past the same group that was out there when they came in. Jamel open the cab door and hopped in while Ne'Sean watched his back.

"Nostrand and Park", Ne'Sean told the driver as he stuffed a twenty-dollar bill through the bullet proof partition.

When the driver pulled away from the curb, a shot rang out causing Ne'Sean and Jamel to duck, and cab driver to step on the gas pedal. The crowd in front of the building shared a laugh as they watched the cab screech around the corner and out of sight.

Chapter 28

Dre being locked up gave De'Quan a lot of solo time to drive around and think about how his life is supposed to go moving forward. De'Quan had been spending more time than he wanted with Shakia, so getting a car was a good move for him. Shakia was crazy, sexy, and cool all wrapped into a nice package they both knew De'Quan couldn't unwrap, because he was Dre best friend and she his sister. The attraction was there, but the reality of the situation as a whole wasn't. Once De'Quan got the car he kept Shakia at arms distance with a million excuses of places to go and people to see, until he took the long drive to go see Pop.

A lot has changed for De'Quan since Pop went to prison, and not being able to talk to him about it was killing him. Pop was moved to Clinton Correctional Facility, a one hundred year old maximum security prison 20 minutes from the Canadian border to the north, and seven hours from New York City. Making the trip by himself would be good for the both of them, De'Quan was pretty sure Pop had a lot to discuss with him, and having Mama K, Ne'Sean and Meika on the visit would not work out right.

De'Quan pulled into the closest town to the prison and grabbed a room in a motel 6 to get some rest. The next morning he drove over to Clinton got processed, and was on the visit floor by 10:15 a.m.

During a week day, the visit room would be light when it came to activity, with the heavier traffic coming in on the weekends. De'Quan made a Tuesday his first visit day, and he planned on staying in the motel 6 for the rest of the week.

De'Quan had to check in with one of the ugliest women he had ever seen at the c.o. desk on the visiting floor, and he was seated at a table close to a window by another officer. De'Quan brought a few things out of the vending machines, and it turned out the wait for Pop to come out took longer than the actual processing De'Quan went through to get in. Hunger took over and De'Quan ended up eating half the food before Pop could check in at the same c.o. desk he had too. When he strolled over to where his son was waiting for him, Pop's face lit up.

"Damn boy, you're almost bigger than me now", Pop said as the hugged and sat down. Pop looked at the garbage on the table and said, "And I see you ate up everything already".

De'Quan smiled, "Man, I was starving Pop, what you want from the machines?"

Pop looked at a few things that were still untouched and grabbed a cheese Danish. "I'm good with this for now, so how was your drive?"

"How did you know I drove here?' De'Quan asked looking puzzled.

Pop laughed and said, "I called your mother the other day, but she didn't tell me you was coming".

"Pop I have something for you", De'Quan said as he shifted in his seat.

Pop didn't expect anything from his son but good news and a good laugh, "What you got?"

"I got some Lewis and Halsey in one thing, and some Hancock and Evergreen in the other. You can mix it up if you want, but trust me, they're both banging separately", De'Quan said with a sly smile on his face.

Pop didn't like what he was hearing.

"Look, you didn't have to bring me none of that. The last thing I need is for you to get into trouble over some petty shit".

De'Quan knew Pop was going to beef with him about bringing him the weed, but he wanted to show Pop he was all grown up now. "Pop I know, but I got this, don't worry about it".

Pop shifted in his seat. The boy is hard headed like somebody he knows. "Alright, don't be doing this shit all the time; these crackers are crazy up here. Go to the machines and heat me up two fish and cheese sandwiches. Put them things in a bag of chips over there while you wait. And watch the fat chick, she's miserable and likes to fuck with people".

De'Quan did what Pop told him to do and when he returned to the table Pop sent him back to the machine for a bottle of water. While the c.o.'s sitting at the desk watched De'Quan and the rest of the visitors at the machines, Pop stuffed the two balloons of weed in his drawers.

When De'Quan finally sat down, they got into a long conversation about the house, and what was happening in the store on a daily basis. Pop sat there and listened to his son, thinking of a good time to ask him about his dealings in the streets. Many nights, he laid up in a cell and thought about the path his oldest son was on.

"De'Quan I need you to be straight with me okay", Pop said once he felt they were comfortable.

De'Quan shook his head yes. He knew it was coming. No matter how many times he went over it in his mind about what he was going to say to his father when the time came, he still didn't know how he was going to tell him what he has been doing in his absence.

"I've been investigating you and your friend's for a while now, and the only thing I know for sure is yah are not selling any drugs in Marcy. Which is a good thing, but people don't just buy G.S.300's out of nowhere without having a job. So fill me in Quan.

"Remember, you're my son, and I understand more than you probably think, but don't lie to me. Now start from the top", Pop said looking his son straight in the eyes.

De'Quan took a deep breath and said, "Pop when you got knocked, I knew I was the man of the house. I didn't want us to have to ask nobody in that projects for nothing. Me and Dre talked about it and we knew we didn't want to sell drugs. It takes up too much time and everybody is in your business.

"I found one of your guns and we used it to rob a bodega", De'Quan said and watched Pop's reaction before he continued.

Pop did not want to show too much emotion until he heard all of his son sins, but he had to flinch when De'Quan said they had been out doing robberies. He thought they were selling drugs in another projects or boro.

"We did a couple of places, brought more guns, and saved up most of the money. Then Grand-Ma Trina's house caught fire, we didn't even know it was money in there. So we did a big hit and gave Mama K the money for the store and we still had something left over", De'Quan said.

"So now that Dre is in jail, what are you doing?" Pop asked.

"I haven't done anything. I can't see myself moving without Dre Pop. I know he got my back and I got his", De'Quan said confidently.

Pop let it all soak in then asked, "Is your brother running around with yah?"

De'Quan knew Pop was going to ask him that, and he also knew Pop would not swallow Ne'Sean being in the streets with him and his friends. He told himself on the drive up there he will have to lie about Ne'Sean's involvement.

"Nah Pop, Ne'Sean is about to go to college and all that soon. There's no way we want him running with us".

"Okay, so now that you have all of this free time on your hands, why haven't you gone to a trade school or something like Mama K asked? These streets aren't promised to anyone as you can see".

"I know Pop...I mean I heard Mama K, but it's like..."

De'Quan stopped in mid-sentence and Pop could see his son was struggling with his inner demons. "I know it is hard son to hold down the family while I'm in here, and living in Brooklyn makes things worst. See son we come from a world where the Real Always Wins.

"You come from a winning blood line, but the times have changed, and the hood is changing right before our eyes. We have to change with it. You already have the vision because you knew it wasn't good timing to go out into the projects and sell drugs after I got locked up for it.

"But I expect you to spend that Real energy you have on something that has a better future for the family, than the one I choose", Pop said as De'Quan hung on his every word.

Pop was always a good teacher to his children and all of the reading he was doing in prison made him feel like he had so much to give them now from it. "Are you driving back home today?"

"Nah, I'm going to stay up here for a few days", De'Quan said looking at the clock.

"Okay good. Then I guess that's enough preaching for today. The visit is over in ten minutes anyway", Pop said.

They talked until the c.o. at the desk stood up and said, "Alight...Visits are over".

Pop shook his head and said, "What I tell you, she's miserable, I'll see you tomorrow son".

"Cool Pop", De'Quan laughed as they hugged, and Pop went back through the thick steel gates.

Chapter 29

With De'Quan being out of town, Rahkem was feeling a burst of energy to go out and splurge a little with De'Quan and company money. The way Rahkem was seeing it, De'Quan just brought a car before he left, so he won't miss a few hundred dollars.

Rahkem stepped out on Fulton Street and brought himself a new Polo outfit, and a pair of Reebok. Once he went home to change, Rahkem took a cab over to Patchen and Quincy to pick up a honey complexion sister named Diamond. Rahkem was feeling lucky tonight, and if his luck was right he might get some Kat from Diamond, or even her real name before the night is over.

Diamond came downstairs did up in a Banana Republic jean suit that hugged every curve God blessed her with. Rahkem broke out in a sweat just watching her walk over to the cab. They went downtown to 44th street to Beefsteak Charlie's, got down on plates of the chicken and shrimp combo, and sipped on long Island ice teas. The conversation flowed and they laughed at each other's jokes like they really enjoyed each other's company.

After diner, they went down to 42nd street to see the new hip-hop movie out called 'The Show'. She was feeling it, he wasn't.

All this pampering gave Rahkem a reason to get bold on her when they got in the cab and dictate the next destination. "We are going to Marcy and Flushing".

Diamond sat back without protesting. If he wanted to go to his house instead of hers, then that was fine with her. Diamond had it on her mind to see where Rahkem lived at anyway, since he was talking all this Willy stuff to her like he making some real money.

As they got off the elevator on Rahkem's floor, they see his brother Tye backing out of the house with a small book bag in his hand. "What's up Tye, what you doing here?"

Rahkem's voice startled Tye, he turned around and slowly put on his vote for me smile and said, "well, well, well who you have here lil bro?"

Feeling good, smelling good, and now his brother was bigging him up for the piece he just brought home. Rahkem knew this was his night. He smiled and said, "This here is Diamond. Diamond this is my brother Tye".

Five seconds of awkward silence filled the hallway as Diamond smiled at Tye, and Tye thought about his getaway.

"What's in the bag Tye?" Rahkem asked after staring at the bag.

For a moment, Tye felt like a cornered cat, and then the thought hit him. Rahkem can't beat him. Tye looked from his brother over to Diamond, licked his lips and said, "I came to pick something up, why?"

Rahkem began to feel queasy inside as bells started going off in his head. "What you came to pick up?"

"None of your business", Tye blasted as his muscles tensed up.

Rahkem and Diamond stood there frozen as Tye tried to push pass them and get to the elevator. Rahkem knew what was in the bag. He just didn't know how much, and he wasn't trying to find out later. Rahkem reached out and tried to snatch the bag out of Tye's hand. Anticipating his little brother might try something stupid; Tye pulled the bag back and hit Rahkem with a left hook to his jaw.

"What the fuck you doing?"

Rahkem crumbed to the floor. "What you do that for?" Rahkem cried out as Diamond jumped back saying, "Oh shit".

Tye told himself fuck the elevator and made his getaway to the stairs. Diamond reached down to Rahkem to help him up, "Oh my God, are you alright?"

Disgusted with himself for letting his brother play him like that, Rahkem let her help him up and he quickly dusted himself off. He made a dash for the stairs and took them two at a time down to the lobby. By the time Rahkem made out the front of the building the only people walking around were crack heads and the project night life. Rahkem didn't know what to do. He walked back into the building and the elevator suddenly open to ruin the rest of his night.

Diamond stepped off the elevator and said, "Aww, I'm sorry Rahkem, but I gots to go".

Rahkem touched his soar jaw and said, "Hold on Diamond that was about nothing. Me and my brother fight all the time".

"That's good and all, but I'm still going home", Diamond said with her mind made up already.

"Come up stairs, and I can call you a cab", Rahkem said, trying one last push to keep her with him.

Diamond bushed him off and made her way through the front door, "Nah that's okay, I'll catch a cab on the ave. Call me sometime".

"Shit!"

From the lobby all the way up to his room all Rahkem could think about is damage control. When he got into his room, he ran straight to where he had the money stashed at. Tye took everything. Damage control quickly turned into Rahkem sitting on the edge of his bed, putting his face in his hands and crying.

*****

The next day Ne'Sean and Jamel were in the park sitting on the benches with their girl-friends when a distraught looking Rahkem came into the park.

"Hey what's up yah…Ne'Sean can I talk to you for a minute?"

Karman looked from Rahkem to Ne'Sean, and he smiled at her, "It's okay baby". Ne'Sean kissed her and said, "I'll be right back".

When they were out of ear shot Rahkem said, "My brother did it".

Ne'Sean was already bored with this story. Rahkem's jaw was swollen and the way Ne'Sean saw it everybody fights with their older brother. "So, what do you want with me?"

Rahkem shifted in his stance, he just got there, and he was already losing his audience, he swallowed hard and said, "Listen man, I don't know how Quan is going to take this, but my brother took the money".

"He did what? Where the fuck is he?" Ne'Sean barked, clearly upset about the news.

"I don't know, I've been looking for that nigga all night and all day, today", Rahkem whined.

"You know you done fucked up right", Ne'Sean said ready to bust Rahkem upside his head.

"Ne'Sean please talk to your brother and them for me, I'm sorry this happen man, I swear", Rahkem said right to break down aging.

Just for him begging Ne'Sean lost his cool and smacked him on the other side of his face. "What you do that for?"

Ne'Sean was furious with how soft Rahkem was, "Man snap out of it. You standing up here crying like some bitch. Just be cool. When De'Quan comes back we'll fix this, now where does your brother live at?"

Rahkem told him and Ne'Sean said, "Aight take your ass home and wait for us to call you". Rahkem nodded his head like an obedient dog and ran off with his tail between his legs.

Ne'Sean went back over to the benches and kissed Karman, "What happen baby?"

"I have to go take care of some business for my brother", Ne'Sean said not wanting to say too much. Ne'Sean liked Karman a lot but she didn't know about how they got their money.

"But I thought we were going upstairs for a little while today?" Karman asked with her bottom lip poking out. She pulled him close to her and started kissing on his ear. Karman's heavy breathing caused Ne'Sean to get a small tingle in his pants, and he knew he had to control himself for now.

"I'll try and be back in an hour, okay".

Karman batted her eyes and said, "Okay, but if you not coming back, you better call me".

He smiled and said, "Okay, yo Jamel we got to bounce".

Jamel looked up from kissing his girl-friend on her neck, with a lost look in his eyes and said, "What, I thought we were going to slide upstairs".

"Yeah, but something came up. Sorry about this Sky, but we'll be back". Ne'Sean said and led the way out of the park while Jamel reluctantly followed.

On the walk to his house, Ne'Sean filled Jamel in on what happened and what he planned on doing about it. Jamel wanted to go back to the benches and finish what he started with Sky, but Ne'Sean was his brother from another mother and no matter crazy Ne'Sean's plans sound to him, Jamel had to go hold him down.

"Here put this on", Ne'Sean said handing Jamel a black hoody.

Jamel took the hoody and started getting second thought's, "Yo man, I don't know why we can't just wait until De'Quan comes back. He'll…"

"Check it Jamel, you my dawg right?" Ne'Sean snapped at him.

"Yeah, but I…"

"Then stop crying about it. I know what I'm doing, and I want to catch this nigga before he spends all the dough". Ne'Sean went underneath the bed and pulled out a Timberland box with four guns in it and a few boxes of bullets as he continued with his rant.

"We'll be in and out of there. You think I want to have a conversation with this nigga, I just want our dough back, that's it".

Ne'Sean loaded up two 9mm's and he handed one to Jamel. He took a $140 out the box for himself and he gave Jamel $60. "What's this for?"

Ne'Sean rolled his eyes, "Just in case we get separated, duuhhh. Now you got dough to get back to the crib. Now let's go".

On their way to Nostrand Avenue to catch a cab, Ne'Sean saw a crack head he knew had a car. "What's up Dornell, what you doing right now?"

Dornell scratched his dirty beard and said, "I ain't doing shit, why, what's up little nigga?"

"You still got a car?"

"Yeah, why you want to go somewhere?" Dornell asked licking his lips. He hadn't had a hit all day and he knew these kids didn't sell drugs, which meant they could pay him in cash, even better.

"Let us hold your car for an hour, and I'll hit you with $30 dollars", Ne'Sean said.

"Aww man Ne'Sean, I can't give your little ass my car. Yah little niggas will probably wrap my shit around a stop sign. I can drive you though", Dornell said.

Ne'Sean thought to himself 'it was worth a try', he didn't a driver's license anyway. "Aight…but you only getting twenty now".

Dornell didn't care; as long as he had twenty dollars in his pocket when they were done, he was good. "Okay, let's go".

Dornell had a four door 84 Buick that had ashes, empty soda cans, and old food wrappers all over the place. Ne'Sean and Jamel kicked some of the garbage out into the street before hopping in.

Dornell pulled from the curb with a little screech and Jamel found himself sitting in the backseat counting the cigarette burns on the seat. "Damn Dornell, why don't you clean this piece of shit up some time", Jamel said breaking the silence.

"Word son, what do you be thinking about, turn left here", Ne'Sean said as he kept his eyes on the road.

Dornell navigated to the left and said, "Man why you got to talk about my wheels like that. She gets me where I need to go with no problems".

"Well if you keep using her as a garbage can she going to go on strike on your ass on a cold winter night", Jamel said sparking a round of laughs from Ne'Sean and Dornell.

"Pull over here", Ne'Sean said pointing to a parking space. Dornell pulled over to the side and Ne'Sean said, "Wait right here. You leave, and you won't get a bonus".

"Why would I leave without my money anyway?" Dornell asked, but his question was ignored as his passengers got out and walked around the corner out of sight.

Tye lived on St. James in a ten family tenement building. The small lobby door locks were broken so they walked right in. "How do you know where you going?" Jamel asked.

Ne'Sean looked over his shoulder as they walked up the stairs and said, "His brother told me stupid, now keep your voice down".

"Why they don't have an elevator in here?" Jamel mumbled to himself as he followed his friend up to the fourth floor.

The dark color walls made the lights on the landing feel dimmer than they were. Ne'Sean walked over to apartment 4a and put his ear to it. Jamel sucked his teeth and said, "What's with the private eyes shit man, just knock on the door".

Ne'Sean gave him the evil eye and pulled out his gun. "Okay smart ass".

He knocked on the door and heard nothing but the sounds of people in the other apartments. After knocking three more times, Ne'Sean gave up and was ready to leave when someone came up the dimly lit staircase. Ne'Sean and Jamel froze as the figure stopped on the landing below and stared up at the two hooded teens.

Ne'Sean couldn't see his face, so he took a shot in the dark and said, "What's up Tye?"

Tye dropped the bag of groceries he was carrying and reached in his waist band for his recently purchased 38 revolver.

"Oh shit!" Jamel blurted out as he tried to scramble in the small hallway.

Ne'Sean already had his gun in his hand, but he didn't anticipate having to use it in a split second situation. He raised it and let off a shot out of fear as he scrambled in the direction Jamel did.

"Shit...little fuck", Tye snarled as he let off three shots in their direction. The gun fire were deafening on the staircase as sounds of panic could be heard coming from the surrounding apartments.

"They shooting! They shooting! Get down...get down!"

"Aww", Jamel cried out as he fell on the stairs. Feeling the heat Ne'Sean turned around and let off four shots at Tye. Tye quickly turned on his heels and dipped down the stairs two at a time.

Ne'Sean turn to Jamel who was gripping his ankle, "Damn son what happen?"

"Shit man, I think I broke my ankle", Jamel said with a pained look on his face.

"Come on son, we have to get out of here, can you walk?" Ne'Sean asked as he helped him up.

"I'm a try", Jamel said, and they began to work their way down the stairs. When they reached the first floor Ne'Sean put his gun in his hand as Jamel held onto his shoulder. He limped out the front door and Tye was nowhere in sight. The faint sounds of a siren sound like it was making its way over into their direction.

"Come on man we got to breeze", Ne'Sean said as Jamel put a pep in his step. When they got to the car Dornell saw the gun in Ne'Sean's hand and almost peed on himself.

"Aww man, what's going on? What happened to him?"

Ne'Sean helped Jamel in the car and quickly hopped in, "Man just drive this motherfucker".

Dornell started up the car and quickly pulled out of the spot, "Where too man", he asked with a nervous look on his face.

"Jamel you think you need to go to a hospital?" Ne'Sean asked not knowing what to do.

"Nah man, let's just go to the crib and put it in ice," Jamel said still holding onto his ankle.

"Cool, take us back to the projects", Ne'Sean ordered trying to calm down.

Dornell kept looking in his rearview mirror like they were being followed, "good man, cause I didn't sign up for all the guns and shit".

Chapter 30

De'Quan had a lot on his mind and it was time to share it with his childhood friend. He called Tammy to see if she was going to see Dre on Rikers Island on a night visit. Tammy said she wasn't feeling well so she was skipping this week night visit. To talk to Dre, De'Quan needed some alone time and Tammy taking a sick day from going to visit Dre is just what De'Quan needed.

After going through the long ordeal of being warned of bringing in contraband and being searched, De'Quan took a seat in a noisy waiting area until he heard Dre's name. He was shuffled into the visiting room and given a table to sit at. Ten minutes later Dre came bouncing out of a sliding door wearing a grey jumpsuit and a pair of Fila slippers. He got close to the table De'Quan stood up and they gave each other a pound and hug.

"What's good man?" Dre said beaming from ear to ear. He hadn't seen De'Quan since the day he came in.

"Ain't nothing, what's good with you?" De'Quan asked as they sat down.

"I'm chilling man. I was expecting Tam to be out here. She didn't come with you?" Dre asked as he scanned the visiting room half expecting to see Tammy pop up.

"She said she wasn't feeling good today. So I gave her the day off", De'Quan joked.

"Oh ok. So what's up?"

"We had to beat up Rahkem", De'Quan said changing is smile into a frown.

"I'm figuring he had it coming for some reason", Dre said bracing himself for a bomb he knew his friend was about to drop on him.

"Fat Pee got more enjoyment out of that than I did", De'Quan said replaying the scene in his head.

"So why yah did it?"

"This motherfucker Rah brother smacked him up and took our money from him", De'Quan said.

Dre's back got straight as a razor, "hold up, what you mean he took our money. How the fuck did he know it was up there?" Dre asked ready to explode.

"That fucking dummy showed it to him", De'Quan said.

They sat there in silence for a few moments, both of them lost in their own thoughts about the lost they took. "What we going to do now?"

"When I spoke to Fat Pee he wanted to bring in Q to take your place, but I don't trust that. Q is good people, but he might freeze up on me and I'm not trying to chance it. We can wait until you come home to do something. By that time, I should have a proper spot for us to hit", De'Quan said.

"Damn son, I want to fuck that nigga up right now. Where's Tye at?" Dre asked like he could go looking for him.

"We have no idea. I was up top visiting Pop for a few days when it happened. Ne'Sean and Jamel took it upon themselves to go to Tye house and they got into a shoot-out with him. Jamel damn near broke his ankle trying to run. Now the nigga Tye is MIA", De'Quan said shaking his head.

"Damn, we got to smash that nigga", Dre said.

"I know this already, but the bottom line is Tye is gone and we probably won't see him again unless it's his funeral, cause the Tye got mad niggas looking for him", De'Quan said.

"Damn son, I got like a month and a half to come home, and when I touch down I wanted to chill. I didn't want to come home and have to kick in a nigga door", Dre said rubbing his head as if he suddenly got a headache.

"I wanted to chill too. I had a few days to build with Pop and he was telling me about some good money moves we could do and now all that shit is pipe dream".

"Yo I can't believe this shit, what's up with Pop anyway?" Dre asked trying to get off the bad thought's running through his mind. Just yesterday, he had a plan for when he came home, now it was slowly flushing itself down the toilet.

Two weeks later Dre found himself sitting on his bunk staring at his surroundings, Black Cee was being released in a few hours and once he left the dorm would be Dre's to run. Dre was going home in fifteen days; he did not feel like running a jail dorm.

Black Cee came out of the shower room half-dressed and ready to roll. He looked at Dre and snapped him out of his trance, "Dre what's up?"

"Ain't nothing, I was just wondering what my girl was doing right now", Dre said.

Black Cee smiled as he put on his sneakers, "Well in two weeks you won't have to worry about that any more".

"Yeah, you right. Plus I was thinking about who might step up now that you bouncing", Dre said.

Black Cee glanced over the dorm room and said, "Well Lite and them are from the Fort and they starting to get kind of deep up in here. They want to fuck with you, cause they feeling your vibe".

Dre twisted up his face and said, "Yeah, but I don't want to fuck with them niggas like that".

"Dre you don't have to hang with them niggas 24/7 like you did with me. All I'm saying is just give them a big portion of the phone time so they'll be comfortable. And when you leave you just pass the torch off to them and they can take it from there".

Dre smirked and said, "I guess you right. Black if this is your first time in jail, then how the hell do you know so much about this shit?"

Black Cee chuckled and said, "Come on son, I'm from Brownsville. Never ran, never will. Half my projects got jail stories. I just paid attention when niggas were talking".

"On The Count!" A female c.o. announced from the front of the dorm causing everyone to pause and waited from her to do a head count. When she got to the back of the dorm where Dre and Black Cee were sitting, she looked at Cee and said, "Smith you ready?"

"If you the one that's walking me out the front door, then I'm ready when you are", Black Cee said with a sly smirk on his face.

She rolled her eyes and said, "Just be ready in five minutes".

When she walked away Black Cee said, "Yeah, she's on my dick".

Dre burst out laughing, "Yo Cee you the illest…I'm going to miss you dawg".

"Smith let's go!"

Dre gave his friend a pound and a hug for a final time. "You know where to find me. If you need anything just get at me", Black Cee said before walking off and out of the dorm.

Chapter 31

With Dre locked up and Fat Pee always tied up with this chick or that situation, De'Quan knew it was up to him to find their next vic. Problem was vics just don't fall out of the sky. He came across a couple of prospects, but nothing solid. To get his mind off his mounting problems, De'Quan decided to take as solo trip to club Esso's. Cursing through New York City clubs on a late night always gave De'Quan a rush and when the streets are bubbling, if you listen close enough, you may be able to pick up some valuable information.

Club Esso's was a two-story structure that gave you a comfortable sense of being in a hip-hop lounge, with a full bar, and section off booths for a more interment setting. The dance floor downstairs jammed to the new 112 feat. Biggie song as De'Quan moved through the crowd and headed upstairs to look in on the mini stage performance they had going for the night.

Mic Geronimo and Royal Flush had the second floor bouncing to their street anthem 'Master I.C.' as De'Quan made his way to the crowded bar to order a double Hennessey.

"Oh, I'm sorry".

De'Quan turns around to see who just bumped into him and he was taken aback by the beauty he just came face to face with. De'Quan smiled, "That's okay, yo trying to order something?"

The girl looked at him up and down and quickly sized De'Quan up. She returned the smile and said, "Yes, will yo help me out?" She waved her hands in a look at this motion.

De'Quan chuckled and said, "Yeah I know, I been trying to get a bar tender for a minute. I got you though, what you drinking?"

"Can you order me a red devil please?" She asked, batting her eyes and handing him a folded up bill.

"Nah, keep your money, this drink is on me", De'Quan said and turned around to get the bar tenders attention.

When De'Quan turned from the bar with the drinks the girl said, "thank you, but you didn't have to do this".

De'Quan smiled, "Don't worry about it; I'm sure you'll hit me back on the next round".

"You confident there's going to be a next round huh".

"Sure am…now what's your name sweetheart?"

"Melissa", she stuck out her hand to shake his. De'Quan took her hand and smoothly caressed hers, "and yours?"

"De'Quan. Who are you here with?"

"My girl-friend and her boy-friend. They're downstairs, hugged up in a booth, so I came to check out the show up here. Who did you come with?" Melissa said as she sipped on her drink.

"I'm here by myself. I was out driving, and this spot looked like it was popping from the outside", De'Quan said, then he looked around. "Do you want to sit down?"

"Sure". Melissa said. De'Quan took her hand into his and he led the way through the crowd to a small table with two empty chairs.

De'Quan and Melissa got lost in each other's conversation for over an hour, until it was suddenly broken up.

"There you are. I've been looking all over for you".

Melissa looked up and was surprised to see her friend standing there. "Oh, I'm sorry, I thought you had company", Melissa joked.

"Well it looks like I'm breaking up your company. Hi, my name is Suge", she said with a bright smile and a wave.

De'Quan returned the smile and said, "I'm De'Quan. I'm sorry; I didn't mean to steal your friend like that".

"That's okay, but we are ready to leave now", Suge said looking over to Melissa.

Melissa frowned and said, "But I'm not finished yet".

De'Quan saw opportunity knocking and he knew he had to answer the door before it walked away. "I can take you home if you like".

Melissa's frown slowly started to fade, "Would you...that would be nice".

"Are you sure?" Suge asked with a skeptical look on her face.

"Girl I'll be fine", Melissa said in a reassuring tone.

"Trust me, she's in good hands", De'Quan said.

Suge looked him up and down, "Okay, you better make sure my friend gets home in one piece, or else I'm coming to find you. Where you from again?" Suge said with a smile, but De'Quan could tell she was serious about her inquiry.

"Don't worry, I'm not hiding, I'm from building 506 in Marcy projects", De'Quan said.

Suge laughed and gave Melissa a hug, "Okay. Melissa call me when you get in".

"Why, you not going to answer", Melissa joked.

"Yes I will, now call me".

"Okay, okay Mame. Now go", Melissa said as she kissed Suge on her cheek.

When Suge bounced back through the crowd, De'Quan said, "Now I feel at a disadvantage".

"Why is that?"

"Cause she knows where I live at, but I don't know where she's from".

Melissa chuckled, "I don't think you're going to give her a reason to come looking for you".

De'Quan laughed and said, "I'm not. You hungry?"

"A little".

"Cool, we can grab something on the way".

*****

"Thank you De'Quan, I really had a good ", Melissa said as they sat in his car out front of her building. "Suge pressed me to come out tonight, so I wasn't expecting to meet anyone, but I'm glad I did".

"No problem. You was good company for me, so I should be the one saying thank you", De'Quan said as he stared into her light brown eyes.

Melissa reached over and gave him a soft wet kiss that De'Quan found himself lost in. Melissa pulled back and said, "call me", as she hopped out of his car and skipped up the front steps of her building.

De'Quan watched Melissa's butt bounce under the skirt she was wearing and shook his head. "I'll be a fool not to call you", he said to himself as he put the car in drive and pulled away from the curb feeling like his realness is what won her over.

Chapter 32

Dre came home to less fan-fare than he did when he had to turn himself in. Tammy waited on the other side of the Rikers Island Bridge for Dre to hop off a transport bus. Dre's prison frown quickly turned into a smile when he saw his pregnant girl-friend waiting for him by the bus stop.

"Hey baby", Dre said as he kissed her than kissed her big belly.

"We missed you so much", Tammy said as a tear slid out the corner of her eye.

Dre wiped it with his hand and said, "It's over now. Let's go home".

They hopped into a cab and took the Brooklyn-Queens expressway back to Brooklyn. Dre stared out of the window as they rode across the bridge and thought about how different the city looked across the East river after 6 months. His mind had been working in overdrive ever since the visit he had with De'Quan. No stash money, with a baby on the way, wasn't sitting well with Dre. He needed to get up with De'Quan and Fat Pee ASAP.

The cab navigated through the light traffic to Marcy houses, giving Dre a quick adrenaline rush. Even though he had only been gone for six months, it still felt like things had changed since he was gone. That is until Dre and Tammy stepped onto the elevator and the strong aroma of piss hit him. That's when he knew he was home.

Dre's mother was in the kitchen when she heard keys jiggling in the door. She put the top back onto the pot and turned around to greet her son. "Thank god you made it out of there, come let me look at you".

Dre chuckled and said, "Let me find out you were looking for me Ma".

They hugged, and she took a step back to look her son up and down, "I was. You hungry, I made you something".

Dre laughed and said, "You cooked, it must going to snow today".

"If I wasn't so happy to see you, I would pop you over your head", She said then pushed him to the side. "Hey Tammy, how's my grand-baby doing in there?"

Tammy smiled as they hugged and said, "Acting crazy in there. I think cause I'm hungry".

"Oh ok, well grand-ma is almost finish in here".

"Oh, so you didn't come home to see me, huh", Shakia said as she came down the hall.

Dre's face lit up, "Stop playing sis, what's up", he said as he gave her a big hug.

"Damn I missed you", Dre said.

"I missed you too".

"Well enough of the mushy stuff, yah get cleaned up and ready to eat, I'm going to start fixing these plates before my Grand-baby starts having another fit up in there", they all laughed and headed to the bathroom to wash their hands.

Blunt smoke seeped out of the windows as De'Quan whipped his Lexus down the Conduit expressway, going from Brooklyn to Sunrise. It was Dre second day home and it was time to take him shopping. De'Quan talked over the music about his late-night encounter with the Spanish beauty he met at club

SOS, in-between pulls of the blunt, before passing it off to Fat Pee.

"Yo son, if I wasn't so Moet'd up, I would have cared about crashing my shit!" All three friends laughed on cue.

Fat Pee took a pull of the blunt, and said, "Yo she got any freaky ass sisters, or is she one of a kind?"

De'Quan switched lanes as they came up on Green Ackers mall, "I don't know son, she left me downstairs on some call me later shit. I wasn't mad though".

For most of the ride to Queens Dre sat in the backseat, taking pulls of the blunt, lost in his own thoughts. Coming home to pressure of having a baby, with no real plan on how he was going to make some money was starting to get to Dre. Tammy was a solid trooper and was very understanding, but Dre knew he had to set her and the baby up proper.

"So how we gonna do this?" Dre asked, breaking up the laughter coming from the front seats of the car.

"We looking at some new spots now", Fat Pee said, as De'Quan navigated through the parking lot in search of a spot. "I'm trying to get up with this Spanish chick from Bushwick; she knows some info on this cat getting it on the dope tip".

"Oh yeah, what's his name?" De'Quan asked.

"Some cat named Diablo", Fat Pee said.

De'Quan found a spot, put the car in park, and lit up a cigarette. "I've been looking around uptown. We hit something up there, it's going to be worth it, you dig. That's why I've been taking my time. I have a feeling about that chick Melissa I met the other night. Cause shorty lives right on 140th street, you know any chick living on a block getting money like that one 9 times out of 10 she's holding something for somebody".

"Word", Fat Pee agreed, "Them dudes are getting money on that block".

Dre shook his head in agreement, "I heard about that block in jail".

"Well whatever route we go, we got to do this soon, cause I'm not trying to have my nephew coming out here hungry", Fat Pee said.

Dre smiled and De'Quan said, "Don't worry; something is going to pop off. Now let's go get my boy fresh".

"That's what I'm talking about", Dre said, cheeseing as they hopped out of the car and bounced to the mall.

Inside Dre made it his business to find some fresh feet's in Footlocker, while Fat Pee played the outside of the store trying to get a caramel complexion cutie number. De'Quan sat down, and then checked his beeper. A number came up he didn't recognize.

"Yo Dre, I'll be back, I'm going to the payphone", De'Quan said, as he passed Dre three hundred dollars and walked out of the store.

"Hello?"

"Yeah, somebody beeped me from this number?" De'Quan said.

"Is this De'Quan?" The soft sultry voice on the other end of the line asked.

"It all depends on who this may be", De'Quan playfully spat.

"Ahh, good one playboy, this is Melissa", She said as she lounged on her couch, dressed in a wife-beater and shorts. "I was hoping you didn't forget the sound of my voice so fast".

De'Quan chuckled, "Nah, I knew it was you".

"Okay, so are you busy?" Melissa asked.

"At the moment I'm out with my boy, but if you're not busy when I'm done I can come pick you up and treat you to a steak or something", De'Quan said, feeling confident Melissa won't turn down a steak dinner.

Melissa smiled and said, "That all depends on what time is later".

"Not too late, but late enough to make it a dinner date if you like".

"I like the sound of that", Melissa said smiling from ear to ear.

Chapter 33

De'Quan parked by the fire hydrant close to the front of Melissa's building and watched the activity that flowed from stoop to stoop on her block. Look outs on every corner braved the cold night air as people coming through to re-up either walked up or pulled into the block to purchase their product. De'Quan kept one hand on his 40caliber resting on the side of his seat, as his eyes bounced from mirror to mirror watching the action around him.

It was no secret Melissa lived on one of the most popular blocks in Washington heights when it came to who had the best product in New York City. The problem De'Quan thought to himself is robbing something on the block, then trying to get off it. Fat Pee was a good driver, but De'Quan knew if any of the look outs got word something was going wrong inside of the building, they would have a major problem trying to get out of there.

After ten minutes of waiting Melissa came strutting out of the building in a pair of knee high boots. Her jeans defined every curve she possessed in the back, and she made sure it all showed under the waist high fur jacket she wore. When she got into the car De'Quan smiled and said, "You look nice".

"Thank you Poppy", She said as she reached over and gave him a soft kiss.

"That tasted good, you hungry?" De'Quan asked he pulled away from the curb.

"Starving, where we going?" Melissa asked as she leaned forward and De'Quan caught it out the side of his eye.

"Don't touch nothing".

Melissa burst out laughing and said, "How did you know I was going to touch something?"

"I felt the vibe that my radio space was about to be invaded".

"Okay I won't touch, unless you want me too", Melissa said.

De'Quan smiled and said, "I want you to touch, but not the radio". They laughed and joked all the way downtown. De'Quan took Melissa to Tad's steak house in the heart of Times Square.

When they finished their meals, they sat at the table staring at each other over drinks until Melissa said, "So tell me something good about yourself".

"Wow that's' a good question. Well off the top of my head, I would have to say I treat people the way they want to be treated. A person shows me love, then I'm going to return that love. What about you, what do you do all day, like do you have a job that takes up most of your days and nights?"

Melissa took a sip of her drink and said, "I work as a receptionist for a firm who represents clients like American Express, and AT&T. Real boring stuff. What about you Mr. Lexus".

De'Quan chuckled and said, "Right now I'm not doing anything until I start this tech school and having a Lexus in New York is nothing. Now if I was pushing a helicopter, then that would be a major thing. So who do you live with?"

She shifted in her seat and said, "I'm on my own, why, you curious about what goes on upstairs?"

Her voice was more intoxicating to De'Quan, than the glass of Hennessey he was sipping on. "Only if you want me too".

Melissa smiled, "I might".

De'Quan felt it. That was his cue to get the bill and get her into the warm car as soon as possible. When they were in the car De'Quan asked, "You ever smoked Hydro?"

"Not yet, why you have some?" Melissa asked.

De'Quan smiled as he pulled the car out onto the flow of traffic, "No, but the one of the few spots in the city is a few blocks from your house".

Melissa knew what he had in mind, but she didn't protest. She just leaned back and enjoyed the smooth ride back uptown.

De'Quan stopped at the weed spot on 145th street, dipped into the store next door to grab them some junk food and juices, and then drove over to 140th street. Even though it was close to 12 o'clock at night, the action on Melissa's block was still going. As he parked the car a thought hit De'Quan, maybe they can follow somebody after they pick up their work from Melissa's block. If they did it like that, they avoid getting into drama with the guys hustling on her actual block. He put the thought in the back of his mind and they headed upstairs.

When they were safely in Melissa's apartment, she instructed De'Quan to have a seat on a beige leather sofa, while she hung up their coats and put on the radio. De'Quan quickly took in his surroundings, as he got comfortable. Melissa lived in a one bedroom apartment on the third floor of a five story walk-up. Being that Melissa lived in a high crime area De'Quan figured her rent couldn't be that much. The inside of her apartment told a different story.

Across from the leather sofa he was sitting on was a matching loveseat, and a glass coffee table in-between. A 40in TV rested in the middle of a wooden wall unit. Pictures of Melissa and her family hung on the walls and De'Quan immediately got the feeling she didn't just let people into her home unless she was comfortable. He pulled out the weed and handed it to her when she came back into the living room.

"So this is the famous Hydro. I've heard about it, but I've haven't had it yet. Is it true they grow this weed under water?" Melissa asked as she sat down on the couch next to him.

"Yeah, in fish tanks and shit", De'Quan said as he pulled out a Dutch master and started breaking it open.

"I hope this Hydro is all that like you and everybody is saying it is, or else we gonna have a problem up in here".

De'Quan laughed as he watched her get up and put on her slippers, then put on the sexy sounds of SWV on the stereo. "If this shit don't hit you like the Hulk, then I'll break out and leave you untouched. How about that".

She laughed as she lit up an incense and brought two glasses of water to the table. "Oh really, you must be really confident about that lah. I hope you're that confident in other areas".

"Oh believe me, I won't disappoint", De'Quan smoothly said, then pulled out his lighter and passed them to her.

"Oh I get to do the honors", Melissa said with a big smile.

"It's your castle, so it's only right", De'Quan said.

She got up and handed it back to him, "That's okay, you can spark it. I want to put on a movie. Have you ever seen 'Tales from the Hood' before?"

"Nah. I've heard of it though", De'Quan said as he lit up the blunt and watched her open up a lower compartment on the wall unit and pull out a couple of video tapes. Melissa shuffled threw the collection in her hands. From the angle he was sitting on the couch, De'Quan's eyes began to stare at a grey package resting in the back of the compartment. The smoke went down his throat hard and De'Quan went into a coughing fit.

She turned around with a big smile and said, "You need some help?"

"Oh yeah", De'Quan said laughing in-between his coughing.

Melissa put the movie on and closed up the compartment. When she sat back down, he passed her the blunt and after four deep pulls, the bud caught her in her throat. Melissa's coughing fit was worst then De'Quan's. Her eyes began to water and De'Quan thought he saw snot coming out of her nose. Melissa put the blunt in the ash tray and dipped off to the bathroom.

De'Quan began to laugh, "I guess I'll smoke this by myself".

De'Quan lit up the blunt, then a thought hit him. He looked over his shoulder than quickly moved to the wall unit. He opens up the compartment and pulled out what he thought was a package, and he was right. De'Quan put the package back, then calmly sat back down on the couch with a hundred things started racing through his mind as he waited for Melissa to come out of the bathroom.

Melissa came back into the living room with an embarrassing grin on her face. She sat down on the couch and reached for the blunt.

"Oh, you think you ready for round two champ", De'Quan said with a slight chuckle.

"Shut up", Melissa joked as she took the blunt and they relaxed into a smooth smoking rhythm while they watched the movie. As the movie progressed, they moved in close to each other, which lead to some light four play.

"Hold on a sec", Melissa said as she hopped up off of the couch and stepped in the back again.

De'Quan thought about the package Melissa had in the bottom of her wall unit, and he had to stop himself just taking it and leaving her house before she came from out the back. That would make him look petty and De'Quan knew if Melissa had one, then she had access to a lot more. If it wasn't in her house already.

Melissa walked back into the living room dressed in a Victoria Secret oriental style, thigh high, silk robe, with her hair draped down to her shoulders. De'Quan took one look at Melissa

308

and his manhood almost burst out of his pants. The look in Melissa's eyes was one of pure experience as she got down on her knees in front of him and in a low seductive voice she said, "How do you want it?"

De'Quan smiled and said, "However you want to give it, your house, your moves".

Melissa smiled and began to undo his pants, smoothly releasing De'Quan's aching hard-on. De'Quan grabbed the remote control and put the TV on mute. Then he pressed play on the CD player button. Total blared out of the speakers asking the world can't we see, what he's doing to them, as De'Quan began to relax and let Melissa suck on him like she found her long lost lollypop. De'Quan had to smile to himself because he knew he hit the jackpot with Melissa.

Chapter 34

"Man, I can't wait till we on that college campus, all the girls are going to be checking for the Brooklyn kid, with the nice handle", Jamel said as he bounced the basketball between his legs, then drove to the basket for an uncontested lay-up.

Ne'Sean picked up the rebound and said, "Who me? Cause I'm the only Brooklyn kid I know with a nice handle".

Ne'Sean took a 12 foot jump shot that went in. Jamel passed the ball back to Ne'Sean, then grabbed the rebound when Ne'Sean missed on his second attempt. Out the corner of his eye, Ne'Sean saw his girlfriend Karmen coming into the park with her two friends Adina and Mimi.

Karmen was looking comfortable in a beige velour suit with a pair of 5411 Reeboks on her feet. Her black Pelle-Pelle jacket was open halfway giving Ne'Sean the invitation to put his hands inside and hug and kiss Karmen all in one motion.

"What's up baby, I'm sorry, I lost track of the time", Ne'Sean said with his winning smile.

Karmen rolled her eyes, "Oh yeah, I see I had to come down here and get your ass. I told you I had to talk to you", Karmen said with a slight frown on her face.

Adina smacked the ball out of Jamel hands and said, "How you suppose to win in college when you can't even hold onto the ball in an empty park?"

Mimi snickered as Jamel tried to take the ball back from Adina, "Don't worry about that, I'll bust your ass". Being a tomboy Adina loved to intimidate other kids in the projects, especially the boys.

"Yeah right Jamel, you too little homeboy", Adina said as she began to back Jamel down to the basket and lay up the ball for two. Mimi hollowed in laughter as Jamel ran after the rebound and slipped on some dirt.

Ne'Sean and Karmen walked away from the ruckus on the court to sit down on the benches. Ne'Sean hopped onto the bench back support, as Karmen leaned in between his legs. The young couple had been seeing each other for the past seven months, and they never had a beef with each other because Ne'Sean had a dream and Karmen was all for it.

Ne'Sean knew Karmen well enough to know when something was wrong with her, he lightly pushed her back to look into her eyes and asked, "What's wrong Karmen?"

She didn't know how to tell him what has been on her mind, "Sean my period has been late for a month now", she said hoping he would catch the hint from that piece of information.

He didn't.

"What does that mean, you hurt or something?"

She shifted her weight and said, "I did one of those home tests and..." Karmen let her words trail off as she watched his reaction.

It slowly started to hit Ne'Sean and his facial expressing began to change, "But I used a condom...Ahh man, Naw. What you saying Karmen, cause we used a condom".

A mist began to form up in her eyes as she said, "I know Sean, that's the same thing I said in the bathroom this morning, but then I remembered the few times the condom broke and I started to cry. I'm sorry Sean".

A million things began to flow through his mind all at once. Ne'Sean didn't know how he should take this news. In those short moments, it took everything in him not to flip on Karmen and blame this whole mess on her. She knew he was about to go to U.N.C. in the summer and something like her being pregnant can derail his whole plan to get his family out of the hood with his talent. They spoke about this.

"Ne'Sean say something", Karmen whined, snapping Ne'Sean out of his trance.

"Who else did you tell?" Ne'Sean asked looking over her shoulder at Adina and Mimi.

"Nobody Ne'Sean. Damn that's all you can say?"

"Karmen calm down, I'm trying to process this shit just like you".

"Damn why you got to curse at me?" Karmen asked looking genuinely hurt.

"Don't tell anybody about this, okay", Ne'Sean said ignoring her. "I'll get the money so you can go to one of those clinics".

"For what!" Karmen snapped as she pulled back from him. "I'm not getting an abortion Ne'Sean. You know that's against my religion. My mother will kill me".

"Okay, don't worry about it K, let me think about this and see what we can do without you violating your religion, and me losing my basketball scholarship. Let's just keep this to ourselves for now", Ne'Sean said as he looked into her light eyes.

A tear trickled out of her eyes and she quickly whipped at them. She nodded, "Okay".

Ne 'Sean kissed her and stood up, "Come on, I'll walk you home".

$$*****$$

Ne'Sean paced his room trying to think about what he was going to do with Karmen. They will never let him go away to college knowing he has a baby on the way. He needed a plan or else everything he worked hard for will end at the drop of a dime.

He paced his room thinking about all the possible scenarios that could go down once they announce Karmen is pregnant. It hit him this is a moment in time where he needed to talk to Pop, because he never judged them and always was willing to find a solution to one of his kid's problems. Not having Pop around for his prime young years was really hurting Ne'Sean on the inside. That's why he made basketball his focus for the last few years, and now he was facing the possibility of losing out on his opportunity to play on a larger stage than his New York City high school and getting his family out of Marcy projects.

When he was tired of pacing his room Ne'Sean sat down on the bed and started counting off all the people in his life who is going to scream at him for getting Karmen pregnant. He couldn't think of anyone who will give them their blessings to have a baby. This was something he needed to take care of on his own. Ne'Sean reached down under the bed and pulled out a Timberland box. He opened it and took out a small knot of money and a 32 caliber handgun.

This will just have to be a secret they take to the grave with them, because he couldn't risk it Ne'Sean said to himself as he counted out his last $487 dollars. Karmen will have to understand this one time they are going to have to do something nobody in the world but them and the doctor will know about.

Ne'Sean sneaked out of his apartment determine to make Karmen see things his way.

Chapter 35

De'Quan weaved through traffic, headed uptown on the Westside highway with the hard sounds of 'Only Built for Cuban Linx' knocking out of the Lexus Bose system. Ever since he saw the package of drugs in Melissa's house, De'Quan had been scheming on how he was going to get to the main stash.

Melissa was making it hard for him, and she didn't even know it. Whenever they were together, she would turn down answering her phone, making her movement centered around him and what they are doing. De'Quan could feel it though, that moment when Melissa is going to need him to take her somewhere other than the store.

When De'Quan pulled up in front of Melissa's building the usual activity with the neighborhood hustlers directing traffic into the building of choice to do their business. He parked and surprised to see Melissa coming out of the building carrying a black bag along with the Gucci bag she had draped over her shoulder. De'Quan's heart skipped a beat as she got into the car and gave him a quick kiss on his lips.

"Hi pappi, can you do me a favor and take me to my cousin house on 160 street and Broadway?" Melissa asked with a smile no man could resist.

"Oh okay, you want to stay over there or something?" De'Quan asked as he pulled the car from the curb.

"No. He wants me to bring him something. So, I was thinking we could grab something from the fish market, maybe", Melissa said.

De'Quan had to maintain his composer. He just was thinking about a shot at seeing where the real work was at, and now that it looked like he was about to get some answers, De'Quan was feeling real jumpy on his insides.

"Ok that sounds cool, you looking tasty in those jeans", De'Quan said as he looked from the road to her thighs.

Melissa blushed and said, "Keep your eyes on the road Mister".

"Si Mame".

De'Quan drove up to 160th street and found a parking spot in-between Amsterdam and Broadway. Melissa readied herself to get out of the car and De'Quan knew he had to think fast.

"I have to use the bathroom".

Melissa froze as if she was thinking about what to do next. "I will only be a second. You can't hold it?"

"I been holding it ever since I left Brooklyn", De'Quan said with some discomfort on his face.

"Okay, come on", she said getting out of the car.

They stepped into the five story walk-up with De'Quan looking at everything there was to memorize about the building and anyone hanging out in front. The first two doors sported broken locks, which wasn't uncommon in the high crime area. They climbed the stairs to the third floor which had four apartments on the landing. Melissa knocked on apartment 3C and waited. De'Quan felt some movement behind the door and an eye appeared I the peephole. Seconds later the door swung open and a big brown skin man with a thick beard stood in the doorway sizing De'Quan up.

He asked Melissa something in Spanish and she replied with a smile which seemed to soften the man up.

"Okay, the bathroom is over here", the man said in a heavy accent.

De'Quan nodded his head as he walked into the apartment and headed for the bathroom. Melissa went into the back of the apartment while the big man at the door closed it and waited in the short hallway.

Once De'Quan closed the bathroom door, he went to the window and looked out of it to see where the apartment was located from a window view. The window was in the back of the building, and from where he was standing, there was no way for anybody to get in through the windows. He turned to the toilet and peed, then stood still for a moment to catch the voices he was hearing coming from the other side of the wall.

The lingo was in Spanish, causing De'Quan to curse himself under his breath for never sticking around in his Spanish classes in high school. He flushed the toilet, and then stepped back out into the hallway where the big doorman was patiently waiting. De'Quan half nodded his head and said, "Thanks man". He pointed toward the bathroom.

The man just stared at De'Quan and let out a deep grunt. De'Quan looked down the hallway but all he could see was half open doors. Seconds later Melissa came out of one of the back rooms and smiled when she saw De'Quan was ready.

"Thank you Bolo", Melissa said to the doorman, then gave him a light kiss on his cheek.

Bolo grunted again and kept his eyes on De'Quan the whole time as he let them out.

When they were back in the car De'Quan said, "I see he's light on conversation".

Melissa chuckled and said, "He only talks when money is involved ".

De'Quan pulled his car out into ongoing traffic, then took a shot in the dark and asked, "What if I wanted to cop some grams from them?"

Melissa was quiet for a moment as she studied the side of his face. "I didn't know you messed with coke".

"Only if my money get's low. My Pops went to jail for selling it, so that's why I don't use it as an everyday job", De'Quan said as he kept his eyes on the road.

Melissa looked like she was in deep thought, so De'Quan let her be as he weaved through the streets and headed to an Italian restaurant on 88th street.

"I'll ask Bolo, but you have to be getting something big, or he won't want to do it", Melissa said once De'Quan parked the car outside of the restaurant.

"I mean I don't have 2 brick money if that what you mean", De'Quan said with a big smile on his face.

Melissa chuckled and said, "I know you not going to want no two bricks silly. I'm saying anything less than a quarter key they not going to want to mess with". She sat back to watch his reaction. Melissa wasn't sure about how much money De'Quan was handling, but him being interested in buying some work from her connection made her open her ears a little wider.

"Ok, how much they charge for a half of key?" De'Quan asked as he finished parking then turned the car off.

Melissa didn't want to give off too much information like she knew the whole operation, "I'm not sure, they charge different. Sometimes it's ten thousand, sometimes nine. I will ask them later. Can we go eat something now?" She joked as they climbed out of the car.

"Anything for that sexy ass accent", De'Quan said as he caught a wind of something real was about to happen in the next few days.

Chapter 36

With so much going on in his life Ne'Sean was beginning to feel like the universe was going against him. Ne'Sean grew up believing ever since Pop went to prison it would be on him to get his family out of the projects. Ne'Sean's world revolved around playing basketball. Taking his game to the next level had been his goal once they knew Pop wasn't coming home for a long time.

He knew running with his brother and his friends wasn't the answer they were looking for to making it out of the projects, and lately Ne'Sean had been keeping his distance from them. Dividing up his time between practicing on the court, helping Mama K out at the store, or hanging out with Karmen. Now that was beginning to look like a bad move, because now Karmen was pregnant. Having a baby was nowhere in his plans, and he had to rectify the situation with her before the wrong person found out about their secret.

Karmen hadn't heard from Ne'Sean in two days and she was beginning to worry he wouldn't want to talk to him anymore because she told him she was pregnant and didn't believe in abortions.

Karmen waited to ten o'clock and when she hadn't heard from him all day again, she decided to go looking for him.

"I'll be back in a little while Ma", Karmen said called out down the hallway as she put on her coat.

"Okay, don't stay out too late", her mother answered as she turned her attention back to her TV show.

Karmen stepped out into the hallway, locked the door, and then was suddenly startled when she saw Ne'Sean standing in the shadows of the building staircase.

"Oh shit Sean, you scared me. What are you doing standing there?"

When Ne'Sean stepped out of the shadows he was wearing a blue hoody, and Karmen noticed he had beads of sweat forming on his forehead even though it was cold in the hallway.

"Come on let's go up to the roof and talk", Ne'Sean said as he led the way up the stairs. Karmen hesitated before following him up the two flights to the roof. When they reached the top, Ne'Sean walked over to the edge and looked down to the front of the building. Karmen walked out onto the roof and immediately felt the cold night breeze brush across her smooth face.

"Sean what's going on?" Karmen asked as she pulled her coat together and hugged herself.

Ne'Sean turned around and said, "We're not having a baby".

His straight face with no chaser scared Karmen, but backing down to this life changing decision, that she wasn't going to do. "What are you talking about? You can't just make that decision without talking to me Ne'Sean".

"Look, I can't have a baby right now. I'll lose my scholarship, and I can't do that", Ne'Sean said wiping the sweat from his forehead with his bare hand.

Karmen snapped, "Scholarship? Nigga fuck a scholarship. So, what am I suppose to do Sean, you know it's against my religion to have an abortion".

Ne'Sean shook his head in denial as he stepped closer to her and said, "Karmen, we're not having the baby".

Karmen was in a rage, "You know what Ne'Sean, fuck you. I'm having this baby, and if your punk ass don't want to help me then you'll pay for that shit".

She turned on her heels and headed toward the roof door. Ne'Sean's reflex's kicked into gear and he grabbed Karmen by her arm with one hand, and pulled out the gun with his free hand.

Karmen saw the gun, but it didn't register that Ne'Sean was threaten to use it to harm her. "Get the fuck off of me Sean".

"You can't have this baby Karmen", Ne'Sean said as they began to tussle. Karmen tried to pull away causing her to slip on the gravel laced roof. Ne'Sean lost his balance and fell forward into Karmen.

Boom

When the shot went off Ne'Sean's heart skipped a beat as Karmen eyes looked to be frozen in time. They crumbed to the ground and Ne'Sean quickly scrambled to his feet. "Oh no, no, no. Karmen get up baby", Ne'Sean pleaded as tears began to form in his eyes.

Karmen's body went limp, and a voice in Ne'Sean's head told him to run. He tried to pick her up, but Karmen wasn't moving. Ne'Sean quickly looked around then bust through the roof door, taken the stairs two at a time as he headed for the lobby.

"Yo motherfucker, watch where you going", A neighborhood dealer barked as he made a sale to a crack head.

"Sorry", Ne'Sean mumbled as he sprinted out of the building and headed straight home.

Ne'Sean sat under the dim light of his bedroom rocking back and forth, with tears streaming down his cheeks. He could not believe he just shot his high school sweetheart. Ne'Sean told himself over and over again, 'It was an accident'; he never meant to hurt Karmen. Ne'Sean knew no one will ever believe him, making the tears come down even harder. He needed to get himself together and come up with a plan.

Looking down on the floor Ne'Sean stared at the 32 revolver resting in between his feet. 'I need to get rid of this gun', he told himself. Before he could come up with a solid course of action, he heard a knock at the door and almost jumped out of his boots.

Mama K and Meika were asleep, and Ne'Sean hadn't seen De'Quan in days. He grabbed the gun off of the floor and crept to the front door. Ne'Sean's heart was beating a mile a minute as one hundred bad thoughts ran through his mind. One thing was for sure, if that is the police knocking at the door, he wasn't trying to go to jail. The thought of going out like this made Ne'Sean grip the handle of the gun a little tighter, as he put his ear to the door and listened for any sounds of voice's and walkie-talkie's. He didn't hear any.

He slowly slid the peep-hole to the side and was surprised to see Dre standing in the hallway. Ne'Sean tried to calm his nerves as he put the gun in his pocket and slowed his breathing down before opening the door.

"You alright man?" Dre asked looking at the beads of sweat rolling down the side of Ne'Sean's face.

"What? Yeah. What you want, De'Quan ain't here", Ne'Sean said wiping his forehead with his bare hand.

"I know", Dre said as he looked around the hallway. When Ne'Sean didn't invite him in Dre gave him the rest of the story. "He called me. He said to come and get you, he needs to see us".

Ne'Sean thought about it, then open the door wider to let Dre in. The hallway was dark as they made their way down to the bedroom. Dre sat on the bed as Ne'Sean closed the door and stood up. Dre was used to Ne'Sean acting weird sometimes, but as he analyzed Ne'Sean standing over by the door he realized he was fully dressed at 1:30 in the morning.

"You were going somewhere?" Dre asked.

Ne'Sean shifted in his stance and said, "Nah. What's up man? I haven't seen De'Quan in days. You said he called you, what did he say?"

Dre brushed off Ne'Sean's funny behavior and got down to business. "He said he was working on something uptown, and he needs us to come up there tonight".

Ne'Sean let Dre's word sink in as the thoughts of the police knocking on the door any moment now crept into his mind. Snapping out of his trance Ne'Sean saw this as an opportunity to get out of the house and get up with his brother and tell him what happened between him and Karmen.

"Oh ok".

"Yo you sure you alright man? You don't look too good", Dre said staring at Ne'Sean as he stood in the shadows of the room.

Wiping the sweat from his forehead and wiping his hand on his sweatshirt, Ne'Sean quickly brushed him off. "Yeah man, you think we need some heat?"

"He might just want us to come and check it out, but to be on the safe side yeah let's bring some.

Marty Mar and Bliss took the stairs two at a time, instead of waiting for the slow elevator. When they reached the roofs landing Marty Mar sat down on the steps, while Bliss remained standing as he caught his breath.

Marty Mar and Bliss were on roll tonight. They just coped from the dealer in the lobby after robbing another person for their wallet. Two fat wallets in one night gave them the options to do big things with the rest of their night. Bliss pulled out the fresh wallet they took from a Chinese delivery man and began to fidget with its contents, as Marty Mar pulled out his stem and began to stuff it with a few crack rocks.

"How much is in that one?" Marty Mar asked as he looked from the stem to the wallet.

Bliss sucked his teeth and said, "Shit, this motherfucker only had 47dollars and some loose change in one of these small pockets. Man what's taking you so long to load that shit up?"

"Shhh, man fuck you being so loud for? When it's your turn to go first, I don't rush you. So, B-E-Z greasy". Marty Mar said as he pulled out his lighter and put the flame to the end of the stem.

Bliss turned his attention back to the wallet, "Damn this nigga had some ugly ass kids".

Marty Mar chocked on the smoke as Bliss threw down the wallet and snatched the stem out of Marty Mar's hand. "Man give me that!"

Bliss put the light to the pipe and as he took a long pull of the crack smoke he got a strange feeling, he was hearing something.

"Yo did you hear that?" Bliss asked as he blew the smoke out. His eyes where bigger than an owl as he looked around the walls of the staircase.

Feeling like Bliss was trying to pull a fast one on him, Marty Mar reached to snatch the pipe out of his hand, "What is that, a joke? Nigga pass the pipe".

"No Shhh". Bliss said, and that's when Marty Mar heard it too.

"What the fuck was that?" Marty Mar asked as he stood up and looked down the stairwell. They both stood in silence as they waited for the sound again.

When they heard the sound again, Marty Mar turned to the roof door and pulled it open. Karmen was half conscious as she tried to raise her head. Bliss freaked out and dropped the stem.

"Oh shit man, I told you we shouldn't have used this staircase", Bliss blurted out as he stared at Karmen.

"Shut up stupid, you broke the got damn stem", Marty Mar snapped. He turned around and reached down to help Karmen up.

"Man don't touch that bitch. Your finger prints are going to be all over her", Bliss snapped as he nervously looked around.

"Man shut up, I saw her around here. She's from out here", Marty Mar said as he pulled Karmen from out of the cold and onto the roof landing. She was still alive, but barely.

Bliss couldn't careless as he picked up the broken pieces of the stem and the wallet and said, "Alright man, that's it. Now leave her right there, and we can call somebody downstairs.

Marty Mar shook his head, "Nah you go, and I'll stay with her".

"What? Are you crazy?"

"Man; just go call an ambulance from the corner, and hurry up", Marty Mar snapped as he put Karmen's head in his lap.

"Alright...alright", Bliss said, turning on his heels and sprinting down the stairs.

$$*****$$

When Dre open the car door, waking Fat Pee up out of a heavy nod, he wiped the drool from the corner of his mouth. "Damn man, what took yah so long?"

Dre hopped into the front seat, as Ne'Sean climbed into the back. "We didn't take that long. Let's go", Dre said.

Fat Pee stared up the car then looked the rearview mirror, "What's up Ne'Sean?"

Ne'Sean turned his attention from looking out the window, "Nothing".

Fat Pee put the car in drive and pulled out of the spot; he drove around to the Flushing side of the projects and cruised pass some police activity that was taking place in front of Karmen's building. Ne'Sean slowly eased back in his seat as he saw the EMT's wheeling somebody into the back of the ambulance.

"Damn I wonder who that is", Dre said.

Fat Pee kept his attention on the road as Ne'Sean mumbled, "I don't know".

Dre shook it off and turned on the radio. They listen to the late-night sounds of Hot97 as they road up to Washington Heights to meet up with De'Quan.

De'Quan had always been a light sleeper, even after a heavy love scene he just put together with Melissa. He lay back staring at the ceiling and listened to the steady rhythm of Melissa's breathing. For the last hour Melissa sound like she was in a heavy sleep. De'Quan smoothly eased his way out of the bed and grabbed his clothes off the floor. He crept out of the bedroom and went into the living room to get dressed. Sitting down on the couch De'Quan stared at Melissa's wall unit as he put on his pants.

The last time De'Quan took a sneak peek into Melissa's wall unit he came face to face with a package that looked to be a little over a half of key. He put the rest of his stuff on, stood in silence for a few moments before opening the bottom compartment of the wall unit.

De'Quan pulled out a small paper bag and quickly opened it. He counted out five wrapped up packages that couldn't have been more than an ounce of cocaine each. De'Quan sucked his teeth and put the small package back. That small amount of drugs wasn't going to solve their money problems.

De'Quan let himself out of the apartment and headed outside to his car.

*****

"Hey Billy wake up. Check this out", Todd said to his sleeping partner.

Billy woke up and quickly tried to focus on what Todd was pointing at. "I wonder where he's going".

"I don't know. You think we should follow him?"

"Yeah, let's see where lover boy is going in the middle of the night", Billy said as he started up the car and began to follow De'Quan.

*****

De'Quan drove to 154th street and parked in the 24hour parking garage, then walked two blocks over to meet up with his brother and two friends, "What's happening?" De'Quan said when he hopped in the back of jeep. He gave everybody a pound and sat back in his seat.

"You tell us. Must be something good you got us out here in the middle night", Dre said feeling restless.

"Word Quan what gives, you found something?" Fat Pee asked.

De'Quan looked around the car and said, "Yeah, remember shorty I've been fucking with from uptown?"

Everybody in the car slightly nodded. De'Quan continued, "Well she took me to her connect about two weeks ago, and I brought some shit from them. I got rid of the work and came back to them".

"Word, so when were you going to tell us that?" Dre asked with some distaste in his voice.

"When I knew for sure we could get up in the house without shorty's help", De'Quan shot back.

"Sounds like you really digging this chick", Dre said.

"Yo Dre I know you tight cause Rah lost our bread while you was gone", De'Quan said going at the root of Dre's attitude.

"You damn right I'm tight, and now Tammy is about to have this baby any day now and I don't even have any money to buy pampers", Dre said.

De'Quan broke the silence in the car, "Nigga, we brothers, so if you think we trying to have you have a baby with no bread to hold yah down then you're crazy. I ain't been around cause I've been working on this, and now I can get these niggas to open up the door without her".

"How much is in there?" Fat Pee asked to change the tone.

"At least two keys and some money", De'Quan said as everyone let his words soak in.

"How many dudes are up there?" Dre asked.

"Just two, one who answers the door and the other conducts the business in the living room", De'Quan reported.

"So you want to do this now?" Fat Pee asked.

"Shit why not. What's up Ne'Sean, you haven't said nothing yet", De'Quan said looking over to his brother.

Ne'Sean shifted in his seat and said, "Uh yeah, I'm good, whatever you want to do bro".

"If you not with this, Pee can come up stairs and up can stay in the car", De'Quan said, staring at his brother still not convinced he was ready.

"I'm good bro, and besides I can't drive like Pee can", Ne'Sean said.

"Okay, yah brought the gun's right?" De'Quan said turning attention back to the task at hand.

"Yeah we got them", Dre said picking up the book-bag he had resting in between his feet and passing it to De'Quan.

De'Quan looked in the bag and said, "Okay cool. Let's do this, Pee drive to 160th street, in between Amsterdam and Broadway".

Fat Pee started up the jeep as De'Quan passed out the guns and everybody put on their game faces.

*****
———

The black car followed De'Quan to the parking garage, waited for him to come out, then followed him to a parked jeep and watched him get into the back seat.

"Wonder what he's doing", Todd said as the stared at the parked jeep. The two partners sat in silence for fifteen minutes, until the jeep suddenly started up and pulled out of its parking spot.

"Okay, let's go", Billy said putting the car in drive and following the black jeep down Broadway. When the jeep turned onto 160th street, Todd looked over to his partner with a worried look in his eyes.

"You think he's going up to the apartment without Melissa?"

Billy looked over to Todd when the jeep pulled over and parked by the hydrant and said, "He might. I think we should call it in".

They stared at the jeep for five minutes until they saw the passenger doors swing open with De'Quan and two other men exit the car, and head into the building. "Yeah we should", Billy said.

Todd grabbed the walkie-talkie and made the call.

Chapter 37

The telephone ringing woke her up out of a heavy sleep, "Hello".

"Ms. Sanchez, this is Lieutenant Hardy", the deep voice said.

Melissa tried to clear the cob webs as she sat up in the bed and quickly looked around her dark bedroom. From the silhouette of the moon coming through the window Melissa could see she was alone.

"Ah, yes what's going on?"

"Seems like the guy you've been dating in on his way up to the Carlito apartment with a couple of friends. Did you know anything about this?" Lt. Hardy asked.

"No sir", Melissa quickly answered as she hurried out of bed and threw on anything that was in arms distance.

"Okay, well we have a team out front of the building".

"Are they going to take them?" Melissa asked as she pulled on a pair of sneakers.

"Well they will be followed and pulled over. If their clean then we will let them go", Lt. Hardy said.

"Okay, I'm on my way there", Melissa said as she hung up the phone and ran out the door looking like a hot mess.

*****

As a light drizzle soaked the rotten apple, the stolen Jeep Cherokee rolled to a stop in front of building 57 on 160th street, between Broadway and Amsterdam Avenue. Everyone in the jeep had butterflies in their stomachs. That wasn't enough to stop tonight show.

"Check your watch Pee. We will be out of there in 5 minutes tops. When we go in, Sean you grab the money and drugs; Me and Dre will hold the spot down." De'Quan said looking down at his watch. It was 4:47a.m.

"Pee give us to 4:52."

Pee nodded, and then set his digital guess watch, as his three passengers hopped out of the jeep and headed for the front door of the five story walk-up. They took the steps two at a time all the way up to the fourth floor.

De'Quan held up his hand to motion to Dre and Ne'Sean, as they caught their breathes, then De'Quan eased up to the door and put his ear to it to listen for any sounds of movement on the other side. He heard a few voices that were rolling over the voices coming from the TV. De'Quan looked at Dre and Ne'Sean and nodded his head then pulled out his 40 caliber automatic. Dre and Ne'Sean followed suit by pulling out their own weapons and readied themselves for what was to come next.

De'Quan performed the secret knock he watched Melissa do earlier and took up his kick in the door stands, as Dre and Ne'Sean stood off to the side in anticipation. Suddenly an eye appeared in the peephole then quickly disappeared with the sound of the locks clicking from the other side.

Bolo snatched open the door surprised to see De'Quan there so late, "what do you..."

Bolo was cut off by the 40 caliber pistol which was shoved in his mouth with enough force to crack some of his front teeth. Dre wasted no time as he pushed past them and ran into the apartment with the fire raging bull and his eyes, "Get the fuck on the floor Poppy!"

A man sitting at a card table weighing some drugs flinched to grab the gun that was resting on the table, but Dre rushed in too fast and tackled the man out of his chair.

Ne'Sean was hot on Dre's heels when they ran into the backroom, and he paused with surprise when Dre tackled the man behind the table. Before Ne'Sean could react to the two tussling on the floor, the bedroom door suddenly swung open and the nose of a shotgun came charging out into the living room. Ne'Sean didn't think; he just pulled the trigger.

The man behind the shotgun took a shot in his arm and pulled his own trigger in the process sending out a loud bang that was deafening in the living room. Ne'Sean cried out in pain as he fell to the ground squeezing his trigger. When Ne'Sean hit the floor, he dropped his gun and immediately grabbed for his leg.

The ruckus going on in the living room caused Bolo to try De'Quan. The second De'Quan took his eyes off Bolo to look down the hallway; Bolo hit him with a left hook right in De'Quan's eye. The shock of being hit out of nowhere caused De'Quan to pull the trigger on his gun as he fell to the floor. Two bullets came out with one whizzing pass Bolo arm, but the second bullet ratcheted off a pipe and hit Bolo in his neck. Bolo crumbled to floor grabbing at his neck.

De'Quan scrambled to his feet and watched as the life slowly poured out of Bolo's body. De'Quan stood still for a moment as he tried to focus. Bolo hit him so hard De'Quan was seeing two hallways. He tried to shake it off as he ran down the hallway and into the living room. Dre was off on one side pistol whipping a guy, while Ne'Sean laid in the middle of the floor gripping his leg. De'Quan quickly looked at the guy lying dead with his shotgun still in his hand, and then turned to his brother.

"Shit let me see", De'Quan said.

"Shit hurts man", Ne'Sean cried as sweat rolled down his forehead.

"I know man, don't worry, you going to be alright", De'Quan said.

Dre finished giving his victim a beat down that made the man pass out. He grabbed the bag off the floor and started loading it up with anything he could get his hands on.

"Dre help me over here", De'Quan whined as he looked around the room for something to wrap around his brother wound.

Dre finished stuffing the bag with all the drugs and money he could take, and then he went into the back room to find a sheet, but he stopped and asked De'Quan, "What the hell happen to your eye?"

"Fucking dude sucker punched me, now can you go find something, so we can get the fuck out of here", De'Quan snapped, visibly tight behind the growing shiner on his eye.

Dre came out of the back room with a towel in one hand and a jacket in the other hand. He handed the towel to De'Quan and stood there staring at the jacket. De'Quan quickly wrapped the towel around Ne'Sean's leg then looked up at Dre.

"What's wrong man?" De'Quan asked as he and his brother looked up at Dre.

Dre turned the jacket around and on the back of it, it said N.Y.P.D.

"Where did you get that?" De'Quan asked with a scared look in his eyes.

"Out the back-room man. Don't tell me these guys are five-o", Dre said.

De'Quan quickly snapped out of his trance and picked his brother up to his feet, "Come on, we got to get the fuck out of here".

$$*****$$

Melissa made the cab stop in the middle of the block and as she climbed out of it the first thing she saw that was out of order was the black jeep parked by the hydrant with its engine running.

Melissa stepped on to the curb and slowly put her hand into her purse. She slowly walked toward the building, but she keep her eyes on the jeep. Then suddenly the door to the building swung open and Dre came running out with De'Quan half carrying his brother as they hopped down the stairs.

Fat Pee watched Melissa get out of the cab and slowly walk up the hill towards the building, but he didn't think anything of it until Dre busted out the front of the building. Melissa stopped in her tracks and slowly pulled her gun out of her bag.

"Oh shit man, look out!" Fat Pee screamed as he raised the gun he had resting on the car floor and stuck it out the window.

De'Quan looked in Melissa's direction and froze in his tracks.

"Don't move De'Quan", Melissa said nervous about bumping into them on the sidewalk like this.

"Who's that man?" Ne'Sean asked with a nervous look in his eyes.

De'Quan looked from Melissa to Ne'Sean, then back to Melissa and said, "Nobody". Then De'Quan turned his gun in her direction and the quiet drizzly night quickly turned into a shooting gallery.

Melissa dove out of the way and fell in between two parked cars. Dre threw the bag on the car floor as he jumped into the front seat and let off two shots into Melissa's direction.

"Come on man!" Dre barked, but his command was interrupted from the back end on the jeep as Todd and Billy let their presents be known in the gun fight. "Drop your weapons!"

De'Quan quickly pushed Ne'Sean into the backseat and Fat Pee couldn't wait any longer as he stepped on the gas with everyone screaming, "Come on man!"

De'Quan slipped when the jeep pulled off, causing him to hold onto the door for dear life as Fat Pee sped down the block heading for Broadway. Ne'Sean grabbed his brother and helped him get into the jeep, but their escape was cut short when Fat Pee drove the jeep onto Broadway and a police car heading to the scene clipped the back end of the jeep and sent it into a 360 spin into a parked car. The loud bang was deafening as the night sky was flooded by the sound of approaching sirens.

Dre was the first one in the jeep to react as he looked into the backseat. De'Quan and Ne'Sean were both knocked out by the impact. He looked at Fat Pee and said, "Shit man, we got to get out of here".

"I can't man, I'm stuck", Fat Pee said as he tried to pull his leg up from its stuck position in between the door and stirring wheel.

The police on the sidewalk slowly tried to make their way to the jeep but when they saw movement in the jeep everyone held their positions. Dre looked around and knew he had to make a move.

A tear slowly rolled down the side of Fat Pee's face as he read his friend mind and said, "Go head Dre, I'll hold you down".

Dre looked around the car one last time before nodding his head and snatching open the car door. Fat Pee stuck his gun out the shattered window and squeezed off as many shots as he could as Dre jumped out of the car and headed across Broadway. The gun fire was deafening in the early morning light as Dre weaved through two parked cars and hit the sidewalk on 162 street with full head of steam.

Dre could feel the heat on his back as he ran toward Riverside and hailed the first cab he saw cruising by. Dre snatched open the door and hopped into the backseat, "What's up Poppy, I'm going to Jersey".

The cab driver half turned to look over his shoulder and said, "New Jersey? No Poppy, that too far".

Dre quickly dug into the backpack and pulled out two hundred dollar bills, "Here Pop".

The cab driver looked at the money and slowly nodded, "Okay". He took the money from Dre then pulled away from the curb as the sirens got louder in the background. Dre kept his eyes in the rearview mirror as he watched two police cars come busting out of the block and headed south. The cab driver drove north and quickly connected to the highway toward the George Washington Bridge.

"Where you go?" The cab driver asked as he moved with flow of traffic.

Dre eased down in his seat and tried to calm his heart rate as he thought about his next move, "Take me to the Hilton by Newark airport".

"Muy bien".

When the cab driver dropped Dre off, he walked around the outside of the hotel and found another cab. He had the cab driver take him to a different hotel in Newark and he found a pay phone.

Tammy picked up on the forth ring, "Hello".

"Tammy, I need you to get up right now", Dre said as he looked over his shoulder.

Tammy felt the seriousness in his voice and sat on her bed, "Dre what's wrong?"

"I need you to pack a bag and meet me in Jersey", Dre said.

"Huh, Jersey…baby what's going on?" Tammy said as she cut on her lamp and moved to the edge of her bed.

"I'll tell you when you get here, just hop in a cab and take it to the Ramada inn in south Newark", Dre said.

Tammy was quiet for a second before she sighed and said, "Okay".

"Tammy don't tell nobody where you going".

"Come on Dre its five o'clock in the morning, my mother is going to be looking for me before she goes to work. What am I supposed to say?" Tammy said feeling frustrated with Dre about this sudden call and move he wants her to do.

"Relax baby, just leave her a note, and say you'll call her later", Dre said.

Tammy thought about it, then got out of her bed, "Okay baby, I'm coming".

Chapter 38

De'Quan opened his eyes and his blurry vision had him feeling like he was on drugs. He tried to wipe his hand over his face but was stopped in mid-motion by a strong set of handcuffs, that were connected to the hospital bed rail. His vision quickly began to clear as he looked around the room.

A uniform officer was sitting in the corner of the room writing in his note pad when he saw De'Quan wake up. He quickly got up and walked to the side of the bed, "Hey man how you feeling?"

"Like I got hit by a truck, where am I?"

"The hospital, what's your name?" The officer quickly asked.

"De'Quan."

"De'Quan what?" The officer asked in a concerned tone.

"Short. How did I get here?" De'Quan asked.

The officer looked toward the door, then back to De'Quan and said, "Hey hold on a second, somebody wants to talk to you".

The officer stuck his head out the door into the hallway and said, "He's up".

Before De'Quan could ask who was in the hallway the room was flooded by men in suits, a cameraman, and a nurse to quickly check his vital signs. The room buzzed with activity as the cameraman set up his camera, and a man in a blue suit took off his trench coat. He laid his coat on a chair and came over to the side of the bed.

"Hi, I'm ADA Mathew Stevens, and when he cuts on the camera I'm going to ask you a few questions about what happen last night on hundred and sixty First Street. First, I will introduce myself, then you. Then I will ask you if you would like a lawyer present during this interview. If you do, then we will turn the camera off and leave. If not then we will continue, okay", he said.

Before De'Quan could respond ADA Stevens turned to the cameraman and said, "Are we ready?"

"Yes sir", the camera man said as he put on his headphones and worked on the focus on the camera.

"Okay, quiet in the room please while we're taping", ADA Stevens said as he fixed his tie and put on his game face.

"Rolling", the cameraman said.

"I'm ADA Mathew Stevens from the District Attorney office of New York County. Today I am conducting an interview with", he looked down at a sheet of paper and quickly read the name off of it. "De'Quan Short. Mr. Short at this time I will ask you if you would like a lawyer present during this interview."

De'Quan looked around the room at all the red and white faces and was immediately uncomfortable. Not one familiar face stared back at his. "Yes, I need a lawyer".

ADA Stevens kept his cool as he said, "Cut the camera off".

The cameraman cut the camera off and everybody began to file out of the room under a mist of grumbles. ADA Stevens snatched his trench coat off of the chair and put his face close enough for De'Quan to see his nose hairs, "that's okay dick head, I tried to help you. I'll get the full story before the judge gives your ass 25years to life".

"Whatever fuck you too", De'Quan said.

ADA Stevens nodded his head and said; "Okay cool; let's go", and he and the rest of his entourage left the room.

De'Quan sat in the quiet room for five minutes lost in his own thoughts until the nurse came back into the room to check on him again, How you feeling?"

"Soar as hell. Where's my brother at?"

The nurse looked over her shoulder, then back to De'Quan and said, "I'm not supposed to be talking to you about anybody else, but I know one of the boys that was in the car with you didn't make it. I don't know if he was a brother of yours, but I am sorry".

De'Quan felt the sincerity in her voice as he nodded and said, "thank you". He let her finish her work, then she disappeared back into the hallway. De'Quan closed his eyes and returned to his own thoughts. She didn't have to tell him who didn't make it; he could feel something inside of him was empty.

Chapter 39

5months later

Dre took Tammy down to her Aunt house in Colombia South Carolina, and they hid out there until Tammy had the baby. They named their baby girl Andrea and found themselves a small apartment in the country part of the city and kept to themselves, with Tammy finding a job while Dre stayed in the house and took care of the baby.

Dre hooked up with a New York guy he met when he did his bid on Rikers Island and his friend helped Dre move some of the drugs they took from the last robbery. Dre made sure he got De'Quan a lawyer they could trust to keep the communication going between them two, because the police had cut off all other forms of communication Dre had with his family in New York once they found out he was the one who got away that night.

Everybody took it hard when it was known that Ne'Sean died in the car from the crash with the police car. Dre was able to speak to his sister after Ne'Sean's funeral, and Shakia filled her brother in on how Mama K wasn't the same and how she refuse to go see De'Quan while he waited for his trial to start. Shakia went to see De'Quan once a week, but their relationship was full of stress once De'Quan came clean about him hanging out with Melissa to get the information on the place they robbed.

To keep her brother off the radar Shakia cut ties with him and everybody used De'Quan's lawyer to send Dre messages. Since the night of the incident, nobody had heard from Fat Pee. They knew he wasn't dead, and he wasn't in jail with De'Quan, which led to the rumors flying around, that Fat Pee is working with the police and hiding in some type of witness protection.

Most days De'Quan walked around in a daze as the lost of his brother weighed heavy on his mind, and today was no different as he was shipped off to Manhattan Supreme court for a another day of ball pen theory and offers from the DA's office for De'Quan to take a twenty year sentence that didn't stop at that number because the life on the end is what the parole board would be looking at.

De'Quan wanted to take his chances at trial, and the DA's office was all for it. They wanted a judge to sentence De'Quan to a hundred years to life, instead of the sweet deal they were offering him.

When De'Quan arrived at the court building, he was taken to the holding area and placed in a cell by himself. He sat on the bench for an hour lost in his own thoughts until a shadow appeared in front of him, "Hi De'Quan".

De'Quan looked up and was taken aback by who he was looking at standing on the other side of the cell bars, "What are you doing here?"

"I needed to see you", Melissa said.

De'Quan got up from his seat and walked over to the cell bars. He looked her up and down and his eyes rested on the detective badge that hung around her neck and rested in between her chest.

"Yeah, well officer Sanchez, you see me. Fucked up and facing life, so now what", De'Quan said.

"De'Quan I never meant for this to happen. I thought you would only make a purchase or two and that would be it. I'm sorry all of this happen and I'm sorry about your brother", Melissa said seeming truly genuine.

De'Quan thought about her words and knew Melissa was the last person he was going to trust at this time in his life. He took two steps back and said, "Melissa I know you didn't come all the way down here to tell me that. You could have wrote me a letter or sent me card".

Melissa nervously shifted her weight from her right foot to her left foot and unfolded her arms. When she did, Melissa opens up her button up sweater revealing her real reason for coming there.

"I wanted to let you know face to face that I was pregnant. I've been wrestling with thoughts of what to do for months and keeping you out of your baby life is not something can I do. I know you probably don't want anything to do with me, but I know you would want to know about your baby", Melissa said.

De'Quan stared at her stomach, then looked into her eyes and said, "So let me get this straight, you saying that's my baby?"

"Yes De'Quan. You the only one I was sleeping with and a few times we didn't use a condom, so something was bound to happen".

"And you want me to do what…Play daddy from prison. How will your cop friends feel about that?" De'Quan said.

"This has nothing to do with the people I work with. I'm here because I don't want to shut you out of your child life", Melissa said.

"The minute you took me up to that apartment, you shut me out. I lost my brother, and now I'm about to lose my life. I don't think your baby story is going to make any of that better," De'Quan said. He looked down at her stomach one last time then walked back over to the bench and sat down.

A tear rolled down Melissa's cheek, "So that's it?"

"Melissa, I have a trial to prepare for and being that you are the DA's leading witness, I don't think it's a good idea for you to be here right now", De'Quan said as he lit up a cigarette.

Melissa stood there in silence for a minute before she wiped her face and said, "Okay De'Quan. You can reach out to me whenever you want. I will never keep you r baby away from you".

De'Quan ignored her and kept his focus on his cigarette. Melissa slowly walked away from the cell feeling defeated. She knew De'Quan was mad at her, but she thought he have a better reception about the baby.

An hour later De'Quan's lawyer showed up at the cell ready to talk strategy, but De'Quan had other plans, "Let me get a pen and paper".

When his lawyer gave it to him, De'Quan wrote a small note and said, "Give this to our friend". His lawyer nodded and stuck the note in his jacket pocket.

Chapter 40

Dre kept his low profile down in South Carolina using side hustles to keep some money coming in, while Tammy worked in a college campus library to keep legitimist money coming in. Their formula was working for them until Dre got the message from the lawyer.

Tammy sat in their small kitchen feeding their daughter when Dre came in with a sad look on his face. "What's wrong baby?"

Dre sat down at the table and said, "I'm going to New York for a few days".

Tammy never was one to blow up on Dre, but at this moment she felt like smacking him with the baby plate of food, "Are you crazy, for what?"

"I need to take care of something for De'Quan. Tammy you know if it wasn't important I wouldn't go up there, but this is serious, and it might help the case".

Tammy chose her words carefully when she said, "but what if something happens to you, what are we supposed to do?"

Dre got up, kneeled down in front of her, and said, "Trust me baby, nothing is going to happen to me. Nobody is going to know I'm there and nobody is going to see me. I'm going to dip in the city and dip out".

Tammy looked into his eyes and knew she had to trust Dre. She never let her trust for the decisions Dre made affect their bond. If Dre felt this strong about something Tammy had to be the rider that she was and support him again, "Okay Dre. Promise me you going to be careful out there".

Dre kissed her and said, "I promise you and you", then kissed their daughter as the baby squealed with joy from her father affection.

Melissa felt a funny pain hit her in the stomach as she woke up and rolled out of the bed. She went to the bathroom and when she sat down on the toilet a heavy rush of fluid dropped out of her body scarring her for a second. Then it hit her, this is it. The baby was coming.

Being by herself was never a plan Melissa had for having her first baby, but the circumstances surrounding her pregnancy were complicated and hard for her to talk to anybody about it. Once she reached six months and couldn't hide her growing stomach anymore, Melissa had to tell her family about it, but she kept the baby father identity to herself.

Getting to the hospital was a move she had been planning on her own for a few weeks and now the moment was happening. Melissa slowly dressed herself, and called her friend Suge and told her the baby was coming. Then Melissa grabbed her carry bag and called herself a cab. When Melissa made her way downstairs to the cab the driver was nervous and excited at the same time as he rushed her to Harlem Hospital.

At the hospital, Melissa was helped up to a pre-screening room until the baby began to force its way out into the world.

*****
———

Dre rented a car in New Jersey and used that as his means to move around New York City and follow Melissa whenever she left her house, which was rare being that she was ready to have the baby any day. Sitting in the car was driving Dre crazy, but he knew it will all pay off in the end.

Dre watched Melissa emerge from her building carrying a carry-on bag and looking wore out like she just had a fight. Dre knew that look from watching Tammy go through it when she was in labor with their baby. He immediately sat up and started the car.

Dre followed her to the hospital and watched as two nurses helped Tammy into a wheelchair and rolled her into the hospital. Dre parked the car and looked into the mirror to make sure the make-up he was wearing looked presentable enough where no one will give him a second glace as he moved through the hallways of the hospital.

Harlem Hospital was buzzing with activity at six o'clock in the evening, giving Dre the cover he needed to slide in and make his way up to the paternity unit. As Dre smoothly moved around the unit, he walked past the delivery room Melissa was having her baby in and dipped into a bathroom for an half an hour.

When Dre slipped out of the bathroom, Melissa had a baby boy and the nurses where working on him to get him cleaned up for his first official visit with his new mom. Dre watched from the side as nurses came and went for one reason or another, and when the coast looked, clear enough for him, Dre made his move.

The attending nurse stepped out of the baby holding room to go to the bathroom and Dre slid right into the room and headed straight for the bassinette that said 'Sanchez boy'. Without wasting any time, Dre scooped up the baby and quickly made his way down a side staircase. Just as Dre hit the first floor of the hospital, a commotion broke out in the main lobby causing security to leave their post at the door. Dre walked as fast as he could out of the hospital without looking suspicious and headed for his parked rental car three blocks down. The only thing Dre could think about was thank god the baby was sleeping the whole time.

Dre put the small boy into the car-seat in the back and quickly hopped into the driver seat. He started the car and before he pulled away from the curb Dre took off the nurse hat and wig, he was wearing. He wiped the make-up off of his face, took a quick look in the mirror and pulled out of the parking spot.

Dre jumped on the highway and headed for the George Washington Bridge leaving New York City in his rearview mirror for the last time.

When Suge made it to Harlem Hospital, she had to sidestep an altercation in the main lobby and made her way up to the paternity ward without anyone asking her for a visitors pass.

"Excuse me, can you tell me what room is Melissa Sanchez in?" Suge asked a nurse at the nurses' station.

"Oh the new mom, she in room 112".

"Thank you", Suge said and walked into the room hoping to see her girl sitting up feeding the baby by now. Instead she found Melissa sleeping like she just ran the marathon.

"What's up Mame'", Suge said waking her up she gave Melissa a hug and kiss and looked around the room.

"Hey girl, wow I must've fallen asleep. I'm so glad you came so you can meet him", Melissa said feeling worn out.

"I told you I got your back, now where's my god child at", Suge said as she took off her jacket and put her bag down in the chair.

"I don't know. They were supposed to clean him up and weigh him and all that, and then they were going to bring him in.

"Let me see what's going on", Suge said as she went over to the baby holding room and quickly scanned the names on the bassinettes.

"Hi may I help you?" A nurse said as she looked up from putting a bottle in a baby mouth.

"Yes, we were waiting for my god son to be brought in the room", Suge said.

"What's the name?" The nurse asks as she made her way down the aisle.

"Melissa Sanchez", Suge said.

The nurse looked around the room and focused on the empty bassinette in the second aisle, "What in the world?" The nurse rushed over to the bassinette and looked inside of it like she was seeing things.

Suge immediately panicked when she read the name on the empty bassinette, "Oh hell no, where's my god son at bitch!"

"If he's not here, then he's supposed to be in the room with his mother…I don't know", the nurse whined as she nervously looked around the room.

Melissa heard Suge yelling at somebody in the hallway, causing her to climb out of the bed and slowly make her way to the door. "Suge what's going on?"

Suge turned to Melissa with tears sliding down her cheeks and said, "Somebody stole the baby!"

Melissa thought she heard the words wrong, but the look on Suge's face told her brain this was not a test, "What?" was the last thing Melissa said before losing her grip on the I.V. pole and passing out in the doorway.

To Be Continued

EverDomo LLC.

Fantasy with an hip-hop twist   **Urban Novel**

Order Form

Address

Sold To	Ship To
Phone	Ship By

Quantity	Item/Description	Price/Item	Subtotal
	Journey to the Kingdom of Soul	14.99	
	R.A.W. Real Always Wins	14.99	
	Winners never Quit R.A.W. 2	19.99	
	Cabin Love/ Letters of Fate	14.99	
	Shipping per book	1.99	

All money orders and checks:

EverDomo LLC

558 Grand Concourse

P.O. box 1484

Bronx, NY 10451

Total	
Shipping Charge	
Amount Due	

All bulk orders and orders from outside the US, please refer to our website everdomo.com, and other sales channels amazon.com, createspace.com & Kindle